TO ASCEND TRIUMPHANT

Twenty-five years ago, Theo Ansgar abandoned the Kingdom of Chalvaren for a hiding place on another world. Some called him traitor. Some, thief. Now his fully grown daughter Mia must return to the land of her birth…and their war.

It was the elf prince Kort Elias who brought her back. Theirs was an instant connection, an inescapable union of body, soul and sorcery, reminding Mia of what she truly is, and what she must become. There is also Magnus, destined to be more potent than any wyrm Chalvaren has ever seen, a three-day-old dragonlet Mia must nurture and then ride. And then there is the Dragonstone, an artifact of power nonpareil. Joined, they can tip the scales of battle against the wraith-possessed forces of darkness, of Mia's own embittered kin. Redemption will be offered, the protected will become the protector, and an ancient prophecy will come to fruition, but only righteous love can conquer all.

CHALVAREN RISING
A KINGDOM OF CHALVAREN ROMANCE

PAULA MILLHOUSE

www.BOROUGHSPUBLISHINGGROUP.com

CHALVAREN RISING
Copyright © 2015 Paula Millhouse

ISBN 978-1-942886-69-3

For Bonnie Gill
Because you loved my dragonlet as much as me

And for Carl
Who bears the mantle of a writer's husband with heroic valiance

ACKNOWLEDGMENTS

Universal stories exist for Readers, so thanks for having a look. I hope you enjoy your time in the Kingdom of Chalvaren. Your kind words and enthusiastic reviews are deeply appreciated.

Special thanks to my own big brothers and sisters: Johnny, Dee Dee, Nellie, Robert, Roney, Lee, & Andy Watkins. You should know our mother inspired this story. I think she'd have loved reading it, particularly the family-centered scenes.

I thank my heavens for Carl, Jason, & Kimberly Millhouse, who taught me what a family is supposed to look like. Love *is* worth fighting for, and I love our love story the best.

Thanks to Lynn, the Triple E's, and my fellow Romance Writers of America sisters and brothers.

I'm grateful to Kellyann Zuzulo for her developmental editing skills.

My deep and heartfelt gratitude to everyone at Boroughs Publishing Group, especially Christopher Keeslar (and all your minions) for finding a place on your shelves for my stories.

And last, a nod to every writer before me who thought it was a good idea to include a dragon to wrangle in their tales—you inspired my imagination.

TABLE OF CONTENTS

CHALVAREN RISING

Chapter 1

"Dragons do exist...?" Mia Ansgar stared at the horse-sized creature. He slept peacefully just outside her cottage door under a protective spell of magic that she'd just helped conjure. She edged around Kort Elias, the strange but beautiful elf with whom she'd cast the spell—the first of her kind she'd seen who was not her family—to get a better look and satisfy her curiosity. "He's awfully small. I thought they were bigger."

"He's only three days old, Mia," Kort said, and joined her inspection. "Trust me. They get bigger. This little guy's egg was stolen, and I'm here to see him returned to be with others of his kind on Chalvaren."

The dragonlet's wings were iridescent black like the rest of his hide, but their tips were swirled with purple and teal. His head was rather equine, Mia decided, with rounded bony horns.

She twisted and peeked up into Kort's sapphire blue eyes. His magnificent face and pointed ears intrigued her, set her heartbeat racing.

She pointed at the beast. "What's his name?"

"This dragon's name is Magnus."

Magnus.

"So, there are truly dragons. My father always said so. But...how did you both get here? To Earth."

"That's another story for another day. The main question is how we are all going to get back to Chalvaren." Kort pointed at the dragonlet. "That containment spell we cast over him won't last for long. I need your help to get Magnus home."

Mia bolted upright. "For the good of the dragonlet I cast the containment spell by melding my aura with yours when we touched, but I don't know how to work *that* kind of magic. Do you?"

He clearly knew how to work many kinds of magic. Kort clasped her hand in his then lifted it to his lips for a kiss. Mia's belly flipped, warm and low, and her body flooded with desire.

It was new for her, this physical reaction if not the reason. Mia wanted a family more than anything else, more sometimes even than she wanted sunshine to warm her skin or air to sustain her life. After years of loneliness living by a human village that reviled and misunderstood her—

A violet aura, her magic signature, cascaded across her skin. Kort's aura spiked, too. His was royal blue.

Handsome, six-foot-something and covered with hard muscle, and *magical,* this elf just might be the perfect male for her. Mia blinked several times, trying to take it all in, to reconcile this sudden change to her overly quiet and lonesome life. For twenty-one years she'd been hidden here on Earth, alone, friendless, with only her parents for company until their death. Now this. *Him.* Out of nowhere.

To mask her discomfort she said, "My mother taught me magic auras are tied to our gods. Yours is blue. Your deity must be Marineth, the demigoddess of peace, unity, and trust." Indeed, Kort had those very words tattooed on his arms in elven runes. She could see them clearly as he pulled her close.

"And your violet aura ties you to Varik. You know about our people, Mia? About our ways?"

She gripped his hand tighter. "Before my parents died they told me other elves would come for me someday. My father didn't say I'd get to rescue a dragon."

"Did your father say why he stole the Dragonstone and hid you away for twenty years?"

Mia flinched. Defending her father's decision might prove difficult in front of Kort Elias, Prince of Chalvaren and next in line to the throne. It was his family that had been deprived of the artifact.

"He did it to prevent a war. A holy war, I think…" Mia glanced down at the sleeping dragonlet and tried to remember all the details. "He said there was a struggle between Heaven and Hell, like the humans believe…or good versus evil, if you want to think of it that way. A wizard who practiced black magic was killed for tapping unsanctioned power, and his wife went crazy. Her actions threatened to tear the seven kingdoms of Chalvaren apart. My father took the Dragonstone so the wife couldn't use it."

Kort nodded then sighed. "He did the right thing, I think. Magic should be used to sustain life, not take it—and she would have gotten hold of the stone. Our allied kingdoms are at peace now…for the most part."

Mia lifted her eyebrow. "Go on."

Kort pointed to Magnus. "That dragonlet fits into the prophecy your father made before he vanished. Magnus is an Aurora-class dragon, tied to the element of spirit."

"Ah, yes. The elements tie all of us together…," Mia said dutifully, smiling. "Fire. Air. Water. Earth. And spirit unites them all. That's the basis of all things, the way our universe is made up. My father *told* me he bred a spirit dragon once. Of course, he was always telling tales."

She looked back at the dragon and swallowed hard. If Magnus was real, as real as Kort Elias, then the concept that her father's tales of magic and adventure might be true as well. Mia's mind flooded with possibilities. "I never believed him. Not really. He had a penchant for dramatic flair.…"

Kort gently cradled her face between his hands. He stared at her, and a thousand words seemed to pass through his blue eyes. Flutters of trepidation strummed her belly.

"Mia. Listen to me. Magnus is the dragon your father created."

She shook her head. "Those were just stories."

Kort turned her to face the dragonlet. "He's as real as you and me, Mia. *Look.* He's the most magnificent dragon ever born to Chalvaren. One day he'll reunite his brethren, dragons who want to protect Castle Elias but are reluctant, afraid, and scattered because of that witch and her black magic. Magnus can bring them together again—if we see him safely home."

Mia recalled the part of the prophecy she'd been forced to memorize as a child. "'Destined to wield the Dragonstone at maturity, a force of magic made real by the blessing of our chief deity, Varik.'" She hesitated and trembled before she went on, glancing into Kort's eyes again. He finished speaking the legend along with her. "'Destined to end a reign of darkness in all the allied lands of Chalvaren.'"

The sudden connection she felt to Kort was too intense. Especially since her father had not been the only one to predict the future. Before she died, her mother Melia had told her things too.

"One day your One True Love will come for you, Mia, and you'll be honor-bound to help in his quest. How will you know him? Only your True Love can help you reverse the spell your father put on the Dragonstone. But if the two of you fail in his quest, you will end forever alone."

Mia pulled away from Kort and turned to stomp off into her cottage.

He pursued. "Wait!"

She threw up a hand to stop him once they were inside. "You said the seven kingdoms are at peace."

"We are, but not everyone agreed with what your father did. Some are loyal to the witch. She uses black magic against us. Killing dragons. Sacrificing wizards. Gathering so much elemental power that even I don't understand what is intended. We have to get Magnus back to Chalvaren. Now, Mia. He's our only hope against h—"

"He's three days old! You must have this all wrong."

"He can't stay on Earth, Mia, no matter how much this world and mine are linked. And neither can we."

She wheeled on him. "We? You keep saying *we* like I'm supposed to believe all this, Kort. That I'm supposed to believe you want me to accompany you back to my homeland and..." *And do what there after our arrival? Rear dragons to fight witches?*

She did not ask. This elf seemed in many ways a perfect match, her One True Love. But was that really what he proposed? She feared she was being naïve.

She turned back and stared at the hearth in the central room of her cottage. Kort saw and guided her over to it.

"Ah. The answer."

The keystone held a fist-sized amethyst embedded in the rock. Kort twined their hands together and touched it, and the jewel lit up, glowing violet with their combined magic.

Mia gasped. Kort chuckled.

"We can do this together," he said. "With the right kind of magic we can blend our auras and blast that artifact out of the stone then use it to open a portal back home. Yes, Mia, I want you to come with me, with us. You're obviously fond of the dragonlet, and he's displayed an affinity for you. He led me straight to you."

Should she do it? It wasn't like she had much choice now. Once the humans in the nearby village realized Magnus had eaten their vicar as one of his first meals, the whole vicious lot of them would come for vengeance with pitchforks and axes. She simply couldn't stay here anymore…but did she want to go with Kort?

"You said we could unite our auras and free the Dragonstone from my father's protections?"

Kort's smile broadened. "That amethyst is the largest chunk of dragon ore ever known to the elves of Chalvaren. The legend around it, if you go in for that sort of thing, is that dragons themselves tore it from the Drakhos Mountains."

It was luminescent, the most beautiful jewel Mia had ever seen. She blinked, her mother's words pouring through her mind. *Your One True Love…* If she was willing to risk being forever alone.

Kort whispered close in her ear, "It's a conduit for energy of all kinds, Mia. Plus it has a special attunement to…" He eyed her meaningfully. "The physical."

She gulped. "So…? How, exactly…? I mean…" She searched Kort's eyes and smoothed her other hand down the skirt of her purple dress to dry her palm. "What are you proposing we do to liberate the thing?"

Kort pulled her into a kiss.

Mia let him.

Their magic auras mingled, and she nearly lost her breath. She trembled in his arms and arched her chest into his. Kort held her tight, his hands drifting down her back. She let the warmth of his body flush through her, and the spark of desire she'd felt earlier when they melded their auras to cast the spell over Magnus burst into full flame. His touch *destroyed* her with need, and she pressed closer, mindless, reveling in the first kiss she'd ever experienced.

He plundered her mouth with his tongue, and Mia reveled in his mastery. When Kort broke away, she arched her neck so he could kiss it. This he did, and trailed hot moist kisses up to the crest of one pointed ear.

"Let me love you, Mia. You don't belong here. You belong with me. Let's use the power of our auras at the height of ecstasy to release the Dragonstone and go home."

At the height of ecstasy? Was he saying they would make love?

Well, whatever this magic was—whatever its intent and whatever its danger—Mia wanted more. All of this had been foretold by her parents. Magnus had led Kort to find her. She was ready to see where he led.

Chapter 2

"Oh. My. God. What have I done?" Mia tried to breathe but couldn't make her lungs work. The wood-fire smell of dragon filled her nostrils, and she was crushed against Magnus's iron-hard chest scales. The dragonlet released a horrifying noise; something off-key, a croak caught between a gravelly roar and the sound of an animal gripped with terror.

"Magnus?" Mia cried. "Where's Kort?"

There came no response.

She held on tight. Tumbling. Spinning. She lost track of which way was up. Finally an impact jarred every bone in her body, and then they were both rolling along the ground, tangled together in a somersault.

Good God, he's going to break a wing.

The perfect man had come for her today, Kort Elias. Together they'd acted to save Magnus, but if the dragonlet killed himself and her in the process of getting back to Chalvaren, her decision to trust Kort would be the worst choice ever.

End-over-end the dragon tumbled, and Mia, nestled under the darkness of his thick black wings, somehow stayed safe as she held on for dear life. They bumped, bounced, and slid wildly as the dragonlet careened across a slick-as-glass surface, colliding with several obstacles that gave way but finally slamming to a sudden stop against a solid wall of stone.

Her head struck the wall. Hard. She moaned, but it didn't sound like her own voice. What she heard was mingled with the memory of Kort calling her name over and over as he made love to her, and her mind returned to the passion they'd shared, to the love they'd conjured, to the magic they'd made. Safe in his arms there, Mia let herself linger in the perfect luxurious ecstasy that had been their first time together.

"Mia!"

She'd helped Kort and Magnus return home. She'd sacrificed her own place in her own world to see them safe. She'd left everything to follow Kort here, and all of that in answer to her heart, in answer to her father's words whispering in her memory. *Each day is a gift and not a given, daughter. Seize every one.* God, she missed him so much.

Again the memory of Kort's strong hands on her body flooded in. She recalled the clean masculine smell of him, like a whiff of sea air touched by balsam and juniper. The sound of his voice whispering her name over and over conjured a smile, and she wanted him again, desperately. He was the way she would one day have a family. She'd wholly given herself to him along with her virginity, and she intended to receive everything from him in return. Of course, right now, until Magnus reached maturity, she was guardian of the Dragonstone.

She inhaled a shaky breath just as Kort's voice, tight with anxiety, pierced the haze filling her mind. "Let me see her, Magnus. Is she alive?"

Mia blinked and discovered the reality of Kort's hands on her, checking her for injuries. He knelt beside her, felt for broken bones, cradled her head in his hands, and his trembling fingers stroked through her hair.

"Mia! Mia, are you all right? Her head is bleeding. Dad! I need your help! Mia, sweetheart, look at me."

She did. Her muscles protested as she moved slowly to sit upright, but Kort's anxious grimace morphed into a smile. He pulled her tight against his chest.

"He did it, Mia! Magnus flew. He saved you. I thought I'd lost you both."

"I thought I couldn't make it."

"It's okay, Mia. I've got you."

Her throat tightened, and emotions assaulted her. Longing. Love. Terror. Anger. Fear. Engulfed by arms like protective bands of steel, she was overcome with relief.

"You're home, Mia. You're safe."

Kort stroked her hair, and she squeezed her eyes shut. Home? This was just too damn good to be true. But she was here. Safe. In her One True Love's arms. In Chalvaren?

Home. He'd said the word *home*, and that was everything Mia longed to hear. She laced her fingers through his long blond hair and gently stroked his pointed ears. He trembled at her touch, and she sighed. She didn't dare speak. She didn't dare open her eyes again for fear that he might disappear, for fear that all of them might disappear like some fairy tale dream. She'd wake again to the nightmare of her cold lonely cottage at the edge of the Earth woods.

Her body shuddered, moved by the very real touch of Kort at her side. Hot as dragon fire, his lips grazed the skin at the nape of her neck and then the hollow of her throat, and she gathered the shards of her courage and opened her eyes, her fears dispelled.

She blinked at the reality surrounding her. Castle Elias. Concerned faces. *Elves.* They looked human, only they had pointed ears and stood taller, their bodies more refined. Nearly every elf carried a weapon and wore some form of armor.

Could this be? Was she really in Chalvaren? She reached up a hand to cover her pointed ears with her hair, a habit learned from years of living in a place where elves "didn't exist," a place Kort had said she didn't belong.

Kort pulled her hand away. "You don't have to hide any longer, Mia."

Magnus groaned beside her, and a hard, steady beat sounded against Mia's ear. Magnus's heart. The rhythm of his life pounded into her, the rhythm of promise. The rhythm of hope.

Her belly flipped, but Kort stretched out a hand to the dragonlet while holding her in his other arm. "You're safe now, Magnus," he said, his voice strong, confident, determined. "No one will harm you here. You're under my protection, little one. Both of you are."

The dragon made another noise, an odd and yet already familiar sound in Mia's ears. She'd known both Magnus and Kort the span of one mere day, yet she felt connected to them like she'd known their souls forever. She heard concern in the dragon's vocalization.

She pushed against him, and Magnus moved, untangling her from his wings and claws. Chalvaren's air filled her lungs, sweet and light, and she lifted her head to look around. She moved slowly, though, the soreness and aching from her adventures making itself known. The dragonlet nosed her with a velvet-soft snout, comforting her.

Mia inhaled, her gaze scanning an enormous white marble hall complete with a framed map on the wall that seemed to cover the whole of a land. A king and queen's thrones, gilded with gold finials of fierce dragons, filled the center of the room. Columns sculpted with the likenesses of Varik—the elves' chief deity—and his six demigods soared up to the ceiling.

Good. If they shared the same religion, she was among friends here, right? Then she gulped. If she'd known she was going to meet royalty today she would have dressed up a little. Done something to tame her mass of golden hair.

The hall of thrones was on two sides comprised of floor-to-ceiling glass, and she blinked in the too bright sunlight. A view of acres and acres of grassy fields led to an expansive blue-green ocean, and arched doors beckoned her forth to explore. She couldn't wait to get outside.

Magnus righted himself and preened, biting at several invisible specks on his hide. He sat back on his haunches and lifted his head, staring inquisitively down his nose at all the elves who'd witnessed his entrance. They said nothing.

The dragon's regal presence seemed to match the vast richness of the room, and despite the damage they'd surely caused a smile bubbled up to Mia's lips. A wave of pride flooded her chest and she reminded herself, *I saved a dragon today.*

Kort helped her upright as the room's occupants drew closer. He led her in front of Magnus then dropped her hand, and Mia wondered how things like this went. Obviously introductions were in order, but the elves' clear suspicion and worry dampened her earlier pleasure. Once again she noticed they were armed.

"Stay back." Kort flung his arms wide in warning. "I know there's a lot to explain here, everyone, but *do not crowd the dragonlet.* He might be the Chosen One of Chalvaren, but he's eaten two people already, and one of them was an elf."

"Son…" A tall elf with long blond hair like Kort's and garbed in indigo robes trimmed with white fleece approached, and Mia's eyes went wide. He wore a crown, and he peered at them with eyes as blue as Kort's, surprise dancing on his handsome face. "If you've gotten your bearings, perhaps you could you tell us your tale? I see you've recovered the Aurora dragonlet despite your mother's edict that you not pursue the mercenary."

Kort tensed, and that reaction thundered through Mia. Something felt off in both the king's words and his son's reaction, so she stepped forward and looked him in the eye. "You weren't supposed to come for us?"

Kort swallowed hard. "My mother didn't exactly like the idea."

From behind the king, a tall, beautiful woman edged closer. Atop her dark auburn tresses lay a thick golden crown encrusted with multicolored jewels and engraved with a family crest much like the one on Kort's father's crown. At the sight of it, Mia's heart fluttered like dragon wings beating to take flight.

The queen moved closer, a vee pinched into an otherwise smooth brow. "Explain yourself, Son."

"My going after Magnus was never a question, mother. It was always the answer. He had to be returned to us."

The queen's expression turned stormy. "And who is this woman you've brought home to court? What is she doing in possession of the Dragonstone?"

Mia looked down at the jewel. They must have all seen what she'd done with it; they were all looking through the portal she'd opened with the Dragonstone, though she hadn't believed they were real until now. But, why were they all looking at her like she'd done something wrong?

"I brought it back to fulfill the prophecy for Magnus," she said.

Kort threw up a hand, quieting the queen. "I know I defied your orders, Mother. I know how this must look to you."

The queen lurched forward, jabbing her finger at Mia, who gasped. "Guards! I want this woman taken into custody."

"Custody?" Mia jerked back. This was the last thing she'd expected. She searched the throne room for a way out. The shimmering portal back to Earth had shut, so there was no escape route there. She scanned next the windows, and then her gaze locked on the arched doors at the other end of the hall. Freedom beckoned in the form of that grassy field, and in the ocean beyond, but the queen's guard blocked her way.

She turned on Kort, fisting her hands. "You lured me here so that she could lock me up?"

"No, Mia. That's not going to happen." Kort wheeled on the queen, his jaw clenched. "Mother, I need you to back off. Don't make her think for one second she doesn't belong here, because she does. With me."

"'With you'? What does that mean, Kort?"

Magnus made a noise and narrowed his amber eyes. He fixated on the movements of several encroaching guards, and a low vibration filled with warning rumbled from his throat.

Mia looked from Magnus to Kort, who repeated, "It's okay, Mia. I won't let them harm you."

She shook her head. "You set me up so that I'd lose the two things I value most: my freedom, and the one thing I'm sworn to protect." Mia's father had warned her there were elves in Chalvaren who were dangerous, but had he meant the queen? Is this what he'd meant when he told her there was darkness here hidden from the light? Had she been wrong to trust Kort? Tears burned behind Mia's eyes at the very thought.

She held up the Dragonstone on its length of golden chain, and the crowd of onlookers scattered, some of them covering their mouths, their terror and confusion apparent. They were afraid of her. But why?

The queen waved her arm. "She will not leave the castle grounds with that artifact, Kort. It cannot fall into enemy hands. No. Matter. What."

Twenty-five massive guards, armored women and men with bows and swords, stepped forward, weapons drawn. They all focused on Mia, who was overcome by the vision of sharp, pointy steel and accusatory elven stares. She swallowed hard, feeling beads of sweat form on her forehead. What should have been an open welcome had turned threatening.

Kort spread his arms wide. His voice was a low, menacing growl. "Stand down, Duncan. You and your men."

Magnus eased in behind Kort, and Mia didn't miss the way the dragonlet lifted both wings to make himself look larger. He raised his tail and switched the spiked tip back and forth until the king held up a hand and the captain of the guard gestured for his men to wait.

"What did you do to Theo Ansgar?" the queen demanded, her face twisted with anger. "Where did you get the Dragonstone, thief?"

"Theo Ansgar was my father. I'm no thief!" Mia shouted back, not backing down from the challenge. "I didn't steal the damn thing. I've spent my whole life protecting it—obviously from people like you."

The entire throne room erupted with whispers and curses. Elves pointed at Mia, their faces hard, animated, or shocked. But what exactly had she said wrong? Was claiming her heritage such a dangerous thing? She'd suspected there would be elves in Chalvaren who didn't think her father had done the right thing by taking the stone, but—

The queen narrowed her eyes. "I don't believe you. And know this, you will *not* give that gemstone to Isa Ansgar. Not as long as I draw breath."

Mia pointed her finger right back at the queen. What did the woman know about her father, and who was this Isa? Her father had never mentioned relatives waiting back in Chalvaren. "I don't know who Isa Ansgar is, but my father warned me elves would come for this stone. He told me most of them would want to take it for themselves. There was only one situation in which I was to relinquish the artifact. When Kort showed up with the dragonlet this morning, he bore all the signs I was to look for. Was that a mistake? Are you going to throw me in chains and take it for yourself?"

How would she guard the Dragonstone if the royals wanted it for themselves? Had she gotten it all wrong by giving herself to Kort? Their union had seemed blessed by Varik—why else would their magic release the Dragonstone?—but now confusion bled into Mia's mind. "Just what the hell is going on here?"

The queen jabbed her finger at Mia. "You show up here kissing my eldest son. You're in possession of the Dragonstone. You're an Ansgar. Your family has done horrible things to our people, and now you dare speak to me like this? I want her in chains!"

Kort tried to intervene, grasping Mia's hand, but Mia jerked back. He turned and yelled, "It's true, Mother. She's from the house of Ansgar, but *look* at her. She's the child of a hero. She will not bring more suffering upon us."

"Her family does little else," his mother retorted.

Mia stood behind Kort, her eyes wandering his body and looking for more evidence that he was the one. The tattoos on his arms bore the elvish words she was to look for, and she remembered his deep bass voice reciting the Dragon Chant with her at their first meeting. He wore an Elias family ring on his hand, and his aura had spiked royal blue in the heat of their passion. All correct. But, could she have gotten it wrong? Had her heart betrayed her out of loneliness, because she'd craved the touch of her One True Love for so long it actually hurt to breathe without him?

I might have missed something, she admitted, blinking rapidly and backing up to eye the queen. Could the woman have known her weakness and sent Kort to steal the artifact after making love to her?

"I never should have trusted you," she growled at Kort, her face burning with embarrassment and fury. "You got what you wanted, mostly. You and your dragonlet are safe back in Chalvaren, as I promised. But now it looks like it's time for me to leave."

"Even if you escaped," the queen said, "you wouldn't survive a day out there—especially after people learned your name. But you won't escape." She glanced at Kort's father. "She can't be allowed off castle grounds. Ever."

Kort faced Mia. His lips were pinched, and he splayed his hands out wide, twitching them in frustration. "Mia, no. You can't go," he begged. "Not now. Damn it, Mother! I just got them home and you're your ruining everything as usual."

"Guards!" the queen bellowed. "I want her in custody. *Now!*"

The only way to save herself and the Dragonstone was to run. Mia turned and bolted. Maybe Kort's mother had spoken truth; she had no idea where to go or how she'd find the resources she'd need to survive, but anywhere was better than being locked up in the castle dungeon, wasn't it? Maybe she could seek out this Isa they spoke of.

An adrenaline spike almost covered the pain in her legs. Mia allowed herself a backward glance at Kort and Magnus, just long enough to see concern in Kort's blue eyes. What would happen to them? Unfortunately, she couldn't stay around and find out.

The queen's angry voice seemed to fill the castle completely. "Stop her! Do not let that woman escape!"

Chapter 3

"And so, we've found an unattended nest."

Isa Ansgar knelt before a clutch of ten dragon eggs nestled securely in a thatch of deep balsam pine needles, straw and gnarled tree roots in the darkening forest of Chalvaren's Drakhos Mountains. She tucked a loose strand of jet black hair back behind a pointed ear and flicked her eyes to the trees in search of the dragon dam. The beast roared off in the distance, and prickling hairs stood at attention on the back of her neck while chills raced down her limbs despite the warmth of her black leathers.

"The mother dragon," she realized, "must have left the nest mere moments before we flew in."

Isa burrowed her hands into the four-foot-tall nest and dragged out two warm eggs. The fresh straw was warm to the touch, sweet and fragrant, and in the fading afternoon light slanting through the tall firs she admired the silver and teal streaks that marbled the hard-as-granite eggshells.

"Eggs of an unknown mating between wild dragons," she mused. "Might there be a spirit dragon among this clutch?"

Her eyes wide with anticipation, Isa smiled at her silver dragon, a regal male now nearly twenty-five years old, young for a dragon but robust with iron-hard muscle and a keen sense of bloodlust she'd nurtured herself. He stood nearly seventeen feet tall, with a wingspan double that, but now the beast crouched down between two enormous fir trees, waiting for Isa's lavish praise and next command.

"Good hunting, VanZanz," she said.

The creature shook his mighty head and rumbled a soft sound of appreciation, but he hesitated before launching himself into the sky. His first thought was always of her.

Isa turned to the two shadow elves she had brought on the hunt today, inspecting her handiwork. How ironic, that she was often protected by her enemies. Whenever one of the seven alliance kingdoms sent soldiers to kill her, she captured and changed them. These twisted and muscle-bound abominations—inhabited by shadow wraiths, demons she summoned from Hell with a grimoire— were now her guards.

The creatures, each more monster than anything else, stood taller than they had as elves. At one time Isa would have feared them. They were not pleasant to look at. Broader, uglier, with sharp teeth meant to cut and tear, their grotesque greenish flesh was a mutation. They didn't need much armor; their skin was hard as granite. Dressed in nothing but loincloths and leg armor, they wore razor-sharp swords at their sides and existed only to follow her orders...and as far as Isa knew, only death could loosen the hold the shadow-wraith demons held over them.

"Time to get to work, boys."

"What is your bidding, Mistress?" one of the pair asked. They still had some semblance of their original consciousness, dominated as it was.

"This dragon's nest is a very nice find." With long, pointed fingernails, Isa caressed an oblong purple-jeweled amulet hanging from her chest. "There should be enough energy brewing in these gestating eggs to make my power complete."

No matter how hard she tried, it was impossible to entirely stamp out an elf's curiosity when it came to dragons. The shadow elves inched closer to peek inside the nest. But as their expressions grew reverent, the frosty malice of greed shivered across the back of Isa's neck.

"They're mine. Back away!"

The warriors immediately retreated and stared at her. Isa's lips twisted, a cold smile daring them to make a move on her prize, but the threat was unnecessary. A protective roar sounded above the trees, and the ground beneath her six-inch metal-spiked boots shook with the vibration.

Isa snapped her head around to look. "The mother. She's closer. That's good."

One shadow elf pointed through the forest. "The dam's caught our scent. If she finds us here, there's no weapon strong enough to stop her."

"No need to fear a dragon when you've brought your own." Isa turned to her silver. "Take care of that for me, VanZanz."

Rather than breathing fire, silvers were tied to the element of water. VanZanz breathed ice, a weapon Isa coveted, and he lifted his enormous horned head and blew out a snort of frosty breath. He tossed his scaled snout in the air and answered Isa's command with an ear-splitting roar. Then, lumbering into the small clearing, his broad wings flapping surprisingly quickly, he lifted into the air and disappeared off in the direction of the mother dragon.

Isa gestured to the shadow elves and the nest. "Get over here and help me search for the key egg. Mother dragons are smart. They hide the egg with the strongest magic, and I want all the energy I can get from this clutch."

The two shadow elves scrambled forward, anxious to see her command fulfilled, and a short time later they returned with an overly large dragon egg, its shell smeared with mud and debris.

"Well done," Isa said. "Collect the rest of these eggs and put them in a circle next to this one."

The mother dragon roared from somewhere nearby. Apparently VanZanz had not yet found her.

One of the shadow elves shook his head. "We don't have time. We have to get you out of here before—"

"Do as I say," Isa snapped. She didn't know the creature's name, didn't care to know. Names led to familiarity, familiarity to attachment, attachment to pain. She'd vowed to never endure pain again.

She removed a pouch from the belt of her black leather pants while the shadow elves, wincing, removed the remainder of the eggs from the nest and placed them as commanded. When the circle was complete Isa's men backed away, their eyes darting between her and the sky.

Isa flicked free a pointed metal spout that she used to empty the contents of her pouch, leaving a trail of glittering dust as she circled the feral eggs. At the same time she said, "The wizard I took this from was number four on my list of seven. He alleged this powder would make my harvesting spell complete." She had been kind because of his gift, killing him before she killed his family so he didn't have to watch.

Isa closed the circle of dust, chanted an elven spell of black magic, and stroked her small purple amulet. At the same time, two roars split the air. The mother dragon answered VanZanz's challenge with an ear-splitting symphony of rage.

Isa jerked her head up as a shiver of ice rushed up her spine. The dragons were close. Too close. Worse, compassion for the dam who was about to lose her clutch waved over her, and she whispered, "Mothers, whether dragon or elf, are not all that different. I understand your fear. Losing a child is an unimaginable horror. Still, I must harvest your dragonlets' magic today."

Trees crashed just out of sight, and the ground shook as the two mighty dragons engaged. Isa's shadow elves huddled together in a crouch, their eyes saucer-wide, their mouths open to expose sharp teeth.

Isa bounced on her tiptoes, her senses heightened from the thrill of the fighting leviathans, from the thrill of seizing the power of the dragonlets. She struck a match and ignited the wizard's magic dust; then, delicately stepping into the circle over the dual rings of purple flame and dragon eggs, she wet her lips in anticipation.

"*Ego sacrifico vobis enim promissio Chalvaren cras,*" she cried. Flames from the wizard's dust flared waist-high, conjuring another smile of satisfaction from her. "I sacrifice you for the promise of my future Chalvaren."

Power built all around and within her. The flames danced and sparkled in reflection upon all the eggs, especially her target. She lifted her knee so that the spiked heel of her black leather boot was poised. With one stomp she intended to crush this egg and absorb the power of the dragonlets into herself.

A gasp made her pause. In her peripheral vision Isa caught the twin looks of horror from her shadow elves. Aghast, they hid their eyes.

"Goddamned weaklings. You could never understand."

Her body throbbed, and Isa glanced down at the egg she intended to destroy. The power around her pulsed again and...dissolved. In the space of a blink, a gust of heated wind had blasted through the clearing, extinguishing her ring of sacrificial fire and squelching her spell.

Isa lowered her shaking leg and searched her surroundings for a clue to what had happened. "What's this? Had the wizard's dust grown old? Or…" Cold disappointment crept down her neck. "That bastard betrayed me just like the rest of them."

Noise from beyond the trees pulled her attention away. The shadow elves beside her backed further into the darkening forest, clearly terrified.

"What's wrong with you cowards?" Isa asked, alarmed. She looked down. Hanging upon her chest, her amulet glowed white-hot at the center, and a blinding beam of purple light burst forth, illuminating the surrounding gloomy woods.

Burnt, Isa screamed. She tore the jewel from her neck, and the stone sizzled in her hand, scorching her flesh. She flung the purple amulet down into the circle of eggs at her feet.

"Bastard!" she shouted. The odor of her own burning skin mingled with the residual smoke of the traitorous wizard's dust. Her shadow elves ran away into the forest, abandoning her to her pain.

VanZanz crashed back down in the clearing, snapping trees with his descent, and despite the fiery pain in her chest and her charred hand Isa smiled. The decapitated head of his enemy dangled from her dragon's mouth, his silver scales spattered with crimson blood.

She thrust her wounded hand in the direction of shadow elves. "Go get them, VanZanz. I do not need them, but no one can know what I do here. We are close and if they were to be found by those from Castle Elias…"

Her dragon did not wait for her to finish, he just tossed his prize aside and took flight.

Isa clutched her injured hand and glared around the wooded glen at her failed spell, pursing her lips and fighting off the agony. She inspected the wizard's inert dust then poked through the ring of eggs and retrieved her amulet by its leather cord. When she peered inside the gem, she raised her brows and her stomach roiled. "Only one thing could ignite this amulet. The Dragonstone of Chalvaren."

But, how? Isa narrowed her eyes, thinking. The mercenary she'd hired to locate the gemstone never returned, and as far as most other elves knew the amethyst was lost or a mere legend. Only Isa had seen it. Long ago she'd held it in her own two hands. Now it was on another plane of existence, in another world. She'd lost the precious stone to her traitorous, thieving brother.

"Damn you, Theo. Damn your soul for taking it from me."

Another thought occurred, and she raised her eyebrows, cocked her head and touched the innocent dragon eggs before her, reverently tracing the silver streaks patterned upon the teal. "If it has returned, Chalvaren *will* be mine. Its ancient power could... Finally, I will have everything I've ever wanted!"

From within the forest came the delightful sound of anguished screams and then VanZanz's triumphant roar. The beast's success was inspiring, and Isa ignored the pain of her blistered hand to delicately collect each and every remaining egg. Though she could not drain their power, she could add to the population of her own hatchery.

"And so, Chalvaren. Now begins your end."

Chapter 4

Mia bolted for the arched doors to the outside.

"Stop!" Kort bellowed, and something else, but his plea was drowned out by a burst of angry growls.

The queen shrieked, her voice mingling with the flapping of leathery wings. This alone made Mia skid to a stop. She turned back, a pit of dread wallowing deep in her belly. Magnus had pinned Kort's mother to the castle's marble floor.

The queen cursed. She floundered, her hands gripping Magnus in a vain attempt to free herself. "Get him off of me, Kort!"

The Queen's Guard turned their weapons on Magnus. The midnight-black dragonlet snarled, exposing razor-sharp teeth, and all the blood rushed out of Mia's face, leaving a white cold stinging sensation instead.

"Wait! Magnus, no!"

Mia changed direction and charged toward the queen. Guards moved to stop her, but she saw Kort pivot and jab an elbow into one's face. The elf dropped to the floor, his sword spinning across the marble as Kort wheeled, sticking out his leg and tripping another.

The path was clear. Mia threw herself on Magnus so that she draped across his head, shielding him from the guards' arrows. Fear speared her chest, and confusion. Again, confusion. Why was the queen so angry with her?

The king's voice boomed through the hall. "EVERYBODY STOP!"

Magnus did not. He whined—a sharp, high keening noise that Mia took as a warning. Beneath him, the queen turned her face away. And then the dragon spoke.

"My princess... My *Mia*."

The beast's voice was a rumble somehow distinct and refined, and its vibration thrummed through Mia's body. She blinked with disbelief. Had he truly spoken out loud?

She looked around. Everyone was frozen, but all eyes were on the Aurora and their shocked expressions confirmed her belief.

Mia tried to pull Magnus away from the queen, but her trembling hands found no purchase on his slick-as-glass scales and slipped off his head. "What just happened here?" she murmured, forcing herself to breathe and turning to her one other ally in the room. "He spoke. Kort, did you hear that? Elven words."

"Yes, Mia," Kort said. "I heard him clearly. He called your name."

The Aurora-class dragon had called her name as his first words and maybe as his last, considering all the drawn sharp steel and arrows trained on his head.

Magnus shifted his shoulders so that his wings lifted and he took on a pose of predation. Mia looked around the hall of thrones at the encroaching guards and begged them to understand. "Please. Gods, *please* don't hurt him."

The guards remained frozen, and Mia knelt alongside the thick column of Magnus's neck where it joined the back of his long jaw. She covered his snout with her hands and prayed to Varik to figure out what to do next. How could she possibly protect him from all those weapons? One drop of Kort's mother's blood would escalate this into an all-out disaster.

The dragon whimpered once and caught her gaze. He nuzzled his head against hers.

"You can't leave the castle with the Dragonstone," the queen announced, still captured but locking her crystal-blue eyes with Mia's. "Even if you are not our enemy, you wouldn't last a day out there against those loyal to Isa."

Mia swallowed hard. "Perhaps not, but I won't surrender the jewel to you. Not after...*this*."

Kort appeared beside her. He knelt down, and in the worst attempt at an introduction Mia had ever witnessed, he raised his palms and nearly lost his balance. "Mia Ansgar...my mother, Queen Elissabet Elias." He nodded over his shoulder and added, "My father, King Lachlan."

The king joined them, squatting down on the other side of Kort. "Mia. I think it's time you call off your dragonlet."

Mia's eyes went wide. *Her* dragon?

Surely this was a capital offense, but could she possibly save him? She would try. "Magnus...this woman is not a threat. I want you to release her. *Now*." She tugged at the dragon's head, but her fingers slipped on the bony but rounded horns. "Magnus, you must not hurt the queen."

Repositioning himself, ignoring Mia's pleas, swishing his long, spiked tail across the polished marble, the dragonlet stared intently down into Queen Elissabet's blue eyes, whimpering. The queen's eyes darkened in response.

Mia pulled on Magnus's head again. "Please, she belongs to Kort. She's his mother. Do not harm her. Please, Magnus, we need her help!"

Every filament of Mia's senses crystallized into sharp focus, so much that the sunlight sparkling through the enormous glass windows and gleaming off metal weapons blinded her. The cloying aroma of polished leather armor assaulted her nose, threatening to choke her. But the warmth of the dragonlet's hide promised a new life, one she wanted to protect, and a tingling sensation coursed through Mia's arms and legs and erupted from her skin in a violet-colored aura. It flowed outward in waves over the young dragon, which she meant for it to calm.

A rush of whispers spread through the hall, and some of the elves backed away. Mia blinked rapidly, not sure what to try next.

The king leaned forward. "That color of your aura is tied to spirit," he whispered. "By the gods, it's tied to *Varik*. Why don't you use the Dragonstone, Mia?"

Mia nodded. "Look, Magnus...look at this." She grasped the artifact by its golden chain and held it out. The dragonlet froze, mesmerized, amber eyes wide.

"Magnus," Mia continued, "you must listen to me." A rush of energy fed by anger and fear flared in her aura, illuminating the jewel, which sparked to life and glowed from within. Ghostfire. Multicolored sparks of elven magic. "Let. Her. Go."

Long prisms of purple light flashed across the queen's face. The dragonlet growled but just repositioned his hold. Mia's stomach seized at his continued belligerence.

"My daddy taught me that dragons love treasure. Is that true, little one? Do you like this jewel? Release the queen and come outside with me, Magnus, and I'll let you wear the Dragonstone. Look at it, Magnus. Look at the ghostfire."

The light engulfed them, and Queen Elissabet gasped, but the power just settled Mia's nerves. *This can work.*

She looked down at Kort's mother. "My father taught me our ancestors' spirits rode on ghostfire. When I opened the portal into Chalvaren, his magic lingering in my cottage associated itself with the Dragonstone and jumped into the jewel. It's how I had the power to bring us home."

She looked back at Magnus and moved the jewel closer. When the dragonlet loosened his grip on the queen, Mia groaned out a prayer of thanks. This was really working.

The beast flicked amber eyes from the artifact to Mia. The noise he made was one of distinct interest.

"You want this jewel," Mia cajoled, "don't you, Magnus?"

The animal shook his head, and a loud snort flared his nostrils.

"Be honest, Magnus. And..." Mia lifted the amethyst and let it swing on its golden chain like a pendulum. "I just want you to release her."

Magnus's eyelids drooped. She had him now, and she knew it.

"I see your courage, little one... Your bravery. You acted to spare me from capture, but I need you to let Kort's mother go."

The dragonlet didn't budge.

"She doesn't understand that we've returned with the Dragonstone to help her." Mia gestured to the queen, her aura flaring purple wisps of energy around her that coalesced on the artifact. "She doesn't know us yet, baby boy. None of them do."

"Mia!" Kort said.

Magnus's lip had curled, and Kort reached out for her, but Mia shook her head. "I won't see him devour your mother as his first official act on Chalvaren." Yet, could she do this? Could she be the first elf to gentle the spirit of an Aurora? Her father claimed this was the proudest of all dragons. The most vicious. The most powerful. The noblest.

"I refuse to see you destroyed, Magnus. Not here, not now that you're finally in the place where you belong." She shoved hard then, trying to push him away from Queen Elissabet, but it didn't work. Magnus was immovable.

Ghostfire flared up between them; colorful particles, glowing sparks of energy flowed around the Dragonstone. Magnus nickered and pulled his lips back again. *Teeth. Sharp teeth. Dear gods, look at all those sharp teeth.*

"By Varik, Magnus, no one will trust us if you injure the queen!"

Painful cramps knotted her legs, but she tugged on the dragon yet again. Then the rattle of a new sword leaving its scabbard reached her ears. It surely reached Magnus's as well.

"Damn it! King Elias, please make them back off so I can help her."

The king lifted a hand to stop whoever had drawn the weapon, but his words were aimed at his wife. "I believe Magnus has made his point, Elissabet. Mia is his to protect. She's obviously tied to him, and you should know better than to show bad manners and threaten any who handle dragons."

Mia's mouth dropped open, surprised by the sudden support.

"Get him off me this instant," the queen growled through clenched teeth. She twisted her shoulders, her hands on Magnus's claws still trying to dislodge his hold.

Kort spoke up, pointing at Mia. "It's simple, Mother. Show the guardian of the Dragonstone and my future bride the respect she deserves, and I'm sure Magnus will comply."

The queen jerked around toward her son, a thin sheen of sweat coating her forehead. Her nostrils flared. "What? *Bride?* You cannot be serious—"

"Kort," Mia fumed, "you're only making it worse!" What kind of family was this, anyway? The woman would never accept her now, or Magnus. Good Lord, this damn dragonlet and her One True Love had ruined any chance she'd ever have of acceptance.

"All I ever wanted was a chance to fit in," she said to the queen. "To find the one place where I can be of service. A family. A home. You promised me a home, Kort Elias," she added, grimacing and pushing her shoulder against Magnus again. "Is that so much to ask?"

Kort shot her an I-know-what-the-hell-I'm-doing-here look.

Queen Elissabet glared at her son then spoke to the dragonlet. "I meant Mia no harm, Aurora." But her voice was full of annoyance, and Mia winced.

"What the heck is wrong with you people? The queen should not have to apologize. Damn it, Magnus, move!" She nudged Magnus harder with her shoulder, putting her full weight behind the push, but leaning into the dragonlet was like trying to move a solid rock wall.

Suddenly, Mia had a different thought. She slipped her trembling hand underneath Magnus's claw and against the queen's delicate skin, risking his razor-sharp talons. Yes, the woman had been horrible to her, but she meant to see Magnus survive.

An unfamiliar but not unpleasant vibration throbbed through her fingertips when she touched the queen, and for a second Mia caught a glimpse of yellow-orange magic flaring about Queen Elissabet's body. The dragonlet bleated out a winsome sound, which meant he'd seen it too. The queen was a wizardess, though her power was across the spectrum from Mia's. Warmth came to mind, but that couldn't possibly be the source of her magic, could it? For now, Mia ignored Elissabet's aura and focused on the dragon.

"Release her," she said for what seemed the hundredth time.

This strategy worked. Upon seeing that she risked injury to protect Elissabet, the dragon lifted his claw. The creature locked eyes with the queen, however, and bared his teeth.

"My Mia," he said.

"Oh, good grief," Mia spat. "Move, you leviathan!" She tugged him backward with all her weight, and this time he came. She stumbled onto her behind.

The dragonlet approached. Mia leapt upright and squared off with him, now standing between him and Kort's mother.

"What do you want?" she demanded.

Magnus pressed closer, his amber eyes wide. Mia jutted her chin in the air.

"Talk to me," she said.

Spectacular to behold, the dragon stood there, all determination and black-as-coal scales rippling with anticipation. Intelligent amber-and-gold flecked eyes locked with hers, and purple and teal wingtips flared wide. Mia swallowed, suddenly aware of how thirsty she was. Magnus was perfectly formed. Perfectly deadly. Perfectly dragon.

"Explain yourself," she commanded a final time.

The beast switched his long, spiky tail, but in anticipation of what? What exactly did he want?

Mia took a step forward. "Kort said my father bred you. He claimed that you are the most important dragon ever in the history of Chalvaren." She planted her hands on her hips, cocked her head, and narrowed her eyes. "What do you want from me?"

Magnus eyed the purple amethyst around her neck, his pupils dilating. The obvious answer was the jewel, but somehow Mia sensed it went deeper than that. Cat-like, Magnus switched his tail across the white marble floor.

"I want *you*, Mia."

"You want me for what?"

"I want you to help me. To help them." The beast tossed his snout at the elves in the room and purred.

Kort was helping his mother up off the floor, but Mia focused on the vibration of Magnus's deep rumble. The sound resonated with something primitive in her soul. She recognized comfort and safety, and also somehow it was a call to action.

"How can I possibly help you?" she asked.

Magnus moved forward as she reached out for him. The Dragonstone became heated, painful against her skin, and she scooped the gem away and offered it to him. A shudder of appreciation rippled across the dragonlet's hide, and Mia spread the artifact's long gold chain up and over his head. As she hung the jewel around his neck, placing it against his chest, a jolt of electricity plowed through her hand, and an iridescent bubble of magic coalesced between them, uniting their minds. At once she knew him and his heart's desire—and she liked it. She wasn't the Chosen one of Chalvaren. The dragonlet was.

Magnus puffed out his chest and admired the amethyst.

"What do you want me to do?" Mia repeated.

The dragonlet moved in close and nuzzled her hand. "I choose you as my rider."

"Your rider...?"

"Mia Ansgar, you were meant for me."

Images of their future flashed before her eyes, projected by the dragonlet, and she gasped. "Flying?"

Yes. They would soar together, rider and dragon.

"More dragons?"

Yes, dozens of dragons. Chalvaren's dragons flew everywhere in the vision she shared with Magnus.

"Is all this true?"

"It can be. Stay with me. Help me."

"I don't understand...." A sensation of disbelief flooded her belly, along with a shaky threat of nausea. Mia wrinkled her brow. "Why me? I know nothing about this place."

Magnus just grumbled, a deep sound like thunder heralding a dark storm.

Mia glanced over at Kort. "*He's* a better choice for you, dragon—a fierce warrior, an elf who knows your ways. He is their future king."

"I am yours," Magnus repeated. "To help him. To free them."

"To free them from what?" Mia's gaze bounced all around, and she drew several quick breaths. Dark, feathery winged images lingered at the edge of new visions they shared, and Mia tracked them with her gaze, struggling to distinguish shadow from light. Alas, the elusive, blue-black apparitions fluttered away.

The stench of rot assailed her nose, and she jerked back from the vision. "What was that?"

"Chalvaren's corruption. Monsters of revenge and greed conjured straight from Hell."

Mia squeezed her eyes shut, pushing closer to Magnus and stroking his chin. She didn't understand, didn't want any part of this. Didn't want tainted the fairy-tale version of Chalvaren that her father painted for her. Yet, more than that, she didn't want to lose her dragon.

"They're coming for you?" She trembled when she put it all together.

Magnus answered with a nod. "Kort Elias is destined to be Chalvaren's future king. I am destined to lead Chalvaren's dragons. But without you, Mia Ansgar, we may never find our place."

Mia stared over at Kort and his parents, lifted her chin and squared her shoulders. "I'll do it, Magnus." She set her jaw and tightened her fists at her sides. There was no other choice. "I'll stay and help you fight their darkness."

Chapter 5

"They've imprinted," Kort said, looking across the marble castle interior at Mia and Magnus. The pair stood waiting for him to acknowledge them, to explain their newfound world, Magnus wearing the Dragonstone, Mia with her fists clenched white.

He turned and addressed his mother and father. "Of course they belong together. I should have known it the minute he led me to her. He found her for us, and then he chose her as his rider. That damn dragonlet's smarter than all of us put together."

"How could he know that, Kort?" Elissabet asked.

"It's obvious that challenging any threat to Chalvaren is part of the Aurora's genetic makeup," the king said. "Some authorities allege dragonlets overhear things while still in the egg. They're so smart they know about our world before they even hatch."

Kort's mother clasped his arm. "You're not furious that the Seven Kingdoms' most powerful dragon is going to a…a novice? He should be linked to a trained soldier. Your father's captain of the guard, Duncan, was next in line to be matched." She tossed her shoulder back to indicate the elf who awaited his next command.

"Your fiancée"—the queen almost choked on the word as she continued—"is the worst choice to be matched to this dragon, as he is nothing but an unruly juvenile. Which means we must put both of them in protective custody. We're honor-bound to protect them now!"

Was he okay with the situation? The last thing Kort could afford was distraction that kept him from protecting Castle Elias.

"Personally, Mother, I'm thrilled Magnus chose Mia. And I intend to protect them myself. No 'protective custody.'" Kort straightened his spine and locked his gaze on his parents, all the more determined. Mia and Magnus would need his guidance and attention, and they would receive that—and more.

He pointed at the castle guards, who stood ready for her next command. "Keep them at bay. They need to understand that neither Mia nor Magnus know our ways. Not yet. I don't want either of them in jeopardy ever again."

He turned away, but his mother blocked his path. "Don't try to do this alone, Kort. Let us help you…for once."

He tossed his head back with a humorless laugh. "Right, Mother. Just like you help with everything else when it comes to me and my dragons."

His father pulled his mother away then glowered down at Kort, lowering his voice so that only the three of them could hear. "If you mean to court Mia properly, Son, and to make her your wife, you might start by showing her how deeply you respect mine."

The jibe cut Kort and he ground his teeth to keep from saying anything else he might regret. It wasn't that he didn't love his mother—he did—but her insatiable need to dictate his life path drove them over and over to exchange harsh words.

He bowed to her then locked eyes with his father. "Of course. You're right. No sense in Mia having to suffer our family relationships on her first night home. But, know this. I have claimed her as my bride. We consummated our union, and I believe Varik blessed our endeavors because our magic liberated the Dragonstone. I even gave her our family ring as a promise. I intend to marry her."

"You did *what?*" his mother asked, glancing over at Mia. "Seven kingdoms of women here on Chalvaren for you to choose from, and you pick her?"

"Yes, Mother, I've made my choice, and I expect Mia to have every right bestowed upon her that the decision entails. Are we clear on that?" He first spoke pointedly to his parents, and then he glared at the surrounding guards. Every elf who still held a readied weapon sheathed it, and as a unit the elves all stood down.

King Lachlan leaned back on his heels, gave a little bounce and widened his eyes. A moment later a smile of merriment touched his lips, and he pointed to Mia. "Very impressive, Son. Not only have you found yourself a beautiful bride, but she's returned the Dragonstone and imprinted with the only known spirit dragon in the realm. While it's true Magnus was intended to be matched up with the next in line of our soldiers, obviously Varik had something different in mind."

Next to his father, Kort's mother swallowed hard. "I never meant for the dragonlet's egg to be stolen. I never should have trusted that mercenary, and now I'm grateful you went after him. But, Kort, we have to talk about this. If you've chosen your princess, things must… Well, things must be handled…"

Had he actually rendered his mother speechless? Kort rolled his eyes, doubting it would last. She and his father had urged him to take a wife. They'd matched him up with hundreds of women from around the kingdom and the seven territories surrounding Castle Elias, but he'd never connected with any of them. If his parents—if his *mother*—contested Mia as his rightful choice…well, their relationship might well deteriorate beyond repair.

He nodded tightly and pointed to Mia, who once again astonished him, a vision of beauty with her waist-length blonde hair flowing down around her simple purple dress. Magnus waited beside her. "You should be grateful to *her* for returning him, Mother. For returning *me*. Without her courage, without her inborn love for Magnus, this conversation wouldn't even be happening."

His father chuckled. "Theo could have planned it this way, Elissabet. Think about it. Maybe he instilled that fire in Mia's heart for the Aurora? You say Magnus sought her out, Kort?"

Kort nodded. "I understand that none of this is easy for any elf on Chalvaren considering the current political climate and the risk of having an Ansgar in the house of Elias, but somehow I know bringing them back here was the right thing to do. Sort out your thoughts and we'll speak later. I'm going to see this dragonlet reunited with his kin before any other disaster befalls us today." Then Kort spun on his heel and strode away.

He watched Mia unclench her fists as he approached. Those eyes, those green eyes of hers that saw so much, nearly did him in. He wasn't sure why, but it was as if she could see right through him, right inside his very soul. He hadn't exactly been ready for something so intense when he went off hunting the missing Magnus, not until he met Mia. Now all he wanted to do was get as close to her as she'd let him.

Of course, that might be the death of him. How could he protect the kingdom when he wanted nothing more than to be close to her?

When she smiled at him, his insides melted into a jumbled mess, and she pointed at Magnus. "He needs to eat."

"Agreed." Kort held out his hand. "You hungry, little one?"

Magnus sat back on his haunches, a healthy snort his only reply.

Mia chuckled, scratching the dragonlet's chin, and Kort quirked his lips. Then he began his standard post-flight inspection and surveyed the little dragon for injuries.

"The first thing you need," he said to Mia, "is to learn is how to check your dragon for wounds." He feathered his hands over the beast's snout and head, then down under his chin.

Mia's blonde brows rose over those sparkling emerald green eyes, and she studied him. "Wounds?"

"Yes, wounds. Little injuries can kill a dragon if they're missed. If they tear off a claw in battle, infection could set in. Because Magnus is so young, his scales haven't hardened completely. If he loses too many, he will be unacceptably vulnerable. Any trauma can cause this to happen."

"Oh," Mia said, moving closer. Three iridescent black dragon scales glittered on the floor, and she bent to pick them up, stared at them and then tucked them away.

Kort traced both hands down Magnus's chest and then his forelegs. "If you wanted to kill a dragon, taking his wings or his tail is sure to do the trick. While muscular and formidable, their wings are essentially their heart, their freedom—and also unarmored. Ground the beast and you've eventually got a dead dragon on your hands."

Mia moved as he did, following his lead, touching the dragon's hide wherever he did. Kort let their hands connect, and her fingers stumbled over his. The contact ignited him, and a memory of touching her back in her cottage flashed through his mind. It had been pure bliss.

Magnus watched with wide, blinking eyes, and Kort moved his hand away, embarrassed. The memory was too potent to revisit here in front of everyone.

"The wings are especially delicate on a youngster like Magnus," he managed to say.

"Look," Mia said, and pointed to a hole at the tip of his right wing. "There. An arrow from the archers in my village?"

Their escape had been more difficult than Kort first hoped, but they three had managed thanks to Mia's magic. She need never fear those bastards again. She need never leave this, her home world, again.

Magnus nosed the soft edge of his purple and teal-tipped wing, bringing Kort back to reality as a whimper rose in the beast's throat. Kort tested the small hole with his fingers and promised, "Not to worry. This shouldn't cause any concern."

Nor did anything else he found. Once he finished checking Magnus and found all was well, he stood up. "Let's take him down to the shore for his first feast, shall we?"

"Okay," Mia said. "A feast? What's that like?"

Kort grinned. "So, you don't know it all? Good. Come with me and I'll show you what I do when I'm not protecting the kingdom or tracking down stolen eggs." He held out an arm for her to take. "Even if you think you know about dragons from your father's stories, the practical reality of caring for them takes experience."

Mia took two steps with him then looked around the hall, surprised. "So, no restrictions on my moving around?" She indicated the guards, who mostly had returned to their posts. "Don't they want me wearing chains?"

"Mother was joking," Kort said.

Mia raised her eyebrow. "She sounded pretty damn serious to me."

"Well, maybe she wasn't joking," Kort allowed. "She just overreacted. There are elves in Chalvaren who will never trust anyone with your last name, but that doesn't mean you made the wrong choice by returning."

"Your mother being their leader?"

"She'll come around eventually. But as long as you're with me and we're in the company of my dragon warriors who are waiting outside, we should be fine." He cast a glance over his shoulder at the royal guard then sighed. "I'm sure some of them will follow us. It's something you'll have to get used to. Castle rules."

"No dungeon, no problems," Mia said and shrugged. Her eyes lit up, and her ample lips turned up at the corners. "Now you can show me around."

Her equanimity pleased him, and he leaned in close and brushed her mouth with his own. She responded and returned the kiss for one simple second, but then she pulled away. Still, all at once his day felt right and filled with promise.

He pulled back when his father cleared his throat. King Lachlan maintained a careful distance, Queen Elissabet sheltered behind his body as both parents eyed Magnus. Kort's father cocked his head, reached into a pocket in his robe and pulled out a...dragonfruit. He held it forward, his palm flat, and looked at Mia.

"May I offer your dragon a treat?"

Mia inspected the spiky, greenish-red offering, while Magnus peered at the man who'd produced it. When she glanced at Kort, he nodded approval. Lachlan shared an affinity for training dragons. Everything Kort knew about the beasts he'd learned from watching him.

Mia whispered in Magnus's ear and urged him toward Lachlan. "Go ahead. You must be starving, little one!"

Magnus still hesitated.

Finally, the dragonlet eased toward the king. Kort eyed Magnus with speculation, but the beast nickered and sniffed the food. Then, with soft, tentative lips, he took the offering and gobbled it down.

Kort thanked Varik the creature hadn't bitten off his father's hand.

Lachlan laughed, a booming sound full of power and love that made Kort lock gazes with him. "I've missed you these last ten days," he said.

Another treat appeared, and this time Magnus took it from the king's hand without reservation. Lachlan eased forward and scratched the horse-sized creature under the chin. "Mia, our apologies for startling your dragon. My wife"—he looked back at Elissabet with an embarrassed grin—"merely meant to provide you with *protective* custody."

Mia glanced at Elissabet, who stared inquisitively back, then quickly again at Magnus. Kort feathered his hand down her back to reassure her.

Lachlan took Mia's hands in his, his gaze locked on the Elias family ring she wore. "Consider Castle Elias yours, Mia. Kort will show you the grounds, get you settled in. We'll prepare the west tower for you for now. Magnus should love the dragon-deck up there, and with that wingspan he should be able to reach it in a snap." When Lachlan looked around at his men and lifted his hand they scurried into action, whispering amongst themselves before branching off to do their king's bidding.

Queen Elissabet stepped forward, curiosity clearly overcoming all that had come before. "Where's your father, child? Your mother, too. Where's Melia?"

Kort pulled Mia close. "Give her some time. We can talk about this later, after—"

"He died," Mia said, spinning the Elias family ring around on her finger. "Both of my parents died three years ago. A hurricane blew in and swamped the nearby village. They went to help, but...the waters claimed them. I searched for them but never found their bodies. I just...I never got the chance to say goodbye."

Mia's big green eyes were full of tears as she told the story, and Kort hated to see her in such pain.

Elissabet reached over and clutched Lachlan's arm. "I'm so sorry, Mia. Your parents...were important to us."

Kort's mind raced. He wondered exactly how important Theo Ansgar had been to his parents, and moreover, why the man had left Chalvaren at all. Clearly there was more to the story than Ansgar deciding to up and steal the Dragonstone and disappear into the ether.

"Kort tells us he wants to marry you," King Lachlan said suddenly. "Are you up for that job, young lady? Being Princess of Chalvaren?"

Mia glanced up and around the room, blinking rapidly. "I...I honestly I have no idea what's involved."

Kort shook his head. "Dad, give her some room to breathe, please." They'd wanted him to pick a wife more than anything, an appropriate goal for royal parents, sure, but he'd yet to find the time to tell Mia what he wanted, what he'd imagined... Hell, he'd just figured it out himself. The day had grown long, and he still had so much he wanted to say to everyone involved.

Mia was staring at the king. "My father... I obviously believe he had good reasons for whatever he did, but I didn't realize he was an enemy to so many people here. I want to help Kort help Magnus, but"—she turned and touched the dragonlet, who nuzzled her hand—"I don't know if I belong here. Especially not as a princess of the land."

"Of course you do." Kort took both her hands in his and stared into those perfect green eyes. Didn't she know how much he wanted her with him? Somehow he'd expected she would after the lovemaking they shared in her cottage. That wasn't the usual, so Mia must know what she meant to him. He'd even told her. He'd shown her when they blended their auras, yet...it *was* a lot to process.

"Don't let them intimidate you, Mia," he said. "Dad, I need you to back off."

"Of course, Son. Of course." Lachlan eased back. "I want you to keep my family's ring, Mia. It's a symbol that you belong with us. That you're under my protection. As was your father."

Mia lifted her eyes to the king's again. "So it's true, your decree cleared his name? Even if some elves still do, *you* don't consider my father an enemy of Chalvaren?" She glanced at Queen Elissabet then back at Kort. "I thought he was mistaken."

"What?" Kort's interest flared, and he looked at his parents. "Neither of you spoke about Mia's father much when I was growing up. All I really remember was that you and Theo shared...well, a history. You flew together as Dragon Riders while young men. Then one day he stole the Dragonstone and disappeared. Or something like that."

Lachlan nodded, so Kort went on. "Surely Mia wants to know the rest of the story from your side. I certainly do."

His father smiled sadly at Mia. "No, my dear. Theo Ansgar was no enemy of mine. We'll talk about it once you get more settled in. I actually have some things that belonged to Theo that might interest you."

Kort swallowed hard. He decided not to push for now; he'd never heard his father sound so melancholy.

"She'll need a wardrobe," Kort's mother spoke up, glancing from his father to Kort. "Ladies to tend her. A guard, of course."

Mia lifted the hem of her torn, dirtied dress. An angry black singe from a burning arrow marred the delicate purple fabric. "This is all I brought with me. My mother made it. I guess it's ruined now."

"It's not so bad, Mia," Kort said, seeing her despair. "Mother's tailor could repair this...?" He lifted his eyes to Elissabet, the request clear on his face; then he gently fingered the fabric of the purple skirt as he inspected it. "I'm grateful that arrow missed its intended target."

"Of course we'll repair your favorite dress," Elissabet said, reaching out to inspect the torn garment. "I'll send my best assistant with some replacements, and I'll set my man on it at once. What else do you need, Mia?"

"Right now? To feed this dragonlet," Mia answered, and she turned back to Magnus.

Kort held out his hand. "Come and take a walk with me. There's something I want you to see."

Mia hesitantly slipped her hand into his, and when she did, his chest swelled with pride. He couldn't just tell her what awaited them outside; he wanted to show her.

"Both of you," he pointed out. "Call your dragon, Mia."

"Magnus, come," Mia called, and she let out a little whistle.

"Good," Kort said as the dragon followed without reservation. Then he gently urged her toward the arched doors overlooking an enormous grassy field. "Now for the *really* important introductions."

Outside, they approached cliffs covered with enormous boulders, ancient rock promontories overlooking the Chalvaren Sea. A gust of ocean breeze caught Mia's mane of waist-length blonde hair and swirled it around her like an angel's nimbus, and Kort smiled and pointed over the rocks to the shore a hundred feet below.

Mia stopped dead in her tracks. Kort turned and faced her, and her broad smile ignited one of his own. Speechless, Mia's mouth opened, and her eyes went wide.

Kort chuckled.

Mia bolted forward, running past him with an expression of awe and anticipation on her beautiful face to stare at what he'd pointed out below. Her excitement tugged on Kort's heart. That smile, that joy dancing behind Mia's eyes... Yeah, this was what she deserved. And, now that she was here with him and things were as-all-right-as-possible inside the walls of Castle Elias, he laughed out loud at her reaction.

"Dragons!" she shrieked happily. She jumped up and down and pointed. "Oh, my god, Magnus, look! Down there! On the shore! Those are the fighting dragons of Chalvaren."

Joy sparkled in her deep green eyes, and Kort's hands trembled. He wanted to see that expression remain; if he had any say in the matter, he'd give everything he owned to witness that look of passion on her face again for the rest of today and for all days. He'd inspired such only when he'd held her and watched her respond to his touch in the cottage, when he'd kissed her sensitive ears for the first time, when she'd called his name over and over, the sound of her voice caught up in shared passion the sweetest thing he'd ever heard.

Magnus moved close, peering down at the shore from behind Mia, and he croaked out a curious whine of surprise and recognition.

Mixed with the chest-busting pride he felt, a sudden sense of dread hit Kort's gut. How perfectly they both fit into his world up here on Chalvaren's cliffs, Mia and Magnus, just like some damn splendid fairy tale. But he needed to show them the beauty of his home, of their birthright, while keeping them both safe from Chalvaren's darkness.

He had no idea how he would do that.

Chapter 6

Mia rushed forward to the edge of the grassy cliff and stopped at the boulders. She covered her mouth with her hand and bounced in place, staring down the steep drop-off to the beaches of Chalvaren a hundred feet below.

An orange sun hovered at the horizon and lit up translucent wings of the beasts flying above the blue-green ocean, and she quietly started counting. *One. Two. Three. Four...* Stunned, she realized the futility of the exercise and simply watched the creatures lofting like flocks of elegant birds in the salt-scented breeze.

"The mighty dragons of Chalvaren. My father spoke truth," she whispered, her belly flipping with joy. "They *do* exist."

She edged closer to the side of the cliff and watched the majesty of their wings as they flew in loops on Chalvaren's zephyrs. Magnus clutched the rocks with his claws and leaned forward to get a better look, while Kort chuckled beside Mia.

"Pretty amazing, right?"

She looked up into his eyes. "You brought me from loneliness to the one place I need to be." She wrapped her arms around his neck, enjoying the hard stability of the corded muscles that strapped his shoulders, then leaned up and kissed him on the cheek.

He turned his face and captured her lips with his. Soft, warm, generous yet demanding, his kiss almost made her forget there were live dragons flying around her. This passion he evoked made her feel alive, like she'd never be lonesome ever again.

He broke away far too soon. "You said you never should have trusted me back there, Mia."

"That was...before. I was second-guessing myself, second-guessing that all this could be true."

"And now?" He embraced her then turned her to face the dragons once more. "What about now, Mia?"

A white dragon soared high above them, swooping through the air and boasting a wingspan Mia couldn't possibly calculate, sunlight sparkling off iridescent diamond scales. She lifted a hand as if reaching for the animal. "No second-guessing you now. The element of air. *So* beautiful."

"Her name is Pure. She's a Wind dragon. My mother rides her."

"Pure," Mia whispered. Then three blue-green dragons caught her eye, sweeping down toward the ocean's surface from the left.

Seeing her reverence, Kort gestured. "Water dragons. That's Poseidon in the lead. He's such a showoff. My dad named him after a character in a book collected from Earth that he keeps in his library. He rides Poseidon now."

It felt so good to be surrounded by dragons, Mia barely noticed as Kort let his hand fall to her waist and he looked down at her.

"How many dragons live here?" she asked. "In Chalvaren?"

"All told throughout the lands my scouts and I calculate there are around a hundred left. That includes dragons in all the seven kingdoms. Four primary elementals serve Castle Elias—well, Magnus makes five—and twenty more feral-class dragons serve in our Dragon Command."

"'Primary elementals'? 'Ferals'? What do you mean?" Mia asked.

"Primary elementals are dragons whose breath weapons are closest to their element of origin. Earth, wind, fire, or water.

Mia turned and stared at him. "I thought all dragons breathed fire."

Kort's eyebrows rose. "Is that what you were taught, Mia? No, far from it." He shook his head. "Okay, so, the closer a dragon's makeup is to its primary element, the more their weapon manifests through that element. So, yes, fire dragons breathe fire. But wind dragons don't. They summon air."

Mia blinked, trying to understand. Seeing her struggle, Kort touched her shoulder and pointed up to Pure.

"She uses her element of air and converts the power of the wind into her weapon. Wind dragons can create a tornado with their roars," he said.

"And water dragons?" Mia looked down at Poseidon, who dove into the ocean and surfaced a moment later, a great wave cresting in his wake. His pack, in close pursuit, caught the wave and rode it, frolicking in the aftermath. Watching brought joy to Mia's heart.

"Water dragons can breathe all versions of water. They can create a soft summer rain shower or spout up great waves upon the sea. Mostly, though, our water dragons help us find fish to eat."

"And what about the feral class?" Mia asked. "Who are they, and do they have combination weapons?"

"An astute observation. The farther away a dragon's bloodline is from its element, the more unique its weapon. A wild clutch of mixed dragons can turn out quite a lot of diversity, but that comes at a price, I think. Their powers aren't as strong as those of the primary elementals."

Mia shook her head, unbelieving. "This is literally a dream come true. I remember days on end spent listening to my father tell me stories of how elves care for dragons and dragons defend their elves, but to be standing here and seeing this for myself..."

"I can't imagine living in a world where they don't exist," Kort agreed. "That must have been hard," he added, glancing at her in concern.

Had growing up as an outcast on Earth been hard for her? Impossibly so. But could Kort really understand? That was why she so badly wanted to fit in here with him. If anything went wrong she would find herself with even less than before.

"Somewhere deep in my heart I always doubted my father," she found herself admitting. "I actually felt sorry for him. I wondered if he was crazy. Still, you should have seen the way his face lit up when he spoke about dragons. Imaginary or not, they brought him pure, unadulterated joy."

The memory of her father filled her with joy, too, especially now that the truth about Chalvaren stretched before her with widespread wings and scales that reflected sunlight with such intensity that tears sprang to her eyes. She and Kort stood side by side, silently watching, and she thanked their people's gods that she was finally sitting on a cliff overlooking the ocean of Chalvaren and its dragons.

It was all too much to take in. She pinched her skin to make certain she wasn't dreaming.

Beside her, Magnus suddenly keened a strange, high-pitched sound. Mia eyed him. Why was he making so much noise? He leaned over the edge of the cliff, spread his juvenile wings wide and let the wind beat against him. Gusts billowed his leathery wings, and...

Mia's first instinct? A smile. She reached out and touched Magnus's wing. Of course he wanted to fly. How could she blame him? She wanted to be down there too, to fly with his brethren, to catch the breezes, to do loops. Her second instinct was—

"Oh. My. God. Can we fly together?"

She eyed Kort, whose smile looked promising enough that she bounced up and down with excitement. Glancing downward, she watched two golden-brown dragons on the beach below ferret through the sand. The distance didn't seem *that* far. They were playing, digging and casting sand and seawater up into the air. One stilled and raised its head to respond to Magnus's call.

Mia looked back at Kort. "Earth dragons?"

His eyes gleamed, and he stood taller, his chest thrust out. "Yes, earth dragons. Terra is their leader, the big female digging in the sand there."

"Terra," Mia repeated. "What's her weapon?"

"She can blow up a sandstorm or a wall of mud, but see her tail? I've seen her strike the ground with it and open a crevasse like an earthquake. They often do that to mine for treasure," Kort said. "Those claws she's digging with are hard as forged iron."

Mia sighed with wonder. "When they're first born, how do you know which element a dragon belongs to?"

Kort smiled. "If we're lucky enough to know the two parents it's an easy guess. If we don't, it's in their coloring sometimes, but we have to observe the dragonlets and make sure they don't get into trouble because mostly we see the truth in their behavior. Wind dragons get right up in the air to test the breezes. Earth dragons start digging for treasure. Fire dragons start setting things ablaze. "

Mia looked over at Magnus. "What about spirit dragons? What do they do?"

"Well," Kort said, "we don't know exactly. But trust me, I'm taking notes."

Magnus had stepped back from the cliff edge. Wide-eyed now, he tilted his head suddenly toward Mia, purred, then threw his black wings wide. Salt air rippled again through the hollow of his wings and threatened to loft him into the sky, and he yipped out another vocalization, a call of excitement to the other dragons of Chalvaren. He did not seem like he was ever going to stop.

Mia laughed and stepped toward him. How could she deny Magnus? How could she even attempt to tell him to contain his exuberance when she felt the same way herself? Every fiber of her being wanted to be airborne, diving down the sheer side of the cliff. But, she had no wings. Could she truly ride Magnus? Even if he was strong enough, would he let her?

"How about the whole riding-a-dragon thing my father spoke of?" she found herself saying to Kort. "Who gets to ride a dragon? Do *you* ride them? How soon after they're born can they fly, and when can they fly with a rider? Is it like breaking in a horse?"

Kort grasped her arm and pulled her back. He pointed toward the sea. "Whoa there, Mia. There's one more dragon I want you to see."

She looked again at the dragons soaring below, and she saw what he indicated. Last but definitely not least was the biggest dragon of all. The red. The dragon born of the element of fire.

She pointed. "Oh, my goodness. He's magnificent."

"His name is Garnet," Kort said.

"A fire-breather?" She bounced from foot-to-foot and grabbed Kort's arm. "Oh. My. God. He's...he's huge!"

Magnus bayed louder.

Garnet the Red soared closer. Mia saw he led a flight of much smaller black and multicolored dragons, and he swung his spiky head toward them. Wariness and trepidation set in upon seeing that warlike face, and Mia's hands shook. She waved her hand to silence the dragonlet.

"Shh, Magnus, don't make so much noise! He'll hear you!"

Garnet did just that. He soared ever closer, and Mia's heart rate doubled. She covered her mouth with her hand. Her third instinct with dragons was apparently sheer terror.

Garnet spread his wings wide and let out a roar. He rose above the dragons he led, who held their course while he twisted and swooped straight toward them.

Mia bolted to Magnus. "Be quiet!" she shouted, but it was a useless command. The closer the fire dragon flew, the louder

Magnus howled, and when the red passed over them he raced out across the field in pursuit.

Mia gave chase through the grass, but Kort thundered up behind her, his strong arms banding around her waist.

"Stop, Mia." He pulled her into his arms. "Just be still."

She struggled against him. "No. Magnus…," she gasped. "He'll… He can't…"

Kort held her fast. His grip was as tight as a vise, and for an instant it stirred memories of lying in his arms, him grasping her hips while he hovered over her, loving her, holding her tight to his naked body. Making magic.

Shaking off the past, Mia turned her face skyward. Garnet circled once in a descent then landed perfectly in the green grassy field, a mere hundred yards away. Magnus flattened his wings to his body and scurried forward to greet the enormous red dragon.

"No. Stop him!" Mia shouted. Every sound was suddenly a roar, and she covered her ears with shaky hands. Her heartbeat thrashed wildly in her ears, ramming cold, hard fear through the rest of her body.

"Be still, Mia." Kort's deep voice was a command, not a request.

She couldn't obey. The two dragons circled each other, and she was certain this was a dance of destruction. The strange sound of Magnus's cry wrenched her soul, and she struggled against her captor. "He'll kill him, Kort! Let me go!"

"No," Kort replied, pressing his cheek against hers. "Garnet won't hurt Magnus. Magnus belongs to him, Mia. They are one and the same. Garnet would give his life to protect Magnus, just like you want to do."

Mia struggled. She reached out toward her little black dragonlet, but Kort refused to let her go. She went limp in his arms.

The two dragons approached each other and hissed. Mia shook her head and moaned. She couldn't lose Magnus now. Not like this. What if Kort was wrong? What if Garnet ate him? Her dragonlet looked so small in comparison to one full-grown. Wasn't he terrified? What if he angered the older dragon like she'd angered the queen?

It was too much. No way in hell was she letting this fire-breather kill Magnus. She tensed her muscles, reared up her knee and stomped down on Kort's foot. He bellowed in pain, released his grip, and she ran forward to intervene.

Her desperate movement was like lightning across the grassy field, but Kort pursued and his long legs outmatched her. He snatched her back at the last second.

"Damn it, Mia! Listen to me!"

She wheeled on him, her face burning hot as dragon fire. "Let me go!"

"No! Stop, and let them be. I know the desire to protect him is strong in you. That's good, Mia. It's right." Kort eased her around to face the dragons, and she lifted her head to watch the inevitable. He held her tight and whispered in her ear, "But Garnet is his sire."

All fight left her, and she relaxed. Kort was right, of course. And this was Magnus's home, his kind. She had to learn to trust him. Still, she closed her eyes, too afraid to watch.

"You don't want to miss this, sweetheart." Kort's whisper was low and hot in her ear, and somehow she found the courage to rip open her eyes.

The two males circled each other, Magnus whining, Garnet growling. The story-high red bared razor-sharp teeth bigger than Mia's own hands, but she gave herself over to the posturing of the two males, stood up straight and faced their first encounter.

"Watch them," Kort said softly. "This is important."

The tension of the meeting was almost too much for her to take. While she wanted to hide, to curl up next to Kort's hard body in some soft bed somewhere, to hide in his strong embrace until this was over, she forced upon herself a calm stillness.

Kort tightened his hold. Gritting her teeth, Mia watched her dragonlet meet his destiny.

"Magnus should have been born here on Chalvaren. Garnet's face would have been the first thing he saw—a familiar face. We'd have prepared a feast for him. He would have spent the first hours of life filling his belly in the company of other dragons. Learning their ways."

Mia flinched. "But that didn't happen."

"No, it didn't. The mercenary who stole his egg deprived him it, but it will happen now."

Mia nodded tightly. Kort loved the dragonlet, too, maybe more than she did. Hell, he'd loved Magnus enough to cross time and space to find him, and then the beast was still in his egg. If anything truly threatened Magnus, Kort would be the first one fighting to save him.

"Garnet has been beside himself ever since Magnus's egg went missing. He's quite territorial," Kort pointed out.

Mia swallowed her fear and turned. The bluest eyes she'd ever seen glittered with anticipation in Kort's rugged, handsome face, and his jaw clenched with determination. His pointed ears, so like hers, reminded her that he too was an elf, and that he knew what he was talking about. More so than she did.

"That's why you came for him," she said.

Kort nodded. "To return him to Garnet. To return him to Chalvaren, sweetheart. Magnus finding you was the best surprise of my day, and I'm glad he ate that mercenary before he hurt you. I had no idea how I'd get Magnus back. Then he found you, and you helped us get him back here where he belongs—and you where you belong."

"He recognized the ghostfire signature on my cottage."

"The signature your father left for me," Kort agreed. "That ghostfire called the dragonlet to you; the elven Ansgar rune above your cottage door was a signal for both of us to find you so you could see this. So you could bear witness to what your father always wanted you to see." He pointed to the two dragons. "Watch them, Mia."

The pair's first meeting played out like a dance of sorts. Mia watched, fascinated. "They're acting like other animals. Sniffing. Testing each other. Posturing. Growling. It's about dominance and submission."

Kort delivered a kiss on her pointed ear. "Yes. Dragons display pack behavior."

"Like wolves or dogs back on Earth."

Garnet circled Magnus. Magnus responded, and growled. Mia understood. Well, the whole wing-raising thing she'd never seen, but these two were dragons rather than the dogs she'd watched before.

"Magnus is yielding to him," she said, her voice light with surprise as Magnus rolled across the grass, exposing his belly.

"Yes. Garnet is his superior. Magnus has good instincts, Mia. He knows who's in charge—and he likes it."

As Kort spoke, he increased the pressure of his hands on her hips. It comforted her in a primitive way, like he was in command of her body. Mia grasped his arms more tightly, telegraphing her pleasure, and she was both surprised and encouraged by the rising passion in his eyes. She took a cleansing breath and caught a wisp of Kort's blue aura flaring on his skin, and it eased her heart rate, gentled her fears. For the first time that day, she felt completely safe.

Beside them, the two dragons exposed their teeth. Garnet leaned down and toppled Magnus with his snout, and Mia cringed, but her spirit dragon rolled, exposed his belly again, and then stilled. Garnet hoisted up red wings, tossed his snout in the air, and roared.

Mia wanted to cover her ears, but she stood still and endured the deafening sound. Magnus called back, a high keening yip. He rolled over again then leapt up on all fours, yelping a playful croak, trying to imitate the big red fire dragon. Garnet sat back on his haunches, lowering his wings, and eyed Magnus speculatively.

The youngster was up on his feet, staring at the older dragon with admiration. Garnet eased back his head, opened his jaws, and roared. It was both terrifying and magnificent. Mia felt the sonic vibration come up from the ground and pulsate through her boots, and she clapped her hands over her ears. She lowered her hands then and really listened. It was a call of pride and happiness.

A smile split Kort's face and he chuckled, a deep warm sound that sound made Mia tremble inside. He kissed her ear, his generous lips soft and warm. A tingle ran straight to her core.

"Good job, Mia."

She smiled back at him. The delicious feeling of his lips on her skin made her squirm her hips, and the sound of his chuckles drew her closer to his body. A new onslaught of emotions and feelings almost took her breath and made her—

Magnus suddenly sat back on his haunches. The midnight-black dragonlet mirrored Garnet's body language, lifted his head to the sky and, damn, if he didn't roar. He roared with all the gusto any youngling could muster, head thrown back, his whole body shuddering with the effort.

"Would you listen to that?" she said with a grin. It was the most endearing sound ever to touch her elven ears. Thank Varik that Kort had come for him. He belonged here on Chalvaren with Garnet and others of his kind. "He's discovered his roar."

Kort stood tall, seemingly more excited than she was. "That's it, little one!"

Magnus hesitated for a moment. He cast a glance back over his wings toward Mia and Kort then tossed his black snout in the air three times before saying, "My *sire.*" He turned back to the red fire-breather and looked longingly at him.

The reverence in the little dragon's voice had stunned Mia. She asked, "Do the other dragons talk?"

Kort's blue eyes sparkled, and his words were rushed. "He's the first as far as I know. There are legends, myths of dragons that speak to elves, but..." He gestured toward Garnet. "They communicate with each other. I mean, we help them understand what we want them to do in the air with signals, with flags in battle, and I know they hear and understand us, but...no Mia. I've never heard another dragon speak our elven tongue. Just Magnus."

Mia bit her lip. "Will the others be upset about it? Will he be a freak like me, unwanted and—?"

Kort shook his head. "Freak? No. *Hell* no. You're no freak, Mia. You're unique, and you belong here like Magnus. Both of you were just in the wrong place for awhile." He stepped forward and tugged her hand, and Mia followed him. "Come on. Let's get these introductions out of the way. Garnet needs to meet you."

Kort motioned to the red with a hand signal Mia had never seen, and the red leaned his head down to smell her. She shivered as he breathed in, seeming to both taste and sense her in a myriad ways with that action.

Tentatively, Mia held out her hand. The huge fire-breather nuzzled her palm, and his snout was warm, moist, and comforting. She couldn't help but smile as she sought the rough scales under his chin and gave them a scratch.

Kort moved forward and spoke. "Let's mount up, big boy. Let's show Mia what it feels like to fly!"

Mia wet her lips, and a fluttery feeling beat about in her belly. "What? Fly? Seriously? On him?!"

Garnet lowered his neck and extended his right front leg. Kort pulled Mia toward him.

"Well, we could walk down to the beach, but we'll get there faster if we take to the air. Come with me, Mia. Let me show you this."

"What about Magnus?"

"No worries, sweetheart. Garnet's got him."

The red growled and eyed the dragonlet before flicking his tail. Magnus scrambled up it to the top of the red's ridged back. Kort lifted Mia onto Garnet's knee then eased himself up beside her. She hesitated until he led her to a position behind the beast's head, in the crook of Garnet's neck. Two bony horns curved back there, serving as handles of a sort, and she swung into better position, grabbing on tight.

She wanted this so bad she could barely concentrate. Garnet was so big, she could only imagine how high he might fly. She managed to secure her purple skirt under her legs with shaking hands, and made room for Kort who scrambled up behind her.

Kort pinned her body with his own against the curve of those horns and wrapped an arm around her waist. One of his large hands spanned her belly, and he pulled her close. When he touched her like that, a spasm of desire speared low in her belly. They fit together perfectly, and Mia leaned back into that firm, muscled chest.

A flush of heat whisked through her. She blushed but couldn't resist wiggling back into his arms. The rigid shaft of his erection snugged close to Mia's buttocks, and he groaned and placed another kiss on her pointed ear. "I can't wait to get you back home, in my bed. What we did this morning was nothing compared to what I will show you tonight."

Mia wanted Kort, too. Despite what had happened with his family, what might still be a tense situation, she wanted to make love to him again. Their connection had been, for lack of a better word, *magical.* He was her One True Love. She couldn't imagine being alone now.

When Kort buried his lips in the hollow of her neck, Mia groaned. "How long is this going to take?"

He chuckled. "A little while. I swear, though, I'll make it worth the wait."

She blushed, knowing he would.

Garnet's scales radiated warmth beneath her, and Mia gripped his muscular neck with her legs then craned back to look back at Magnus. Her dragonlet was secure, his black claws dug tightly into the fire dragon's deep layers of red scales.

"So, let's go," she said, and increased the pressure of her grip around Garnet's ivory white horns. Her knuckles showed the same white.

Garnet rose to his full height, twenty feet from talon to horn, and took bounding steps until he was running. The air whipped through Mia's hair, which she'd neglected to secure, but it was too late now. The dragon ran full speed toward the edge of the cliff, spread his red wings, and leapt.

Just like that they were flying. Her massive, fire-breathing mount stroked salty air currents with his wings, and Mia shrieked, squeezing her eyes shut. Chalvaren's wind surrounded her, and she suddenly respected gravity on an entirely different level.

Kort laughed and nudged her with his jaw. "Have a look around, Mia."

The warmth of his big body behind her and the heat of the incredible dragon below tingled her every nerve ending. She dared a glance to the world below and sighed with pleasure. Safe in Kort's arms, she didn't want to miss a single moment, not one detail.

This is really happening. I'm flying on dragon-back in Chalvaren.

"I never expected it to feel so right, so where-I-was-meant-to-be," she murmured as Garnet cleared the cliff. Castle Elias shrank below her, its spires disappearing into tiny flagged dots. A gleaming city by the sea appeared, all its secrets seemingly opened for her to drink in.

Kort pointed to a range in the distance. "The Drakhos Mountains."

"That's where the Dragonstone was harvested before I was born," she replied.

Her stomach vaulted as Garnet flew higher, but she ventured another peek far below. Farms dotted the hilly landscape, and sheep, cows, and livestock she didn't recognize dotted green pastures. They swooped nearer, and elves below turned to look at them.

"Our people live down here," Kort said. Mia wanted to wave but instead held on tight.

A broad river, fed by blue-green water from the mountains, wound down to the sea. A tiny boat with a sail navigated its way along the water and drew her eye to sunlight sparkling off the waves. The briny aroma filled her nose.

"The Sea of Chalvaren," Kort murmured in her ear. "From where we draw much of our sustenance."

Cheerful houses decorated the landscape in vibrant colors and various shapes. Crops grew in the patchwork quilt of tidy tended gardens, with sunlit blue and red and yellow flowers. Kort waved at the male elves working the fields, and Garnet roared, and they waved back.

Mia's mind unlocked memories of her father, stories about the freedom of flight. She'd never missed him more than now, and some part of her grieved for how she'd never believed his tales about Chalvaren. But this place was real—as real as the mighty red dragon between her legs, as real as the prince holding her in his arms.

I wish he was here now to see all this.

Garnet soared up into the sky again, and his great wings spread some fifty feet wide to catch air currents rolling in from the sea. Mia took a breath, tasting the sweet, clean air. Flying with the dragon counted as the most incredible sensation she could ever recall, second only to sharing her body with Kort. The ecstasy he'd provided felt like flying, and she closed her eyes for a moment, remembering him moving over her, within her, whispering her name in her well-kissed ears.

Once his mother saw how much she loved Kort, maybe she'd come around?

As if reading her mind, her prince laid a gentle kiss on her ear, and Mia shivered, astounded he'd provided her with such breadth and depth of emotion and experience all in the span of one day. She trembled though she wasn't cold, primal instincts simmering within her. A vortex of pleasure twisted and raged inside her, and every fragment of her being screamed that this was where she belonged: safe and warm in Kort's arms.

"You okay?" he whispered softly in her ear.

She wasn't, she realized. Not exactly. She was worried. She'd always worried she was destined to be alone, a raw wound ripped through her heart after her parents left her stranded on Earth with no others of her kind, no one to understand her or her family's ways. The stark contrast between that and this newfound connection she shared with Kort was…unnerving. Could she let herself believe she would somehow fit in here, that he really wanted her above all things and not just Magnus and the power of the Dragonstone? Or was that foolish?

She bobbed her head up and down in answer and pressed closer to Kort, and he nuzzled her neck with hot, moist lips. The last thing she needed was to burden him with her fears. He was who he was, and the good here far outweighed the bad. Even if she somehow ended up alone.

"I'm so much better than okay," she called to him, and in almost every way it was true. "No wonder you love this."

Kort nodded emphatically then let out a whoop of satisfaction. Mia shut down her fears and held on tight.

Chapter 7

Kort surveyed his future kingdom as Garnet flew a wide arc around the city.

"So, this is Chalvaren. My father's Chalvaren," Mia said in front of him, a catch in her voice.

Kort adjusted his hold, pressing her taut stomach with the flat of his hand, and pointed out landmarks. "Yes. Look! My father's market. His pride and joy."

"Why is it so important to him?"

"A long time ago both our fathers fought to secure the port of Chalvaren under Elias territories. At first it was purely a military move, a strategy to make certain the lands where the Chalvaren River meets the sea are secure. My parents then established this market as a place of trade to enrich all the alliance kingdoms. All Chalvaren's peoples bring their wares here for shipping and sale."

"All Chalvaren's peoples?" Mia echoed.

"Elves aren't the only citizens of Chalvaren, Mia. Our world is known as Chalvaren, as is the main city of our Elias territories and our Kingdom. Our kingdom's citizens are mainly elves, but dwarves live in the north in other kingdoms, and there are other peoples here as well."

"Others. Okay," Mia said. "Will we get to meet them someday? And I want to look at that map again when we get back to the castle."

"We'll see." Kort gestured to the right with his head. "The Drakhos Mountains and the Chalvaren River. Everything. First impressions?"

The marketplace bustled below with merchants hawking their wares. The countryside stretched out to the rivers and the sea. The fluttering flags, which included his family's royal crest, heralded a grand kingdom. God, he loved it here, and if her sighs of appreciation were any indication, Mia would too.

"It's incredible. I never thought I'd see this. I'm..." She shook her head. "I never dreamed my father's stories were real."

The awe in her voice had him wondering why her father had deprived Mia of her birthright. Why had he run from Chalvaren? Did she know the answer? In time he'd earn her trust, and maybe she'd share all her secrets with him. He looked forward to the process.

"Definitely real," he said. "No fairy tales here."

Appreciative of Garnet's desire to show off for Mia and Magnus, Kort rubbed his mount's neck then craned back to check on the younger dragon. Magnus had dug into Garnet's heavy layers of scales with his claws, and he was anchored, moving his head about here and there, watching everything with rapt attention.

"Magnus looks happy, no?"

Mia's nod was tight. Kort tried to imagine what she was thinking, but then she wriggled. It was almost more than he could take, the warmth of her body rubbing against his erection. The friction felt good. Too damn good. To distract himself, he turned back to eye the dragonlet.

"He can't fall, can he?" Mia asked.

"Well, he's certainly full of surprises, but no, he shouldn't. And Garnet won't let anything happen to his son," Kort pointed out.

Garnet rumbled a soft growl of agreement.

Magnus had his wings folded close to his back, and he peered precariously over his sire's side at the ocean below. The dragonlet thrust his snout forward into the wind, and Mia called out, "I think he's smiling."

Kort chuckled and turned his attention back to her. "He's probably thinking about flying. All he needs is a day or two in the company of his kin and he'll learn. He'll learn to land, too. Hell, he'll learn everything—even the right things to eat that aren't meddling mercenaries." He leaned close and nuzzled Mia's neck again, her long silken blonde hair streaking out behind them.

She stiffened. "What...what if everyone rejects me because of my name? Like your mother did."

Kort clenched his jaw. "If anyone contests your rightful place beside me I'll see them in chains. But they won't. My father is on our side."

"You sound awfully sure. But what if you're wrong? What if you're wrong and Magnus goes to protect me and won't stop? What if Magnus kills another elf?"

Here he was, attempting to spin out a vision of how their lives would play out in perfect harmony, Magnus holding court with dragons he would someday lead and Mia holding court with her fellow elves, and all she could contribute was fear and negativity? He bit back annoyance. "Let's just give this some time, Mia."

She sighed. "Just tell me my coming here wasn't a huge mistake."

The sadness in her voice tightened around his chest like a band. He'd rather have her argue with him than feel defeated. "In order for you to fit in here," he pointed out, "we'll both have to make some changes."

"Changes...?"

"I chose Dragon Command for a reason. It's a hard life filled with endless hours of work: caring for dragons, drilling them and their riders, tackling the logistics of supplying them wherever they need to be. But it's an honest, clean life. No politics. No head games." He sighed. "The last thing I want is to become like my mother."

She stared at him. "Why would you have to change any of that?"

The innocence in her voice reminded Kort that Mia knew nothing of the realities of Chalvaren, realities he instantly hated. Refusing the luxuries of his heritage had been a joy all these years, a joy like ignoring his mother's associated demands. But he suddenly wanted to give Mia those comforts he'd denied himself. All of them.

"Because you deserve the best that Castle Elias has to offer."

"What does that mean?" she asked.

He didn't want to go into the political and emotional issues tied to his mother's understanding of his responsibilities. Building a family with her and truly becoming a worthy heir to the throne meant resolving his roles. He'd have to endure castle politics. Dress up in silks like his mother always wanted. Deal with other monarchs in the seven-kingdom alliance. Leave the day-to-day dragon care to others while he sat inside the castle listening to boring ramblings of state. The boy in him hated it. The man in him thought anything was a worthy sacrifice for Mia.

He tightened his grip on her waist and placed a kiss on the lobe of her pointed ear. "It means all this is yours, Mia. I want to share it with you."

Of course, there was still Isa to deal with. With her on the loose he couldn't abandon his military responsibilities. Not yet. Especially not now that the Dragonstone was returned. Mia's one remaining blood relative on Chalvaren was public enemy number one—her aunt, Theo Ansgar's sister—and the appearance of Mia and the artifact would likely bring an intensification of her aunt's evil.

Countermeasures began to fill Kort's head. First he'd speak to his father in private. Maybe they could come up with some way to better secure both the Dragonstone and Mia. He'd coordinate with Duncan, too, the captain of the guard, maybe even bring in Lucan Brix, the castle wizard. At all costs he would keep Mia protected, shielded, hidden.

Surely she would want to meet Isa, though—a terrible idea. Her aunt represented her only living link to her family. Kort's thoughts churned for an answer but found none. Damn, she'd likely be furious when she found out the truth. Or would she? How important was this particular tie? From the earlier exchange with his mother it seemed Mia didn't know about Isa. Or had she just been holding something back from him?

Dire discomfort gnawed at his gut. Gods, what had he done by asking Mia to come here? Had he done the wrong thing, gotten so caught up in the prophecy and his own desire that he'd acted rashly? Mia controlled both Magnus and the Dragonstone. When she found out her one remaining relative was Chalvaren's greatest enemy, what would she do? Where would her allegiance lie?

He had to trust his gut instinct. Her innocence assured him Mia would choose wisely. His mother had been wrong—dead wrong—to fear her. Though his own aura was tied to the demigod Marineth, and thus one of his struggles had always been trust, Kort believed in Mia. She could never be a threat to Chalvaren.

Garnet interrupted his thoughts by circling the shallows near the beach. A silvery school of fish scattered when the great dragon's shadow eclipsed them, and Magnus whined. Kort understood instantly. The little dragon was hungry.

"It's time for his first feast," he told Mia. "Way past time. Hold on."

Nearby other dragons dove for fish, and Kort grinned when he heard his warriors cry out with each success. He leaned forward and tapped Garnet's neck three times, pointed to the water and their potential meals then grasped Mia tight in his arms. Garnet dove, plummeting toward the sea.

Mia shrieked. Magnus croaked, which was embarrassing. Kort felt bad for the dragonlet's pride. He knew dragons preferred to roar.

Garnet did just that, a deafening sound that split the silence of the golden afternoon. Fish in the school scattered and jumped. Garnet flapped his wings faster, extending sharp claws down into the sea, and skimmed up two huge wriggling bluefin. Kort laughed out loud and patted Garnet's neck.

"Take us in, old man. Magnus needs to eat."

The fire dragon turned and glided silently toward the beach. Kort stared at the steep white cliffs rising from the beach to Castle Elias above, and in particular the Elias royal family flags whipping in the wind.

Garnet back-winged once he was above the shore, tossed his catch onto a bed of waiting seaweed and then descended, light as a feather. He touched down on the sand so elegantly that Kort never felt a thing.

"A perfect landing," he praised.

Garnet lowered his leg, and Kort jumped to help Mia down, spinning her around before he let her feet touch the sand. Her soft curves felt good in his hands. Her laughter erased his previous fears, and then she leaned in and kissed him; quick, hard, demanding.

She tasted like sunshine and sweet morning dew. Kort wanted her back in his bed. The kiss freed him from worries yet shackled him to desire. He could have kissed her full lips all afternoon, made love to her right there on the shore, but Magnus chattered out a complaint of curiosity and Mia broke away to check on him.

Damn dragonlet.

Kort pulled Mia back in front of him and encircled her with his arms. Garnet twisted toward the gasping fishes flopping around on soft green seaweed, roared, then turned his head toward his son and nudged Magnus down off his back.

"Watch them," Kort prompted.

Magnus croaked again and clambered down off Garnet's back. He shied away from the wriggling fish at first, flailing on the shore against their sudden eviction from the sea, but their jerky movements brought the other dragons.

Mia leaned over toward Kort. "Magnus doesn't understand what to do. Do we need to clean it for him or something?"

"Wait," Kort said, pulling her close, and he was pleased when she relaxed into his arms. Her soft body, so close, so tantalizing, made him crazy with need. The soft curve of her hips elicited a groan of appreciation.

To their right, it only took the dragonlet a second to catch on. He studied Garnet's movements intently, his tail twitching behind him. He and Garnet circled the flopping fishes in full-stalk mode. Finally, the red nosed a fish out of the seaweed. It protested violently, flopping here and there, trying to find the sea. Magnus tried for a grown-up growl. Kort felt a smile of almost-paternal pride.

Mia's stomach growled audibly. "That fish would feed two people for a week."

Kort feathered one hand down to her belly. "And it's a mere snack for a growing dragon. Do you like to eat fish?"

"Are you kidding? I love most anything from the sea." She folded into him like she belonged there, and together they watched the dragons.

Magnus chattered out an un-dragonlike sound and dodged away from a flipping fish again. Garnet snared it in his teeth and gobbled the thing whole. Magnus sat back on his haunches, blinked his amber eyes rapidly and watched, then suddenly dove into action. He tore into the other fish, mimicking his sire's gusto if unable to manage the same one-bite ingestion.

Kort let out a laugh and nuzzled into Mia's hair. "Magnus will be fine, see? Speaking of which, is that a dragon I hear roaring in your stomach?"

Mia smiled and covered her belly with her hands.

"We need to eat too," Kort said. "You must be starving. I know I am."

"Yes, I'm starving, just like— Well, maybe not *just* like him." She looked away from the feasting dragons. Magnus was not exactly being clean. Scales flew everywhere. When he looked up, he had sand in his teeth and a long strand of wet green seaweed hung down from his snout.

Kort chuckled. "When they're finished here we'll go back to the castle, and if I can keep my hands off of you, we'll find something to eat."

She blushed, and he adored that pink color.

Magnus edged away from the slick green strand on his snout, pawed at it with a black claw and stumbled face-first into the sand. Mia covered her mouth and laughed, doubling over when the little black dragon raised his snout and pawed desperately at the sand in his eyes. Garnet made a noise that sounded like a groan of exasperation and promptly ushered Magnus down to the water to rinse off. Then they looked like they were about to go get more fish for themselves.

Kort turned Mia's attention toward a flight of incoming dragons and their riders above the beach. "I think we've been spotted."

Mia bristled. "Who are they?"

He put his arm around her waist. "Don't worry. Those are our protectors—the Dragon Warriors of Chalvaren."

Chapter 8

Dragons filled the afternoon air with squawks and roars of excitement, and not only beasts with riders landed, but free-flyers came in to check things out as well. Magnus and Garnet were back on the beach and dealing with their fresh catch.

Kort rubbed Mia's arms, trying to soothe away her tension. "Those without riders are ferals who live near Castle Elias. They're not technically in the service of the king, but they stay close for protection and proximity to our dragons." He pointed around as the beach grew covered with nearly twenty-five dragons of various sizes, shapes and colors. "Water dragons are usually blue, like that big female there in the shallows."

"Are all wind dragons white, like Pure?" Mia asked. "Fires red and earths brown?"

"Yes." Kort nodded. "The free-flyers, the ferals, tend to be other colors, as usually they're mixtures of the basic elements."

"So, *wild* dragons?" Mia surveyed the beach. "What are they all doing here?"

Kort looked over her head at Magnus, who was still focused on his meal and didn't look up. "That bizarre yipping he sounded earlier on the cliffs was a call. He lured in all of these who weren't already here. I've never seen anything like it, Mia. He lured in that whole wing!" Kort indicated the Dragon Riders, who patrolled the shore, armed and ready for any threat to the castle. "It makes sense, though. The spirit element unifies all others. Collectively, these dragons mean a stronger defensive force for Chalvaren and protection for the castle. Magnus has united them already, and he doesn't even know it."

All the dragons crept nearer. Mia looked up and smiled.

"You said he was unique. Are they bowing to him?" she asked, leaning forward to watch the animals interact. "He doesn't look like any of them. Not at all."

Magnus gobbled down more fish, his black wings with purple and teal tips closed tight on his back while his sire strutted nearby, crimson wings raised in a menacing show, hissing out licks of smoke when one lone coppery-brown earth dragon edged too close.

"When we were kids," Kort said, "my father read legends to us from the scrolls in his library that foretold an Aurora with the gift of speech who would hatch one day to unite all of Chalvaren's dragons."

"Wait," Mia said. "The others are fighting each other?"

"No, but things are not as they used to be. Something's been driving off the females. Someone's been raiding their nests and they're spooked. Uneasy. They rarely come together like this anymore."

"Yet Magnus drew these in?"

"Yes. Spirit connects every living thing, and so he will connect and lead the elementals as prophesied. He must."

Mia glanced over at the dragonlet. "Seems like a lot to shoulder for someone who can barely manage a fish."

Kort wanted to speak with his Riders, to talk about Magnus and what the dragon meant to their struggles, but first he had to introduce Mia properly so that there was no misunderstanding of her role and what she meant to him. He didn't want any repeats of what had happened in the hall of thrones.

He beckoned to his men and then timed the kiss well. Just as the elves dismounted, turned, and made their way across the sand, Kort took Mia in a passionate embrace.

Surprisingly, it remained a sensual experience, even with others watching. This woman moved him beyond all else. Whether Mia sensed the political importance of the kiss didn't matter; the way she responded to him did. She went up on her tiptoes and leaned deeper into the kiss than he expected, deeper than he'd hoped. She was his, her kiss said; and by Varik, Kort had to admit it, he just wanted to get her back in bed.

But that would have to wait. He not only needed her in love with him but safe.

He turned to inspect his crew and saw he'd achieved his intended effect. The Riders stopped dead in their tracks, jaws agape. Silence fell, followed quickly by whispers, nods, and subtle gestures.

He knew they'd cast him in the role of Last Elf in Chalvaren Who'd Ever Take a Mate—he'd refused so many prospective brides that surely they believed this day would never come—so it was gratifying to see hard faces soften. Some warriors showed curiosity, others relief. Yes, he knew he'd take some ragging for the public display of affection, but it was worth it. Especially since he knew Mia would prove herself a worthy princess.

She sighed against him and buried her head in his chest. Her flushed face burned with heat, and the proximity of her pointed ears made him wet his lips with anticipation. Twisting, he whispered that he loved her. Soon everyone would know.

He turned her to face the crowd. "Everyone! Come and meet Mia—and Magnus, her dragonlet."

"It looks like they're in shock," Mia whispered.

Kort shook his head and gestured for all to come meet her.

His brothers led. Everyone else followed.

"Mia, meet Ian and Quinn Elias." He pointed out his siblings, two young elves still long and lean with youth, who had moved to the front of the assembly. One brown-haired, and one blonde, the pair pointed at Mia's hand and murmured vigorously to each other. They'd spotted the king's ring.

"I think they like you," Kort whispered, rubbing Mia's back. "But how could they not?"

Ian pulled his dark brown hair back behind his pointed ears and spoke first. "Who's this beauty that's caught the eye of the most eligible bachelor in Chalvaren?" Fourteen years old this year, the youth stepped nearer and inspected Mia. Quinn held back, though the thirteen-year-old's mouth dropped open when he saw the sun flash off the Dragonstone hanging from Mia's neck.

Kort had just started to answer Ian's question when the sound he dreaded most split the golden afternoon: a high-alert horn. He whipped his head up to the eastern tower of Castle Elias, and his mouth went as dry as the sand they stood on. Every elven warrior turned and scrambled to action, dashing Kort's hopes for proper introductions. They rushed to their dragons, mounted, and took to the air.

"Kort," Mia demanded, clutching his chest, her body rigid. "What's wrong?"

"An intruder in Castle Elias airspace! Get back to Garnet. RUN!"

The feral dragons on the beach scattered, roaring as they lofted into the air. Kort dragged Mia with him while he searched the sky for the threat. If they were caught on the ground… His imagination ran wild.

Garnet growled a sharp warning at Magnus, who scrambled up his back while bleating in alarm. The red thundered toward Kort and Mia, hesitating only a second while they scurried up his leg and into place. He lofted himself into the air, gaining position against any approaching disaster.

Kort leaned backward, gripping Garnet's neck with his legs while he scanned the sky. He spotted the intruder and gasped, his heart hammering against his breastbone.

Mia turned to look at him. "What's wrong?"

"There." Kort pointed to the tiny silver shimmer high in the clouds, a winged shimmer, a harbinger of death, a reminder of something he'd long ago lost due to his mother's lack of foresight. "It's a silver. An ice dragon. That's Isa Ansgar's dragon," he added.

Mia shook her head. "I don't see anything."

He wrapped her body with his. "It doesn't matter. When those horns sound it's a warning an attack is imminent. We can't risk being caught out here. We don't know how many dragons she's brought with her, but we take this as an act of war. To the castle, Garnet. Now! I want Mia underground and Magnus secured. Then we'll deal with VanZanz."

This was no drill. By every treaty ever, that silver flying into Castle Elias airspace meant war. Kort had trained years for events such as this, even with the idea of protecting assets like Mia and Magnus, so at least his warriors were prepared. Still, his heart rate escalated and sweat sprang up across his palms. Isa Ansgar loved to intercept elves unawares, kidnap and torture them. Her silver specialized in killing full-grown dragons on such occasions and left their bones behind to fester and rot, but until now she'd operated in ways that war would not be declared. Not that it mattered, Kort supposed; every alliance kingdom on Chalvaren had a bounty posted for the pair.

He dug his heels into Garnet's hide, urging the red to fly faster. There was no way he could engage Isa and VanZanz with Mia and Magnus—or his brothers—out in the open like this. The first priority after hearing the early warning system was the safety of the royal family.

Kort reared around to watch the castle's troops. Yes! Perfect—a well oiled machine! The evacuation of non-fighting personnel below took less than a minute, and four armed warriors now accompanied his two younger brothers, all of them upon Poseidon, the king's powerful water dragon, which was rising to follow Garnet.

Kort turned toward the safety of the fortress. "There!" he shouted, pointing to an open area in the semi-transparent walls of the castle. Garnet dove for it, and Mia dropped her head. A moment later they were through, as were his brothers, and Kort turned to witness the five-inch-thick dragon ore–tempered glass slide closed and click into position behind them. Nothing was getting through that.

"Secure!" he called out.

"What's happening?" Mia sounded confused. "Who the hell would dare to attack this castle? Where are you taking us?"

"To the bunker."

Garnet swooped along a cavernous hall, turned and circled. He touched down on a marble floor next to a series of heavy metal doors where guards rushed out to assist. Kort scrambled down and whisked Mia off the dragon. He held out his arm to Magnus, who stayed hooked to Garnet's back.

"Magnus! Come!" he bellowed.

The little dragonlet hesitated. Garnet growled at him and dropped his shoulder.

"Now, Magnus, listen to Kort," Mia called. She whistled and waved her arm, trying to get him to follow, and finally Magnus scrambled down behind her.

Kort grabbed Mia's hand and led her toward two open metal doors where a red light beckoned. His two young brothers blew past, their guards in hot pursuit, in through the safety of the doors and disappearing down that corridor. Kort escorted Mia and Magnus through, but then he turned back.

Mia put a hand on his arm. "Don't you dare leave me here alone."

He spun around, frustrated. "You don't understand. I *have* to go." He regretted the words as soon as he said them, but how could she possibly understand? He'd wanted to ease her into understanding the dangers of Chalvaren. They'd barely been together one full day. He didn't want to go, but he had no choice. It was his job to protect the castle, and this attack changed everything.

She shook her head. "No. I don't understand. But if you go back out there, I'm coming too."

He pointed down the corridor into the bunker. His father stalked their way. "Go with him, Mia. He'll keep you safe."

Mia fisted her hands at her side and planted her feet. "No."

"This is not up for discussion," Kort said. "I have a job to do, and I'm going to do it. Now go inside with my father."

"NO!" she shouted. Magnus grumbled beside her.

Kort bit his lip as King Lachlan approached, trying to balance the contradiction of his soon-to-be princess. At once he wanted to hold and comfort her, but he had to get back out there, to mount Garnet and seek out the silver dragon who dared enter Castle Elias airspace, an intruder who threatened her as much as the royal family. "Stay here, Mia."

She glared at him. "I don't want to stay here without you, Kort. If something needs to be done, maybe I could help. I won't lose you too."

Sirens blared. Lights flashed. Kort's father blasted past them, ignoring their argument. He commanded the men at the doors to work them shut, which they did. The heavy metal doors ground toward each other.

Kort rushed to the door. "That's not how we drilled this, Dad."

King Lachlan wheeled around and held up his hand. "You hadn't chosen a bride at that time, and like it or not you're part of this royal family, so deal with it."

A flash of anger and trepidation burned through Kort. If he couldn't get out to stop the silver and Isa, something could go wrong. His men were competent, sure, but he'd trained his whole life in order to lead them. He wasn't about to stand down now.

"I won't just sit around here waiting—"

"No, Son, you won't." King Lachlan shook his head, lowered his voice to a growl and pressed his fingers into Kort's arm. "You're going to help me figure out why in the hell Isa Ansgar has the audacity to fly her silver anywhere near my castle. Something must have changed. She's no fool."

Kort glanced at Mia, whose face was ghost-white. Had Isa somehow sensed the Dragonstone? Was she risking all her power on a desperate bid to claim it? Hoping for some last-minute reprieve he glared at Lachlan and asked, "Do you have positive confirmation she's present?"

King Lachlan nodded, a grim frown mangling his lips. "Not just from the east tower, either. I've got another eyewitness…along with what's left of his partner." He snatched his arm away. "Now, Son, get Mia settled inside the chapel with the others. And see to Magnus. Then I need your assistance with the interrogation."

†††

"So, they're expecting us. How delightful."

Isa gave VanZanz a playful pinch as they hovered above the castle. She'd hoped to catch her deserter minions before they neared Lachlan Elias's territory, but that apparently wasn't to be. Below, elves and dragons loyal to King Elias scurried for whatever safety they could find, many headed toward the security of the fortress itself.

A flash of purple on the beach drew her attention, and Isa narrowed her eyes. She eyed her burned and blistered hand before a smile snaked across her face. "They…they've got the Dragonstone, VanZanz." She pointed at the shore, at the red dragon whisking the flash of purple away. "That fire dragon demands to be dealt with, my friend. I'll save him for you when we come to our reckoning."

Of course, it wasn't just the fire dragon here. Far too many of the beasts congregated on the beach for her liking. What had they been doing down there, and who was in possession of the Dragonstone? Could it be that her brother had returned at last? Had he summoned these and…? Where *was* Theo? She wondered about him for a moment, and something like nostalgia pricked at her heart. She shook it away.

Isa watched the red dragon streak toward the castle and disappear behind the reinforced glass with her prize; then she glanced down at the shore. The dragons there, some of them feral, some of them with Elias's warriors on their backs, flew straight toward her. An arrow whizzed past her head. Another buried itself deep in her thigh, and she winced, having long ago trained herself to ignore pain. But VanZanz roared and turned to retreat from the projectiles.

"Oh, I don't think so," she cried out. "Wait, dragon! I've got something for them before we go."

She patted her chest and screamed out a spell of defiance. As she turned her silver back toward Cumberlae, black shadows born of dark magic flew from her chest and clouded the skies, dark-winged accomplices who descended on her approaching enemies. "Yes," she mused, "that should be a good deterrent."

She had not destroyed her deserter shadow elves, but this trip had been worthwhile nonetheless. Isa clucked to herself and murmured, "Who *was* that, VanZanz?" In one brief moment she'd finally seen a flash of purple and the blonde elf who dared display the jewel like a beacon of reckoning. A blonde female elf. Not her brother.

Well, she would find out. Isa's thoughts drifted to her spies far below on the ground, even now in King Lachlan's castle and no doubt comforting Elissabet Elias and Elissabet's brother, Lucan Brix. Isa laughed out loud and urged VanZanz forward on a sea-breeze toward home.

"Soon, Elissabet. Soon you shall know my vengeance. You and your family have a hallowed place reserved at my home, and I cannot wait for your visit...."

The silver roared and caught higher air currents, swooping them off and out of harm's way.

Chapter 9

Anger and confusion burned in Mia's mind, and she stomped her foot. Kort had taken leave of his senses if he'd thought for one second she was going to let him leave her barred behind some damn door. Her parents had done that to her—left her behind to help someone else—and they'd died, abandoning her in a world of humans who hated her and her ways. Was Kort just like them: giving yet thoughtless?

"If I lost you, what would I possibly do here without you?"

He held out his hands in what looked like a vain attempt to explain himself. Mia just bristled and turned to Magnus, whose entire focus was upon the closed door separating them from Garnet. The dragonlet whimpered.

Kort took her arm, the look on his face determined. "Wait, Mia. Let me explain."

"Back off, Kort. I need a moment here." She pulled away and went to her dragon, running a hand across his scales. "Are you okay?"

"I am uninjured," Magnus answered. He directed a wistful glance toward the door. "My sire…?"

The concern in his voice emboldened her, and Mia ran her fingertips up the delicate scales on Magnus's neck. She found the soft spot under his chin, mimicking what Lachlan had done earlier and scratching him there. The truth was that she didn't know what Garnet faced outside, but it couldn't be good, and she didn't want this juvenile distracting him in battle. That wouldn't do anyone any good.

She moved close to whisper into his ear, "Garnet has an important job, Magnus. We cannot interfere with his work, not in any way. Your sire protects Castle Elias and, if we distract him, he may fail. Our needs will have to wait until the danger has passed."

"But what if he should need my help?"

Such loyalty. Mia was touched. She glared at Kort, but the look of concern on his face took the edge off her anger and she sighed, wishing he'd just told her what the hell was going on.

"I suppose warriors like yourself and Kort always want to fight in times of danger, but you are not yet trained. Your job is to remain steadfast until you are. Otherwise you might be a liability."

The dragonlet considered her words and nodded. Then he asked, "May I stay by the barrier? In case my father calls for my help."

Mia glanced toward the door and nodded; she could see no harm in it. "Of course. You guard this side of the door. I'll go check on Kort's family. If Garnet calls for you, go to your sire and listen to him."

Seemingly assuaged, Magnus sat straight-backed on his haunches and eagerly eyed the door. Mia laid a gentle kiss on his muzzle then turned to talk to Kort.

"He's holding his position in case Garnet needs him. You show me how *I* can help."

Kort guided Mia down a flight of stairs. "The family is stationed at the end of the hall here, in the chapel."

Mia looked at him. "'The family'?"

Kort dragged her forward, but she pulled him to a stop. "This is *your* family. As in, these are the dearest people in your life, right? Your father wanted you to come down here with the rest of them. Why wouldn't you want to stay here and protect them when asked?" She held her breath, confused and nervous, but Kort didn't answer. If he truly felt separate from his mother and his brothers, if he truly could ignore what was best for his family, what did that say about his character? There was so much she didn't know about him.

She stalked down the torchlit hall. "Unbelievable."

Kort ran up and grasped her arm. "What's so damned unbelievable, Mia?"

She turned to face him. "So, you're the kind of guy who rushes forward into battle without any regard for what you leave behind. My mother must have been dead wrong about you being the one," she grumbled. "Just because you showed up and knew how to help me liberate the Dragonstone, I'm not convinced that proves anything. If you don't value family the way I do..." She threw her hands up in the air. "Or maybe I just misunderstood."

She shook her head, cursing herself for jumping into an intimate relationship with Kort and then berating herself for wanting his hands on her body even now, in the midst of this argument, in the midst of some sort of crisis above. Perhaps the prophecy was only about whom she would find irresistibly attractive. Such a ridiculous concept seemed appropriate given all the other events in her life.

Kort towered above her. "Misunderstood what, Mia? What the hell are you so angry about?"

"That you would run off without me. That you would leave me alone in the middle of a crisis." She hesitated and eyed his hand on her arm then looked back up into his handsome face, hoping he'd accept her challenge and prove her wrong. "That you wouldn't think about me before you acted."

He did challenge her assumption and almost obliterated it with one action. Pulling her close, Kort kissed her, and Mia's anger melted away when his generous lips touched hers. She…just wanted him. Kort. Her loyal protector. Valiant. Rallying to prove her angry words wrong.

He broke away and whispered against her lips, "I'm here, Mia. I'm right here, and I'm not going anywhere. And don't make assumptions when you don't know what you're talking about, Princess."

"Don't call me that," she hissed as he again pulled her down the hallway. "I'm not your princess yet." But he'd accepted her challenge and Mia saw that he cared, so she tightened her grip on his hand and hurried along with him.

He led her into a room that held an altar, prayer benches, and that was full of lit candles. Silver, gold, and copper mosaics of Chalvaren's seven gods loomed on the walls, and four people kneeling at the altar lifted their heads at the disturbance. A priest in a white robe standing at a pulpit looked up from his prayer book.

Queen Elissabet knelt at the altar, and she smiled when she saw her son. Mia understood why. He was safe at her side and out of harm's way. On that goal, the two women agreed.

"Come and join us." The queen pointed to an empty seat beside her. "Ian. Quinn. Brite. Greet your brother's princess. This is Mia. Mia *Ansgar.*"

The two young men stood. They couldn't have been much older than twelve, or perhaps fourteen? Like they had on the beach, they stared at Mia with open admiration. A tiny girl with dark ringlets of auburn hair and her mother's eyes also peeked out from behind Elissabet's indigo robe. Mia's heart melted at the gentle and vulnerable look of her.

"Greetings, Mia," Ian and Quinn said in unison, their hands behind their backs. Without the armor they wore on the beach the boys were the spitting image of what Kort must have looked like at that age, and when Mia raised her brows, Ian nudged Quinn and his brother hissed back, blushing. From there, their shoving descended into a small skirmish. Mia couldn't help but smile.

"This is no time for horseplay," Kort growled.

His brothers stood to immediate attention. "Sorry," they mumbled in unison and studied the cool tiled floor of the prayer room.

Kort approached and addressed them directly. "Name your orders here, princes of Chalvaren."

The boys transformed into men. They drew sharp jeweled daggers, squared their shoulders, and stood with feet planted shoulder-width apart. "To protect our sister and mother, sir."

A flash of movement caught Mia's attention, as well as the gentle rustling of Elissabet's velvet robe. Brite stared up at her brothers, surprise and fear blazing across her perfect little face peeking out from around her mother.

Queen Elissabet stroked the child's hair. "It's okay, Brite. We're safe."

Brite Elias turned the biggest, bluest eyes upon her that Mia had ever seen. Dressed in a flowing pink gown, she was the spitting image of her mother, yet Mia saw Lachlan's features in that face, too.

Kort pressed past his gangly brothers and knelt to scoop the child up in his arms, and Brite lit up as he did. "Kort! The bad dragons have come. Are you all right?"

Kort's face softened, and he kissed his sister's cheek. When he pulled back, the two stared into each other's eyes. Brite splayed one tiny hand wide against her brother's face and then lit up the room with her smile.

Mia regretted every harsh word she'd uttered earlier. She'd obviously gotten things all wrong.

"I'm fine, baby girl," Kort said, so softly that Mia almost didn't hear. "And what is your job here, Brite? What are you going to do in a situation like this?"

Brite's tiny voice was firm. "Listen to my brothers and do as Mommy says."

She couldn't have been four years old yet, but Brite Elias was quite possibly the most beautiful elf Mia had ever seen. She kissed Kort's cheek, and he stood up, cradling her in his massive arms.

"Welcome Mia in to pray, Brite," Kort prompted.

The little girl eyed Mia over the large mound of Kort's shoulder. She looked to Kort then her mother, who nodded, and the little princess turned to Mia as Kort set her down on the floor. She skipped toward Mia and held out her hand, beckoning Mia forward with a smile.

"Mia. Come and pray with us."

As soon as Mia clasped Brite's hand, she knew she was home. Without another word, she knelt beside Kort's family to pray for Castle Elias and for the safety of their dragons.

Chapter 10

Once Kort got Mia settled safely beside his mother in the chapel, he went to find his father. Passing Magnus, he saw the dragonlet had an ear pressed to the huge sealed doors to the underground complex. Good, he decided. Things were as they should be. There were dragons keeping watch on both sides of the door.

He rounded a corner, and Duncan, his father's strident guard captain, joined him on his walk. Kort took the opportunity to growl out commands as they approached the interrogation chambers. "I want a full guard on Mia at all times… If I'm kept from her for any reason, she's to be with my father."

"Understood," Duncan said. "And her dragon, of course."

Kort nodded curtly and stopped at the heavily fortified door of the interrogation room, hesitating before going in. "What have we learned? Anything?"

Duncan frowned. "Just that Isa Ansgar knows about the Dragonstone."

"I assumed," Kort said. "That's why she showed herself and her silver dragon—to rattle us, and likely in the hope of snatching it if we acted too slowly." So much for the simple joy of returning Mia and the artifact to their homes. But still, how could Isa have learned so quickly? Had she been using her magic to watch them? Were spies loyal to Isa in Castle Elias at this very moment?

Kort followed the guard captain inside the interrogation room, which was split into two vast but separate sections, and he blinked his eyes rapidly as severe lights revealed two former mercenaries, soldiers hired in service of Castle Elias. A shudder of remorse rippled through Kort's chest. He didn't recognize either of their twisted faces, but he recognized their tattoos— elven runes not so unlike his own inked into their bodies. Confusingly, Duncan had chained one to a sturdy metal table in the first room, and the man lay there limp. What the devil had happened to him…?

A soft moan caught his ear, and Kort peered through the archway into the further room. The other elf lay collapsed in on himself on the cold stone floor. The interrogation chamber seemed unnecessary, with its shackles and stainless steel tables, hard stone walls and severe overhead lighting; from the look of this elf's injuries, and from all the blood on the floor and the odd angles of his body, he needed to receive medical treatment immediately.

Duncan pointed to the prisoners. Kort thought he noticed a flicker of something strange behind the guard captain's eyes. Or maybe he was imagining things.

"These two barely escaped with their lives. The far room, as you can see, holds what's left of the mercenary the silver attacked. I've never seen anyone live with injuries so grave. Still, your father insisted we keep him until he dies, so perhaps we can understand what happened and what threats our castle faces."

Kort looked closer at the second body, and suddenly he understood what he'd seen in Duncan's eyes: true disgust and aversion. The fallen elf was missing most of his right arm, and dark red blood pooled on the grey stone floor below him, but the most disturbing feature was the horror etched across the maimed elf's disfigured face. Kort lifted his hand to block the stench that permeated the still air, gagging, acid roiling in his gut. The silver had done this. How was the mercenary still alive?

He looked away. The far elf moaned again, and Kort fisted his hands and asked, "Where's my father? These men need medical attention or…or to be set free." No one should look like that. Not ever. "What the hell happened here?"

King Lachlan strode into the interrogation room. "As you see. Dragon attack…and maybe worse."

"They need help," Kort said. He turned to see his father's eyes were red-rimmed with grief. Lachlan bore a soft spot for all elves, but doubly those who strove in the name of the crown. "And why is the first man in chains?"

The king grasped Kort and tried to pull him out the room. "Tell yourself it's not possible, Son. There's no help for these two. I was wrong and—"

Kort planted his feet and stared over his father's shoulder. "These were elves who served the crown. We owe them much, Dad."

"I know, Son. But, until we know what we're dealing with, they must stay contained. No help for either of them." King Lachlan looked over his shoulder. "I'm afraid it's too late for Nerian, anyway. Dear God. It would have been more merciful if the dragon had finished the job. How did that dragon not finish the job?"

His father's voice was heavy with despair, and Kort swallowed hard. "Nerian…? And Arden Demar. What has happened to them?" He clutched his father's hair, feeling helpless against the waves of remorse and anger that swamped him. He had trained the men himself in the fine art of warfare. They'd eventually become mercenaries in a group of ultra-elite soldiers who hired out to noble causes throughout the kingdoms, vowing to give their lives if they must in exchange for the glory of taking Isa's. Lucan Brix, his uncle and one of the castle wizards, had fortified both elves with magic spells of stealth and strength…but they clearly had not been enough.

"They sacrificed everything for us. For our family," Kort said. He closed his eyes as he remembered the day they'd eagerly left the fold to assassinate Isa Ansgar, which had seemed the only option against her terrible magic and more terrifying crimes.

Lachlan clung to him. "Yes. They suffered for our plan. Isa Ansgar did this." He pointed to the breathing thing that was once a comrade-in-arms. "That's black magic, Son. We can't fight that sort of horror. We do not have the power."

Kort grabbed his father's arms. "What about Arden? Can we question him? Did he learn any—?"

King Lachlan shook his head and cut him off. "Look at him. She's cursed him, driven him insane. We can't get him to talk. All he does is snarl and moan and shriek when anyone comes near."

Kort turned away, defeated. A moment later a new idea raced through his head. "Wait. You say we do not have the power? What about the Dragonstone? Maybe Mia can use it to help break that spell. Was it not meant to destroy black magic? To liberate us all from darkness?"

"Can she do it?" Lachlan asked, and swallowed hard.

"I think so. She wants to help us, Dad, and I doubt anyone else can manage the artifact's power. You saw how she commanded the portal open with its magic."

Kort took off at a run back to the chapel. His mind was awhirl. Did the Dragonstone have the strength to counter this black magic? Moreover, could Mia wield it? Greater even than that, did he really want to expose her to this particular horror? She'd said she didn't want him fighting this battle without her. Now it seemed she'd be doing something he couldn't.

Maybe somehow they could do this together. And maybe, if Mia joined her power and that of the Dragonstone with the magic of the castle wizards, maybe they could finally stop Isa Ansgar once and for all.

Chapter 11

Mosaics portraying the deities of Chalvaren covered the walls of the chapel, and these gods seemed to watch over Mia and Kort's family while they held vigil. A robed priest spoke soft words aloud from thick vellum pages of a gilt elvish prayer book at the front of the room, but Mia silently offered up her own.

Help them, Varik. Help me help them if that's why I'm here—and please, don't let anything happen to my dragonlet. Keep Kort safe under Your watchful eye. Keep them both out of harm's way.

Flames flared atop white pillar candles as everyone prayed, but Mia stilled and silently stared at the prayer book Queen Elissabet slid into her hands. "Thank you," she said as she noted the kindness in Kort's mother's face.

The queen nodded, apology in her blue eyes. "I'm glad you're here, Mia."

"Have you ever seen him? Varik, I mean?" Mia asked. Her father had spoken of such things being possible.

The queen raised her brows. "Do you mean, like, in a vision?"

Mia nodded.

Kort's mother stared at her for an overly long moment. "Have you? Is *your* magic strong enough to visit with the gods, Mia?"

Mia froze then shook her head. She'd dreamed of seeing him, but no, she'd never had the privilege. The queen would think her daft or a braggart. She'd only meant to try to connect with Kort's mother, not raise more questions.

"My husband says he sees Varik from time-to-time," the queen admitted. "Early in the morning hours during his prayers. But no, I've never had that sort of vision—and sometimes I think the king exaggerates."

Mia glanced at Queen Elissabet and registered the woman's strong orange aura, both by sight and by a warmth upon her own skin. The intensity and sensation reminded Mia of her mother's long-ago lessons, that certain elves wielded magic and that you could tell what they were best at by the colors of their nimbus. Its hue represented both attachment to a certain god and manifestation of certain traits both positive and negative, both masculine and feminine.

Queen Elissabet's aura was almost hot. Many elves knew simple spells—like Mia—but wizards practiced magic on a much higher level. The difference between a wizard and a lesser caster was like the difference between a doctor and someone administering first-aid. Wizards tended to have a stronger connection to the gods. Was Queen Elissabet a true wizard? If she were, wouldn't she have seen a vision of a god if anyone had?

Mia squeezed her hands together and searched her memory for what she knew. Her own aura was tied to Varik, violet, a color her mother said represented grace, intuition, protection, and nostalgia. Elissabet's orange nimbus was tied to Octavianus, the demigod of energy. Balance, courage, and warmth were traits of such an aura, which was good to know considering how damn mean Elissabet had been in the throne room. Kort's blue aura was linked to trust, peace and unity, and to the demigod Marineth. But if Elissabet had never seen her patron deity... Maybe demigods weren't strong enough to show themselves in visions?

Mia's chest suddenly tightened as she remembered how the queen's aura flickered when Magnus pinned her to the floor. If she was a wizard, why hadn't she used her powers to stop him? Had Kort's mother acted with more cunning than fear? If so, was that whole intense drama a test to see where Mia's loyalties lay?

Mia swallowed hard, like a stone had lodged in her throat. One thing was for sure: Chalvaren was teaching her lots of things today. Suddenly, knowing everything else was paramount.

Magic followed the matriarch, so it made sense that Kort had some. Of course, mothers did not dictate which magic their children inherited; that was ultimately up to the gods. That explained how Kort's aura could be blue. Memories of her time with Kort raced through her mind, warming Mia and forcing an unbidden smile to her lips; she'd been drawn to him because she trusted him. Still, there was so much about him that she didn't know.

"Tell me about your magic, Elissabet."

The queen shook her head, ignoring the question. She turned away to tend Brite, shushing her two boys at the same time then resuming her former silence, staring at her prayer book and occasionally looking up at the priest.

Impatience prompted Mia to whisper again. "Lachlan said someone named Isa *Ansgar* was responsible for this attack. Who is she?"

Elissabet eyed her—not with contempt but relief. Relief for what, though?

"Not to worry," the queen said. "She can't possibly know who you are, Mia. Actually, thanks to your father's quick thinking, she won't even know you exist."

Mia shook her head again. "But why did she attack today? Who is she? Our last names are the same. I need to know what that means."

Queen Elissabet straightened her spine, obviously perturbed. "You truly don't know anything about it?"

"No."

Elissabet chuckled but speared Mia with her eyes. She tapped the wooden pew in front of her with a long, slender index finger. "Isn't that fitting?"

"What?" Mia snapped.

"It's so like Theo to have not told you. But certainly your mother warned you. Surely Melia warned you why you should never come here, Mia?"

"Quit speaking in riddles! Your secrecy doesn't help anything."

The queen just stared at her and then pointed at her daughter, directing Brite to pay attention to her brothers. She leaned close to Mia and said, "Isa Ansgar is your father's sister. She is your lone surviving relative on Chalvaren."

"My father's sister?" Mia repeated. "But, why would she attack? Why does this mean I shouldn't return? They never told me they left anyone behind..." She dropped her gaze to her hands, which clenched the pew in front of her. If she had family here, maybe her place was with them instead of the Eliases.

"Some questions are best left unanswered," Queen Elissabet said sadly, her expression a haunted look that turned her beautiful features gaunt. But the idea conflicted with everything Mia believed.

The queen's face darkened further, and she cast a meaningful gaze across her three children. "Maybe Theo counted against Isa surviving. Maybe he told you less so that you didn't have to suffer. But, Mia, you must now understand. Isa Ansgar means to see every Elias dead."

The queen's penetrating stare made Mia feel as if she were somehow responsible for this danger, this threat. But how could that be possible?

"Did bringing the Dragonstone back to Chalvaren put me and your family at odds? Is that why you...overreacted when we first met?"

"If you do anything foolish, if you let Isa get her hands on that artifact or that spirit dragon, you may as well kill us all yourself."

Mia sat up straighter and frowned, but before she got the chance to collect her thoughts, to question the queen further, Kort burst into the chapel. He looked around for her, his face a mask of worry and desperation, and then he bolted forward and held out his hand, curling his fingers in a signal for her to join him.

"Mia. I need you to come help me. I'll explain on the way."

All questions vanished as she rushed to his side.

Chapter 12

The castle was warm, brightly lit from sconces on walls that were embedded with tiny chips of luminescent dragon ore. Kort grasped Mia's hand and led her back to the interrogation room.

The sensation of her fingers twined with his, bare skin against bare skin, sparked a memory of desire. He ignored it, fitting his hand to the curve of her waist and guiding her underneath an underground archway. "Okay, you said you wanted to help. I want to see if you can break a spell of evil with the Dragonstone. Do you think you can do it?"

"How?" Mia asked.

"I'm not sure, exactly, but I think two of our warriors have been cursed. Lucan Brix will know better. He is our castle wizard, and together, maybe you and he can use the magic in the artifact to break the spell."

"Of course. Anything."

Her assurance pleased him, as did the fact that she kept pace with him through the maze of underground tunnels.

A moment later she said, "Lucan Brix? He was in my father's stories."

Kort nodded, unsurprised. They rounded a corner. "There he is, with my father."

Indeed, Lucan Brix waited outside the interrogation room, huddled close and speaking in low tones with the king. He possessed an affinity for magic, and an affinity for dressing the part. The goatee Lucan wore pointed toward his heart like an arrow. He wore a moustache and had wiry, spiky eyebrows. As elves weren't known to sport facial hair, Kort really didn't want to know what weird magic caused Lucan's to grow. A black velvet robe covered the wizard's lithe, muscular frame, and he cut a tall, imposing figure in the dimly lit hall, and when he looked up, the skin on his bald head shimmered with a silvery aura.

Kort stopped in front of the wizard and lifted his and Mia's entwined hands. "Mia, meet our resident wizard, Lucan Brix. He's the man who sent me to find Magnus. He's also my mother's half-brother."

Mia said nothing at first. Anticipation roiled off her, though, and not fear, which emboldened Kort.

"You're responsible for sending Kort my way?"

Lucan smiled. Light danced off multiple gold hoops piercing the lobes of the wizard's pointed ears, and a bright diamond stud graced the sharp tip of the left. "Yes. And I understand you're responsible for helping my godson return with the Aurora."

Mia never missed a beat. She pulled her hand from Kort's and held it out to shake.

Lucan took both of Mia's hands and gently twisted the Elias family ring on her finger, then brought Mia's hand up to his lips and pressed a kiss to the back of it. Kort tensed, flooded with sudden and irrational jealousy.

"Princess," the wizard said in a sibilant hush.

Mia stamped her foot. "Not yet."

Kort stared at her, surprised. What was it going to take for her to accept her role here, to really believe that she was the one with whom he wanted to spend forever?

Lucan's eyes shifted, and the wizard lifted a hand. "No worries, young prince. I can see she belongs only to you. It's written all over her magic."

"Don't forget it," Kort growled.

Mia arched one brow and glanced sardonically from Kort to Lucan. "First, thank you for sending him to save my dragonlet. But now I hear you want my help with a spell." She stepped back and eyed the wizard. "Your aura is silvery, so that must mean you're a dreamer. Cool and graceful with a penchant for neutrality."

Lucan did not reply to that. He just stared into her eyes. "Mia is it?"

Mia bobbed her head, her lips a firm line. "My father spoke of you, Lucan, but you're not nearly as scary in person."

Kort stared. Had Lucan known Mia's father? What sort of history had they shared?

The wizard's eyes gleamed, and he laughed. "Oh, I do miss my Theo."

Mia's gaze fell. "I miss him too."

Lucan peered closely at her. He swept a hand along her head, following the curve of her skull but not touching her. "You have your father's eyes, Mia—and a touch of your mother's magic, I believe."

Mia shrugged. "They taught me simple spells using herbals, potions for healing. Nothing spectacular."

Lucan looked back to King Lachlan. A deep, knowing chuckle rumbled in his chest. "'Nothing spectacular'? No, not Theo. He simply yoked you to the most powerful artifact known to our kind." Mia pulled her hand away and reached for Kort, whose father lifted an eyebrow as the wizard continued, "I'll bet that's stirred up some friction for you today."

Both Lucan and King Lachlan smiled. Kort did his best not to snarl at them and their usual amusement regarding his mother.

The wizard returned his attention to Mia. "Child, you have returned the Dragonstone to Chalvaren. And the Aurora. And my godson. And now you must help me counteract a spell—if you will."

Mia edged backward. "I would, but I don't know how. I know nothing of counterspells."

"I'll help you," Lucan said.

"I'll do anything the king asks," Mia stated, glancing over at Kort's father as if for approval.

Lucan raised wiry brows and glanced at Kort. "It will not be pleasant at first," he said, stepping back as though to size her up. "You are hearty, Mia, and of good stock, but the question is...how much can you take?"

"How much of what can I take?"

Kort fluttered a nervous hand down the small of her back. He was glad she would help, but he didn't want her in any type of danger. Just how much would this counterspell entail?

King Lachlan stepped forward. "Mia, two men escaped our enemy this afternoon and came here. I believe the reason she invaded our airspace was to recover or kill them. Lucan thinks that you can counteract the...trance she's put them under, and if we can talk to them, bring them back from the grip of her evil spell, we may unearth vital intelligence we need to stop her. They are in the interrogation chamber."

"Stop her from what?" Mia asked, and Kort's chest tightened. Mia obviously knew more than she was letting on. Had his mother talked about Isa? What exactly did Mia's expression mean? Was she angry about being told so little?

Mia surprised him, gently touching his chest with her hand. "Your mother told me. In the chapel she said someone named Isa Ansgar wants every Elias elf dead. Is that true?"

Lucan's lips thinned. "And others besides the Eliases, such as Elissabet and myself. She means to kill everyone here, Mia. We intend to stop her, of course."

Mia drew back, crossed both arms and looked down the corridor as if she'd heard something. She tapped one booted foot against the stone floor then returned a steely gaze to Lucan.

"Why?" she said. "If she's intent on what you say, I want to know why."

"It's complicated," Lucan replied, waving a hand through the air as if in dismissal.

"Why *now*?" She turned to Lachlan. "Why on my first day in Chalvaren ever is this relative of mine, this woman that you all paint an evil sorceress, suddenly such an issue?"

Kort looked upward and shook his head. He wished he knew. "Somehow she knows the Dragonstone is back."

"What are her points of contention, exactly? Have you all negotiated with her?"

"There's no negotiating with Isa Ansgar, Mia." Lucan waved his hand through the air as if swatting away flies. "Death. Destruction. Black magic. Those are her tools. And what Isa wants is our heads. If you help us, you will join the list of her enemies—as will that dragonlet you love. But he is in danger anyway."

"*No one* threatens my dragon."

Mia's purple aura had pitched brighter. Kort put his arm around her and pulled her close. She came willingly as he said, "Enough with the scare tactics. Let's see what we can learn, wizard."

Lucan palmed Kort's shoulder. "These are not scare tactics. She deserves to know everything. Or do you not want to tell her this part?" The wizard's eyes cut back to Mia as Kort shoved his hand away. "I don't suppose he's had the time to fill you in, has he?"

"I've seen enough to understand—"

"Understand?" Lucan bellowed a hard laugh. "I've been at odds with your aunt for over two decades, and I still don't understand everything. But you must know that if you join me today, if you really want to serve Chalvaren, there is no turning back. Your aunt will become your enemy."

Mia's gaze hardened. "She may be my aunt by blood, but I do not know this Isa you speak of. If the woman means people harm...well, I see no problem with helping you deflect it."

Kort breathed a sigh of relief. He'd witnessed Mia's courage when she helped him contain Magnus and bring the Aurora home, and now he was seeing the goodness of her nature. A pang of passion roared through his body—for her, for her strength, for her loyalty. God, he just wanted this over so he could take her someplace safe, someplace quiet, someplace where he could make love to her again. Where he could make her his princess.

Someone was coming down the hall. Mia turned her head, then Kort, and Queen Elissabet swept into view, her children in tow. "Enough with the debate about who might anger the evil witch of Chalvaren. Let's get on with this."

She directed her children toward King Lachlan, but Kort intercepted Brite, swiftly scooping his sister up in his arms. He joined his father against the back wall of the corridor, as did Ian and Quinn. Lachlan sheltered them in his arms.

Elissabet took Mia's hand and took two steps. Then she sighed and turned. "Lucan's right, Mia. You need to know that Isa will sense it if you go through that door. I cannot promise it will end well, child."

Kort grimaced, but Mia seemed undaunted. She raised her chin and nodded once, and Lucan and Elissabet looked relieved. The auras of all three—purple, silver, orange—flared brighter.

Mia headed toward the interrogation chamber. "Let's get on with this."

Chapter 13

Mia followed Lucan and Queen Elissabet through the door. Inside the interrogation chamber, Lucan reached out one long gnarled finger and pointed to the first alleged victim of her aunt's black magic, an elf chained to a table who stared back at them with milky-gray eyes. Mia had seen old men with cataracts like this, but this elf was not old. He was ugly, green and covered with robust bulging muscles.

She approached, but the elf lunged forward, snapping his chains tight. Lucan rushed Mia out of harm's way and into the next room.

"We'll leave the one in chains for last," the wizard said. "This chap needs our attention more."

Mia followed Lucan's gesture. When her eyes hit the wounded man, his right leg missing, his left arm bloody and shredded, she wrenched free, fell to her knees and vomited. Wiped her chin. Closed her eyes, blocked out the terrible sight. The devastation of that elf's body! It was too much. Gods, he must be near death. She hoped he was. She prayed he was.

Her belly roiled again, and she dragged her hand across her mouth, fighting to still her thrashing stomach. "What could you possibly want *me* to do?"

Queen Elissabet helped her stand. She put her hand on Mia's arm, and a flicker of yellow-orange sparks tinged Mia's skin and settled her nerves. "He's in terrible pain, Mia, trapped in this half-death. We have to end it for him. Mercy. That's the only option."

Mia dropped her shaking hand from her face. "End it for him? What? How?"

Kort's mother gestured to Mia's neck. "The Dragonstone, child. Last rites. They will release him."

Mia stood tall and pulled the artifact from beneath the neckline of her dress. "Show me what to do."

The queen led her forward to where Lucan knelt beside the dying elf. Mia and Elissabet knelt, too. A single tear coursed down Mia's cheek.

Lucan flourished gnarled hands wide over the maimed elf's body, leaving a silvery glimmer of a wake. His voice startled Mia.

"Nerian Llewellan!"

The dying elf groaned and tried to raise his shaking head. Mia saw that his eyes were cloudy like the other captive's, but there were brief moments of clear green iris that increased her agony for the man. Tears spilling down her cheeks, she clutched the Dragonstone tight. The artifact flared with ghostfire, set ablaze by the purple aura snaking out of the end of her fingers. Mia glanced at Elissabet, who nodded and gestured toward Lucan.

"Listen to him," the queen advised.

"Nerian," the wizard was saying, glancing briefly at the Dragonstone and seemingly satisfied by what he saw. "You chose to serve Chalvaren as a proud and worthy ally."

Nerian writhed. Somehow, his mangled body managed a nod. Mia's heart threatened to tear apart in her chest, but Lucan kept speaking.

"A silver has taken your body, warrior, but the death that waits to claim you has weakened the hold of the evil spell upon your soul. Your bones will rest in the Garden of Elves here at Castle Elias. Have you anything to tell us? Any last words for your family?"

Mia didn't know Nerian. Why was she crying for him? She'd wanted Chalvaren to be a place of comfort, but this was terrible. One of Mia's tears landed on the Dragonstone. It sizzled in the heated ghostfire, and multicolored sparks of energy burst forth. These encircled the fist-sized amethyst then seemed to dive off the jewel into the chest of the maimed elf, whose cloudy eyes cleared fully. He reached his good arm up to Lucan, groping for contact.

The wizard responded. He grasped Nerian's hand and spoke a prayer. Somehow his strong baritone comforted Mia, eased the grief flowing through her body for this lost and dying man. *Last rites.* Mia had never heard them spoken aloud; she'd only read the ritual silently from a prayer book when her parents were taken by the sea. She'd had no one to read them with her. Now she had companions.

Queen Elissabet put a hand on the small of her back, and yellow-orange warmth flared through Mia. The queen's touch held further comfort, reminded her of the concept of home. Elissabet's touch and Lucan's voice each held supernatural power doubled by the potency of ritual and tradition.

"Tell my wife I love her," Nerian whispered. "And my children …"

Tears flowed freely from Mia's eyes and spattered the elf's broken body, and these too became multicolored sparkles. When they touched Nerian, his suffering disappeared.

"It is done," Lucan said.

Queen Elissabet nodded, and her gentle voice filled the intimate space left by Nerian's pause. "Your children will celebrate their father as one of the fiercest warriors Chalvaren has ever known. I swear it."

Mia's heart threatened to collapse.

The maimed elf seemed to go limp. "I feel no more pain." Then Nerian sputtered, "I see them, Lucan!"

"Who, Nerian? Tell us who you see."

"The dragons, Lucan. The dragons in the stone." The dying elf reached out his one good hand as if to grasp the Dragonstone. Mia cringed, and Elissabet held her fast. Nerian looked longingly at the artifact and said, "They call me. They ask for my knowledge to join theirs. Wizard, I must go."

"Then go. Join them, my good man."

Nerian reached again for the Dragonstone, and Mia let him clasp it. She wanted to rip the chain from her neck, give it to him, and run. But she stayed put. She stayed, channeling the magic that was breaking this spell of pain and death, and as dozens of tears flowed down her cheeks, meeting and sizzling upon the artifact, Nerian Llewellan gasped his last. She felt his soul meld with the Dragonstone and strengthen it.

She scrambled backward as the elf's empty husk tumbled onto the floor. Elissabet and Lucan both reached to help her up.

"What the hell just happened here?" she asked, but she didn't need them to answer. "His soul. The stone. Collective knowledge. Collective power. It's the only way to stop true evil."

Lucan crossed his arms, a glimmer of silver dancing about him. He glanced at Queen Elissabet and murmured, "I believe my godson has found us an apt pupil."

The queen used her thumbs to wipe away Mia's tears. She cradled Mia's face in her hands then sighed. "Indeed, Lucan. Theo's firstborn will be a perfect piece when we reestablish the High Elven Council of Magic."

The power crackling between Lucan and Elissabet both intrigued Mia and scared her to death. She didn't have time to think long, however, as Lucan gestured toward the first captive.

"Let's see if we can counteract the spell on the living."

Chapter 14

What was taking so long? Why had they demanded he stay behind?

Impatient, Kort left his father and siblings in the hall and strode through the white stone doorway to the interrogation rooms. Inside he saw Mia, Lucan, and his mother walking out of the far chamber. Mia's troubled green eyes wrenched his heart, and he wondered what exactly had taken place while he waited.

"Nerian?" he asked, his heart hoping for a miracle that his head knew was impossible.

Elissabet and Lucan both shook their heads, but he could glean from their expressions that at least Nerian was no longer in pain. He could see the elf's body lying limp upon the floor.

His mother, Lucan and Mia approached, moving as a unit toward the first mercenary who now lay writhing in chains near the table in the center of the room. Kort moved to Mia and tried to pull her close.

"Leave us. Now," Lucan commanded, gesturing to the door.

"No," Kort replied. "I'm not leaving her."

His mother grimaced. "There's no time to indulge your anger issues, Son. Stand aside. Go collect your father, but stand back."

Lucan took one side of the chained elf with the milky eyes, and Queen Elissabet took the other. Mia hovered between, a wild look of bewilderment on her face.

Kort pulled her close, but she pulled away and her glare startled him. He didn't want her suffering like this. He didn't know what she'd seen in that other room, but from her expression he gathered that it hadn't been good. "Come outside with me, Mia."

She held up a palm and shook her head. "Back off, Kort. You need to do as they say. Go wait outside."

Her words were like a blow. Maybe it was fatigue, but maybe this was his worst fear: He'd dragged her into something horrible, something that would poison her happiness for the rest of her life. Mia now knew the depth of Isa Ansgar's darkness, the intensity of her hatred for his family and friends.

He backed away, turned and strode to the door. There he called to his father, who joined him. The door was locked after Kort waved to his siblings. They needed to be reassured only a little more than he himself did.

✝✝✝

Lucan and Queen Elissabet set to work. Mia hovered at the periphery, watching them and ready to do whatever they asked.

The first elf had been easy. He had been dying, and all Mia did was feel for him and be a conduit for the Dragonstone. Apparently her focus had helped Nerian join his soul with the artifact. The process had felt dignified and just, with Lucan administering last rites and Elissabet supporting all with the warmth of her aura. This other situation was a totally different level.

Their captive hissed at them and fought against his shackles. He looked…bestial. Nearly naked except for a loincloth and boots, this elf's flesh held a greenish-grey pallor. Was he dying too? Even though the chains secured him to the table, occasionally Mia thought she saw something squirming under his skin.

The room reeked, and the closer she edged to the afflicted elf, the more she recognized the stench of death that rose from him. Mia cringed to see the way his muscles punched out from his flesh in wrong places, and his ears flapped out at an unnatural angle from a head sparsely decorated with long stringy strands of greasy hair. His cheeks resembled the jowls of a rat.

"Arden Demar?" Lucan's voice boomed with authority.

The elf flinched and turned milky eyes toward the wizard. His wailing response was inarticulate and caused Mia to flinch.

Lucan and Elissabet each placed hands on their captive's sinewy green arms, and he screamed again. He struggled. Mia backed away and stumbled into someone. She reared around and found Kort, who looked pointedly at his mother.

"Mia doesn't need to be part of this," he called, tugging on Mia's arm.

She snatched it away. "No, I'm staying." Whatever the hell was going on here, she sure wasn't leaving now, not if anyone thought she was the afflicted elf's—the *kingdom*'s—only help. She took the Dragonstone in both hands and willed her aura into it. Whatever power resided there, she wanted all of it focused on whatever was happening.

"We need her. This is as bad as we thought," Lucan said. He cast Mia a glance before his worried gaze returned to the bizarre, misshapen elf. His inspection of the afflicted warrior intensified, and Mia grimaced. She saw Kort look uneasily back at his father, a hefty sword now gripped in King Lachlan's hands.

Arden became a writhing mass of flailing arms and legs. His pelvis bucked up from the table to the point his back nearly broke. Arden lunged forward then, at Mia, a howling sound tearing from his lips and showing pointed teeth as sharp as a dragon's. The chains snapped taut but Mia raised her arm to deflect something that leapt out from the stinking red-black depths of Arden's mouth. The flutter of its blue-black transparent wings assailed her skin with cold drafts of rancid air. A shadow? A demon? Was this the same type of wraith Magnus had shown her in the hall of thrones when they shared his vision of Chalvaren's darkness? When he'd asked her to help them? Those shadows had borne the same winged creatures, the same stench of rot. She tightened her grip on the Dragonstone.

Kort dragged her clear as Queen Elissabet lunged forward, a burst of orange light leaping from her hands, and the queen intercepted the shadow wraith and wrestled it to the floor. "*Tenebris increpationem*. Back to darkness, wraith. You'll do no damage here today."

The shadow screamed and turned on her.

Mia broke free of Kort's protective grasp, shouting, "*Savla regina Elissabet, Varik*. Save the queen!" The spell came from somewhere that she didn't recognize, somewhere deep in her psyche, and it worked; her magic aura sprayed from her splayed fingertips and joined Elissabet's in a sizzling hiss. Sparks flew and surrounded the demon.

The wraith struggled to break free and reach them, black and feathery, but together Mia and Elissabet worked to subdue it. The creature howled in anger and malicious intent, but united the women were too strong, and the thrashing shadow creature finally disintegrated, its screams dissipating with its fractured particles of essence.

"Whoa," Mia said.

Queen Elissabet nodded, a smile playing across her lips. Then she tossed her head back toward Lucan and Arden. "Look, Mia. There's more. The last one channeled a portal through Arden into the castle. You game?"

Mia gave a tight nod.

Behind them, Lucan was dealing with another specter that had burst free from the captive elf. It loomed twice as large as the last, but Mia leapt forward to engage. She thrust her palms in front of her, opening her hands, and the blast of her purple aura sent it sprawling. It rose a moment later, however, fluttering toward her.

Instinct told her to run. Mia refused. "You will not take anyone else, devil."

The Dragonstone warmed on her chest, bursting alight with ghostfire that she directed toward the specter. Elissabet's magic joined hers, and the combined light energy seared the shadowy creature into oblivion.

"More?" Mia yelled, hungry now for the fight. The queen had said there were more.

She whipped around to see another shadow wraith leap from Arden's body, this one three times bigger than the last. Lucan struggled to contain the demon within his silvery aura, but the damned thing filled the room with shrieks and stinking wings of ashy soot, blackening everything and threatening to suffocate everyone. Mia sucked in a tight breath as Lucan threw a bolt of silver magic at it, and Elissabet flooded the chamber with orange. The wraith knocked Elissabet to the ground.

His silver aura blasting wide, Lucan shouted, "*Lux Chalvaren disperdens.* Show me the light of Chalvaren!"

From her place on the floor, Elissabet screamed out words of a different spell.

Mia stood dumbfounded, frozen in place, enveloped by terror. Her lips moved and she repeated the words she heard the queen speak. First just a whisper, she increased her volume to a fevered pitch. "Light of Chalvaren. Light of Chalvaren. *Lux in nos Chalvaren.*"

A horrible sound caught Mia's attention, and her feet shuffled backward despite her resolve. The sound came from Elissabet, not another spell but a scream of anguish. At the same time the massive black wraith shifted and struck out at Kort and Lachlan, pinning them to the far wall. The two men clutched their throats, gasping for air as the shadow wraith forced them to their knees.

"Mia," Kort gasped, using the last of his breath. "Flee!" He collapsed, and the shadow wraith rose above him, intent upon something even more dire.

"Oh, *hell* no!" Overcome by fury and desperation, Mia grasped the Dragonstone. Ghostfire poured forth, and Mia stalked forward toward the wraith, toward the man she loved and toward his father, both men collapsed before the umbral abomination. Arms wide, she directed the multicolored ghostfire onto the snapping, howling beast. It was all she could think to do.

Behind her, Queen Elissabet lunged to her feet. Mia saw orange magic join her own, and she felt her skin warm with Kort's mother's gentle aura. It was the boost she needed, and she kept advancing.

"*Murmur cessant!*" This from Lucan, whose angry words of defiance boomed behind Mia, supporting both women with flashes of mercurial silver that erupted from his fingertips to surround them, Kort and the king.

Mia's ghostfire now fully surrounded the shadow wraith, and it turned away from Kort and Lachlan. Mia leaned forward and growled, "Come on. Come and get me!"

It surged at her, its jagged, feathery wings reeking of purulent death. Crow-like, the shadow wraith screamed, its voice gravelly and deafening, but Mia kept it the target of her ghostfire. The wraith bent, let out one final agonized scream, and collapsed into a billion black molecules of oblivion. Behind them all, Arden Demar collapsed back onto his table with a clatter of chains.

The ghostfire receded back into the Dragonstone with an affirmative snap, and Mia rushed to Kort.

"Are you okay? Kort, look at me!"

God, she'd never forgive herself if he was hurt. She reached for his head. Cradling it in her lap, she searched his body for injuries. Queen Elissabet rushed to kneel beside her, tending to Lachlan, slapping his cheeks, speaking to him, trying to rouse him and crying out his name. But Mia's eyes were only for her prince.

"Look at me, Kort!"

He groaned, and his eyes fluttered open. In that second Mia knew she'd never be able to live without him. She knew in that exact moment she loved Kort Elias, and that thought terrified her more than the wraith. Still, she leaned forward and brushed his lips with hers.

Kort slowly embraced her. His lips found hers and took them with authority. She kissed him back with all the fierceness of a love nearly lost.

"Are you okay?" His voice was a husky whisper, and he pulled her against him with arms that were surprisingly strong for all he'd seemingly been through.

Mia nodded and hid her face in the hollow of his neck. They sat there together, shivering, holding each other. No one in the room spoke.

"Is it over?" Mia asked finally, continuing to stroke Kort's jaw.

Elissabet nodded from where she sat on the floor. "For now."

King Lachlan shuddered. "Bastard nearly suffocated me."

The queen kept one hand on her husband but held out the other to Mia, who reached back to take it. The two women clutched at each other in newfound solidarity, and the gratitude—and strength—the queen conveyed with her beautiful blue eyes moved Mia. This was definitely a woman she wanted to know better.

Lucan's deep voice cast a shadow over their victory. "It's not done. Not until we get some answers out of this prisoner. I want to know how Isa Ansgar conjured these shadow wraiths up from the depths of Hell. Such has not been done since Malachai was alive. "

Mia sighed, nodded, and closed her eyes.

Chapter 15

So, the shadow wraiths had been conjured from Hell? An actual Hell, then. That meant these elves believed in Heaven and Hell much as Mia understood them. Her parents had taught her the concepts as a child, and moreover, of a struggle between the forces of good and evil, but to see something as vile as those shadow wraiths burst free from another elf was beyond what she'd ever imagined—and beyond horrific.

She wiped the sweat beading on her forehead and looked around the bright interrogation room. Elissabet had asked for a moment to check on the children outside. King Lachlan was assessing the threat to the castle, which left Mia alone with Kort, Lucan and their prisoner.

Her limbs were sore from exertion, and Mia tucked her arms tight to her body and leaned back against the flat cool stone wall. She remained watchful of Arden Demar, not taking her eyes off him until Lucan and Kort were satisfied he was harmless. If another one of those demons lurked inside him...

Of course, Arden had changed since the fight. The mercenary now looked like any other elf she'd met here in Chalvaren, though maybe after a bad hangover and a case of influenza to boot. He'd been unconscious after the struggle, but they'd roused him for interrogation. It was difficult for Mia to tell if he was the same as he'd been before his fateful journey to Isa's lands.

Fury rolled off Kort as he questioned the prisoner. "You left Castle Elias eighteen months ago with a job to do, assassin. Where have you been?"

Mia winced, but Lucan wasn't much kinder. He loomed over the broken mercenary and bellowed, "How many more shadow elves does Isa have?"

Arden responded, barely a whisper. "I can't remember."

Lucan held out a chalice for Arden to drink. "This serum should refresh your memory."

The battered elf took giant swallows and almost choked, but finally he appeared sated.

The solution smelled of sage and jasmine mixed with dragon's bane. The acrid smell settled on Mia's taste buds, and she frowned. Was that a truth potion? These wizards really used magic like nothing she'd ever seen. Of course, this issue with Isa Ansgar was like nothing she'd ever seen. Maybe she didn't belong here. Her vision of any happily-ever-after in Chalvaren hung by a precariously thin thread.

"She wants you dead, Lucan," Arden whispered, drawing Mia's attention.

"Tell me something I don't already know."

"She captured one of the strongest wizards from the southern alliance last week, Laudegrance Smarr." The captive elf groaned, and tears spilled out of his bloodshot eyes. He buried his head in his hands as he continued, "She killed his whole family and forced us to watch! She—"

Kort leaned in and gave Arden a menacing stare. "You did nothing to stop her, mercenary?"

Arden threw up his hands in a feeble gesture of failure. Mia's belly tightened, but she couldn't turn away from hearing the rest.

"It was as if we were all paralyzed. Such magic!" He shook his head, obviously confused. "She's at once kind and then malicious. Thoughtful and then driven. A single word of discord, and she sucks the life from you. And she has command over...*things.*" Arden grasped Kort's arm. "Black as coal, with wings that carry pestilence and evil. Sh-she lets them eat at your soul until—"

"Shadow wraiths," Lucan hissed. He shot Kort a meaningful glance. "Yes, we've seen." He tapped his chin, his brown eyes calculating as he paced the room. "But where did she find the power to do this? With the help of those things she can make any one of our soldiers her minion."

Mia stood rigid against the wall. There were more of those winged black things lurking in Chalvaren? No wonder her father took her away from all this!

Lucan caught her expression and nodded. "She's fighting us with the darkest arts. We'll have to reconvene what's left of the magic council and tell them what she's doing."

Mia dropped her hands to her sides, and her voice was barely a whisper. "Why?"

Lucan sighed. "Because it is the only way to stop her."

"No." Mia shook her head. "Why is she so angry? What did you do to her?"

Kort spoke up, gesturing to Lucan that he would explain. "Twenty-five years ago, Isa and her lover Malachai slaughtered ten dragons in tearing the Dragonstone from the Drakhos Mountains. The High Elven Council of Magic found out and captured them. Isa claimed losing the dragons was an accident, but the Council refused to listen. They uncovered Malachai's plans to kill my father, corrupt the wizards on the High Council, and rule Chalvaren from a pulpit of darkness. One—Alastair Krogh—administered the spell that dismembered Malachai. The Council disbanded afterward, amidst complaints that so much magic convened in one place was the temptation that pushed Malachai over the edge."

Lucan whipped around and stared at Kort, his black robes following in a swish. "That's not *exactly* what happened, but Alastair did stop those two lunatics from taking control of all of Chalvaren with the unsanctioned power of the Dragonstone. Of course, his actions also ensured that Isa Ansgar would declare war."

"Revenge?" Mia said, trying to understand. She posited her best guess at what had happened: "The wizards from the seven kingdoms of Chalvaren responded to a crime involving harvesting the Dragonstone. One punished the offenders, but not every wizard on the Council agreed on the punishment and so they split afterward. Isa Ansgar's grief turned to hatred, and this afternoon's attack was that hatred made manifest. She's been doing this for some time, causing strife wherever she can. But this is her first overt attack."

Lucan grumbled something that sounded like a confirmation before, "There were other issues involved in the disbanding of the Council, and in Isa's rage. Fear, I suppose. A subsequent attack five years later. But she's lain semi-dormant for many years now—or so we thought."

Mia inhaled, lowering her chin. "Other issues?"

Arden acknowledged her for the first time, pointing at Mia with three outthrust fingers. "Only three wizards remain on Isa's list of those to be punished, but remember, she won't stop there. Anyone in alliance with those wizards will die as well."

Mia thought for a moment. This was her aunt. This was her father's sister. From the sound of it Isa was simply angry that her beloved was killed without a fair trial, or at least without a consensus regarding a capital punishment. It sounded like her beloved had been the original force behind any evil. No matter how deep she'd sunk, perhaps Isa could be reclaimed. Wouldn't that be what Theo Ansgar would want? Hadn't he always talked about the power of love and redemption? Mia's mother certainly had.

She took a deep breath. "I could try to talk to her. Maybe she'd listen to me?"

Lucan roared with laughter.

Kort stood. "No, Mia. Lucan's right. It's generous of you to want to help, but that witch won't listen to reason."

"Who else is on Isa's list?" Mia asked, wondering where she would strike next. "Which other wizard?" Mia held out her fingers and began to count. *Lucan. His absent brother Alastair. And...?* Her knees suddenly weakened as she realized.

The door opened behind her. King Lachlan strode in, assessing the room. Elissabet followed, leading Magnus. All of them stared at her.

Mia looked up at Kort's mother, her eyes growing wide. "You. Isa. The Council..."

Elissabet slid a glance Mia's way and nodded as she strode toward Arden Demar. "Yes, Mia. I'm the third remaining wizard Isa wants to exterminate. Lucan, Alastair and I are the last of the original Council. And without you and the Dragonstone, she will likely succeed in destroying us."

Was this why Kort came for her, to save his mother and his family's court wizard? Mia draped exhausted arms around her dragon's neck. She'd believed Kort, believed he was her destiny and that he cared for her as much as she did for him, but now, after hearing this...well, it was easy to imagine other motives. And even if he did love her, was the rest of the family simply interested in using her and the power of the Dragonstone?

She squeezed Magnus and considered fleeing with him.

†††

Kort grimaced at his mother then glanced at Mia, who stroked Magnus's head and spoke excitedly in his ear. The dragonlet growled softly then purred, and Mia's expression changed. Joy replaced the anger on her face, and that eased Kort's heart a little. At least the dragonlet could still make her happy.

Kort addressed his father. "If Isa can capture soldiers and possess them with those hideous things... The other men we sent. She must have a small army by now." He trailed off, horrified, and glanced back to Mia. What he saw instead was Magnus's teal-and-purple wings disappearing out the door.

His heart quickened. He needed to follow them. To reassure them. But how? Mia was furious, and rightly so. He should have warned her before bringing her back to Chalvaren about all the danger here, danger that involved her possibly wronged aunt. How could he ever make this right?

"Shadow elves. An army of shadow elves..." Kort's father shook his head and sighed. "Well, at least the castle's safe for the moment. Isa is gone. I ordered the guards doubled, though. I do not doubt she will return. She was likely not just pursuing these two"—he motioned with his head toward the two elves they'd freed from shadow—"but assessing our weak spots. Things will only get worse. Elissabet and Lucan, you must consider yourselves in constant danger from now on, even here in the keep."

Kort's mother nodded. "I must speak to my contacts in the Southern Alliance. If Laudegrance Smarr and his family have truly been killed..."

Kort eyed the door then crossed his arms. "We must protect our dragons—and see that they protect us. I'll arrange new tactics with our riders."

Elissabet approached Arden, still chained upon the table. She smiled at him then looked back at Kort. "See that Mia gets settled in, Son. That's your first duty now that she's found her place here at Castle Elias. There are others who can see to our Dragon Riders."

Kort threw up his hand. "Mia will never agree to stay now."

Lucan eyed him. "Did you not warn her what she was walking into?"

Kort shook his head and diverted his eyes. "I needed her help to return here, and we had so little time. The villagers near her home had formed a mob and…" He paused and eyed the door again. "The truth is, she is better off in Chalvaren. No matter what, Mia should be here beside me where I can protect her. She *will* be my future queen."

Lucan said nothing, just let out a long, low whistle.

Kort's father took his arm and led him to the door. "Things will work out. Go to her, Son. Give her this."

Kort took his father's offering, a small golden-hinged box. He opened it, peered at the revealed ring's square of perfectly faceted dragon ore surrounded by baguettes of clear, shimmering diamond, and he stepped back in surprise. "My grandmother's jewel? You want Mia to have this?"

King Lachlan gestured toward Queen Elissabet with his shoulder and whispered, "Jewelry solves most issues with your mother." He shrugged, and his sheepish grin touched Kort's heart. "It was her idea, actually, but it's your choice, Son. It's your ring to give. After what I saw of Mia's courage today, you'd be a fool to let her get away."

Nodding, Kort looked at his mother, who flashed him an expectant glare and waved her hand as though to dismiss him before turning back to Arden. So, she fully approved of Mia now? Well, that made sense. His father was gentle and generous with family, but no way would he have given up this ring without Elissabet's agreement.

Kort shook his head, awed as always by his mother's changeable nature. She was always shifting, scheming, planning. He never doubted her loyalty to his father, of course, but she'd paid the same mercenary who eventually stole Magnus's egg to locate the Dragonstone. Maybe the part his mother played in his returning that artifact was larger than he'd realized. And, Lucan too! The castle wizard had been more than willing to send him after Magnus. Had both Lucan and Elissabet known he would find Mia too? Had they hoped she could be brought under their control to fight Isa?

He shook his father's hand then turned toward the door. His first goal was to recover his future princess.

Chapter 16

Above the bunker in the main castle Kort found Duncan, who pointed toward the open doors leading out to the cliffs. "Mia's gone out there with Garnet and Magnus. I thought it was okay. Your father sounded the official all-clear."

"No one gets near her. Or the Aurora," Kort said. "For their own protection, Duncan. Not until I say it's okay. Things are more dangerous than ever."

The head of the castle guard nodded. "As you wish. It shouldn't be hard to manage. Your mother's assigned my wife as Mia's lead lady-in-waiting. Shayleigh will see that everything is in order in the west tower and also be sure to keep her safe." He gripped Kort's arm. "The elf who's still alive. What did he say? Did he have any useful information?"

Kort would not be delayed. "My father will give you the details. I need to find Mia." He paused a moment to add, "She will be a great addition to our fight against Isa, Duncan. She…has great magic."

Duncan looked surprised. "I guess this was meant to be, then. At first I was surprised the Aurora chose her."

Kort sighed. "It's rare for a dragon to make the choice to imprint, I'll admit. I know you were next in line, Duncan, but don't worry. There'll be another hatch soon."

"How amazing you found her," the guard captain murmured. "For the mercenary who stole the Aurora egg to go to the world where Theo Ansgar fled… What else can I do to help you?"

"Send my personal belongings to the west tower within the hour. I'll meet you there. After she's done outside, I plan to get Mia settled and…welcome her properly. I've already been delayed too long."

The guard captain nodded and smiled, clasping Kort's palm and forearm in a grip that was sure and friendly. Then the two men parted.

Kort stalked toward the main doors of the keep, considering the weight of his grandmother's ring in its small golden box tucked deep in the leather pouch hanging from his belt. How would Mia react to such a gift? It was a ladies ring, something spectacular Mia could be proud to wear at court. The promise behind it represented more than the king's ring and the protection of the royal family. This engagement ring meant Mia was his princess and his alone.

Expectation of her joy tickled the corners of his lips, but as he strode through the grand castle doors his smile fell away. Mia was not waiting there. Instead, several of his warriors, their dragons beside them, were gathered in a circle in the green grassy field. They pointed skyward and shielded their eyes from the sun. The white wind dragon Pure sat off by herself at the other edge of the field, her body posture rigid, looking up with everyone else.

Kort looked up. Magnus soared above him, black wings spread wide. Airborne. Flying.

Impossible.

A flash of blonde hair feathered out behind the dragonlet, and Kort's chest tightened. Magnus didn't know how to land properly.

He shielded his eyes from the bright sunlight and rushed forward into the crowd. "Who authorized that flight?"

His only answer was a thunderous roar. Garnet flew mere wing-beats behind the little black dragon, calling out to him as if in challenge to attain further heights.

Kort gulped in jerky breaths, and the pressure in his chest nearly drove him to his knees. He fought off the weakness and stormed through the crowd, shouting, "Who allowed this without my permission? We've just sounded the all-clear and a dragonlet is given permission to take his first flight?"

The warriors nearest him jerked to attention. Kristoff, Kort's second-in-command, caught his gaze and called out, "Damndest thing. Those three tore out through the castle doors and she mounted him before we could even introduce ourselves. They didn't ask permission to enter castle airspace, they just...took off."

"They can't be up there without assistance," Kort said.

"He's not quite got the hang of things yet," offered a new voice.

"He'll kill her if he's not careful," said another.

Ian and Quinn had appeared behind Kort, who looked back at his brothers in annoyance. The two shielded their eyes, pointing toward Magnus, talking excitedly.

"Oh. Look at that. He can't even turn," Ian said, bouncing from one foot to the other.

"How's he gonna land? What kind of dragon can't turn with the air currents?"

"He'll have to take to the sea…but the tide's out."

"Well, maybe Garnet will catch her if she falls."

Kort shoved past his brothers, a snarl forming on his lips as he stared helplessly at the sky. Somehow, he knew, he would eventually have to learn to trust Mia in situations like this, to give her the independence she needed if she was going to live here in Chalvaren and be his wife. But, no. Not like this. Not with an untrained dragon who didn't have flight training or know how to save her if she fell. And if Magnus fell…

Garnet roared out a warning. Magnus was flying even more haphazardly and had neared the cliffs. The Aurora faltered and twisted. Mia shrieked then righted herself. The spectators groaned collectively.

Kort raced through the crowd of his warriors, headed for his best option. "Pure! Help me bring them in!"

The white wind dragon extended her leg for him to mount. Kort scaled it and secured himself behind her neck.

"Up, girl. Get me up there now!"

The white dragon took two steps forward and leapt into the air.

As they took position beneath the inexperienced duo, Magnus caught sight of them and frantically beat his wings, swerving away. Kort realized what he'd done and grimaced.

"Easy, girl," he said to Pure. "Don't spook him. He doesn't know what it means to fly yet, let alone what it means to fly in formation."

He gave Pure a signal to pull back, and she did, but Magnus was still frightened. The Aurora croaked out an attempt at a roar, Mia screamed and thrashed her legs to counterbalance the juvenile dragon's sudden jerky movements, and the pair disappeared downward over the edge of the cliffs. Kort's only solace was that Garnet held course and went with them. But Magnus was still trying to get away, confused and flying into certain disaster. The dragonlet's stupidity and overreaction could cause any or all of them injury or death.

"Follow them, Pure," he called out. He leaned forward on the beast's neck and sighed. "Get closer. There may be something we can do to help."

Below the cliff edge he saw that Garnet had hung tough, flanking the dragonlet who still shrieked in fear and fought his way out over the ocean.

"Magnus!" Kort yelled. "Do not go out there!" But the warning was surely swept away by the wind, rough air currents wafting up from the water that the Aurora hit at the wrong angle, twisting his wings and being knocked backward. Giving a pitiful roar, the dragonlet was wrenched suddenly into a sideways spin.

Kort urged Pure forward to intercept. "Get them, girl. Save them."

The white put down her head and dove.

The tide was out, so the beach stretched far away from the cliffs. Pure bleated a roar of contempt as Magnus descended toward the sand below. Sure, it was soft, but a fall from this height would kill anyone. The Aurora had to correct his spin.

"No," Kort growled. Magnus wasn't managing. He couldn't catch air. Kort locked his gaze on Mia and ignored Garnet's red wings beating in his peripheral vision. He pressed his body tight to the diving white dragon and prayed. Somehow Pure had to catch them.

He readied himself to stretch, to grab Mia when the time came. *If* the time came. They might be dead before he could do anything.

"Faster, girl! Go! Get me close enough to leap over and—"

Pure screamed out a defensive roar and abruptly pulled up.

"NO!" Kort shrieked, confused and desperate. "Don't stop now!"

Garnet blew by, his massive red body missing Pure by such a narrow margin his wake buffeted them. The white tried to correct, to counterbalance with her tail, but this sent her into her own spin. Kort struggled to stay with her. His boots dug into her scales, fighting the force of correction as she again found her balance.

"Mia!" Kort called, looking downward. He reached out as if his one hand could span the distance and catch her and Magnus, as if he could protect them, as if he had any control over their impending disaster, but they and Garnet were too far below, and Garnet was still too distant from the Aurora to do any good. Isa Ansgar wouldn't do them in. Kort would only have himself to blame. His own stupidity and impulsive behavior had done them in. By giving chase, by trying to save Mia, by trying to stop them he'd made things even worse. Mia and Magnus careened down wildly toward the sand, and he was helpless to stop it.

"Varik, no," he whispered. "Don't let this happen."

Time slowed to a crawl. Every muscle in Kort's body tightened as he watched his future plummet toward the earth. Images of himself, Mia and Magnus flashed through his mind. Mia's soft body under his, the way they'd made love before returning here to Chalvaren, the way they should have made love again. Magnus growing to adulthood, leading the dragons of Chalvaren with the Dragonstone strapped to his chest. Mia's gentle smile as she said "I do" and became his princess....

Tears sprang to his eyes, burning as Magnus spiraled downward toward the shore. "Fly, damn you! Fly, dragon! FLY!"

Garnet roared. Mia screamed out words so loud Kort heard. Then Magnus somehow corrected and pulled himself out of his dive. Mostly. He was now descending at a much less deadly angle.

"Yes! Fly!" Kort screamed, his eyes fixed on Mia and Magnus. "Fly...!"

Ten feet from impact, the Aurora threw back his head and roared, a mighty sound that thundered through the air. He kicked back his feet and caught the last remaining current of air wafting up from the ocean, and he rose.

"WOO-HOO! YES!" Kort heard Mia shriek. The skirt of her purple dress billowed out behind her as Magnus arched up one or two feet above incoming waves, sped out over the ocean then let out another glorious roar.

Kort blinked twice. Whenever he closed his eyes for the rest of his life he'd see the image of that pair, after coming so close to death, speeding safely over the water toward the setting sun.

"Thank the gods," he whispered. "Hell yes, Magnus. Hell, yes."

Above, a crowd of warriors on the cliffs roared cheers of approval. It took Kort a moment to realize what the sound was, but when he did the noise bolstered both his relief and his love for Mia and her mount. The damn dragonlet had done it, and now the beast was a mere streak of black soaring toward the setting sun, looking more competent with every beat of his wings. It was the most incredible thing Kort had ever witnessed.

Pure roared beneath him, stretched her neck, and dove in pursuit of the little black dragon.

"Hell, yes!" he heard Mia scream, her blonde locks whipping out behind her. Magnus let his tail down to skim the turquoise water, blasting sea spray high into the air. Above, the crowd screamed with joy.

"Showoff!" Kort yelled, laughing. Tapping his heart with his fist, he corrected his seat on Pure and urged the wind dragon to catch up. He couldn't wait to greet them both, couldn't wait to hold both Magnus and Mia in his arms. He also couldn't wait to strangle them for engaging in this stupid stunt.

Garnet appeared on his left, giving Pure the wide berth she deserved, and the two mature dragons caught up with their juvenile quarry. They flanked Magnus, and when Kort stared at Mia, his heart racing at as fast as his dragon, she laughed, spread her arms and then had the nerve to wave at him!

Kort waved her back to the castle. She stuck out her tongue, but Magnus seemed to understand and allowed Garnet and Pure to direct him. Their destination was the dragon-deck of the west tower, the relative seclusion and safety on the wide expanse of sun-warmed stones of the lowermost part of the spire. Kort finally allowed himself to breathe.

"Take us in, girl," he said as he patted Pure's neck.

Garnet landed first, a guttural growl gurgling from his throat, and Pure touched down a moment later. Kort slid off the dragon's back and ran forward, looking back over his shoulder to see how Magnus would do. The Aurora seemed to be handling the descent all right, circling and diving, but in the last ten feet he pulled back and squawked.

"Down, Magnus!" Mia commanded, her voice fierce. "Open your eyes!"

He didn't, and he struck the sun-warmed stones at an odd angle and rather high speed, crumpling and sliding crookedly toward the far edge of the platform. Kort raced after them in hot pursuit, but they thankfully stopped before going over the edge.

Mia hopped down, her feet firm on solid stone. She gulped air, her cheeks vibrant red. She doubled over then reared back up and shouted, "That was fantastic!" Her eyes shone with excitement and vigor. With life.

Kort wanted to strangle her. "You're grounded!" he bellowed.

Mia stepped back, anger burning in her eyes. Her chest heaved and her hands shook, but she lurched forward and pointed a finger in his face. "You have no right to tell me what to do, Kort Elias!"

Kort recoiled, struck by the bitterness of her words, but she needed to know how foolhardy that stunt had been and so he threw out his arm to point at Magnus and said, "You stay off that damn dragon until he learns how to land. Hell, until he learns how to *fly*. Are you crazy?"

Mia stared at him. "How the hell's he supposed to learn if he doesn't try?"

"Without you on top of him!"

"He's my dragon. He asked me to come."

"You could have *died*, Mia," Kort found himself whispering. He heaved in deep breaths, conflicted as to what to say next. Her flushed skin demanded his attention, and he wanted to kiss her. She was so beautiful like this, hot, angry, and full of life. In one breath he wanted to turn Mia over his lap and spank that supple little ass, and in the next he wanted to take her into his arms, comfort her, and tenderly tell her of his concern and love for her. Hell, she both infuriated him and left him speechless.

She planted fists on her hips, her knuckles white. "Better I die on dragonback because of my own stupidity than fighting shadow wraiths because of other people's political mistakes."

She wheeled away, her long blonde hair whipping out as if in punctuation. Stomping toward Magnus, she reached out and hugged him. The coos she gave the dragonlet were low and comforting…and sexy. Hers was the softest, sweetest voice Kort had ever heard.

"We'll get it right next time," she cooed into the dragonlet's ear. "Never mind him."

Garnet moved close, and Mia placed her hand on his neck. "Thank you for the escort," she said. Then Kort's traitorous red dragon let her scratch him under his chin. The beast purred, and Kort could have kicked himself for having acted like an ass when he could have contained his temper and turned the moment into a tender reunion and kiss. He alone had been the one to turn this into a confrontation.

Mia walked over to Pure, who waited on the opposite side of the stone deck. "Thank you, wind dragon," she said as she offered up her hand.

Pure leaned down and sniffed it. She let Mia stroke her scales for a moment; then the dragon shuddered, pulled away, and flew back down to the yard in front of the castle.

At least someone is still on the side of reason, Kort thought.

Mia clasped her hands and watched the dragon fly away. She said nothing, just moved to the edge of the tower and stared down into the fields.

Kort went through the usual post-flight protocols, assessing both Magnus and Garnet for injury. He stroked Magnus from tail to snout and found a couple of scales out of place, but they were nothing that wouldn't grow back. He smoothed the beast's hide and leaned in to whisper, "Damn good job, little one. I've never seen anyone pull out of that sort of dive."

Garnet yawned, folded his wings onto his back, and stretched out on the sun-warmed stones of the deck. Magnus did the same.

Satisfied the dragons would survive, Kort dragged his gaze to Mia. All he wanted was to hold her in his arms, to connect to her in a private and intimate way, yet he'd angered her in at least a hundred ways since they met. He'd never wanted to succeed at something so badly yet failed so completely. How the hell was he supposed to get through to her now?

Easing over to the banister, he saw that Mia stared out over Castle Elias lands. Warriors below practiced drills with their dragons, while others soared above the ocean on patrol. Mia flinched when he approached, and she kept her back to him, her posture rigid. He deserved as much, maybe, but still he hated it. He wanted to explain.

"I yelled because you scared me."

"You'll need to work on that."

"I..." He sighed, embarrassed and angry. He didn't know how to proceed. She meant everything to him, this young woman. She scared him to death and inspired greatness at the same time, was everything he didn't know how to handle.

She pointed down at his warriors and their dragons. "You must be used to barking orders to keep them organized."

He conceded that truth with a silent nod. She didn't look over, but the comment seemed somewhat conciliatory. At least that was something. The golden strands of her hair danced in the wind, and he moved closer to touch them. She seemed so...so perfect here. So perfectly beautiful in the light of the setting sun of Chalvaren.

"I'll show you what to do. We'll start tomorrow."

"No. We won't." She turned to face him, her expression pained, and her words struck him like a slap. She pivoted and walked away from Kort, calling over her shoulder, "I'm not staying until tomorrow."

Chapter 17

Isa Ansgar's spiked boots clicked out a determined tempo as she stalked through the ancient gray stone halls of her manor at Cumberlae. Her heart beat out an echoing staccato rhythm. She'd turned VanZanz out to pasture and her bed called for her to rest, but she had something more exhilarating to attend. A plan had come into her mind, and now it was all she could think about.

"If the Dragonstone is back in Chalvaren, I have the means to use this shard to tap its energy."

She grasped her aching, blistered hand and eyed her purple amulet, careful to not let it touch her bare skin again as she made her way toward the altar room, toward the shrine she'd erected to her dead lover. She didn't need the main piece of amethyst at all. She could channel the magic from where she was and would finally see her Malachai again.

Shadow elves joined her progress, fell in line behind her.

"Tonight," she told her followers with a smirk, "we raise our hero from the grave."

They raised their voices in flat-sounding cheers, but Isa ignored that detail and kept walking forward. Most of the possessed elves were too stupid to speak. The problem with using shadow wraiths was that they sapped their victims of their minds and free will...but then she wasn't interested in civilized warriors, even if it meant they could never understand what tonight would mean to her. This savored reunion was an end to the cold and bitter loneliness she'd endured for two decades. Malachai had given her access to the shadow wraiths, and she used the dark, birdlike demons to assist her in raising him from the grave.

She had reached her inner sanctum. The shadow elves surrounding her stood at attention. "Leave me," she hissed.

All obeyed except for the two enormous creatures who guarded this, her favorite room, both armed with precision compound bows and poison-tipped arrows. They really were magnificent, the best Castle Elias had offered up to kill her. She'd hand-picked them. She doubted they even needed their impressive weapons, but nothing was getting through to her prized possessions.

One of the pair was slightly smarter. He spoke and welcomed her with a flourish of long, muscle-bound arms that ended in claws. "Mistress, your temple?"

Isa flourished her hand toward the doors. "No disturbances. Understood?"

He bowed. She nodded, pleased, refusing to tolerate anything less than total obedience.

The two hulking shadow elf guards unlocked and heaved open the massive black doors. Isa breathed a sigh of satisfaction and went inside. This was it, the place she loved. The place where she would effect the magic to bring back her beloved.

A long red carpet led from the heavy doors to the altar ahead. As she eyed its length, she took note of the room, decorated to her exact specifications. Her eyes took in the perpetual lights shining down from soaring ceilings that illuminated her prized possessions: two golden urns in the center of the room—one large, one small—gleaming on that altar covered with red velvet.

Isa smiled. "After tonight, Chalvaren will belong to me."

She stepped into the chamber and the room's two guards followed, shadow elves with their grayish-green skin and hairless heads and their shadow wraiths half erupted from their shoulders, screeching for her success.

"Thank you, gentlemen," Isa said, laughing, tossing raven black hair over her shoulder. She sauntered down the carpeted aisle to the altar, her amulet swinging from her uninjured hand. "All is well with the altar, I presume?"

They hissed, bowing and groveling.

"Yes," the smarter one said. "Your altar awaits your attendance, Mistress."

While alive, Malachi had told her she deserved adoration from every living creature. Living out his belief had become a religion of sorts for Isa, and as soon as she raised him from death she'd show him how his creatures loved her and craved her approval.

"Malachai will be proud of your loyalty and faithfulness. I will see you both rewarded...but for now you must leave me to pray alone."

The pair bowed deeply at her dismissal, loped down the aisle toward the door and fled the room.

Isa relaxed her shoulders as she heard the door shut. "Alone at last."

A tickle of excitement coursed through her belly, and at her command a feathery demon bled out of her mouth and right ear and materialized upon her shoulder in the form of a blue-black raven. It was her shadow drake, a shadow wraith that had bonded with a raven wholly and completely, a ritual Malachai completed just before his death at the hands of Alastair Krogh. Malachai had loaned Isa the creature, and now their connection reminded her of him in a most sensual way. Whenever she suffered with bouts of conscience or regret, the shadow drake reminded her of her single most important mission: to raise her beloved from the grave.

She reached out and stroked the shadow drake. "With Malachai at our side, the remaining members of the once-great High Elven Magic Council of Chalvaren will bow at our feet. All of Chalvaren will grovel for forgiveness!"

The black-winged fiend cawed out in triumph.

"First, my amulet," Isa said. She ignored her blistered hand and laid the amethyst on a silver, three-pronged pedestal in the middle of the velvet-covered altar. This was only a shard of the Dragonstone, but Malachai had carved it from its parent himself. "With the Dragonstone back, this shard might just be all I need."

Her shadow drake lurched around on Isa's shoulder and let out a vigorous cry. Isa took her time, though, dropping to her knees on plush black cushions laid out in front of her. She could barely contain her excitement, but there was ritual to consider. And she wanted to savor her triumph. She'd spent twenty years imagining these next few moments.

The pendant lay before her on the altar. Isa bowed her head against steepled hands and whispered reverently, "Come to me, my Malachai."

At first no reply came, but she was not upset. She'd been here before, and no magic she'd stolen from either the wizards or dragonlets had been powerful enough to raise him. But this time would be different. With the power of the Dragonstone channeled through her shard and her will to bring her beloved back to life…

"Failure ends tonight, Malachai. Let me see you, my love."

Still nothing. She eyed the purple amulet and allowed herself a moment of doubt. Was it strong enough to do the job?

Yes. It had to be.

"I *will* find the right spell to channel the Dragonstone's power," she whispered.

Rising, she took down a nearby torch and lit three thick, black, round candles. Once the flames burned high, Isa returned to kneeling. She watched the candle flames and the golden urns intently, her brows raised, her heart beating in her chest like a trapped sparrow.

"Malachai, return to me."

The candles gusted, and her belly tightened. *Yes. Good.* He'd disturbed the thin veil between their worlds before, and it had begun like this. She was on the right track.

"I miss you, Malachai," she continued. "Come back to me tonight…and bring back our unborn child."

Isa lost herself for a moment in memories of him: her lover, her wizard. Apprenticed to him at the tender age of fifteen, she'd found his views of magic exciting. And he'd been so handsome. Malachai had stood tall, with long thick black hair like hers. He'd cut the finest figure garbed in his leather armor and always outfitted with sharp, deadly weapons.

"Yes, the weaker elves of Chalvaren contested your rise to power," she murmured. "No one approved. But they did not understand. Might makes right in this world. In *every* world. It is how you stop people from hurting you—something my brother never understood. But he never craved power or wielded magic like you, my love. Theo was content to be second best, a king's second-in-command and never a king. I'm not surprised the coward stole the Dragonstone and ran."

Her shadow drake danced on her shoulder then leapt toward the altar. Isa kept talking, barely noticing.

"As children Theo and I often competed for the honor of conjuring the most remarkable spells. Sometimes our results produced very different things. Theo made it clear he worried about my affinity for darkness. And I loved my brother then…until I met you." Her brother had tried to warn her not to get caught up in black magic, and he'd tried to get her to come home again from her apprenticeship. She'd refused.

Isa grimaced. Who would have ever thought she'd find herself lost in the dark depths of despair and grief that governed her life for the past twenty years? Thinking of Theo and the happy days of childhood was…painful.

Her shadow drake cawed. Isa stroked his feathers then swept her fingertips across the golden urn on the altar. "My family's heritage bore strong magic, so it seemed appropriate for me to pursue you, Mal. I gave myself to you willingly, ceded to your every whim. Now I want you back beside me."

Isa narrowed her eyes on the dancing flames of the candles set around the room, and her gut tightened as she recalled how her dark wizard was taken from her.

"Why didn't you stop them, Varik?" she asked, bowing her head. "Since you didn't, I must right this wrong. This might well be sacrilege, but I cannot see any other way. I must have him back."

She understood the harm her actions would cause, but without Malachai, without the child she'd lost, what was the point of life? Damn the consequences, she wanted her man at her side. Malachai had hated everyone else on the High Elven Council of Magic for their weakness of mind. Now she did too.

The shadow drake ruffled its wing feathers and cawed out a wicked sound.

"Come to me, Malachai. Bring our son, and together we will crush the House of Elias and all who side with them. Tonight, a new chapter in the history of Chalvaren will be born of my pain and tears. I lift my pain up to you!"

Isa relished the black magic, the ceremony. She stared through the candlelight at the golden urns on the red velvet altar, and they vibrated to life. She flourished her burned and wounded hand through the three candle flames and screamed out her beloved's name, and wisps of black smoke rose from the largest golden urn, swirling up and around the altar and coalescing into a fraction of a tall male form. Her shard of the Dragonstone sparkled, and Isa let herself smile a genuine smile of delight.

Malachai.

Isa beckoned him forward. "Yes, husband, come to me. Bring our child." She saw their future beginning again tonight.

She stood and reached for Malachai's hand, his outline still only a smoky curling image hovering above his golden urn. Tears fell from her eyes. This was the closest she'd ever come to seeing her wishes fulfilled. He was forming! Her mind raced forward to plans for the night, plans for victory over the rest of the world.

"Yes! Channeling the power of the Dragonstone is working!"

The amulet flickered out.

Isa squeezed shut her eyes, her throat thick. *Please, no. This can't be happening again.* But it was. A cold breeze shifted through her manor, chilling Isa's skin, and the candles on the altar gusted out.

The pain of her blistered palm suddenly doubled in intensity. Isa screamed and drew back, doubled over in pain. She cried, "No!" and her chin quivered, but the wisps of smoke heralding Malachai's return nonetheless sank back down into his golden urn. Her shadow drake slithered its cold black wings back inside her, and the thing wound itself back around her heart.

Despair overwhelmed her. How could she be so wrong again? Then she gazed upon the golden urns and collapsed back upon the black cushions before the altar, realizing exactly what she had to do.

"I must take it from them. Nothing is powerful enough to raise the dead but the Dragonstone."

Chapter 18

Mia mumbled several choice obscenities she wished she'd used on Kort as she strode through the double arched doors that led into the west tower of Castle Elias. "What the hell was he thinking, yelling at me like that? Has he lost his mind? I'm not staying here another minute and listening to domineering rants about what I can and can't do. Tell me I'm grounded just as Magnus is learning to fly? I'm getting out of here. He can keep his castle and his ring and his family if he thinks I'm putting up with that behavior for another sec—"

She almost changed her mind as she absorbed the vast interior of the tower.

"Oh, I could definitely live here."

The décor was a warm mix of wood and stone, interior buttresses soaring high to arched stone ceilings. Mia eased forward, tempted to forget everything except the beautiful space, the scene a powerful distraction from the earlier drama. And—Mia touched her belly as her stomach growled—what was that incredible smell? Was it a stew? Comforting aromas of food and life assaulted her nose and led her further into the tower.

Mia touched the back of her fist to her lips, and wished it wasn't all so beautiful, so welcoming, so homey. Soft carpets covered the stone floors and begged for bare feet, so Mia kicked off her boots and wiggled her toes. It was sheer heaven. A fire burned merrily in a nearby fireplace, crackling and drawing her attention to the fine stonework surrounding the hearth.

"It's all so gorgeous…," she murmured.

Well-lit circular staircases ascended to multiple upper levels. Mia spotted a little library nestled along the stone walls, a reading nook placed just below a curved window. What did Chalvarens read, though? What had her father read?

Nostalgia hit her full on, but Mia cast her eyes downward to study the floor. She couldn't stay. She wouldn't. Not after what she'd seen in that interrogation room. Not after Kort yelled at her for flying and—

"Where *is* that smell coming from?" she found herself muttering as she followed her nose.

Two elves looked up from their work in an open kitchen: one brown-haired female and one gray-haired male sporting a white beret. The aroma of what they prepared was almost intoxicating.

"Come into the kitchen," the female said. "Queen Elissabet told us you must be famished. We're almost done."

Mia couldn't make her legs move. She stood there dumbfounded, exhausted, frozen.

"From King Lachlan's cellar," the woman continued in a soft voice, bringing two glasses filled with a chilled, light-colored, bubbling liquid. "He thought you'd enjoy a sample of the mead he brews. We understand you've had a long day, Princess."

"Mia," Mia corrected as the woman curtsied. "Please call me Mia." She took the glass and somehow managed an awkward smile while staring into the kitchen toward the aromas that called to her aching belly.

"And I'm Shayleigh." The woman pointed behind her to the busy man in the white hat. "Our chef, Thorvid. Don't tell him I said so, but his creations are a delight for the soul *and* the body. He's not much for conversation when he's working, though."

Mia's eyes lingered on Thorvid's bustling activity. "What's he cooking?"

"Some of the prince's favorite dishes. We thought they would be a wonderful way to welcome you to Castle Elias, Mia. Are you hungry?"

Some of Mia's tension eased away with Shayleigh's gentle welcome. She admitted, "I could eat...an entire dragon."

Shayleigh laughed, and then so did Mia.

Mia got her legs to move, and she took a seat at a small wooden table. When the first taste of Lachlan's honeyed wine hit her tongue, its dry, mellow, fruity flavor brought her soul to life. Sparkles of little bubbles effervescing up the flute tickled her nose, and she giggled. She took another sip and the stress of her earlier conflicts began to melt away.

"Oh. This is really good. He brewed it himself?" she asked. Then her stomach growled again, demanding attention.

"Dinner won't be long," Shayleigh promised.

Kort's deep bass voice filled the room. "Thank you, Shayleigh. Is everything in order?"

The woman headed across the room with the other glass of mead, and her subsequent exchange with Kort was quiet, but Mia didn't stay to listen; she took her glass and fled back into the tower.

She wandered around, sipping her mead and peering into each room. The furnishings all looked comfortable, soft and inviting. The fabrics married rich and varied hues—warm reds, deep greens, complementary neutral shades. And the bathrooms were outfitted with plumbing, hot and cold running water, elegant and luxurious fixtures!

"I can at least stay one night, right?" she found herself saying. "Queen Elissabet knows how to outfit guest quarters. And they've gone to a lot of trouble making dinner. It would be rude to leave now, right?"

To tell the truth, it wasn't just the food. Mia longed for conversation. She'd been trapped on Earth without friends, without family, without *anyone* after the deaths of her parents. The idea of her own kind for company was almost as appealing as Kort had been, with his handsome face, strong body and complementary magic...

She turned and walked back to sneak a peek at Shayleigh, but Kort was still talking to her, damn him. Mia wanted a friend so badly it overwhelmed her, but she didn't want to deal with him now. Not at all. So she headed back out into the tower.

Climbing the stairs, Mia peeked through windows that looked out over Chalvaren from at least a hundred feet up. One bank of windows surveyed the dragon-deck, and she saw Magnus sleeping beside his great red sire.

Magnus. Her whole reason for being here.

Well, one reason anyway. She'd also hoped to create a family and find a home that actually wanted her.

Kort's deep bass voice sounded below, and she climbed back down the steps to find him speaking to several armed and armored elves who'd joined him in the vast main room outside the kitchen. Were they the guards she had been promised? What would they have to protect her from tonight? Or tomorrow? Moreover—Mia frowned—what might she have to protect them from?

"Duncan ordered us to rescue these from the dragon paddock," one soldier said; then the men carted in a scant few belongings that Kort directed them to stow near the door.

Kort. Where was he planning to stay tonight? They'd made love to come here, and the experience had been near perfection, but that didn't mean he could take what he wanted whenever he chose. He didn't seem the type to force himself on an unwilling woman…and yet, she knew him so very little. And he called her his princess. Did that mean he actually thought she was his?

Mia's stomach growled again, reminding her of Thorvid's food. What did Kort love to eat? She wondered, and hunger mingled with desire as gulped down the last drop of Lachlan's royal mead and watched Kort organize his things. Was he as discriminating in the kitchen as he was gentle and sensual in the bedr—?

She tore her eyes away, refusing to acknowledge her heart's desire. *I need a meal, a hot bath, and a good night's sleep. That's what's wrong with me.*

Kort ventured a glance her way, and his eyes pierced her soul. He was so handsome, directing the soldiers with his belongings. When he'd lectured her earlier, after Magnus faltered, she'd seen his expression. She'd felt his fear. Had he been right to suggest she remain grounded? His delivery of the ultimatum was pompous and ridiculous, but had it come from the right place? Was she simply reacting to her discomfort at the intensity of their relationship, which had begun not much more than a day before?

She turned away, not wanting to deal with any of it. *What I really want to do is curl up in front of that fireplace and take a nap.*

Couches stretched out before a crackling fire in a hearth big enough to fit Magnus. The heat flooding the room warmed her skin, and the king's mead warmed her belly, but Mia told herself to stay alert—or at least to stay true to herself.

Kort dismissed the guards, and they left. Shayleigh brought Mia another glass of mead.

"Would you like me to show you around, Mia?"

"I'll take care of that," Kort said, appearing beside them. He kept his distance, but Mia felt his eyes burn into her and a blush of heat rose up her throat and stung her face.

"Mia and I have some things to discuss, Shayleigh. If you and Thorvid are finished...?"

"Of course, Your Highness. I'll see if I can round him up. There's enough food prepared for a few days now, and more of your father's mead chilling in the kitchen." Shayleigh moved forward and took Mia's hand in her own, which was warm and comforting.

"I've left clean clothes for you up there," she said, and she pointed to a separate set of five wide stairs that led up to another level Mia hadn't already seen. "Some things the queen picked out for you by hand. That's the master suite, and there's hot water for a bath. I'll be downstairs when you need something. Please, call if there's anything at all."

"Okay." Mia thanked her, and the woman fled back to the kitchen, leaving her alone with Kort.

Mia fidgeted, tapping her foot, and she moved to turn away from him, but at the last second she paused and searched Kort's face. She wanted to reach out and touch him, but she held back. She opened her mouth to speak but hesitated. Her heart hammered in her chest.

Kort lifted his glass of mead to his lips and drained it. Mia watched the muscles in his arms flex with restrained power, flinched, and turned her eyes away.

"These are best eaten now, young man."

Chef Thorvid had appeared at the doorway to the kitchen flourishing a silver tray filled with tiny morsels of food. His pointed ears stuck out from under that white beret-style hat which covered long gray hair, and there was a merry twinkle in the rotund old man's eyes. As he set the tray of goodies on a counter, he gestured toward two waiting stools. "Introduce us, Kort."

Kort's face split wide with a grin. "Mia, I want you to meet Thorvid. In Chalvaren, the smart elves come running when Thorvid says it's time to eat."

He gently grasped her arm and escorted her to inspect the chef's offering. Mia went willingly, curious about the food. Kort scooped up two small pastry shells filled with diced green vegetables and a cream sauce, held out one of the treats and offered the first bite to Mia in a gesture that felt more than a little intimate when she held his deep blue stare and took it.

Kort popped the other in his mouth, closing his eyes as he savored the morsel and sighed. When he opened them, a spark of appreciation glowed in his expression, and his fingers were shiny with sauce as he jabbed them at the chef.

"Thorvid's served our house since before I was born, and he works magic. Pure magic."

"No magic here," the old man scoffed. "Just fresh vegetables from my garden, the best cheeses from our farmers, and maybe a touch of love."

"Thank you," Mia said, taking another pastry. She couldn't resist. She didn't want to offend, after all. And when the salty morsel hit her tongue, her taste buds reeled with delight. Heaven!

Kort popped another pastry in his mouth and offered Mia the tray, chuckling. "I know, right? He's the best."

Despite their earlier exchange, Mia couldn't take her eyes off him. Damn it. How dare he be so handsome? So generous?

"Wait, did he say fresh vegetables?" she realized. She raised her brows and turned to Thorvid. "Did you say garden? You tend a garden?"

"Someone has to feed this castle." The old chef smiled broadly and took Mia's hands. "I believe your father used to tend a garden here, no? So you have an invitation for a tour. How much do you know about herbs?"

She flashed him a conspiratorial grin.

Thorvid turned to Kort. "That's a very good sign, lad. Mia, come and see me when you get settled."

"I will."

Then Mia remembered that she'd never be able to take Thorvid up on his offer. She was leaving, wasn't she?

Shayleigh arrived with a stack of paperwork. "Come on, Thorvid. We must go check on the queen's orders."

The chef groaned and followed her to the door. "Make sure you save room for dessert," he said on his way out. "You'll love it."

Kort escorted the elves away, and Mia listened while he spoke to someone else out in the hall. More guards, she supposed. So she sighed, sat down on one of the stools and ate another heaping helping of Thorvid's hors d'oeuvres.

Before long, her nose led her into the kitchen where two red-lacquered pots bubbled merrily away, and a basket of golden-brown crusty bread waited on the counter next to a dish of fresh yellow butter. Another dish held pungent-smelling cheese.

"Goats. Do they have goats here?" she asked aloud. Wouldn't dragons eat goats?

Mia lifted the lid off the biggest red pot and inhaled the tantalizing scent. Roast beef simmered there, thick hearty gravy glazing vegetables that gently bubbled alongside, and the delicious smell pummeled her empty tummy. A spoon waited nearby on the granite counter, calling to her to grasp its silver handle and dive in.

"Just a taste... I have to eat, right? Who knows what I'll need my strength for later?"

By the time Kort rounded the corner and strode back into the kitchen, Mia had her mouth crammed full of bread and roast beef. She couldn't do anything but stand there wide-eyed and chew.

His handsome face split with a smile.

"Hand over that bread, woman. I'm starving too."

†††

They had not heeded the warning. Stuffed with Chef Thorvid's meal, neither Kort nor Mia had room for the decadent desserts the merry elf had prepared.

"Maybe later?" Kort said.

He patted his full stomach and eyed Mia. She nodded, so he led her out into the room with the red couches and the roaring fire. There they collapsed on opposite ends of the furniture and didn't talk. Finally alone, they sat in silence and watched the logs burn.

Kort sighed. The feeling was extremely congenial. He was glad Mia hadn't brought up leaving again. Maybe Thorvid's culinary magic had swung things back to a point where she'd forgive him his outburst? His father's promise to prepare the West Tower had also apparently proved to her satisfaction. He wondered how such a tiny woman could cause him so much discomfort, so much terror. Images of her falling from her dragon manifested in his mind, but he shut them out.

Mia popped up and went to the window, staring out onto what Kort knew was the dragon-deck. When she returned, she was wringing her hands. "I guess he won't come to any harm with his sire sleeping next to him...."

"Doubtful," Kort agreed, going over to the fire and adding three logs. Then he rejoined her on the couch.

The silence between them soon made him squirm.

"Are you warm enough?" he asked.

She didn't answer.

Kort crossed his arms and tried to settle into a comfortable position. The new one didn't feel any better. He realized he wasn't going to find any comfort until he had Mia back in his arms again, and that was... Well, what the hell had she meant that she wasn't staying?

"I should have told you everything," he admitted, steepling his fingers.

She glanced up with incredibly deep green eyes, and she sighed. Her expression was suddenly forgiving. "You didn't exactly have time."

"No," he agreed. "I didn't."

She diverted her eyes and slid back, increasing the distance between them on the couch. Her lips formed a thin line.

"I..." He wasn't good with apologies, but he'd try. "I'm sorry."

She shook her head. Her words were almost a whisper. Simple. Quiet. "You didn't start our parents' war."

Quiet, agreeable... This beauty sitting motionless and stoic beside him frightened Kort more than a full-grown feral dragon on a rampage. "Our parents' war?" he echoed.

"Yeah, our parents started this." She held open her hands. "I see now why my dad took the Dragonstone from Chalvaren. It's too powerful in a time of strife. He obviously had good reason."

"Why did he take you too?" Kort asked. "Why hide you from us? We searched and—"

"If his sister had access to this thing...," Mia interrupted and then drifted off. She fingered the chain against her neck. "I mean, you were in that interrogation room. You saw what happened with those shadow wraiths. "

Kort drew his brows together. "Yes. That thing wanted to turn me to ash. You...you stepped in and suddenly I could breathe again."

It was true. She'd saved his life more than once today—which added to his confusion. He was the one who usually did the saving.

Mia averted her eyes. "Lucan and your mom helped, too. It wasn't just me."

Kort shook his head and reached for her. He wanted to touch Mia again, to feel her skin under his fingertips. "Don't hide from your power. It felt like that was all you, Mia—like you literally gave me back my breath. That shadow wraith meant to kill me. It meant to kill us all. Hell, Mia, you saved the king of Chalvaren and his whole family today."

She looked up, but her plump lower lip trembled as she touched his hand. "You could have died. We could have all died. I was terrified."

The warmth of her skin lit a cold dark place inside his heart. He laced his fingers through hers and said, "That's how I felt when I saw Magnus plummeting to the ground with you on his back." He inched closer, searching her eyes for understanding. He just wanted her safe and here in his arms. "I'm sorry I yelled at you."

His arms arched out and he drew her in for a kiss, but she shook her head of golden hair and pulled away. Leaping up she cried, "No. We can't do this!"

She ran for the window again, looked out at the dragons. Kort bolted upright and followed. She wasn't getting away so easily.

Mia pointed through the windows. "He's back where he belongs now, and so are you." She turned and regarded Kort, her expression tense. "But I can't stay. I don't belong here. Maybe Lucan can send me somewhere safe, but your mother's right, Kort. It's too big of a risk for me to be here with the Dragonstone. I...I must go."

Kort took her arm and gently pulled her close. He glanced at Magnus outside. "He'll never make it without you."

She shook her head and tried to pull away. "He'll be fine. You said so yourself. It's not my job to train him."

Kort hung his head for a fraction of a second. He never should have yelled at her. Here she was, risking her life and trying to help, and all he could do was yell at her? Remorseful, he lifted his chin and met her stormy eyes. "I was angry when I said that, and it's not entirely true. Sure, I have more experience training dragons, but the way he responds to you is amazing. He's learned more in a day than...well, more than I expected he'd learn in weeks. And I don't doubt that you're a part of that, Mia. He imprinted with you and loves you."

Mia looked away. "No. I can't... I can't do this."

He had to find some way to convince her to stay. While it was true that he didn't know much about women, and that all he ever managed to do was enrage his mother, the queen, one thing was etched solidly in Kort's mind: He wasn't going to let Mia go anywhere else. Not without him.

"Yes. You can." He touched her chin with one finger, turning her face back to his. "You can stay and help us, Mia. You can stay and we'll help you."

The shadows from the flickering candles intensified a sudden rage in her face. "No! The only reason you brought me here was to use the Dragonstone. You wanted to protect your family and bring back Magnus. You obviously need my magic, whatever it is, to stop Isa!"

His gut spasmed. Guilt snaked through his thoughts and he shook his head, his throat tight. "What? That's not why I did it. That magic I sensed in you... Mia, I'm in love with you. Didn't you feel it when we made love? I couldn't fake that connection. Our destinies are—"

She jerked away. "I'm not a child, and I'm not stupid." She held up the fist-sized amethyst on its chain around her neck, and when she did, tiny sparks of multi-colored ghostfire buzzed to the surface. "You're lying. Here, take it! That's what you need, not me. I have to get out of here."

Kort flinched and stumbled back a step as she yanked its chain up over her head and thrust the Dragonstone at him.

No, no, no. This isn't right. How can she be so angry at me?

The shadows on her face seemed to increase the appearance of Mia's hatred for him. She held the amethyst higher, but Kort raised his hand in protest and forced himself to speak.

"I...I never even believed the damn thing existed before I found you! Before *Magnus* found you," he pointed out. He lowered his hands and tried to steady his voice. "Seriously, Mia, I had no idea. All I knew was that I wanted you more than any woman I've ever seen. I still want you. I always will. You must be my princess and my eventual queen."

She advanced on him, holding up the Dragonstone as if she hadn't heard. "My father may have charged me with protecting it, but it belongs to you and Chalvaren. Don't you see? I don't want it, Kort. I don't want the responsibility."

He recognized the emotion that twisted her beautiful face and darkened her eyes, but she was more powerful than she realized. She had to accept that fact, or it would doom them all. At the very least it would doom him to being without her.

"Don't be afraid, Mia," he whispered.

She blinked rapidly, as if trying to clear her thoughts. "It doesn't belong to me!" she muttered, staring at the Dragonstone.

"You're right, Mia," Kort said, realizing it was true. It ultimately belonged to Magnus. This jewel could see him reunite the scattered dragons of Chalvaren, but not if she left.

He took her firmly by the arm and turned her to look outside at the dragon-deck. "It belongs to *him.*" He jabbed one finger at the dragonlet.

Mia flailed against his grasp. "I'm not fighting Isa. From the sound of what happened—"

Kort moved closer, towering above her, wanting her to calm down. "No one said you had to fight Isa. And you think Isa Ansgar is the only sociopath on Chalvaren who wants that thing? I guarantee you she's not. But the fighting is our job. The only thing you have to do is see Magnus to maturity."

"But there'll be more of those shadow wraiths." Mia shook her head, her eyes wild. "No. I'm leaving, and you can't stop me."

She turned her back, but Kort held her fast by the arm. She did not struggle.

"Where, Mia?" he asked. "Where will you go?"

Mia leaned back against him. She fought for breath and shook her head, and he caught the scent wafting from her long blonde hair, like a mixture of soft honeysuckle and spicy cinnamon.

"There's nowhere far enough I won't find you," he whispered. "Nowhere that Magnus won't follow."

"No!" she cried. "You belong here. They can't do this without you, Kort. And Magnus... You train him. He'll be better off."

He pulled her closer, aching to take her lips in a kiss but restraining himself. "Neither of us will ever be better off without you. And you will never be better off without us."

She turned and stared at him, and he caught a flash of desire simmering in those deep emerald eyes. And yet, there was still fear and determination.

"If you won't stay for Magnus," he begged, offering his heart, "stay for me."

"This will never work."

Yes. It could. He felt like he could make anything work with Mia at his side, and he just needed to convince her of the same.

He turned her to face him completely. "I'll make it work. Whatever it takes. You want to relieve yourself of the artifact? Fine. If we can't find anyone else who can wield it, or if you ask, we'll talk to my father and lock it in some hole somewhere. Hell, maybe we'll take it up to the Dragon Shrine in the mountains and throw it back down that godforsaken crevasse where it came from. The important thing is that none of this means anything to me if you go. *If you go, I will follow.*"

She looked shocked. "But your crown. Your country."

He shook his head. "I'll abdicate."

Mia sucked in a gasp. "No. You can't give all this up. What about your brothers? What about Brite? What about your parents?"

He sighed. "I made up my mind back in your cottage, Mia. When I made love to you, when we made that connection…well, everything about the old life I led here slipped away. You're the most important thing in my life."

He stopped talking, realizing that if words couldn't change her mind, maybe actions could. He looped the Dragonstone back around her neck, pulled her face to his and kissed her.

She didn't pull away, responding hesitantly at first then winding her arms around his neck. The kiss deepened and she tangled her tongue with his, lifting up on tiptoes to meet his body with her own, clasping his face with both hands.

I got through. She's terrified, yes, but this can work.

"Stay," he groaned. His body was ablaze with desire, and when she ground her soft belly against his erection he shuddered. The intensity of that touch was almost too much.

"We need you, Mia. I need you."

"Kort. I can't—"

"Yes. You can."

Her hot-blooded challenges drove him insane with desire, as did her soft touch. This connection was primal. He'd never felt this way with anyone, and he damn sure wouldn't ever let her go.

He spread one hand across the small of her back, dipped and scooped her knees up into the crook of his other arm. God, she felt so good, so *right* there, and she moaned his name against his lips as they kissed.

He carried her up into the master bathroom and broke the kiss long enough to sit her on the edge of the suite's enormous tub. After he turned on the hot water, he ripped off his shirt.

"What…what are you doing?"

The innocence of her question nearly drove him insane with need. "First I'm going to clean you up," he promised. He left unsaid what would come next.

He reached for a container of soap next to the faucets, breathed deeply of its floral scent and held it out for approval. Mia sniffed it, nodded, and watched him intently as he tossed the contents into the water. A riot of bubbles swirled up along with steam.

"And once we're done in here…" He gently took her hands and lifted her to standing. He sought her lips again, teasing her mouth open with his tongue. "I'm going to show you exactly why I want you to stay. We're going blend our auras again, because I want to explore exactly what that means. And I think you do too."

"I won't stay…," she said, trembling at his touch, but when he reached for the hem of her flowing purple skirt she helped him lift it.

He bunched the fabric in both hands and removed it. As the garment came off, she attempted to cover herself with her hands. He lifted those hands away.

"Let me see you, Mia. Beautiful."

She was naked now, with nothing but the Dragonstone hanging from her neck and long strands of blonde hair cascading over her breasts and hips. Kort drew in a tight breath. Gently he cupped an ample breast and kissed her again. His other hand fluttered down the curve of her waist to her buttock, and he squeezed her tenderly, wanting to grind her sleek curves against him.

She sighed his name, arched her soft body against his chest. He nuzzled her pointed ears, and she gasped and pressed herself closer. His aura sparked to life. The blue glow zipped across his bare skin. As did her own purple magic.

"So beautiful, my Mia…."

Her hands suddenly went to work on his trousers. "Take these off," she demanded, loosening his belt. "I'm dying to see you too."

He let her hands lead the way, and he groaned when she encircled his erection with her delicate fingers. Stepping out of the confines of his pants, he shoved his boots off along with them, never breaking contact with her body. Then he picked her up and stepped into the ankle-deep bath. He knelt with her in his arms in the steaming water and let the rising heat engulf their bodies and stoke their passion.

†††

"Kort," Mia gasped as he kneaded her neck with his lips. If he asked her one more time, she knew she'd stay. But Kort wasn't talking now.

He washed her body with fragrant soap. Slippery fingers traced paths of pleasure across her aching, heated skin. She poured some in her own hands and followed his lead, and groans of satisfaction confirmed what he liked—like the growing flush of his royal blue aura.

"Mia, don't stop."

His husky voice urged her on. She slid her hands up and down the length of his cock, and lower, to his sack. The day's worries vanished as his hands found her center, one working in from the front, one from behind. He washed her, then, and the slow sensuality of his fingers remained long after the job was done.

She leaned her head forward on his chest and closed her eyes, agonized pleasure stealing her breath. Her focus should be on pleasing him, but when he slid two soapy fingers inside her and circled her bud with his other hand she lost the ability to think. She leaned into each lightening stroke of his fingers.

"Yes. More, Kort. More."

"That's right, Mia. Let me feel you come for me."

The erotic huskiness of his voice triggered something primal in her exhausted mind. There was only this, only this handsome, hulking man hovering naked in front of and above her, working her into a frenzy of emotion and ecstasy. Her violet aura danced across her skin and mingled with his blue one, a visual confirmation of their bond.

Kort chuckled as their auras met, the sound deep and sexy in her ear. Mia ground herself harder against his hands, and when he increased the concentration of his strokes she was blinded by the lightning of her first orgasm.

"I *love* you, Mia," Kort growled.

Her body tightened around his hands, and wracking spasms of pleasure engulfed her. She went boneless, and he eased her backward into the swirling, bubbling tub. He kissed Mia's mouth, and when he came up for air he whispered her name over and over in her ear.

A few moments later, he turned off the faucets.

"We're not finished, are we? I want more." She sat up and eyed him, licking her lips. But, should she be doing this? She'd never be able to leave if she let him have her body and heart like this. Mingling their auras sent her into a place of ecstasy she'd never dreamed she could feel.

Kort turned slowly, a feral look of passion hooding his crystal-blue eyes. A smile played on his lips before he said, "Sweetheart, we're just getting started." He twirled a strand of her blonde hair around his fingers and gently tugged. "I'm going to focus on this gorgeous hair of yours next, and those beautiful ears. Let's see where *that* leads us."

Okay. Whatever happened, one thing was for sure: Mia wasn't wasting a second of whatever time they had left together. If this was to be the last night she spent in Chalvaren, she was damn sure going to make the most of it.

She lunged forward onto her knees, sloshing hot water all around their bodies as she reached for him. He met and engulfed her in his arms, and his tongue, hot and moist, followed his lips as he kissed her ear. Self-conscious about those for her entire life, the fact that he adored them stripped away her reservations. His desire for her—for *all* of her—melted away Mia's worries.

Her need for him—for *all* of him—showed her the way.

†††

Kort washed Mia's hair with the focus of a dragon upon a rare gem. If she left him tomorrow, he vowed she'd remember this night for the rest of her life. But he wasn't about to let her leave.

He knelt in the tub and lathered Mia's tresses, massaged the tight muscles in her neck and shoulders. She arched into the attention. She deserved it, and he lavished it on her. It wasn't like he was suffering, either. Touching her ears was a treat. The smiles she flashed him told him he'd found her soft spot, and he exploited that.

Seducing her gorgeous body drove him to the brink of madness, but he made himself wait. He wanted her so satisfied that by the time she woke up tomorrow there'd be no chance she'd want to leave. The hold she had over him made him ache with desire. He wanted her to feel the same in return.

Fragrant conditioner next. He worked the slick salve through her hair. He rinsed the excess. She knelt and helped him. So much hair. He wanted it dried, soft, and covering the length of his body as she lay upon him.

He led her out of the tub and to a wide bench in front of a vanity. The mirrored wall revealed everything in stark detail, like how his tortured erection rose high, demanding attention, yet he focused on her.

Lush fluffy towels helped him dry her hair and their bodies. She twisted, came up on her knees on the cushions and took his engorged cock in her hands, then put it to her lips. Pleasure blasted his body, and he gripped her hair and tugged her closer.

"Mia. Oh, God."

Her lips destroyed his well-composed control and he ground his hips forward. Her violet aura pulled him in. Restraint wasn't possible.

She moaned as she licked, and the vibration tore at him, raced up his nerves and through his scrotal sack, up his spinal cord until he thought his brain would explode. His aura flared a deeper blue, and when their blue and purple magic fused the gratification he felt only strengthened. How was that possible?

Her soft, ample lips stroked him, and her inexperienced tongue lashed the pulsing head of his cock. Her hand pumped the base and he struggled to hold back. Yet he didn't want to. Especially not when she took him all the way into her mouth.

He tried to pull away, but she devoured him and held on.

"Mia, stop! I won't last!"

"Don't want you to," she managed, and she took him in deeper, increasing the suction of those damned determined lips.

Kort threw his head back, convulsing with pleasure. The ecstasy of his aura blending with hers was blinding, so severe. Damn her!

This was supposed to be about her. And what was he doing, fisting her damp mane of gold hair in his hands, urging her to stay in place, to keep her mouth on him?

Mia let out a moan of pure feminine satisfaction and increased her pace. If he didn't stop her now, he was going to explode.

"I want you, Mia," he groaned through clenched teeth, the insane pleasure of release threatening to erupt at any second. "Let me have you, sweetheart."

Her vise-like grip denied his request.

Kort glared down her curves and traced his hand along Mia's back, around the globes of her perfectly round buttocks. He squeezed and kneaded her ass, loving the tactile softness of her clean, silken skin.

She wriggled but didn't stop. He dipped long fingers between her legs, finding her slippery and welcoming as he glanced back down at her head. He spread her lubrication across her swollen bud, and Mia moaned and ground herself against his fingers. She was really enjoying this.

Her purple magic twined further with his. He tried to pull back, but there was no stopping it now. "I'm going to come, Mia. If you don't—"

She giggled and pushed hard against his hand.

He increased the circles he was making with his fingers, and her giggles turned back to moans. Their auras danced blissfully around their bodies, and Kort's hands shook. The muscles in his legs bunched, and his stomach tightened. He fisted her hair and tugged and deepened the pressure between her legs with his other hand.

She came. The spasms of her swollen sex vibrated against his fingers, and the feel of that pushed his body past the point of no return. His sack tightened and he exploded, losing all control of his pulsing cock. He didn't want control anymore anyway. All he wanted was Mia.

He tried to pull back, but she kept sucking and licking, moaning and consuming every last drop.

Astonishing, his still rock-hard cock demanded more attention.

"I'll never get enough of you, Mia. I'll never get enough of this magic we're making."

He swept her up and took her into the bedroom. There he settled her atop soft linens, turned her around and positioned her on her knees. He spun around behind her, knelt on the mattress, and tested her wetness with his fingertips. Still ready. Still slick. Still desperate like himself.

Smiling, he moved into position. Grasping her hips in his hands, he pulled her close—but not close enough.

"Tell me to do this, Mia. I want to hear you say the words."

She turned to face him. Her lips were red, swollen and sexy, and the triangular tip of her tongue peeked out and wet them as she nodded, pushing backward against his flesh. The tip of his cock wedged snugly at her entrance.

She whimpered. He worked the head inside her, but that was all and she cried out.

"More."

"Say it, Mia." He had to have her say the words. He needed to hear them from those sweetly bruised lips. If she wanted to leave, she'd never ask. If she didn't ask, he'd have his answer.

Her eyes widened and she pushed backward, trying to take more of his cock. He caught her hips and held her still.

"Ask. Tell me you want me."

She opened her eyes wide then nodded. "Make love to me, Kort. Now."

Those were the words he was dying to hear, and he surged forward into the depths of her tight, slick folds. Ah, gods, how could this possibly feel better than her mouth? But it did. And her words and the reality of her heat blistered his soul.

He edged out of her, and she whimpered again, her aura spreading across her back in colorful waves and urging him on. Mia spread her arms wide, dug her knees into the linens and slammed herself backward just as he thrust. He drove himself inside her to the hilt, and Mia cried out his name.

From that point on, it got no gentler. He wouldn't deny her this. He would never deny her anything she asked. The first time they'd shared their bodies had been for the benefit of something greater than themselves, but this time was…even more powerful. This was something they both needed, a hard, deep coupling that would tie them and their magic together for a lifetime. Kort reached around between Mia's legs and found the center of her sex and stroked her swollen bud in time with his thrusts. He surged forward and she met him, the pair increasing their frenzied tempo until they both crashed over the edge together into an impossible blinding orgasm.

Trembling, they both collapsed onto the bed. Astonished by the depth of his emotion, Kort moved over her and murmured in her ear, "You're mine, Mia. I swear, sweetheart, I will *never* let you go."

†††

Mia felt it too, this heart-wrenching link to Kort. His words were everything she wanted to hear, but should she dare let her heart believe? She wanted to, with all her being, just as she'd wanted to believe since their first meeting, but a soft nagging voice of worry clenched at her soul and threatened to ruin everything.

Something will take him away from you.

Was it because of her mother's prophecy? Was she doomed because her mother foretold the possibility of failure, or was she simply unworthy of real love because she couldn't silence that insidious voice? The fear that she'd always be alone remained strong within her despite all of Kort's fine words and finer lovemaking.

As he slipped in behind her and wrapped Mia in his strong arms and warm embrace, she took in a deep, trembling breath and let fatigue sweep her off to sleep.

Chapter 19

Kort opened his eyes to a satisfied, sleeping princess. *His* sleeping princess.

"Incredible," he murmured.

Mia's face lay inches from his own on the soft, white linen pillow. Her green eyes were closed, but her angelic features drew a renewed ache to possess her from deep inside his bones. Yet he didn't want to wake her.

Moonlight cascaded through the window and sparkled in her blonde tresses. He reached out and brushed his thumb over her lips. Plump. Sweet. *Contradictory.* This softness belied her strength. He closed his eyes and remembered her generous mouth on his body, a series of memories he would take to his grave. He refused to bemoan the obvious. Mia Ansgar had crawled inside his soul and hooked claws securely around his heart.

Good God, man, you've fallen in love. No wonder she terrifies you. But the realization made him smile. He had a future kingdom to run, and while that responsibility loomed over him like a question mark, Mia's strength and beauty were gifts that he treasured.

Her long, moonlit tresses lay in a pool of silvery blonde all around him, covering his bare chest. He fingered the soft strands, gently pulling them to his nose. He inhaled the soft flowery scent of her, and it quickened the beat of his heart. He'd never loved another woman before. Sure, he'd had relations once or twice, but those couplings hadn't been love and there had been no emotional ties. Not like this.

"You will make the perfect princess, though you don't even know it yet," he whispered.

Mia arched backward and stretched her soft naked body toward him, yawning. Her eyes remained closed.

"Are you still sleeping?" Kort asked, winding fingers through her long blonde hair.

"Mmm. Wonderful dreams, I'm sure."

She pressed soft naked buttocks against him, and he wondered why the gods had smiled on him with such favor. And, how could he be ready to go again so soon? But with one determined move of his hand on her leg he pressed his rock-hard erection into her.

She gasped and wriggled closer. "Yes, Kort, *please.*"

They proceeded to sate their early morning desire. She cried out his name a few moments later, and he spoke her name too. It would forever be on his lips.

Their auras sparked, but with less intensity this time. Kort wondered why, but he assigned the decreased visibility of their magic to fatigue. He snuggled next to Mia for a few moments until he heard the rhythmic breathing of deep and satisfied sleep take her from him; then he whispered, "You belong right here in my arms, Mia. Always. Let my love be enough to convince you."

He eased out of bed and walked over to the window. Torches on the outer wall illuminated the outline of the two guardians of Castle Elias. Father and son, Garnet and Magnus still slept outside on the dragon-deck, though Kort could not say what they had done while he and Mia were making love.

Kort's eyes darted back to Mia, and he couldn't help but imagine the children that would come of this passion he held for her. "How did this happen so fast?" he murmured, but the answer eluded him and he swung his gaze back to the dragons. Some things were simply meant to be.

He pulled on pants and walked out onto the deck. Easing past the sleeping dragons, he made his way toward the stone rail that rimmed the tower's overlook of all Chalvaren. The landscape was alive under a clear, starlit sky.

Garnet opened one sleepy eye, and Kort glanced at him then nodded. The dragon turned over and resumed his snores next to the dragonlet.

Kort knelt in front of the rail and looked up into the stars. "Varik," he said, acknowledging the chief god of Chalvaren's elves. "I've come to thank you for these generous gifts. I'm not very good at this. Still, gratitude has never been far from my lips for wars won, for the granting of all things that are right in Chalvaren. For the elements, the dragons, the kingdoms..."

Yet, questions littered Kort's mind. So many questions. Varik was a generous god and a wise spirit, a deity he prayed to for wisdom in war. That was his usual request, not for wisdom or courage in love. What if the things Lucan alluded to, the fears his mother held, manifested? What if Isa's powers grew overlarge and she consumed all? What if she took Mia from him? The dragons? His family, and their future dynasty? Kort squeezed shut his eyes, leaned his arms on the banister and steepled his fingers as a flush of hot adrenaline spread through him. His head spun.

He prayed first for Magnus, and that was easy. He'd recited these words of protection over the entire fleet of dragons since he was little. Lachlan had taught him the words; Lucan explained their importance and Elissabet reinforced that. Though he'd rarely prayed where anyone else saw him since becoming a man, Kort still prayed this way before a battle to inspire the troops.

He prayed for Mia then, but his words felt selfish.

"What if Mia's right? What if my desire for her puts her life in danger? I could not justify that, Varik."

He wanted her so much, but he wondered suddenly if he was worthy of her love in return, a love that might sustain him for years to come when he himself was only putting her in peril. A cloud of fear and sorrow lingered over his words.

Above him, within one of the constellations of stars hovering above the castle, a threadlike image coalesced. Kort inhaled slowly, transfixed. *Varik.* And the god's voice sounded calmly in Kort's mind.

"You hold Mia Ansgar up to me as the love of your life?"

"Yes." Kort nodded up into the heavens. "Yes, Mia Ansgar. And I beseech you to bless her soul for me."

The wisplike threads between the stars coalesced, forming an image of Varik not so unlike Kort's own. A warrior. A leader who wanted good for his people. Kort's heart thudded, and he watched with rapt attention.

Varik's image gestured. "You pray for many souls, my son. As you should. But I see conflict inside your heart. Wherefore for Mia? Do you doubt my gift?"

"No." Kort shook his head. "I believe you made her only for me, and I am grateful. However, I fear for her life."

Varik sighed. "You are wise to do so."

"How can I protect her?" Kort asked. When Varik was silent he added, "You've charged me by birth with the responsibility of ruling this kingdom. How can I do that without her at my side?"

"You cannot," Varik replied. "Be assured that without Mia you will never succeed."

Kort fisted his hands and swallowed. "This evil that has beset Chalvaren... I ask for courage to defeat Isa Ansgar and her shadow elves. Why haven't *you* stopped her? I...I need you to show me the way through this conflict. Her black magic plagues our world with hatred and despair."

"Yes, it is a great sadness," Varik agreed. "Isa's sacrilege is a test of faith and fortitude for all elves."

"Give me the wisdom," Kort begged. "The knowledge and courage to stop her."

"You possess both already, Prince. But you must use them."

Kort nodded, thinking about Nerian and others who had fallen in the conflict. "I want to. The loss of one more soul to her sorcery will be impossible to bear."

"Lay aside your childlike resistance," the god commanded.

"How?"

"Trust the others I've sent you. Empower them each to their greatness, Prince, and you shall find yours."

"What if they fail? If I don't see to things myse—"

"Face your weakness, Kort. Challenge your own doubt. I tied you to Marineth for a reason."

"Letting go isn't one of my virtues," Kort whispered. He'd lived his life in control, directing others as necessary, making certain Castle Elias's dragons and warriors were trained and equipped for any martial eventuality. He frowned, wondering if their similarity was the reason he and his mother clashed so often. But now was not the time to wonder such things, so he quickly admonished himself and looked up into the indigo sky. "One thing more, Varik. Thank you—for Mia and for the Aurora. Help me teach him to land before he kills himself."

He stared at the moonlit sky. The deity had faded and the stars appeared normal now, but the essence of his god was always near.

He'd known that his entire life. Kort took it on faith that Varik would hear him, and also that Varik would give him everything he needed to succeed.

"This must be what my father feels like every night," he muttered. How often did Lachlan search this same starlit canopy for Varik's grace? How often had his father prayed for him like this or others for whom he held responsibility? The thought filled him with regret for every foolish move he'd ever made, regret for the stress he'd put upon his loved ones.

With a heavy sigh he shook off the chill of remorse and stood tall. Varik had said he already possessed what he needed, and the trick to success was collaboration and trusting others around him. If that's what it meant to rule, to care for those he loved and respected...

"I'll do it. I'll find a way to empower everyone I can who's loyal to the crown."

He walked back to the dragons. Kneeling down beside Magnus, Kort caressed the beast's velvety soft head. Tiny buds on Magnus's skull poked out like stones, buds that would become enormous horns. The Aurora had so much growing to do, and Kort couldn't wait to see him mature. The first thing he'd do once the sun came up was get Magnus back in the air and help him figure out how to land safely. Then he'd get Mia up there too.

The dragonlet sighed, took a deep, sleepy, contented breath, and turned over onto his back. Kort scratched the dragon's tummy, a light-hearted smile tickling his lips.

"Sleep tight, little one."

A flutter of movement caught his eye from the window. He looked up and saw Mia watching him, illuminated through the glass by silvery-blue moonlight. How long had she been standing there? Her long blonde hair almost covered her naked curves, and he mimicked the dragonlet's sigh of contentment as he stood and admired her beauty and body.

Her face split wide with a grin. She placed her palms against the glass as if trying to connect with him, so he strolled back toward the arched doors leading inside the tower. He was reluctant to leave the sanctity of the dragon-deck but eager to move forward with his plans. He'd prayed enough. Now was the time for action.

Mia met him at the door.

Kort raised his brows and took her hand, kissed her then led her back to the bedroom. "Are you okay?" he asked.

"You were praying out there?"

"I was thanking Varik for Magnus. I was thanking him for *you.*" She blushed and dropped her gaze to the floor, so Kort leaned forward and lifted her delicate chin with his fingertips. He added, "I have something for you."

She giggled and stroked her fingers across his chest. "Haven't you had enough yet today?"

He grinned but shook his head. "Mmmm. No, never. I'm not likely to ever get enough of you."

Their gazes locked. Mia cupped his cheek with her hand and ran her thumb across his lips. "Was...was all of that real last night? The hunger I felt for you, the passion, that power I felt when our auras collided?"

"Every bit of it."

She laughed, and it was a welcome winsome sound. "I dreamed a handsome prince stole me away from loneliness."

He kissed her passionately then said, "I hope that is true. But, playtime later. This is serious."

She nodded, so he led her back to the bed. He knelt while she sat, covering herself with the sheet. He kissed the back of her hand and said, "I should probably wait to do this in front of a thousand people, because that's what I feel you deserve, but I also don't want to wait."

Mia stared at him, her eyebrows drawing together. "Wait for what?"

He fished around in the leather pouch on his belt, and a moment later he produced the golden box his father had entrusted to him. Drawing it open, he revealed the ring with its square-faceted shard of multicolored dragon ore, its deep indigo background surrounded by baguette diamonds. "Marry me, Mia."

Her emerald green eyes popped wide with disbelief. "Your family... They...they're not going to object? Isn't there a protocol for choosing a princess? Are you allowed to—?"

"My parents gave me the ring to give to you," Kort interrupted. "*Marry* me. I've suggested as much before, but this is official."

Her eyes cut away from him and then she bolted, streaking from the bed, clutching the sheet around her in her haste, leaving him kneeling there expectantly. She disappeared into the bathroom, slamming the door, and a click of the lock followed. Kort hesitated for only half a second before he leapt up and followed.

He stopped, staring at the door. His first instinct was to get to her and comfort her. He'd thought those two little words terrified *him*? The look of terror they'd inspired in Mia's eyes put his own inhibitions to shame.

He tapped softly on the door. "Mia. I *love* you, Mia."

He tried the knob. It would not yield. Incredulous, he stepped back and sized up the barrier between them.

"Open this door, Mia. Please."

Silence was the response, and it roared in his ears. He wheeled around then turned back toward the door. He wanted to plant the back of his fist in its hardwood, but he didn't.

"Mia," he tried again. "Let me in."

Nothing.

He thought better of tearing the door off its hinges, though he inspected those. Breaking the door down like some uncivilized beast wouldn't present his case well at all, so he decided to wait. He'd planted the seed, and now he had to let it grow. He simply needed to trust her to share his feelings.

"I'm afraid," a small female voice called from the other side of the door.

Kort sighed. It wasn't in his nature to admit fear, or to show it, but the thought of anything separating them or of him losing Mia because of dishonesty was terrifying. So he said, "I understand. I'm afraid too."

The soft click of a lock sounded. Mia opened the door, and she peered out at him with a crooked smile that nearly flat-lined his heart.

She opened the fingers of her right hand. "You're not afraid of anything, Kort."

"That's not true," he said. "I *am* afraid. I'm afraid if you refuse me, if you say no, if you leave this land I'll never find what I have with you with any other person ever. We have a future to live together, Mia. A spirit dragon to guide. Our own children to rear someday. A dynasty to rule!"

Mia burst into sobs and rushed into his arms. "That's everything I want, Kort. All of it. But I'm so afraid to believe we can do this. With Isa—"

"Of course we can do this," Kort interrupted. "Don't cry, Mia. Please."

He scooped her up and strode back to the bed. He set her down gently, laid a chaste kiss on her forehead and again took a knee. As she placed her hands on his shoulders he murmured, "I don't have every answer we need. We'll have to discover those together. It's true that things will be difficult for awhile, but...this life can be more than amazing enough to make up for the bad."

There *were* good things here, and he was dying to show her.

"There are too many good things here on Chalvaren for you to miss, Mia. Let me show you. After we save this world, let us enjoy it together."

Mia sniffed, wiped her face, and blinked several times. "Maybe," she said with a laugh.

"Marry me, Mia." Kort held out the ring again. "Be my future queen. You belong with me and you know it. I swear to give you a lifetime of love and passion like we shared last night. A life of fortune. A life of *dragons*. A life you don't want to miss out on. Hell, I'll build you your own castle if that's what you want. We can love each other there, raise dozens of babies and dragonlets...."

She reached for the ring, and his gut spasmed. Her aura flared both clear and purple as she touched his fingers, and that all-encompassing current flowed through her into him, soothing his fears.

"Say yes to me," he said as their eyes met.

"I'll wear the ring, but we have to give this some time. I mean, before a ceremony and all that. To make sure. Are you willing to do that?" Mia asked, even as tears flowed down her cheeks.

Kort pulled her close, and they toppled onto the bed. He didn't care that she wanted to wait. Maybe he should have given her more time in the first place, but everything seemed to be moving so quickly with Isa's attack and the difficulties with Magnus flying.... Now that she'd agreed to wear the ring—and as long as she stayed in Chalvaren—he would find a way to make everything work.

He nestled Mia in the crook of his arm, and she held out her hand to receive his grandmother's ring on her finger. Kort dried her tears with the back of his hand, kissed her cheek, and then pulled the covers up over them both. They were silent awhile, and he traced her fingers with his own while she admired the ring.

"Do you think others have this—what we have together?" he murmured, twining their fingers. "I've never experienced anything so strong, never heard of anything like it."

Mia giggled then stared at him. "I certainly hope so, for their sake! Of course, I'll have to make some girlfriends here before I can question anyone about their sex lives."

Kort chuckled. "But seriously, Mia. I've never heard anyone I know talk of anything like this. It's so…what's the word…?"

"Intense," she answered. "Good though, right? What we share is good? The way our auras join together when we make love?"

He sighed heavily and kissed the back of her hand. "Yes. It's good. Powerful." He shook his head and added, "Imagine if we could do that outside the bedroom."

She smacked his shoulder. "You wouldn't dare!"

"What? Expose our sex magic? No. We're keeping that weapon to ourselves."

She laughed. "I prefer the term 'blending auras.'"

"I like that," he agreed with a yawn. "My princess and I 'blend our auras.'" He then touched her engagement ring and looked deep into Mia's eyes, sensing that something was amiss. "Are you worried about something?"

"I have no concept of what it means to help you rule a dynasty."

He chuckled. "Well, you don't have to do that until after you marry me—and after I ascend to the throne," he added. Reaching over, he pulled the blankets up around them as they snuggled down for sleep and gave a less mirthful laugh. "Until then, just watch my mother. No one's ever made ruling look more effortless."

Chapter 20

"What have I done to myself now?"

Mia spun Kort's grandmother's ring around her finger and watched prisms dance in reflected sunlight on the dragon-deck. The heirloom engagement ring weighed heavy on her hand, and the night's activities weighed heavy on her mind. All that magic they'd conjured...! A heated flush flowed up her neck to sting the tips of her pointed ears, and she eyed Kort from under her lashes. Good Lord, even the sight of the man drew erotic memories.

The way he'd held her. The passion they'd shared. The total satisfaction of making love to this rugged prince undermined every rational thought, concerns that told her to run far, far away from Chalvaren and abandon the country to its destiny like her father had. Yet Kort transfixed her with his passion, tangled her in some web of longing that she didn't understand. She wanted more. More of him. More blending of their auras. More of *everything*.

How am I supposed to resist all this elven magic?

"Please," Kort said, holding out a mug. His handsome smile induced heart palpitations like tiny dragon wings fluttering in her chest. "Have another cup of Thorvid's coffee. He'll be insulted if he thinks we're not indulging ourselves."

Kort had proved not only an attentive lover, but also keen to what would make her happy in the day. While she'd wanted to sleep and luxuriate in the privacy of the tower, he'd balked and dragged her out of bed to this—dark and robust cups of hot coffee. *Wonderful.* They'd watched the sun rise over Chalvaren together in the company of the dragons and sipped the aromatic brew while they looked down at the castle grounds.

Garnet and Magnus soon flew off the dragon-deck, with Magnus secured tightly on the big red's back. Mia again admired the deep purple stone on her finger as she sat and watched them fly.

"We could go back to bed," she suggested. Her body was still suffused with pleasure from the magic of last night, and yet she could think of other things to try. "What's the worst that could happen? Garnet will take care of Magnus, won't he?"

"You look nice this morning, Mia," Kort said, smiling in amusement and ignoring her suggestion.

She giggled. "I *love* these clothes."

She'd braided her long blonde hair, and the garments Shayleigh left out seemed as if they were sewn specifically for her body. Soft, camel-brown, low-nap velvet trousers lay over beefy socks of wool and fit snugly inside gorgeous thigh-high brown boots that Mia rubbed her palm down. Tough on the outside but soft as a lamb's butt on the interior, she wiggled her toes in them and grinned. Her tunic was colored ecru, soft with unnecessary ruffles that reached her waist, and the color nearly matched her blonde tresses. She'd tucked the Dragonstone inside the tunic next to her chest and tried to forget the artifact's significance for the nonce.

"Here," Kort said, presenting her with a beautiful golden dagger with a jeweled hilt. "This should stay with you at all times."

"Oh, yes. I like that very much," Mia said.

Kort helped her secure the knife in a sheath that hung from her new leather belt. "Now, my dad's expecting us for breakfast. Let's go tell them you're staying."

††††

Kort led Mia down the circular tower stairs, his heart beating faster than usual. His parents waited at the bottom, a phalanx of guards in tow, and Kort catalogued each man present. Sizing up Chalvaren's protectors was second nature, but it was even more important today. He was introducing the woman who would be his queen.

He named everyone to Mia and then turned to his mother.

"Good morning," he said formally, kissing Queen Elissabet's hand. His mother had pulled her auburn tresses away from her face in a ponytail, and her eyes shone brightly upon noticing Mia's engagement ring.

The king, dressed in black trousers and a soft black sweater, kissed Mia's hand in the same manner. "Let's hope it's better than yesterday. I see Kort's convinced you to accept his grandmother's ring, Mia...?"

"He's very determined," Mia agreed, then softened the statement with a smile.

The foursome entered the castle proper. They passed through an arboretum, and Kort had to corral Mia back to the group. She showed a particularly keen interest in the plants of the queen's greenhouse, and Kort wondered if his mother would let his wife tend a garden there.

Elissabet noticed Mia's interest and said, "This is one of my side projects. As I remember, your parents both gardened. Did you inherit any of their talent?"

Kort smiled as Mia bobbed her head with excitement. "I could spend all day in here!"

His mother gestured outside, to a huge patch of ground that was sunny and lush with vegetables, flowers and herbs. "That's Chef Thorvid's garden. He mentioned you'd like a tour. I'll arrange it if you'd like."

Mia looked about ready to explode from excitement. "Yes, I'd like that."

"First," Kort said, escorting them along, "a tour of the castle. Then breakfast. We're starving."

King Lachlan named off significant rooms as they navigated the fortress on the way to the main formal dining room. Ian, Quinn, and Brite waited there, at a table set for fifty. The youngsters flocked forward as one, a chattering mob.

Brite ran over first and held out her hand. "Come and eat breakfast, Mia!"

Mia scooped Kort's tiny sister up into her arms. "Good morning, Brite. Did you sleep well last night?"

The girl nodded. "Mommy says you're going to be my sister, Mia. Is that true?"

Brite fingered Mia's engagement ring and Kort tensed, but Mia just smiled and nodded in agreement.

"I never had a sister before. Only brothers," the child whispered conspiratorially, and Kort was pretty sure Mia didn't stand a chance against her cuteness.

He led Mia to a seat and sat down beside her, and suddenly he realized how ravenous he'd become overnight. Thorvid's breakfast didn't disappoint. Eggs, pastries, seeded crusty bread with jam and butter, and bacon filled their bellies and strengthened their souls. The royal dining room was silent as everyone indulged, Kort not just in delicious food but the closeness of family as well.

"I want to show Mia the hatchery," Brite said, licking a smear of jam from her fingers.

"As soon as she's finished eating," King Lachlan replied, gesturing to Brite's plate with his fork. "You need to finish your breakfast too. You'll need your strength if you want to help Mia fit in, Brite."

The child happily did as her father required.

"Hatchery?" Mia hesitated mid-bite and searched their faces.

"For our dragons, Mia," Brite said.

Mia's emerald green eyes flashed toward Kort. "Oh yes! I definitely want to see that."

Kort grinned, stuffed his mouth with another slice of Thorvid's bacon and chewed. "It's got history, Mia. Magnus's history."

Ian and Quinn both groaned.

"Just a bunch of eggs," Ian muttered. "We just want to see Magnus. I've got an idea for helping him get that first turn down. My dragon is the best, and I want to show him how it's done."

"Your dragon doesn't know a turn from a loop. My dragon's so much better than yours," Quinn laughed. He buttered another piece of toast then crammed it in his mouth.

"Boys, finish your food. There'll be time enough for all that this afternoon," Queen Elissabet admonished.

The pair groaned again but dug in, and they polished off their breakfasts with gusto.

Queen Elissabet turned to Mia. "Lucan and I thought you might join us for some magic training this morning while Kort works with Magnus?"

Mia glanced at Kort. When he nodded she said, "Of course."

Kort stood, offering her his hand. "But first let's go see the nests."

Mia hastily gulped down a silver chalice of ice cold milk, wiped her lips, put her napkin on her plate and took his hand. As they left the table, Brite asked to be excused. Her mother agreed, so the little girl raced ahead, her two gangly brothers in hot pursuit, all three children chattering away like dragonlets in a nest.

"Wait for me, Brite!" Kort's father called, moving ahead of Kort and Mia.

The girl ran back and took his hand. "Hurry, Dad. I want to see if my dragon's ready to hatch."

Kort shot Mia a glance of pride, and he smiled when she tugged on his hand in an attempt to keep up.

†††

Mia quirked her lips and looked around. Torches lit the walls of this secret area of the castle, clear glass sconces burning with incandescent shards of dragon ore. The stonework was spotless, not a mote of dust anywhere, and the aroma of clean juniper and balsam floated on the air. Imposing guards blocked the entrance, but they stood aside to let the royal family pass.

"It's beautiful down here," Mia said. "How far is the hatchery?"

Castle Elias's secret interior glowed with an ambiance of peace. Mia clung to Kort's hand as they followed Brite and King Lachlan down a flight of stairs, rounded a corner and stepped into a hall that seemed to go on forever. Illuminated insets ran the length of the walls. Most insets were arched and made of stone, and each glowed a different color such as red, yellow, or blue.

Kort brought her to a stop in front of the first small alcove, and they peered inside.

Mia gasped. "It's a nest?"

She reached into the well-lit hollow and touched straw with her fingers. A smile teased the corners of Kort's lips as she then looked down the corridor. At least a hundred alcoves lined the sides.

"Dragon nests?" she said.

"Of a fashion."

Mia raised her brows. "Where are the dams?"

"Every egg in Castle Elias's hatchery is a foundling, Mia."

"A foundling? I don't understand." Surely there were female dragons. Wouldn't they come after their young? Her belly flipped at the thought of a hundred angry mothers rampaging Castle Elias to claim what was rightfully theirs. "Did you steal them?"

Kort's expression twisted. "No elf true to Castle Elias would ever touch a natural nest, and I'd have the head of anyone who did."

"Then…these were all abandoned?"

Kort shook his head. "Rescued."

Mia frowned. "From what?"

"Something's killing the mothers before the dragonlets hatch." Kort leaned against the stone wall, crossed his arms, and sighed. "When we find the body of a female, we do our best to find the nest before it can be raided. We're not always successful—most nests are fully destroyed by the time we find them, reducing Chalvaren's natural population of dragons. But the females are adapting. They don't put every egg in their nests anymore. They hide at least one from every clutch, and sometimes we find those. We call these key eggs."

Mia raised her brows. "But don't all the eggs need to stay warm?"

"It's a risk, yes, but they usually choose their hardiest. This plundering of nests has spread far and wide. It is threatening the very existence of Chalvaren's dragons, and the mothers are doing their best to overcome."

Mia gave a cry of horror and stared down the long hall, sorrow engulfing her as she imagined so many motherless dragonlets. "Is it another type of creature, something new and unknown? Maybe even another type of dragon?"

Kort shook his head. "I believe the nests are being raided in order to harvest the dragonlets and their elemental powers."

"Not some*thing* then." Mia narrowed her eyes. "Some*one*."

Kort sighed. "Given the state of devastation at the nesting sites, and the number of fully grown female dragons murdered, I'm convinced it's the same black magic we saw yesterday. I think Isa Ansgar is doing it."

"Why?" Mia's angry question echoed down the hall. A strong protective instinct flooded her chest, and she eyed the row of nests suddenly worried about her own dragonlet. "Why would she—why would anyone—do that?"

"To become stronger," Kort said. "To magnify their magic."

"Isa's harvesting dragon eggs to become more powerful? That's unforgivable," Mia said. "No matter what happened with her beloved—"

Queen Elissabet appeared and interrupted. "Yes, *unforgivable.* Killing a dragon is a capital offense on Chalvaren. Lachlan and I decreed it soon after we married. They're a natural resource, a gift from Varik." She glanced at Kort. "After you left us with Arden yesterday, he confirmed your suspicion—which is probably why Isa didn't want him or Nerian to reach us. They were at a site in the mountains and she raided a nest. She's become many times more powerful already than she was, and Lucan and I think we know what she's trying to do."

Mia crossed her arms and lowered her voice. "Something worse than just killing your dragons, getting more powerful and destroying the way you defend yourself?"

Elissabet and Kort shared a glance. Kort seemed unwilling to go into further detail.

The queen glanced down the hatchery's illuminated hall toward her youngest child and husband who held hands and visited each alcove. She turned back to Mia and Kort and said, "Chalvaren's force is back up to thirty dragons. With the return of the Aurora, that makes thirty-one."

"What kind of monster kills baby dragons?" Mia demanded. "How long has this been going on?"

Kort and Elissabet's long faces told her all she needed to know, and she fisted her hands. Her belly pitched with nausea and an urge to race back to find that Magnus was safe. She didn't, though; she just stood and contemplated all that was happening in this world. As she did, Kort and his mother walked down to the next alcove to join Lachlan and Brite.

Mia turned her attention to the alcove beside her. Reaching into the nest, she reverently touched its red and golden egg, the thought of any dragon suffering too much to bear. But, wait. Wasn't Kort's family in charge here? She thrust out her chin and hurried to catch up with them. There had to be more that could be done to combat whatever was killing those mother dragons and taking their eggs.

She reached the royal family. Before them were two blue-speckled eggs as small as her own thumb, and Mia's heart leapt when she saw how tiny they were. She could hardly imagine the size of the dragons inside.

"I have so much to learn," she whispered, studying the nest. "These...must be the size of hummingbirds when they're mature?"

"They are messenger dragons," Queen Elissabet said. "Their speed and agility allow us to communicate quickly across long distances. But don't be fooled by their size, Mia. Their sharp beaks are laced with poison. One intentional bite can immobilize a full-sized dragon."

Mia smiled, pleased. It seemed there was so much from which dragons needed protection. Who would have guessed?

"Who else knows about this?" she asked, bringing herself back to the matter at hand. "The killing of feral dragons and the thieving of their eggs. Isn't there more that can be done?"

Kort kept silent, gazing intently at the nest before him. His eyes were stormy and his posture stiff, and his father spoke instead.

"Everyone knows, Mia. And there's an understanding between my family and all our subjects. We pay a bounty for any information about poaching."

"Is that enough?" Mia asked.

"The castle also runs programs for those who wish to be trained as Riders. We have here in Chalvaren the foremost authorities on all breeds, so elves would be wise to come to us rather than take matters into their own hands. After military training and approval there is a lottery for commoners. When a rescued egg hatches, I select one name. That elf, assuming they are capable and worthy, is inducted into our Dragon Command."

Mia nodded. "So, you share the power and the glory. It's a way to be sure your people are loyal to both you and the dragons themselves."

"Yes, Mia. Exactly," said the king. "Except if they want to destroy the beasts and absorb their power."

Mia was a silent a moment. "How long does it take for a dragon egg to hatch?"

Kort turned. "It varies." He touched her hand, and a tremor of excitement zipped through her fingers. "We wait with all the anticipation of new parents until any egg shows activity. Then we do our best to help the hatchling. When the call goes out that an egg is near hatch, we assemble our wing of mature dragons and bring them inside for the first feast. Then we hope for the best."

Mia looked back toward the guards at the entrance of the hatchery. "So, this is where Magnus's egg was stolen from? How? And why did it happen when it happened?"

Kort sucked in a breath. He glanced at his mother, his expression severe. The queen glared back, and Mia remembered how the two were at odds. "We knew Magnus was close to hatching. His egg showed increased signs of internal movement. When I made the final rounds that night, every guard had been slain, his throat cut. As soon as I realized Mother's mercenary had stolen the egg, I demanded Lucan send me after him."

Mia frowned. "Who was assigned to take Magnus when he hatched?"

"The next royal in line is Brite, but that privilege was suspended because she's too young for our military needs. Magnus would have gone to a soldier."

"So... I've singlehandedly upset everything." Mia bit her lip. She reached out her hand to Kort and grasped his forearm. "I'm no warrior."

Queen Elissabet took that moment to jump in. "You may not be a soldier, Mia, but we can focus on refining your magic. The stronger it is, the more you will be able to work with Magnus. Together, then, maybe we can all come up with a solution for stopping Isa."

Mia glanced at Kort, realizing part of her still hoped her aunt could be saved. Maybe she could learn enough magic to change Isa Ansgar's mind. Wouldn't that be what her father would want? Wouldn't that be preferable to simply her destruction?

"He *did* draw in all those dragons yesterday...," Kort was saying to his parents. "Magnus will unquestionably be their leader when he's mature."

"Will Brite get a dragon?" Mia interrupted. "I mean, since she would have gotten Magnus."

Both Kort and King Lachlan nodded. Kort said, "As a princess, she'll have her pick as soon as things get back to normal. As soon as there are enough dragons to go around."

"But you don't know when that'll be. That could take another twenty years." Mia glanced at the child, who played next to her father, moving from one nest to another. She felt sad for Brite, but she also suddenly craved the sight of her dragonlet. Whatever else happened, she and Magnus were destined for each other.

"I don't think she'll have to wait that long," Kort said, leading Mia over to inspect three impressively large, white-as-milk eggs in the next alcove. "These wind dragon eggs are showing promise."

"We put the breeds together when we can identify them," Queen Elissabet pointed out. "It's not an exact science."

They discussed the condition of the eggs for a few moments before Mia asked, "What about a breeding program? You told me my father genetically engineered Magnus. What was that all about?"

King Lachlan's face brightened. "Twenty years ago, Theo and I worked on just that, Mia. But I'm afraid that once he left I couldn't duplicate any of his magic. It's too bad. His secrets died with him. That's one reason I want you to study his journals. Maybe you can make sense of his notes."

Ah yes, Mia was reminded, her father had abandoned his king and his people, and her aunt was decimating the rarest creatures for her own personal gain. No wonder Queen Elissabet had reacted so harshly to her appearance at the castle. It was a miracle she'd been accepted here at all.

The queen held out her hands. "As far as a breeding program...yes, we want to get back to that. The problem is, our mature dragons are stressed. They've stopped producing viable clutches. I think they're afraid."

"I think they're angry," Kort interjected. "I think they're furious that we haven't found out what's going on with the feral dragons, and I think that if we don't solve the situation soon they will revolt. At the very least they'll stop listening to us."

Which was why he thought Magnus could help, Mia realized.

"So," she said, "that brings me back to my original question."

Kort and the queen lifted their eyebrows.

"What are we doing to stop this insanity?"

King Lachlan sighed. "At the moment? Nothing. As you saw, our expeditions to Castle Cumberlae have been...fruitless. Or worse."

Mia recalled the two elves possessed by shadow wraiths, and the memory infuriated her. Somehow there had to be a way to get through to this Isa. She curled her hands into fists. Maybe she should go to Isa herself? Talk to her, offer her mercy for her crimes? Could she do that? Otherwise there would be no choice but destruction.

"You said I had to learn to focus my magic before anything else. Will you show me how?"

Queen Elissabet grasped Mia's hands, and a spark of warmth tingled through Mia's skin from the queen's aura. "Yes, Mia. We'll do this together. For the future of the kingdom. For the future of dragons."

Mia met the queen's blue eyes and gave a vigorous nod. Suddenly, being one of the royal elves of Chalvaren appealed in a new and delightful way. Whatever she had to do to redeem the Ansgar name, she silently vowed she would make things right.

Chapter 21

Easing out of the pasture, Kort signaled to Garnet, who corralled Magnus behind him in the heavily fenced field. The pair of dragons sat observing his actions, while ahead on the road was a local farmer, an elf with a nervous gray goat hooked to a cart of squawking birds in a large square wooden cage.

"Oren!" Kort called. "Chef Thorvid says you're the perfect man for this exercise. Did you bring what I asked for?"

The farmer stepped forward, and Kort shook his hand before peering at his stock. A smile broke across his face as he did. "They're big and fat just like Thorvid alleged. A tasty treat, I'm sure. Thank you for helping me."

The farmer shielded his goat's eyes from the dragons and comforted the beast with soft words. "Of course, Your Majesty. I'm honored you called me at all. Thorvid said today's needs were pressing, so I came as soon as I could." He glanced around the pasture then his eyes darted back to the dragons. "That's the Aurora? The one the whole town's been gossiping about?"

Kort crossed his arms and stared at the dragonlet with pride. "Oren, meet Magnus, Garnet's offspring."

Oren took another look at Garnet and Magnus and shook his head. "I'm afraid I've failed you, Prince. My birds won't even make a decent snack."

"They're perfect for Magnus's first lesson," Kort argued. "How high will they fly?"

The farmer frowned. "I've seen them get up to twenty feet, maybe, but these are ground birds, Kort. I don't understand what you want."

"This exercise is about the mechanics of the hunt." Kort gestured toward the tree line at the far end of the pasture. "I want you to release your birds there. Let's see what Magnus can do."

Oren scratched his head but obeyed, guiding his gray goat and wagon down to the end of the field.

"Garnet, take Magnus out there," Kort directed, taking a seat on a sloping rock to watch the show. A moment later he lifted a hand to signal the big red to start the hunt.

Garnet nosed his little black charge out into the middle of the hunting pasture. Oren had loosed his twenty birds at the end of the enclosure and taken his goat off the field, and Magnus was instantly drawn to the fracas of fat, chattering chickens. He lowered himself close to the ground in full-stalk mode.

"Look at all that natural instinct," Kort called out, chuckling, then crossed his arms and leaned forward, elbows on knees, watching.

Magnus swished his black tail back and forth, wiggled his hips, curled himself into a tight knot of muscle and then stormed at the noisy birds. The flock scattered and took flight, racing up and away for their lives, but Magnus leapt, stretched his wings, caught air and lunged for one of them.

He missed. Kort winced.

The fat birds crashed back to the ground, unable to maintain flight but still landing on their feet and scattering. Magnus growled, a low rumbling sound, and lunged again. Once more the dragonlet missed his target and turned up nothing but dust, rolling across the pasture in a tumbling heap of flailing wings and screeches.

"Damn," Kort said.

"That's not pretty," a voice said from behind Kort, who looked up and saw his father.

"Dressed in that robe with the hood up over your head you certainly don't look like a king, Dad. Testing your guards again?"

Lachlan chuckled and sat down beside him. He pulled a fragrant pouch of tobacco from the robe, passed Kort a hand-rolled cigar, struck a match and held out the flame. After Kort used it, Lachlan lit his own. The two men inhaled.

"Your mother forbids my smoking in the house as a general rule—and Duncan's guards need to be challenged every once in awhile."

"The castle guards should never let their king out of sight. I'll speak to him," Kort grumbled.

His father smirked. "Just doing my part to point out our defensive shortcomings. Now…what exactly are you trying to accomplish here, Son?"

Kort shushed him, and the two watched Magnus chase Oren's clucking white chickens around the end of the field with no success. Well, with very little success, none of it having to do with catching a snack.

"Well, it's some improvement over yesterday," Kort pointed out. "At least he's getting more agile in the air, if he does keep overshooting the chickens. But if he can't figure out landing, Mia will never get to fly him again. I won't let her."

His father eased back on the sloping, sun-warmed rock and took another puff of his cigar. "Hmm. Never known a dragon who couldn't land…or a woman who took kindly to the word no."

Kort grimaced. "So you see my dilemma. I thought the birds might be just the right incentive."

Magnus took to the air again, chasing a particularly agitated bird. Kort and Lachlan leaned forward as the dragonlet lofted himself upward, then back when the bird swerved and dove to the ground. Magnus pursued, nipping at the bird's gangly chicken legs. Then the dragonlet fumbled, rolled, and squawked louder than his escaping snack.

King Lachlan tried to suppress laughter. He covered his mouth, but his shoulders shook with amusement. That mirth was contagious, and soon an explosion of mutual hysterics overtook both him and Kort.

"This is serious," Kort finally said, straightening his shoulders and sitting upright.

"I've never seen anything so ridiculous," King Lachlan gasped, wiping tears from his eyes. "A dragon who can't catch a chicken!"

Kort shook his head and stood, taking one last puff of his cigar before grinding it out on the rock. He then signaled Garnet permission to hunt the chickens as well.

The big red dragon's scales flashed in the sunlight as he stood and flapped across the field. The chickens scattered as before. Up, up, up they flew, trying to dodge their pursuing predator, but Garnet caught three white birds in his jaws, swallowed them whole, and landed with perfect precision a few feet away from Magnus.

The dragonlet stared at his sire with awe. Garnet looked at him and then again at the flock, and Magnus raced in. The chickens blasted up into the air, and Magnus pursued.

Lachlan got to his feet beside Kort, raising his arm. "I think he's going to do it this time, Son."

Magnus targeted a straggler that raced for a tree, snapped his jaws but missed. The tree came closer, and the dragonlet flew on a collision course. Magnus extended his hind claws and grasped one thick branch near the trunk of the tree, recovered from the fact that his wings got snarled in the branches and proudly sat himself upright twenty-five feet above the ground, calmly observing the field of chickens below.

Kort sighed in disgust. "Great. Now's he's stuck up the damn tree. This is impossible." He planted his hands on his hips and stared up at the dragonlet. He'd wanted this to work so badly, this failure pissed him off to no end. Riding Magnus was clearly a threat to Mia's life. And yet, his father was right: He'd never once met one woman who wanted to hear the word no. He grunted, "How am I supposed to trust a clearly incompetent charge?"

Nearby, Garnet stared up at Magnus. Oren waited too, standing patiently near his wagon at the end of the field. Kort was just about ready to give up.

He raised his hand to give Garnet the signal, but Lachlan grabbed his arm and said, "Give him a minute." The king's eyes were trained on Magnus. "Patience is as much a virtue as boldness."

Kort glanced back at the treed dragonlet. He took in a breath as Magnus shifted his hold on the branch, lowered his head and focused on a trio of white clucking fatties scratching up bugs in the grass. The beast narrowed his eyes as if intense concentration.

"*That,* Dad? You really think he'll do it this time?"

Magnus went into action. Swooping out of the tree, he touched down inches away from the chickens, who squawked, wings flapping, jerking upward into flight. But not before Magnus snapped his jaws shut on two of them.

"He did it!" Kort yelled.

Lachlan laughed softly. "Yes. And, Son…? Magnus pulled that hunt off with style. Just in time, too."

His father motioned, and Kort glanced over to see Mia walking across the meadow, Queen Elissabet close on her heels. Mia came straight into his open arms, while Elissabet joined her husband on the rock.

"Duncan's put out a full alert. He's looking for you."

King Lachlan laughed loudly and pulled his wife onto his lap. "I'm starting to worry about him, Elissabet. I got away really easily. Why's he so distracted these days?"

"You shouldn't push him into such a frenzy. It's embarrassing to have to explain away your bad habits." The queen glared pointedly at the cigar remnants on the ground, and Kort moved behind Mia and wrapped his arms around her waist. They all watched Magnus and Garnet chase the remaining chickens together, and Magnus made three perfect landings.

"I suspect he's just showing off for Mia now," Kort said.

"That's amazing." Mia's green eyes were bright with excitement. "You taught him that today?"

Kort shrugged. "I bought the birds from Oren the farmer over there. Magnus taught himself. Funny, how proper motivation changes things." He looked at her beautiful face and lifted a long strand of her golden blonde hair to tuck it behind her pointed right ear. "How was magic practice? Were they hard on you?"

His mother whispered something in his father's ear, and King Lachlan burst into laughter. Kort raised his brows and focused on Mia's wince.

She fiddled with the ruffles on her tunic, unable to meet his eyes. "Lucan will never let me near his things again. I don't know what happened! One minute his prize gecko was green, and the next thing I knew... Well, there were pink feathers attached to his hide. My god, the man was livid."

Kort chuckled. "Lucan *loves* that gecko."

"Let's just say Mia needs more practice," Queen Elissabet offered.

Mia lifted her shoulders and let out a long, exasperated sigh. "What use will I ever be to Chalvaren if I fail at magic? I'm no warrior. There's so much to be done and I can't even manage the simplest spells."

Magnus suddenly bounded across the field toward them. Fuzzy white chicken feathers, the remnants of the morning's work, covered his hide, and Kort made a decision. "That's enough for the day. Let's take the dragons down to the beach for a swim. We can get Magnus cleaned up...if you're willing to do some work?"

Mia glanced out toward the water, clearly thinking about her aunt. "Is it safe?"

"I think so," Kort said. "We'll be careful no matter what."

Mia's face brightened, and Kort was pleased. He waved for Garnet to finish up then asked his parents, "Want to join us?"

Lachlan and Elissabet stood, clasping hands, whispering between themselves. His mother actually giggled, and Lachlan held up his palm. "We're going to...ah, see if we can't give Duncan and the guards another hour or so of hide-and-go-seek. You go on ahead. We'll see you later."

With that, his parents turned and walked away. Kort took Mia's hand and said, "Okay, just the four of us, then."

They met Garnet in the middle of the field. The big red needed a bath too, maybe worse than Magnus. Mia burst out with laughter and plucked white feathers from his scales, laughing again when a gust of wind swirled the feathers up and away. The sound fortified Kort's heart.

Mia climbed up Garnet's neck, and Kort clambered into place in front of her. She wrapped her arms around his waist, splaying her fingers across his stomach, and the muscles there tightened at her touch. Kort could hardly think about anything else.

"To the pools, Garnet," he commanded, and the mighty red heaved himself forward.

"What about Magnus?" Mia asked.

The dragonlet ran behind them. Spreading his wings, he mimicked his big red sire and thrust himself up into the air in a wobbly flight.

Kort grinned. "Our destination is only a short flight away. The exercise will do him good."

†††

Mia assessed the natural tide-pool below as Garnet descended. "Is this a lake?"

"Sort of. It's a lagoon fed by the ocean," Kort said. "It's always full at high tide. A volcano erupted eons ago and left these natural indentions in the earth. That black rock is lava cooled by the sea."

"It's incredible," Mia said, looking down at the blue-green seawater sparkling against the black background.

"My father claimed this tide-pool and made it a natural sanctuary shortly after he and my mother got married. It's our own private paradise. Predators can't get in from the ocean, so it's perfect for swimming. Do you know how to swim?"

Mia loved everything about the sea, and a dip in that blue-green water seemed like the perfect way to shed the morning magic lesson's disappointment. The smell of the ocean brightened her spirit, and she couldn't wait to get in. "I do. One of my favorite things, actually. We lived by the sea when I was younger."

"Good," Kort said. I'll need your help with some chores."

He tapped Garnet's neck, and the great red dragon eased down to a dark sandy shore upon the far side of the black rock perimeter. Mia looked up in time to see Magnus gliding in. The dragonlet's approach was way too fast, and he splashed clumsily into the pool, dousing them with seawater.

"Well..." Drenched, Mia looked over at Kort and held out her hands. "We'll count that as a landing of sorts."

Kort nodded, shaking his head. "Let's get them cleaned up. I have an idea."

They shed their boots and stripped down to their underclothes. The sight of Kort in his, with all that tanned muscular skin exposed, ignited liquid heat through Mia's belly and down to her core. A slow smile built on Kort's face when he looked at her, and his skin was flushed. She rather liked that. She assumed it was because of her near naked body.

He grinned, bent down, scooped up a generous handful of coarse black lava sand and called Garnet over. Then he showed Mia how to clean a dragon's scales. "They love it," he said. "The seawater kills any parasites, and the hard nature of the rock can work wonders on their hide."

He worked on Garnet, and Mia pulled her attention away from Kort's rippling muscles long enough to attend her own dragon's hide. But she was still scrubbing white feathers off Magnus in the shallow end when Kort finished. He'd already worked Garnet's crimson and gold scales until they shone, and she was only half done.

He caught her exasperated expression and shrugged. "I've been at this at least twenty years longer than you. Don't worry, you'll catch up."

"Easy for you to say." Mia harrumphed and wondered how he moved so fast and elegantly across Garnet's hide. Turning back to Magnus she called out, "You think he's healthy? I mean, Magnus looks good to you? He certainly looks good to me."

"Yes," Kort said, coming over to help. "And I suspect he'll grow fast, Mia. His appetite is enormous."

He was already bigger than an eighteen-hand draft horse, and she could swear he'd grown more robust, more muscular overnight.

She stood back, knee-deep in the lagoon, and stared up at her dragonlet. Magnus purred with the praise and rose tall and proud. Mia snuck a peek at Kort's tattooed shoulders. Firm muscles rose and fell and pulled taut as he worked, and she licked her lips and tried to divert her attention back to Magnus, who luxuriated in the attention of his hands.

She had to reach up on tip-toes to clean the dragon's back, over which she peeked at Kort. He stood waist deep in the water, watching her, a hungry stare burning behind his eyes. Mia met that hungry stare even as Kort strode around through the water toward her.

"You know what would make him look even better?" he asked.

"What?" she said, her focus glued to him, though his nearness made her movements jerky.

"You."

Mia grimaced. "But you said—"

Kort shook his head. "I was worried yesterday. Today...let's try something."

He didn't give her the chance to reply, only snared her about the waist and lifted her onto Magnus's back, staring up at her, bright appreciation glowing in his blue eyes. When Magnus lifted his head, craned his neck and nuzzled Mia's hands, she petted the dragonlet and scrubbed another chicken feather off a spot she'd missed.

Kort walked away from her toward the shore. Looking at the Aurora, he formed a hand signal and said, "Magnus. *Come.*"

The dragonlet followed.

Mia flexed the muscles in her legs to cling to Magnus's long neck. She liked sitting up here and had a wonderful view of the sanctuary and Garnet, who swam in the furthest end of the secluded pool. The huge dragon's bathtime activities made her giggle. Who would have guessed a two-story creature could act so much like a dog?

Magnus followed Kort out onto the sand, water dripping down his hide. Kort smiled and said to Mia, "Let's do this."

He patted the back of the dragon's knee. Magnus lifted his paw and bent, making Mia pitch forward and grab his neck with both arms to avoid falling off. In two deft steps, however, Kort scaled Magnus's leg and seated himself behind her. He tapped the beast's neck twice and said, "Magnus. UP!"

Mia turned, warmed by his nearness. She ventured a smile as Kort's legs, like solid granite, gripped her hips and locked her down.

"This feels good," she ventured.

"For me too. Now, okay, Magnus. Take us up."

"Fly?" Magnus asked.

Both Mia and Kort caught their breath. It was still such a shock to hear the dragonlet speak in that deep baritone voice.

Kort tapped Magnus's neck twice and squeezed his knees together. "Yes. Fly."

The Aurora hesitated then took off across the sand, spreading open his wings as he ran. Mia caught her breath, but the dragon caught the air. Up, up, up, he lofted. Soon they were zooming over the water, and Mia's heart caught fire. The wind streaming through her hair tickled every nerve ending on her exposed skin.

"Turn around," Kort ordered, and he gave the command signal with his hand. When Magnus veered right and circled, Kort moved behind Mia and changed the position of his knees. He wrapped Mia's bare waist tight with his arms, pointed at the pool and commanded, "Land there, Magnus. On the water."

The dragonlet dove, and Mia shrieked with joy as they plunged into the center of the pool. Cool salt water rose up to cushion what was a fairly stable landing, and Mia dove off Magnus and into it. Kort's strong hands grasped her waist and a moment later she surfaced. Magnus bobbed just a few feet away. When Garnet roared with approval, the dragonlet turned and swam toward him.

Laughing, Mia pulled Kort close, kicking her legs to stay afloat. "That was incredible!"

Kort swiped water from his eyes and kicked his own legs. "I know, right?"

Mia wrapped her arms around his neck, their chests colliding, and she kissed him hard and sudden on the mouth. Pulling back she said huskily, "I think he's learning to land. Now all we need is a pool of water for him to aim for."

Kort laughed. "I think he's got the hang of the descent, actually. And...you looked good up there. Want to go again?"

"Hell yes!"

Kort whistled, and Magnus swam over. The dragonlet dove then came up underneath them, their weight nothing for him in the water, and Mia grasped his neck tightly with her arms as he headed for shore. Kort was showing him all the training signals again.

Spreading dripping wings and catching air, the dragonlet raced into the sky. Laughter bubbled up from Mia's chest as he circled back toward the tide pool, and Magnus shifted his wings, tucked his claws in tight, and dove again. This time was just as coordinated as the last, but this time he was coming in at a steeper angle. On purpose. Kort had apparently taught her dragon to land, built his confidence, and set them free. He was playing!

Mia shrieked loudly with glee. The shock of the plunge stole her breath away, but Kort found her hand and led her back to the surface where he laughingly kissed her. She eased backward and smiled at him, and they bobbed on the surface of the sunlit lagoon, their arms and legs entangled beneath the swells.

"This is fantastic!" she repeated.

Kort grinned. "Want to go again?"

She whistled for Magnus herself this time.

Chapter 22

Back at the west tower, as the dragons retired to the deck for a nap, Mia followed Kort straight inside to find that the shower in the master bath was spacious, sparkling clean, decorated in textured tiles the color of sand, and lit from above. Two showerheads released hot water over their naked bodies, and Kort traced demanding hands over her skin.

Mia moaned and pressed herself to him. Erotic warmth and wetness pooled between her legs while she slid soapy hands across his broad, muscular back, massaging him and delighting in the way his body felt. He pulled her more fully into the hot jets of the shower.

"Mia...," he moaned, and his desperation speared her belly with fire. His muscles clenched as her fingertips danced across his skin.

"Oh."

He'd dropped to his knees in front of her. He pressed her back against the wall, one large hand spanning her belly, holding her in place. Her aura materialized, and Mia blushed. It was useless to try to contain her excitement, if today the glimmer on her skin seemed transparent, less powerful.

"Oh, yes," Kort continued, his gaze rapt. He slid fingers up her thighs, spreading her legs, then lifted her left knee up over his shoulder. When he slid two fingers through her curls, gently opening her, her breath hitched and she adjusted her stance.

"Definitely yes." Mia's head lolled against the tile shower walls as he clamped soft, warm lips where his fingers had worked magic. The stone tile was cool on her back in contrast to the fire he ignited with this intimate kiss, and she tangled her fingers in his long blonde hair.

A chuckle of satisfaction vibrated through Kort's mouth as she pressed her hips closer.

"*So. Good.* Oh my god," she whispered. "That feels so good."

His next move felt even better. The leg she stood on quivered when he added a finger, reaching deep inside her until he found an ultra-sensitive spot. Mia panted, the feeling so exquisite, so intense that an explosion of sensation engulfed her. Her body went rigid but Kort didn't stop, and Mia came, and came, and came, until she went boneless from the insane pleasure.

Kort supported her shaking body. Too dazed to speak, Mia threw limp arms around his shoulders.

"Oh, no. You're not done yet."

He turned her around, grazed his expert fingers up her sides, stopping briefly to cup her breasts, to pinch her taut nipples, then lifting her hands above her head. His royal blue aura swelled across his muscular arms as he pushed her hands flat against the shower tiles and spread her legs with his.

"Now let's see," he whispered, "if I can inspire you to do that again, hmmm?"

He nudged the tip of his iron-hard cock against her entrance with one hand and grasped her hip with the determined fingertips of his other, holding her firmly in place as he slowly but firmly worked the thick head of his erection just inside her slickened folds.

"Tight. So hot. Mia, you burn me like dragon fire."

Mia came back to life with the sound of those husky words in her ear. Her tummy twinged, and she wanted more of him inside her. *All* of him. So she angled her hips back and Kort thrust deep inside.

"Dear gods, Mia."

Her body sparked into motion. She used the shower wall for leverage and gyrated against him, forcing him deeper with each push, and a moment later Kort froze, as still as a statue, and took a tight breath between clenched teeth.

It was Mia's turn to chuckle. "Feels good?"

"Mmm…hmmm. So damn good." He grasped her hips with two tight hands, pulled out, then thrust back in.

Kort set the rhythm, and Mia answered his every move. The sensations torched her body until she thought they'd both explode, a blazing inferno of pleasure, and groans took over instead of coherent words…until they climaxed together. Then his words filled her ears.

"Mia, I love you."

She wanted to see his handsome face. Turning around, her eyes caught the glimmer of the engagement ring on her left hand, and she cupped his chin in her hands. She loved him too, and she'd finally realized there was no use in fighting it anymore. "I love you more," she said, and kissed him deeply.

He indulged her then broke away and nuzzled her neck, placing a kiss on her pointed ear. "So glad you decided to stay."

†††

As she came out of the bathroom, Mia froze. Anger flared in her belly. She'd left the Dragonstone in the bedroom, on the dresser in front of the mirror, never once considering it might attract attention. Now, reaching out to—

"Don't touch it, Shayleigh."

The elf started and drew back her hand. She whipped around and said, "I'm sorry, Princess. I was tidying up and thought I'd polish it for you."

Mia's face burned, not sure if she'd been rude or appropriately protective. She crossed the room, picked up the Dragonstone and slipped the chain over her head. "Thank you, but I don't think it's a good idea for anyone else to touch it. I…I wouldn't want you to get hurt."

Shayleigh shook her head. "Of course not. I'm so sorry."

The maid left the room, and Mia grasped the artifact with a sweaty palm. Surely Shayleigh was honorable, right? Elissabet wouldn't allow anyone dangerous to remain so close to the royal family, would she?

She walked to the bed and sat down for a moment to calm her wild imagination. As she rolled the Dragonstone's purple facets between her fingers, an idea formed in her mind about how to secure the artifact from others who might covet its power.

"I'll go to Lachlan."

Chapter 23

Queen Elissabet arranged to have Shayleigh deliver Mia's newly restored purple dress. After she put it on, Mia inspected the repair and found the tailor had erased every sign of damage from those flaming arrows. Giggling, she smoothed down the skirt and spun around the room feeling just like she imagined a real princess should, lighthearted and full of joy.

That day seems so long ago, she mused, remembering her flight to Chalvaren with Magnus and Kort, *but it's only been two days.* Adoring the way the gauzy fabric felt between her fingertips, she checked the dress in the mirror one last time. It was her last link to her mother, who had made it for her.

"Are you ready to go, Mia?" Kort called. He ambled into the master bath where Mia put the final touches on her appearance for the evening. She was excited. They had a date with his father—in the king's library.

Kort stopped mid-stride and admired her. His hungry expression was pleasing.

"I'm ready. Yes," she said, but fidgeted with her purple barrette. She'd pulled her locks back from her face, and her pointed ears jutted out. But that was a good thing. She was among elves here, among her own kind. Finally.

Kort reached for her hand and stilled it. "You look amazing." He kissed her ear, and for a moment she wished they could skip past going to the library. She never seemed to tire of his hands or lips on her body.

"Let's go before those ears of yours get us both in trouble," he said, obviously reading her thoughts, and the warning pleased her again. She took his hand, and the two of them left the west tower.

When they joined King Lachlan in the great library, he stood to greet them and suggested they finish off the evening with some of his homebrewed mead. Servants brought in a bottle and glasses, set them on the main table and vanished almost as instantly.

"Kort tells me you worked on your dragonlet's landing skills all afternoon, Mia," the king said. He took her arm and escorted her toward a wall of several looming bookcases. "How does it feel to fly him?"

Mia fought off a wave of self-consciousness about the way her flight experiences with Magnus started. "It's such an amazing day that I'm not sure I can describe it. What about you? Tell me about *your* dragon."

King Lachlan did not respond, just turned and led Mia further into the room. Distracted, she didn't press him any further.

"Holy hellfire of Chalvaren, would you look at all those books." She stood perfectly still, staring at Castle Elias's real treasure trove, the contents of twenty-foot-tall shelves that lined the library's sixty-foot walls. Those had to hold thousands upon thousands of tomes. "It would take a lifetime to open every one."

Lachlan offered her a knowing grin and spread his arms. "I want you to feel welcome here. This room is at your disposal."

"Well, what's the history behind all these books?" Mia asked, her fingertips gingerly touching several spines.

The king watched. "This archive is a hobby my family has worked on for many generations. My father before me, and his father, thought access to knowledge was a king's best ally. These hold not only Chalvaren's history but histories of many other cultures. It's quite a collection. You might even find a section from your homeworld, Mia."

Mia searched Lachlan's blue eyes and saw nostalgia there. She touched his forearm and said, "Thank you for inviting me in to play."

"Of course. I want you to be part of this family in every way."

The king strode along the impeccably clean stone floors in front of the bookcases, and Mia followed. As they walked he said, "So, you tried your hand at spells today? Elissabet told me your command of the language of spellcasting and our science of studying magic is commendable."

"I may understand the language, but the mechanics, not so much. It really was a pitiful session, I'm afraid," Mia said, though she was warmed by his praise. "You know about Lucan's pink gecko? He may never recover. Still, I'm looking forward to tomorrow's agenda. We're going to enchant all the castle weapons, every arrow tip and sword with what we learned from the wraiths in the interrogation room."

The king smiled, and Mia knew he was picturing Lucan's pink prized lizard.

She followed him through the library and decided that Lachlan Elias emanated something special that she could not name. She didn't know why, but she loved being with him. He radiated...confidence, perhaps, and gentlemanliness, and she suspected his eldest son's greatest wish was to be like him.

"I need to speak with you about the security of the Dragonstone," she finally said.

He stopped and turned. "Has something happened?"

"Not exactly."

"Go on, Mia."

"I'm sure it's nothing, really, but...how loyal are all of your subjects?"

Lachlan tapped his lips with two fingers. "You're suspicious. I admit I've always feared Isa's ability to manipulate or dominate others. Or buy them. And if Isa got her hands on the artifact..."

"I'm worried about just that, King Lachlan. We can't let it happen." Mia clasped the king's forearm. "I want you to help me come up with a plan. The idea that some spy of Isa's might get it in a moment of my weakness is untenable. It's just too powerful for any one person to guard alone."

Lachlan sighed. "That's probably why your father took it away. Tomorrow at first light you and I will work on a solution. But...tonight is about celebrating small accomplishments. Agreed?"

Mia glanced at Kort, who was waiting and reading books on a shelf some thirty feet away. She felt a weight lift from her shoulders and nodded in agreement.

The king reached up and removed an enormous, red, leather-bound and gold-gilded journal from a shelf above his head. "I have a special gift for you tonight, Mia." He turned and presented it to her. "This is the first of your father's journals."

Mia's aura spiked, and she couldn't find any words. Her knees threatened to collapse, both under the emotional weight and the actual physical weight of the volume. Suddenly lightheaded, she wanted to sit down. But she accepted the gift and searched Lachlan's eyes for meaning.

He gestured. "Most of it contains Theo's scientific documentation of his breeding experiments, notes about his magic, but you'll find some personal material as well."

Mia stared. "Seriously? My father wrote this?"

Lachlan nodded, a smile tugging at his lips. "Aren't you interested?"

Mia's fingers tingled, and she lovingly traced them over the book's pages of elegant text. Her purple aura was flaring even brighter. "I'll never find a way to convey my gratitude for this treasure."

Lachlan placed his hand on her shoulder and turned her toward the bookcases. "I want you to continue his work if you're able. It'll take time, of course, to understand his spells." He pointed to two more volumes on the same shelf, one bound in yellow leather, one in blue. "Once you're done with the first, those will be waiting. I thought you might like to read by the fire while my son and I discuss future military and political strategy over our nightly game of cards."

A night of reading? Oh, the day couldn't possibly get any better. Mia reverently pressed the book close to her heart then followed the king to a soft settee with green velvet cushions.

A servant poured each of them another flute of mead, and Mia settled down to devour her father's book. She hadn't even noticed Kort left until she spotted him return with Magnus.

"Garnet's out flying patrols and hunting," he said as he led the dragonlet into the room. "I thought Magnus might be better off in here with us. He's exhausted," Kort added, moving to Mia's side. "Ian and Quinn are already in bed, and Mother and Brite are occupied in the kitchen making cookies with Thorvid. So it looks like it's just us four all night."

Lachlan petted Magnus and scratched him under his chin. When the dragonlet purred, the king produced a dragonfruit that Magnus gobbled down and then pointed to the soft woven carpeting laid under the settee in front of the fire, inviting Magnus to curl up beside Mia. Then he and Kort moved to the other side of the room.

Mia went back to reading her father's journals, searching for clues to the mysteries of Chalvaren while she absentmindedly stroked the soft head of her sleeping dragonlet.

†††

Kort kept one eye on Mia, the other on his hand of cards. He'd played this game against his father for years and maintained a losing record. Tonight was different, though, and he intended to win. The wager on the table was a small plot of land in his mother's arboretum. He wanted to claim it for Mia.

The king had seemed pleased by the suggested wager, which thrilled Kort deep in his heart. All he'd ever wanted was to please his father, and for his father to be pleased that he was looking after Mia…

The other thing that thrilled him was Lachlan had dealt him the dragon of fire, and the dragon of water to start. Kort kept his expression even. The rules of the game were simple: the four suits represented the basic elements, like all good things on Chalvaren. The cards were numbered 2 through 10, with the royal knight, queen, and king at the top of each suit. The trump card for each suit was its elemental dragon, and Kort had two. Players simply built their best hands out of what they were dealt, not unlike in life.

While the rules were simple, the strategy was complex.

"Beating you is *going* to happen tonight."

"You thrive on competition, Son. Make sure that temper of yours doesn't get the best of you."

Kort discarded a ten of fire, and searched his father's eyes.

King Lachlan considered his own hand then drew from the deck. He raised his eyebrows. "Mia's important," he said, studying his cards again, setting down his flute of mead then throwing a knight of earth onto the discard pile.

Kort focused in on the way his father set down his glass. Did Lachlan already have the other two dragons of air and earth? If so…

"You have no idea," he said, ignoring the discard and drawing afresh.

Lachlan's lips thinned, which Kort took as a good sign. "I understand more than you give me credit for. Like…you're afraid you'll lose her if she finds her place here casting magic."

Kort wouldn't be dragged out of focusing on the game, but he did admit, "I don't want Mother and Lucan to put her in harm's way."

Lachlan nodded and took Kort's discard. "Well, your mother told me she's sure Mia is a wizard, regardless of what happened earlier today. That's a good thing if they want to rebuild the Council."

Kort shook his head. "A good thing? I don't like the idea of Mia having to protect us, not even if her magic is strong and she learns to control it. I won't—"

"Allow it? That's folly, Son. You can't keep her from being what she is."

Kort's jaw clenched. "She wants to serve Chalvaren, but she's afraid. And here's the thing…" He discarded another queen, leaned forward and whispered, "Isa is truly something to be terrified of."

"Mia seemed strong enough yesterday," King Lachlan pointed out. "I thought that shadow creature was going to kill us. Mia intervened."

Kort sat back in his seat and stared at his cards. "Well, what about if the Dragonstone falls into Isa's hands? If that happens, none of us will—"

Lachlan scoffed. "Mia and I will prevent that. But you have to trust her, Son, just like you trusted Magnus today. Your mother and Lucan are doing the right thing in training Mia. You must accept it: She is important here not only to you but to all of Chalvaren. We must every one of us put ourselves in danger if we are the one who holds the key to salvation."

Kort's father snapped up Kort's discarded queen and tossed away a knight of fire. He set his glass of mead down then thinned his lips. Kort keyed in on that expression, his heart racing. What other cards did his father have? Was this already over?

Kort drew a fresh card, deliberated on keeping it then threw away a different one. He glanced over to Mia and the snoring dragonlet but saw his father's eyes focus in on his discard. King Lachlan snapped it up, sorted his hand then splayed the cards wide on the table. He puffed out his chest and rapped the cards with his fingers, triumphant.

Kort looked down and narrowed his eyes.

King Lachlan snared his flute of mead and leaned forward. He gestured to his hand, fixing his gaze on Kort in a challenge to reveal his own. "My other suspicion is that Mia isn't used to taking orders. She's not one of your warriors to command."

Kort smiled. "We're working on that." He laid out his cards. Three dragons, and two kings. He'd won.

Lachlan groaned. He studied Kort then leaned back in his chair, a glimmer of satisfaction in his eyes. "Nice play, Son. You've been paying attention."

Kort heaved a deep breath. "Everything I know about winning I learned from you."

Chapter 24

It was ten days later that Mia met Kort for what was now a regular afternoon swim in the tide pools. The castle had not been bothered again by Isa Ansgar, and Mia's lessons were proceeding apace. As were Magnus's.

"He's nearly doubled in size. To think a diet of fish and chicken could pack on that much weight!" she said, patting the dragonlet's stomach with pride.

"Magnus is definitely thriving. Looks like you are too," Kort said. "You seem happy, Mia, and that makes me smile."

She was. She was certainly happy with their daily routine, and she wondered why she'd ever questioned joining him here. They'd slipped into the rituals of daily life at Castle Elias like she'd always lived there, and she adored the way the last ten days passed without incident. She had never mentioned leaving again. She didn't like the argument the idea drew between them. Kort clearly hoped she never would leave, and Mia was beginning to feel like this life with him might, in actuality, be everything she'd always wanted. What she'd hoped it would be when she first took the portal from Earth.

Garnet had flown them here to the lagoon after magic practice, which had been...well, typical in the fashion that she'd left Elissabet and Lucan feeling like she would never really meld with their vision of how magic should be conducted. But she decided to keep her angst to herself.

"Our afternoon swims are good for him," Kort said, pointing to Magnus. "Dragonlets do well with ritual."

That seemed true. Magnus was a quick study, and he showed off whatever Kort taught him in morning training sessions.

"I bet you do too," Kort said.

"You should ask Lucan for his take. Magic training isn't exactly working out so well. Not as far as he's concerned."

"What?" Kort asked.

Mia shrugged and lowered her eyes. "Nothing really. Just trying my best to succeed. Not doing so."

Thankfully, Kort did not pursue the subject farther. "What were you and my father up to yesterday?"

"Discussing the extra security we put on the Dragonstone."

"Ah." Kort gave a half laugh. "I assumed you were bargaining for more gardening space."

"Hardly." Thorvid had helped her set up a small sunny garden plot of her own inside the queen's arboretum, but Mia did much more than that. She practiced with Elissabet and Lucan in the mornings, held lunchtime meetings with Thorvid where they discussed the castle's gardens and herbs, and talked long into the night with Lachlan about Chalvaren's history. "We had much more serious work in mind, thank you very much.

"I *am* working on a special plot for medicinal herbs, though. My father left specific instructions in his blue journal about some of the local flora. Chalvaren's plants are different species than the ones he taught me to tend back home, but I think they share many common traits."

Kort shook his head. "You'll soon be taking care of the whole castle with your potions and mixtures."

She was, in fact, interested in developing her healing abilities, so it made her happy that he encouraged her. He found it difficult, she knew, to keep up with her excitement about plants.

"Well," she said, wanting to compliment him in return. "Magnus has shown remarkable improvement in Garnet's care under your supervision."

"Yes. I'm taking them out further every morning. He's doing well. *Very* well. He's even begun to fly in formation. Tomorrow we're planning a long-range flight to search for feral dragons to recruit."

Mia watched Magnus and Garnet swim together in the depths of the tidal pool, alternately fishing and then sunning themselves on heated black lava rock. "Is that dangerous?" Every time Kort brought up long-range flights, her belly twisted with fear. "Maybe I should come too."

"It's not that far," Kort said. "But Kristoff, Maddix, and Shyla documented a full hatch of water dragons. I'm hoping Magnus might help bring them into service. We even came up with a signal for that bizarre yipping sound he makes when he gets wound up, which he can do now whenever I ask. He's so damn smart."

"So, you'll be somewhat close to the castle?" Mia asked.

"I'll be back before you're done with magic practice. We have to get back so he can have his lunch. I can hardly keep him fed."

"Good." Mia paused. "I'm glad Magnus is doing better than I am with spells. Did you know Lucan has a—or, rather, had a—wand? He won't let me near the damn thing now. One of the spells I tried this morning set it on fire…. It's not funny! He loves that wand," Mia said morosely when Kort howled with laughter.

Kort didn't stop, so Mia swatted him. "I'm the world's worst wizard's apprentice."

Kort stifled his laughter, but Mia felt awful. It had been ten days. She'd never get it right. The magic she'd practiced on Earth was much less complicated, and the magic she'd practiced with Kort had been…well, much more *natural*. She blushed even thinking about it, despite the fact that they'd done far more in the nights since coming to Chalvaren.

"I'm sorry," Kort said, which made Mia laugh. He'd been right. It was truly comic how she'd set fire to Lucan's prized wand. Ridiculous but comic.

She lowered her head, thinking of her lessons. "Lucan and Elissabet. I'll never fit into their mold. I just like the days we work on power blending. That feels natural to me. Nothing else. If I could just give up on—"

Kort touched her arm. "No. You'll find your way. Give it some time."

She lifted her head and sighed, considering his words.

"Just because my mother and Lucan haven't figured out how to control your magic doesn't mean you're a failure. They've been practicing magic for decades, so it's been a long time since they were in the position of learning. You're new. You'll find your way. I know it."

Mia looked up and smiled at Kort. Maybe he was right. She wanted to think he was. She wanted to get her thoughts organized on spellcasting so she could weave her love of medicinal herbs into elixirs to help the citizens of Chalvaren, not only to heal sickness but to promote wellness. Practicing magic that sustained life and enhanced it would make her valuable to the people. It was something of her own, and maybe it was simple, but she fancied the idea of conjuring a potion that enhanced the notion of love. She practically beamed when she thought about it.

He thumbed her chin. "*There.* That's what I love to see, your face full of wonder and possibility." Standing, he offered her his hand. "Now, we need to get these dragons back to the castle. I've got an idea for…something adventurous in our bedroom after our shower, and I have a sneaking suspicion you'll excel at this particular activity if you're game. It involves power blending, Mia, and I want to see your aura again. Desperately."

She visualized repeating their recent afternoon ritual. It was her favorite part of the day, actually. How could it not be?

She blushed and whispered, "I read something hidden deep in the king's library about power blending. It was related to…to sexual positions. Maybe we can try a couple?"

He pulled her close, and his voice was low and sultry. "I like to see that shade of pink coloring up your ears. Anything to make that happen."

She took his hand and stood. "Let's get to it then."

†††

The sex was good. Better than good. Yet their auras didn't blend at all, despite Kort's willingness to try the new positions. Afterward Mia found herself near tears, her worried prince beside her, reassuring her that they'd figure out whatever was blocking their connection. But it seemed to be getting worse.

"I just don't understand," Mia moaned. "This was supposed to help…you know, everything."

"Stop. We're fine," Kort said. "That was incredible sex, Mia, and maybe you're trying too hard. Worrying can sometimes get in the way of what you're trying to accomplish." He stood up to drag on his trousers.

Mia cringed. Was he right? Was she worrying too much? She tugged the bed sheet away and pulled on her tunic. "What do *you* worry about, Kort?"

"I… It's ridiculous, really."

"No!" She shook her head and pulled him back beside her on the bed. "Tell me. Nothing's ridiculous. The text I read in the library said if there was a block between lovers they should 'explore.' You know, talk things out. Employ any means possible to release tension."

The mortified expression on his face made her wish she'd never brought it up. "You think we have a *block*? Well that makes me worry right there, Mia."

"Well, I'm afraid," she admitted.

"Of what?"

"That I'll lose you."

He heaved a sigh. "Well, I'm afraid you'll never agree to marry me, that our future dynasty will never exist. I don't want anyone else, Mia. I want you. You've accepted my ring, but we haven't spoken further about plans and…"

"I've all but given up on the idea of leaving," she offered.

He bolted upright and strode across the room. "'All but'?"

"I don't want to. But that doesn't change the fact that I'm afraid I'm destined to be alone." Tears poured down her face, and she could not get them to stop no matter how hard she tried.

He turned and walked to her, knelt before her, took her hands. "Okay. You really want to know my fears? You'd better brace yourself to hear. I'm afraid that I'm not doing enough to protect you, that I'm failing to protect the kingdom because I'm so entranced by you. I…I've become less since I found you."

She sucked in a gasp.

"That's right, Mia. But it doesn't have to be that way. I can't keep my mind off you, but commit to *us*. If I know you'll be with me forever I can shift my focus. I can be everything I need to be, can protect you the way that I want. But I need you to commit."

His words struck a hard blow but she was grateful for his honesty. And yet, she could only commit when she was ready, and she wouldn't take responsibility for his lack of focus. If it even existed. "But…you do your job. You're training dragons every day. You're—"

"Not like before." He shook his head. "Not like I should be. Oh, hell, Mia, I used to sleep in the dragon paddock before you and Magnus came. I was in tune with every beast down there. I was nothing of a prince, was simply a Dragon Rider and their commander. I knew the answers my men needed before they even asked questions. Now...well, I've changed. I'm going to have to name a successor."

She cringed. "So you regret this."

He sighed. "I didn't say that."

"But that's what you mean."

"No." He ran his hand through his hair and looked at the bedspread. "What I mean is...I'm having trouble resolving my roles. Yes, the dragons and my warriors need me, but you need me too. So does the kingdom. I have fought that responsibility far too long, as my mother will tell you. But you and I have a family to build when you're ready to commit, and I want to get started. With you. Doing this."

"But you resent this. You're giving up a role you love." The sadness of his sacrifice pinned her soul to the floor.

"Mia." He took her chin and stared into her eyes. "I want to be with you. I guess I'm just having trouble letting go. Like you're having trouble letting go of *your* fear. That prophecy you spoke of— what your parents saddled you with—was unfair."

Mia trembled with the truths they were sharing. Could they find a resolution? If she married him tomorrow, would that fix their auras? Would it remove the block? Would it promise a perfect future for her, the perfect future that Chalvaren promised in so many other ways?

"I don't think a piece of paper is going to give us our answer," she said at last.

"Fine."

His intonation was harsh, and when Kort stood up and turned away from her Mia cringed. She wanted them to find their way through this, back to the magic they'd shared at the beginning when everything was new and uncomplicated. But what could make that happen?

"I could help you resolve your conflicting roles...if you'd let me," she suggested, her voice small, almost quiet as a castle mouse.

Kort turned back, shaking his head. "How, Mia? That conflict is entirely inside me."

She stood up to face him. "I don't have all our answers right now, but I know this. I want you and all your flaws, just like I hope you want me despite all my worries. Yes, I'm asking for more time to make it official, mostly because I'm terrified you'll be ripped from my hands just as I accept you and then I'll have to face a world without us. And, yes, I'm terrified the Dragonstone will tear this kingdom apart and I'll be powerless to stop it. But Kort, think about it. If we help each other through our issues instead of turning away… Well, the idea that love is worth fighting for despite all the odds we're facing—isn't that the whole damn point of everything?"

Kort reached out, clasped his hands behind her neck and pulled her to him. "God, Mia, if I lost you now I might not survive. That's the problem. But, yes. I do believe our love is worth fighting for. I do believe that our magic blended can overcome all that's bad."

His words were everything she needed to hear. She was terrified, but they could find a way through this. They just both had to continue to believe.

Chapter 25

It was really happening this time. Isa Ansgar had crossed into Castle Elias airspace with a squadron of twenty-five shadow elves on dragonback flying behind her in perfect formation.

"Today, VanZanz, we reclaim the Dragonstone."

She urged the silver forward with a kick of her heels, soaring close over the mountains below. Clutching his neck with her arms, her body plastered close to his scales, Isa cast one last glance behind her and waved her black leather–clad arm forward. Her wing of dragons and robust shadow elves eclipsed the sun.

Four figures walked the road from town back to the castle. A copper-colored earth dragon ambled along behind, stopping periodically to scratch the soil.

"Look there, VanZanz." Isa thrust her head forward, clutching her silver. "It's the king himself and his children. Take him!"

VanZanz dove.

King Lachlan looked skyward and spotted her. He drew a sword first, but then he seemed to pause. Changing his mind, he rushed his three children toward the safety of the castle. The east tower remained silent, however, with no dragon patrols coming to his rescue, and the terror emblazoned on his face spread warm satisfaction through Isa's body.

One lone female, a brunette, someone loyal to Isa, lifted her hand from the turret of the east tower. Isa raised her hand in response, in camaraderie. Then, euphoric, Isa urged her dragon onward with a war whoop.

Turning, Lachlan brandished his blade and thrust his children behind him. Isa couldn't fault him there; losing a child was a nightmare. She wanted to leap off her dragon and behead him herself, but she held back. For the moment.

"Yes, Lachlan," she called as her squadron descended ahead on Castle Elias. When its defenders saw the faces of their own people and realized these shadow elves were the very mercenaries they'd dispatched to assassinate her, her revenge would be complete. "You will understand what real loss feels like today. How many will die today for their loyalty, VanZanz? I'll leave you with nothing but ruins."

Some soldiers rushed out of the castle, but several of Isa's dragon riders gave chase and decimated them. One attacked the nearby earth dragon, and the whooshing sound of leathery wingbeats filled the air. Isa smiled as she heard the creature shriek in pain.

Lachlan darted his gaze back and forth, and his expression was one of shock and rage. "You go too far, Ansgar!"

Isa pointed. "I've breached your pitiful defenses. Finally, your unworthy head will be mine along with the artifact. Beg for mercy, Lachlan, and hand over the Dragonstone. Maybe I'll let your children live to serve me."

A red dragon suddenly appeared, flying in from seaward, a little black dragon soaring behind and yipping out some kind of alert. Lachlan's oldest son rode the great red, and Isa saw they were coming straight for her.

The king was cornered, so she thrust her arm skyward. "Take down that fire dragon, VanZanz."

She kicked the silver hard in the ribs, and he swung his mighty head around, spread his wings and leapt into the sky, his challenging roar splitting open the silence of the afternoon. The prince pointed to VanZanz, and the prince's fire dragon lowered his nose into the wind for a charge.

Isa laughed. "How I love a surprise."

†††

"This is bad. This is really, really bad," Mia said, wringing her hands and stepping back from the table and her magic lesson.

"Damn it!" Lucan yelled, leaping forward to counteract what she'd done.

Mia frowned. "I don't know what happened!"

She moved out of the wizard's way, smoothing her fingertips down her navy blue linen tunic. Spell practice had gone well until she apparently said several words wrong, forcing another disaster upon a prized bird of Lucan's. She'd turned the damn thing into a frog! She stifled her initial giggles, but Lucan's shocked reaction nearly put her into hysterics.

Elissabet admonished her with a frown and moved to help. "It's not okay to get this wrong, Mia. We might not be able to change her back."

Mia pulled away so nothing else went wrong. "Forgive me, Lucan. I'm tired. When will King Lachlan be back from town? Brite and I made plans to visit the hatchery. We think those little water dragons are close to hatching, and she wants me to help reinforce their nest."

The queen smiled. "I expect them any moment. Remember, though, we have an appointment tonight to discuss the menu for—"

A deafening roar rattled the panes of glass on the walls of the room. Mia glanced around, surprised, as the wrongness of the sound raised hairs at the base of her neck. "What was that?"

Queen Elissabet hurried to several windows overlooking the road to town. When her knees buckled and her hand flew to her mouth, Mia and Lucan rushed to her side.

"Dear Varik! No!"

Mia pushed the queen aside. As she scanned it, at first the bizarre scene didn't make sense. Terra flapped wildly, her wing obviously broken, and Lachlan hid Brite and Ian and Quinn underneath a nearby dead dragon's wing.

A dead dragon?

Mia looked up. The sky was dark with other dragons ridden by grotesque green shadow elves.

"She's attacked," Lucan growled, his silver aura spiking bright as he wheeled around and grasped his wand.

"Lachlan!" Elissabet shouted, bolting for the door.

The two wizards moved as one. They rushed outside, leaving Mia to follow as she could.

The trip down the long castle halls was onerous, and Mia could barely breathe as she ran. Outside she saw Kort. He sat astride Garnet, his bow drawn, an arrow nocked. Behind him, Magnus was yapping out a warning.

Not far behind them, Kort's Dragon Riders flew in from the sea.

Chapter 26

Kort's heart raced as he nocked an arrow enchanted by a spell Lucan and Elissabet devised after the wraith encounter in the interrogation room. Garnet pivoted, evading Isa's silver, and Kort let fly straight at his enemy's head. The arrow flew true...but the silver blocked the missile with a flapping wing.

Isa and VanZanz twisted in midair and looked to renew their attack, but Kort only had eyes for his endangered father and siblings below. "Get them to safety, Garnet. Help my father!"

The big red roared and exhaled a red-hot mouthful of flames to clear them a path. A shadow elf who'd flown too close was caught in the blast, and he was knocked from his mount and plummeted to the ground, ignited and screaming. Isa and VanZanz seemed to pull back and watch, as if she intended to see her minions do all her work for her now that she'd seen he could actually do some damage.

Kort raised his bow and took aim at another shadow elf, while Garnet continued to breathe fire that kept attackers from getting too close to the king. "Good!" he shouted. "Again! More, Garnet! This is what you were born to do!"

The big red roared again, sharp teeth exposed, and swung around for another attack.

Kort loosed another magic arrow, which buried itself in the torso of a shadow elf. The thing clutched the missile, howled, and slid off its dragon, and a dark-winged specter lofted up out of its body to dissipate into thin air. *Good.* His mother and uncle's spell had done its work. Every warrior in Castle Elias had been equipped with the enchanted arrows; every sword and spear likewise bore magic to even the fight.

Kort watched as the elf's body returned to its normal shape then struck the ground, hard. That mercenary would not be rising again in any form.

Magnus flew better than ever, avoiding direct attacks and yipping a constant alarm, calling for allegiance from any friendly dragon in the vicinity just as he'd been taught. Kort fired arrow after arrow, and more of Isa's shadow elves fell.

Soon other Dragon Riders joined them, the ones who'd been on patrol, summoned by Magnus's call.

"Now," Kort yelled. "To the king!"

Garnet flew over Terra's floundering body, maneuvered sideways, and Kort leapt off. The earth dragon looked bad, even though she was still alive. Her coppery wing looked beyond repair, and there was no way she could carry the royal family to safety. She might even have to be put down.

Kort signaled then fired up into the sky, targeting shadow elves with his enchanted arrows and keeping them away as Magnus touched down beside him. "Dad! Mount Magnus. He's big enough to carry you all now. Get the children to the castle."

Lachlan pulled the children from their hiding place and swung into action, dragging himself onto the dragonlet's back, towing Brite securely under his arm, sheltering her tiny body with his cloak. Ian and Quinn scrambled up behind him. Kort jumped on as well, backwards, facing Magnus's tail and gaining a perfect firing position nestled behind his wings. He targeted anyone who soared close and sent them veering off to find safety.

Yet, Kort had been wrong. Magnus couldn't quite get airborne, not with his heavy load. But he could still run, and run he did. While Kort laid down a suppressing fire of arrows, the dragonlet shot off toward the castle.

Only when he was behind stone walls did Kort survey anything but his enemies. That's when he saw Lucan, Mia, and Elissabet storm onto the field.

†††

"Bastard," Isa hissed, leaning back on her silver's neck. Her dragons still fought, but many of her shadow elves lay dead and her objective had escaped. "Their king and his children hide like cowards,

VanZanz." Then, espying who marched onto the battlefield: "What's this? They actually dare to intervene? Two master wizards in one attack? *Perfect.*"

Victory from the jaws of defeat. Isa had no qualms about settling for these rather than their king, as this pair would work just as handily as ransom for the Dragonstone, which was surely stowed someplace impervious to her magic. As she leaned forward, however, Isa caught sight of a tall blonde elf girl who lingered behind. "So, they've taken in an apprentice as well? Lovely. We'll take her too, VanZanz."

Isa urged her silver to the edge of the courtyard, and she barked out an order as she expertly leapt off his back. "No more holding back, VanZanz. I want that fire-breather down, in chains, and dying."

The silver rose to do her bidding, and Isa turned to face Lucan Brix and Elissabet Elias. Triumph would yet be hers.

†††

With Magnus and Kort off the field and no doubt locked inside the bunker now with Lachlan and the royal children, Mia relaxed just a fraction. Still, she shadowed her teachers, enraged at Isa's attack. She lent her purple aura to Lucan's and Elissabet's, the two wizards targeting the remaining shadow elves who fought so hard against the standing castle defenders.

Kort's warriors were impressive. Each Rider and dragon did his part, and the sight emboldened Mia. They could contain the carnage and maybe even win.

Then Garnet engaged the silver.

Mia swept her gaze across the bloodied battlefield to watch the two mature dragons fight. The sound of their roars shook the ground, and Mia's knees trembled with the vibration. She thrust her hands over her ears.

The two beasts clashed. Where Garnet offered blasts of fire, the silver countered with frost and blistering steam boiled up wherever the breath weapons met. Two enemy dragons winged too close, and they screamed in agony as their wings were caught in the cloud. The pair plunged to the battlefield and were dead on impact.

Mia stepped back and looked away, disgusted by the carnage, but a moment later she heard Garnet roar in pain. Looking up she found the silver had covered his wings in hoarfrost. Frozen, the red tumbled toward the ground, which luckily was not too far away. Still, his wings looked frozen solid.

No!

Mia ran forward, Elissabet at her side, only to be intercepted. A female elf, apparently the leader of this assault, stood before them. Dressed in black leathers, with waist-length black hair, the woman turned and watched the end of the dragon fight. She was so close that Mia saw a tattoo of three tears under her right eye.

Isa?

VanZanz landed and again hit Garnet with a blast of his breath weapon. Mia shrieked, but Elissabet dragged her backward before she could bolt for him.

"No. Not alone. Isa will kill you if you give her the chance. She's more powerful than I've ever seen her. Get behind me, Mia, and stay there no matter what. Lucan. At my side!"

Mia shadowed both wizards, and the three of them blended their power and cast bolts of energy at Isa. The witch just laughed and ripped open her vest. A cloud of wraiths flew out, but Lucan and Elissabet zapped away each successive demon, and Mia got one too. Her gaze swept across the field toward Isa again, and toward the struggling dragon.

So, this was indeed her aunt. Isa had thrust out both hands, and she chanted, low and menacing, and her strange words drew chills from Mia's limbs.

"*Ligare Ignis Draco. Adferunt mortem.* Bind the dragon. I want him bleeding and suffering before he dies!"

A rigid black webbing studded with three-inch barbs shot from her fingertips. Mia blanched and struggled to escape, but Lucan grasped her arm along with Elissabet. The pair wouldn't let her go to Garnet's aid.

"Mia. No. Stay with us."

Mia gulped in air. What kind of magic was this? She shook her head and drew back, watching Isa manipulate matter out of thin air. Watching Magnus's father tortured and defeated.

Razor-wire shot from Isa's hands. It encircled Garnet, biting through the ice which held him fast. As the black magic tore into his scales, the massive animal roared in pain. Mia's belly spasmed and she broke free of Elissabet and Lucan and bolted forward to help. No one else was going to.

"*Stop it!*" she shouted at her aunt. She covered her face, too shocked to watch Garnet suffer.

Isa turned. Seeing Mia she almost laughed; then she turned her attention to Lucan and Elissabet. Bracing her legs, the wizardess threw out her palms and hit the pair with a blast of crimson energy. As it surrounded them, neither Elissabet nor Lucan seemed able to move. Isa was somehow imprisoning them with light.

Mia reacted, dragging the Dragonstone from her tunic. She wasn't sure what she could do, but if she— Only then did she realize her folly. This gem was nothing but paste, a decoy. It looked authentic, sure, but the real artifact was inside the bunker with the king, nestled securely in a safe she and Lachlan designed together, safe from Isa's attack. There was little point in carrying it until she truly knew how to control her powers.

But Isa doesn't know that.

Mia fisted the jewel and thrust it above her head to catch the sun. She sparked her aura and encircled the stone with prisms of light that reflected over the courtyard, and this was what accomplished Mia's goal. Isa saw it and froze.

Mia swallowed hard but held her position. Her distraction had dissipated Isa's energy blast, and Lucan and Elissabet struggled free. The two fell to the ground, dazed and gasping, which meant Mia had to move, had to shield them with her body. Lucan was rising, but it didn't seem like the queen was able.

"If you attack them again," Mia growled, "you'll have to come through me."

Isa strode forward, her blue eyes blazing with malevolence and furious need. The woman looked like Mia's father, though with long, straight, ebon hair. The resemblance brought a pang to Mia's heart.

Isa pointed. "I want that artifact. Give it to me."

Mia trembled but stood tall. Could her aunt know who she was? No, that was impossible. Unless…

She shook off Isa's icy stare, removed the imitation gem, swung its chain above her head and flooded it with the energy of her aura. "Call off the attack and it's yours," she cried. "Take your demons and leave my chosen family alone."

"Mia, NO!" Lucan screamed. "Don't give her the jewel."

Isa gave a half bow, seemingly amused. "Yes. Give me the Dragonstone and I will leave what's left of your family alone."

Mia ignored Lucan and threw the amethyst, hard. It soared over Isa's head. The wizardess hissed out a curse then turned and raced after it.

Wheeling around, Mia grasped the queen's arm and began dragging her toward the castle. "Lucan. Help me. *Now.*"

Lucan leapt into action, scooping Elissabet up in his arms, and together they all ran toward the safety of the fortress.

Mia whipped her head around for one last look. Was Isa leaving like she'd promised? Unfortunately, it seemed someone else had shown up.

"No. They can't be out here," she said. "That's not possible."

Chapter 27

Garnet's screams of pain hit Kort first as he returned to the battlefield. The magnificent red beast writhed on the ground, bellowing in agony, unable to stand up, unable to fly, and Kort's gut knotted in a fist of anguish. How had he allowed any of this to happen? Wasn't he the one responsible for protecting Castle Elias from attack? He and Duncan.

He searched the battlefield for the wizards. For his princess. *Thank God.* Mia was hurrying Lucan and his mother toward the castle.

"Good," Kort said, glancing down at Magnus. "Now for Isa. I saved three arrows, and I intend to bury one in her heart."

The witch was running away, looking at the ground. Magnus glided down in front of Garnet. Kort leapt off him and knelt in firing position, calling, "Go back to Mia, Magnus. Protect her. Get her back to the bunker."

But Magnus didn't listen. The dragonlet saw his wounded sire, and nothing could keep him away.

Isa suddenly called out. VanZanz descended, and the witch clambered up onto his neck, a glint of purple from her neck. Kort saw it and recoiled, unable to take his shot. What had Mia done?

The silver took to the air. As he did, Isa turned back and gestured then shouted to her minions. It seemed clear that her target was Magnus, so Kort screamed out a warning, but the dragonlet didn't listen. Isa cast her hands wide, and another burst of razor-wire netting flew from her palms. It covered Magnus, and two remaining shadow elf dragon riders flew in and lifted the bundled Aurora off the ground.

Kort shouted as all Isa's dragons turned to go home. Magnus yipped and screamed, thrashing against Isa's bindings. Kort sacrificed two of his last three arrows and more shadow elves fell, but VanZanz circled back, stretched out wicked-looking hind claws and snatched the netted dragonlet from his riderless captors. Then the silver flexed strong shining wings and soared off toward the last rays of sunlight limning the Drakhos Mountains. He was chased by all the remaining Dragon Riders, but they would never catch him; that silver was a monster.

"Magnus!" Kort screamed, and crashed to his knees. He fired one last time, his target Isa's back. The arrow missed but buried itself in the hide of the silver, who seemed not to react at all.

"Magnus! NO!" Mia suddenly appeared, and she raced out past Kort, reaching up as if she could stop what was happening. She threw out her aura as if it could somehow grab back her dragonlet. She couldn't, though. The Aurora was gone. The sound of Mia's anguished voice was torture. He'd failed her. And Magnus's helpless bleats faded into the distance.

"Somebody do something to save him!" a voice called out. It was his mother, and she looked not toward the Aurora but Garnet. The red had been left behind, bound, wounded, but apparently forgotten in Isa's triumph.

Kort's chest sank as if trampled by a thousand dragons. Garnet wheezed, his body contorted, his wing bent back at an awkward angle. The red was in great jeopardy. Bent backward like that, the wing might never heal, which was a death sentence. Shimmering black metal wire constricted him also, and the fire-breather moaned.

Kort ran to Mia. Her face was ashen, her eyes still locked on the sky where she'd last seen her dragonlet, but she took his hand and they spun around, racing toward the struggling Garnet.

Lucan flashed past them, his mother alongside. The two began peering at the barbed netting on Garnet that shimmered first black then silver.

"What the hell is all over him?" Kort demanded. He'd never seen anything like it.

His warriors landed nearby and rushed to assist, but the net was clearly magical. Garnet writhed, and the more he fought, the more the net restrained him and cut into his scales. His breathing became increasingly ragged.

Kort shuddered. He couldn't lose Garnet; he simply would not survive. Red and gold dragon scales littered the ground, and the mighty fire breather bled dark crimson-black blood. Kort reached out to tear the binding away, but a blast of black magic slammed him backward into the air. He writhed and tried to right himself after landing, but two elves had to help him to his feet.

He twisted to face his mother, Mia and Lucan. "Help me get it off him before he dies! Lucan! Help him! ANY OF YOU! You're wizards!"

He reached out again, this time to comfort Garnet, but Elissabet slapped his hands away. "*No.* Don't touch him, Kort."

Lucan spoke then, shouldering Kort behind him. "Keep him back. Out of my way."

Mia grasped Kort's arms, but he snatched free. "What the hell is it?" he fumed, moving forward again, searching Lucan's worried face. "What spell did she cast? I've never seen anything like this!"

Lucan didn't answer. Instead, he began a chant and drew out his wand. The tip, fitted with a Drakhos diamond, flared to life, and as the wizard's voice grew louder it finally blasted an energy surge toward the magical metal netting that rent the silver-and-black web in two places. Kort shielded his eyes from the intensity of the flare.

Elissabet flooded the great red dragon with her orange healing aura, and Mia pulsed with her purple aura, combining it with the queen's. Garnet's eyes lifted open. The dragon seized, struggled, then stilled.

"Get him out of there, Lucan," Kort commanded. This had to work. The wizard's magic *had* to prove stronger than whatever held his dragon near death. But his hopes vanished as the black webs seemed to grow back and tighten. The great fire-breather barely managed a scream of rage.

"Garnet," Kort said, and his hands trembled. "Be still."

Pure appeared behind them, and the wind dragon lifted her head and let out a roar, a wail of grief. Poseidon joined her, and then all the others.

"Again, Lucan. *Help* him," Kort commanded.

The wizard walked around the dragon, chanting, lifting his arms and waving his wand. Another blast of white magic jumped from the diamond and more web vanished, and this time Garnet dragged his head free. Kort raced forward to stroke the beast's cheeks. "Yes! More, Lucan, more!"

Garnet offered labored gasps, resting his snout on Kort. Maddix and Kristoff rushed in, lending their strength, shouldering the great dragon's neck in case that helped Garnet breathe. The wizards worked. The dragons roared. Then Garnet dropped his head, all the life seeming to rush out of him.

"No. Garnet, no! Breathe, old man. Breathe for me!"

Lucan and Elissabet began casting again, but the webs grew back as fast as they were removed. The horrific stench of searing flesh and scales burned Kort's nose. From the corner of his eye he caught the shimmer of blonde hair running from the field, but he didn't have the heart to call Mia back to watch the last gasps of his dying dragon.

Chapter 28

She wouldn't let this happen.

Mia ran, her leg muscles burning with the effort to get down into the bunker, to get to what she needed. Once she slipped and skidded forward on the polished but unforgiving stone of the castle floor, but she was up again before the burns on her knees and wrists had time to register.

She banged on the door with both fists. "Let me in! Let me in! Somebody open this damn bunker!"

King Lachlan appeared from the other direction, striding forward with a full guard.

"Please! King Lachlan, help!" Hot tears streamed down her face. She ran to the king and clutched his arms in desperation.

The guards had drawn weapons, but Lachlan growled for them to be put away. "Mia, are you okay?"

"I was wrong, *so* wrong. I must have it. Take me...take me to it. Garnet! Lachlan, he'll die if—"

Lachlan swung her around, and together they waited for the bunker doors to be opened then darted inside. Mia ruminated on her good fortune in finding him so quickly. She'd set this up so that only she and the king could retrieve her objective together.

They burst into the hall where the safe waited behind one of the alcoves in the hatchery. Lachlan entered his code first then gestured at Mia. "Go ahead, child. Hurry!"

With trembling, bloodied fingers, Mia dialed in her code and flipped the mechanism. The heavy mechanical safe's gearwheels ground, and four inch–thick metal doors wheeled open with a hiss. Inside, suspended on a pedestal, glittered the real purple amethyst.

Mia thrust her hand inside and grasped it. Brilliant ghostfire snapped to life with her touch, engulfing the artifact. "I've got to get back to Garnet," she whispered. "This has to work."

Lachlan helped her don the necklace and ushered her forward toward his guards. "Duncan," he called, "take Mia to Garnet's side. At once!"

The captain of Chalvaren's guards did not hesitate, and soon Mia was rushing with him out of the bunker toward the dragon, toward her destiny, toward the job that only she could do. Toward her true magic.

†††

Kort's legs quivered with fatigue from holding up his dying dragon's head, and fury threatened to overwhelm him. Lucan's attempts to free Garnet had proved pointless. It seemed Isa's conjured evil would win out.

One of the razor-wire filaments touched Kort's flesh, and the pain was so intense that it stole his breath. If this evil hurt him like this, what was his dragon suffering? "GET IT OFF OF HIM!" he found himself shouting. "GODS, HELP US! IT'S KILLING HIM!"

Lucan again buried the tip of his wand in the black netting and it receded for a second, but only for a second. Useless. Queen Elissabet moved in front of him, her blue eyes glistening with tears, and she gently cupped Kort's chin.

"We cannot save him, Son. Move away. I won't lose you too."

Kort's chin quivered at the sight of her tears, at the sound of despair in his mother's voice. He pushed down an instinct to scream at her and simply begged. "Mother, help. Please. By Varik, if you've ever loved me, help me hold his head up so he can breathe."

Tears trickled down her heart-shaped face, but she moved next to Kort and helped support Garnet's neck.

Lucan continued to work, chanting out counterspells, but every lashing he removed was replaced by two more. Elissabet spoke low and soft encouraging words into Garnet's ear, but the sound almost tore Kort's heart from his chest and he swallowed hard, trying to dislodge the hardening lump in his throat. If he was going to lose his dragon, he'd be damned if he didn't do everything in his power to ensure Garnet suffered as little as possible.

As Mia hit the courtyard and saw the fallen, elves and dragons alike, a fleeting thought drifted through her mind. *This is what Hell must look like.*

Then, *My fault. This is my fault.*

Blinding hot tears fractured her vision, but Mia ran anyway toward Garnet. Toward the wizards who might help her do what she was meant to do. Toward Kort, the love of her life. She raced toward her destiny, toward ultimate success or ultimate failure. This would be the test.

She skidded to a stop in front of them, planted her feet wide and screamed out, "*Varik! Deposco meo utere priuilegio Chalvaren magicae. Salvare illum.* Save Garnet. *Expugnare vincula.* I claim Chalvaren's magic as my birthright, invoke the power of the Dragonstone to succeed where otherwise I might fail. Save him. Save Garnet. Destroy his bonds."

All heads turned. Mia's knees buckled as a surge of magic consumed her. Her purple aura mingled with the ghostfire of the Dragonstone, and a blinding rainbow light covered everything in the vicinity. Lucan stopped his futile attempts at casting and stared. Kort and Queen Elissabet both nodded mutely, desperately.

"Yes, Mia!" Lucan shouted. He moved forward and touched the Dragonstone's golden chain with the diamond tip of his wand. His silver aura surged, flooded the wand, melded with Mia's purple magic, and was channeled through her.

Garnet bucked wildly at first, and Queen Elissabet dragged Kort away to safety. Maddix and Kristoff rushed back and covered their eyes. Then Mia's white magic took hold. Her power ripped through the conjured razor-wire and those deadly restraints vanished into specks of swirling ash.

Garnet collapsed. The dragon didn't move. Didn't respond.

Elissabet led Kort by the hand, and they two encircled Mia and Lucan, lending their auras. The queen's healing energy engulfed Mia and warmed her, but it was no use for Garnet, who did not seem to move. Pure and Poseidon flocked forward, drawn by the magic, but they moaned out soft sounds of grief as they reached the big red's body. Mia swiped at the tears blurring her vision. She had been too late to save him.

"No!" she shouted. She refused to accept this. She stalked forward and touched the dragon's head, waved the Dragonstone around him and coated him with its ghostfire. The magic surrounded her, building, and her hands caressed the great red beast. "Garnet, wake up. Magnus needs you. *We* need you."

The dragon spasmed. Mia recoiled when he opened his mouth, and Kort dragged her backward, away from those sharp teeth, but she wrenched her arm free and streaked back to him. She barely heard Lucan say, "Let her do this, Kort. We must not interfere."

The last remnants of razor wire were gone, leaving only bleeding scars and loose dragon scales. Mia stood tall, walking around the big red, throwing out her arms and trying to let the magic do its work. Something was happening. Something was definitely happening.

Garnet struggled to stand. Ghostfire burned all across his hide, and soon the worst of his wounds knitted together. The fire raced across his injured wing, repairing it, making it whole again, making it perfect. Mia's mouth twitched. Something like a smile threatened her mouth, and her heart pounded harder than ever. She was truly beginning to believe he'd be okay.

"Garnet?" Kort tore free and caressed the big dragon, tenderly removing hopeless clumps of torn scale and smoothing others back into place.

Mia glanced over. Tears streamed down his beautiful face, and her heart thudded against her breastbone. "Easy, Kort. Be careful. The healing is not complete."

Garnet turned eyes upon Mia, moved his head close and laved her cheek with his enormous raspy tongue.

She wrapped her arms around his neck. "I'm so sorry, Garnet. I'm so sorry that this happened."

The witch. Isa took him, a voice said suddenly in her mind, and Mia fought shock as she recognized the big fire-breather could now speak. He closed his eyes and nuzzled her, adding, *I could not stop her, but we must give chase. She means to kill Magnus. She means to kill my son.*

Mia spat out a curse, and Queen Elissabet took her arm. "What is it, Mia?"

Didn't the queen hear the dragon too? Didn't anyone besides her? Mia glanced around and began to believe that Garnet's voice was for her mind alone.

She looked into Elissabet's eyes. "Isa means to kill Magnus. Garnet said we must pursue her."

Kort nodded. "Yes. The Dragon Riders and I shall go after them immediately."

Lucan rushed forward and gripped him by the arm. "No! Not now. We wait. We cannot—"

"No! No more waiting. I've waited long enough," Kort growled, glancing around at the Riders who surrounded the proceedings. "All these years we've waited and waited, wondering if Isa would find her way back to sanity, praying that no more violence need be suffered. From this moment I will wait no more. Warriors! Mount your dragons!"

"Kort. Wait!" Mia called.

He pulled her close. "I'll get him back, Mia. I'll see Magnus home before the moon sets tonight."

She sighed. "I'm coming with you."

His eyes widened, and he shook his head. "No. You stay here. Protect Garnet. He needs time to heal. Please let me do this alone, Mia. It is the job I was always meant to do."

Mia wriggled in his embrace. "No. I'm coming—"

"For once listen to me, Mia." Kort caught her face in his hands and kissed her. He pointed to his mother. "Protect her. Take Garnet underground. Learn more about your magic."

She pulled free. "No, Kort. I won't leave you unprotected. For you to fight Isa without a powerful magic-user—"

"I'll take Lucan, if he's man enough." Kort glared at the wizard, who nodded. "And Duncan…?"

The king's captain stood taller, obviously eager to join the fight.

Kort stepped forward and brushed his lips across Mia's. "Please. Stay here with my mother. With my family. Protect her. Protect all of them. And Garnet."

He called his Riders to action then ran to Pure, bellowing out commands. Lucan followed, and together the pair mounted the great white wind dragon. Pure leapt up into the air, and she winged away toward the Drakhos Mountains, Chalvaren's remaining mounted warriors in formation behind her.

Their exodus should have been one of the most incredible sights she'd ever witnessed, but the image only amplified Mia's anxiety. She watched the squadron leave, miserable. This wasn't what she wanted. She wanted to go after Magnus herself, and her belly clenched at the thought Kort might never come back.

She fisted her hands and looked around the battlefield. There had been so much loss here today, and she refused to indulge the terrifying idea it might not be over yet.

Queen Elissabet eased up behind her. "So, are you planning to start blindly obeying my son now? Because if you are, you'll never make any sort of leader. Kings require queens who are their equal, and I know you do not want to stay here without him. You are right to think that this was a rash decision. His father will not approve."

Mia bit her lip then glanced up at Garnet, who watched the darkening night sky. "To wait here blindly is too much for Kort to ask. If my aunt gets her hands on him…"

Elissabet nodded. "You must follow him and watch, Mia. And if anything happens…there is another wizard. He lives deep in the mountains. His name is Alastair Krogh."

"Lucan's brother…?" Mia remembered the wizard's name from the interrogation room, when Lucan confirmed Alastair as the wizard who'd killed Isa's Malachai. "Then he must be your brother too."

Elissabet nodded. "My half-brothers, both of them." Mia saw a flicker of sadness in her eyes; then the queen grasped her hands and said, "Seek out Alastair, Mia, if something goes wrong. If anything happens to Kort, tell Alastair I'll help him assemble the Others. Tell him what Isa has done, that she has abducted the spirit dragon, our Aurora. He's my oldest ally. Say that, whatever resources are necessary, whatever price he names, Castle Elias will pay it. We must stop Isa. It finally has to be done."

"But…Alastair started this, right? He killed Isa's lover."

"On one level that is true, Mia. On another it was Malachai who began everything. Regardless, I'm afraid Alastair Krogh is the only one who can end this."

Mia shook her head and turned to Garnet. "Can you fly?"

The great red dragon looked down at her and nodded. He raised his wings, opened and inspected them. *Your magic healed my wounds. I will do whatever you require.*

"Garnet knows Alastair's location," Elissabet said, walking over to brush a hand along the dragon's flank. The great red swung his tail back and forth and flapped his wings, clearly testing his strength and health.

"Swear to me you'll protect her, dragon," the queen whispered. When Garnet lowered his head in response, she caressed his snout and said, "Go, Mia. Go and watch my son. Find your dragonlet—and my brother."

Mia grasped Elissabet's hands and tried to sound upbeat. "Tell Brite I'll bring her brother home."

Elissabet pointed. "Go!"

Garnet extended his front leg, and Mia scurried up. She took hold of his ivory horns, gripped his neck with her knees, and urged him forward.

"Take it slow, old man."

Garnet snorted in disdain and lumbered forward. Then he roared and ran. The power of the mighty beast flexing beneath her, coupled with their mutual anger, was intoxicating to Mia as he leapt up into the air, but soon she hung on for dear life. The injured dragon was winging them skyward in pursuit.

Chapter 29

Kort screamed a war cry into the darkness, but his words were lost in the wind. This was all on him. If he'd acted long ago and put Isa down himself, none of this responsibility would lie at his feet. But it did. And so where his father's mercenaries and his mother's negotiations had failed, tonight he vowed to end this. It was long past time. He was almost to Castle Cumberlae, Isa's stronghold.

I'll snap her neck with my own two hands.

Lucan's body went rigid behind him, and the wizard pointed over Kort's shoulder. Kort looked left then right and then up, but all he saw was darkness. And then VanZanz.

"The witch. She is on us," Lucan said.

Isa began casting her spell, and down fell her wicked net of death, larger this time, and everywhere. Kort reared back and tried to turn Pure, but he wasn't fast enough. The web burned his flesh and, worse, it snared Pure's wings.

"Get out of the way!" he shouted, trying to warn the others. It was futile. Poseidon and Pure both bellowed, and he heard the screams as sorcerous razor wire caught every dragon in the flight.

Wails and squawks sounded all around him. Warriors cursed. The smell of Pure's coppery iron-rich blood registered in his mind. Kort couldn't breathe, but Lucan sprang to life, snatching out his wand and searing away Isa's conjured bindings. He could just cut Kort free, and then the wizard used surprisingly strong legs to push Kort out from under the snare.

"Damn it, Lucan! Don't!"

Kort reached out, but his uncle's face was determined. Lucan pushed him again, and then used both legs to kick him entirely off Pure's back. The last thing Kort saw was tentacles of razor wire swarming across Lucan's face and bald head, and the last thing he heard was Lucan's screams.

Then he fell.

†††

"KORT?" Mia saw him fall. Yes, it was Kort plunging to the ground. One second he was tied tightly to Pure's snow-white hide by black magic, the next he tumbled toward the ground. His blue aura flared bright, making him look like a meteor blasting across the sky.

"Garnet! Catch him!"

The red began a nosedive. Could he do this? Mia wondered. Could he catch him?

"Faster!" she urged, plastering her body against the dragon's hide, becoming one with the mighty beast as he swooped down like a red falling star.

With little time to maneuver, Garnet twisted and arched underneath Kort, angling to catch him. Mia gasped as Kort struck a wing, but then Garnet had him, Kort hanging on as the dragon tried to slow their descent and not crash headfirst into the earth.

It was close. Garnet pulled up at the last minute, digging his spiked tail into the soil as he made the final turn, and using his enormous hind claws to slow them. Mia lurched off his back at the third jounce. Soft mounds of tall grass broke her fall, scratching her legs, but real pain registered in her chest as the breath was knocked from her lungs. Still, it could have been worse. She pulled her legs to her chest and inhaled sharp breaths as she rolled to a stop.

She lifted her head when Garnet roared. The big dragon now tumbled end over end, rolling and bouncing, his wings tucked in tight. Dust and gravel clouded the air around him as he crashed to a stop, and the giant beast roared again.

Mia winced and covered her ears with her hands. She leapt upright then lurched forward into a full-blown run.

"Garnet. Is Kort okay?"

He was. He lay safely tucked inside Garnet's wing, and Mia used her fingers to check for a pulse, which she soon found. Kort was just out cold, if his skin was bloodied in the crisscross pattern of Isa's razor wire. The sight drew a black fury from Mia's heart, and she vowed her aunt would pay.

Garnet lifted his head and searched the starlit sky, but silence screamed back and it remained empty. Had the others all plummeted to their deaths? Had they been captured? They were all gone, every single one of them lost to the witch.

The dragon mourned them with a low, soulful, whining roar. Mia's chin quivered and twisted. Big soppy tears pricked behind her eyes, and she fisted her hand up to the empty sky.

"I'm coming for you, Isa. I'm coming for you, for my people, and my dragons!"

Chapter 30

The Dragonstone hung from her neck, the Aurora was bound and in her custody, and she had Lucan Brix, number six on her list of most-wanted wizards. Soon he would be strapped to a stainless steel table and… Isa's insides quivered with joy.

She surveyed her catch once they landed back in the safe confines of Cumberlae. Pleased with the harvest, she offered her remaining shadow elves a rare smile of satisfaction and set them to the task of confining her prisoners. "Not bad, men. Not too bad at all. How foolish of them to give chase. Didn't they think I'd circle back just in case? Didn't they think I'd be waiting? Haven't they learned anything about my power? Well, soon they shall. All in all, a good day's work."

The shadow elves set to work dragging her prisoners below, and Isa took some time to refresh herself. Not too long, though, as she was eager to get started on the next phase of victory. She soon stalked through the fortress of Cumberlae and into her favorite room: the torture chamber.

Turned her attention on its newest occupant, Isa smiled at him. "So nice of you to finally join me, Lucan."

The wizard said nothing, just twisted his hands into a less than gentlemanly gesture, an elven insult. But the response just made Isa laugh.

"You cut Elissabet's first-born free. While I would have preferred him in attendance at tonight's festivities, the sight of him falling to his death warmed me, Lucan. That was some of your best work. How does it feel to own the title of prince-killer? Assassin?"

Lucan ignored her, which was annoying.

"Yes, resort to silence, as if you don't have a tongue," she muttered. "But you do, Lucan. And you will gladly sing before the night is done."

Lucan just curled his upper lip.

Isa circled the torture table and stroked one long red nail up his body, feeling his surprisingly powerful muscles clench as she did. Leaning close to his bejeweled ear she whispered, "You've done well to avoid family. That's served to be the undoing of most of your fellows. Like Laudegrance Smarr. You should have heard his wife *scream.*"

Lucan averted his eyes, but not before Isa saw the hate in their deep brown depths.

"So...I know where Elissabet is, but let's talk about your eldest brother's whereabouts, shall we?" Isa hissed. "Ah, yes, Alastair. When was the last time you two broke bread?"

Silence was Lucan's answer. Isa's mouth twitched, and she flicked her wrist toward three waiting shadow elves, each of whom held a polished knife, pliers, or oversized shears. The abominations guffawed and fought for first position, all wanting to earn Isa's favor.

She pointed at the third. "Time to light the sacrificial fire, boys. Let's start with the branding iron, shall we, Shamus?"

His once-straight elven ears jutting out sideways from his flattened head, the repugnant creature howled in delight and slithered a gray tongue over pointed teeth. He lumbered over to the hearth on bare feet, struck a match and lit the tinder. Once the flames rose high enough, he thrust his three-foot metal branding iron into the base of the fire. Then he growled and whined until the iron glowed hot and red.

Chapter 31

"I don't know if I can fix this, Garnet."

Mia squeezed her eyes shut briefly before assessing Kort's wounds. Thankfully he slept, which meant he wasn't in pain. For the moment. She'd collected the herbs she remembered from talking to Thorvid. The fauna and flora of Chalvaren were becoming familiar, but still, it was easy to second-guess herself, especially when she was also guessing at the problem. She'd channeled every memory of lessons with her father, and finally she thought she had the healing mixture right.

Maybe. At least for the burns.

The sun wasn't up yet. Morning was still a few hours away. Mia shook her head and glanced up at the dragon. "I don't understand. I don't find any internal injuries. He's breathing, so why won't he wake up?"

The fire-breather shook his head. *Perhaps it is mental, Princess. Perhaps he feels shame. He fears his comrades have all died. Failure like that is not something Kort can tolerate. He has never tolerated failure.*

Hearing the dragon's thoughts was still surprising to Mia, and she didn't know why that had changed, but she had more important issues to focus on at the moment. She knelt and poked at Kort's chest, saying, "Well, he'd best get over it and come help us now. Grieving in silence won't serve anyone today. We've a wizard to find, and his laying about like this just won't do." She stood and eyed the dragon. "Can *you* wake him?"

Garnet shook his head. *I've tried. I've beseeched him since we landed. You should rest, Princess. This is a situation that will resolve itself.*

Mia surveyed the burns on Kort's chest, arms, and legs. The ointment she'd created stank to the heavens but it had closed his worst wounds and he wasn't bleeding anymore. Still, her warrior slept.

"You say you think it's grief that keeps him unconscious?"

Garnet sighed, or made a sound very like a sigh. He gave no other response.

Mia fisted her hands. "Well, maybe he just needs the night to heal his mind. I'll let him rest. But what about you? Will you hold still and let me tend your wounds? If I can get that wing-tip covered with this salve, I think it will heal by morning."

Garnet reared back, his lips curled away from his huge white teeth. His eyes glittered, and he stared at her with revulsion. *I don't think so.*

"You'll feel so much better!" Sure, the stench was a sacrifice, but still… Mia looked up at the dragon, expecting him to understand, but Garnet backed away when Mia dipped her fingers in ointment. She held up her hand, but he skidded away like a small child, lifted his magnificent head, and covered his nose with his injured wing.

No.

She shook her fist at him. "That was not a request, dragon. Get over here and let me help you. We've no time for an infection to set in. You need to be at your best when Kort wakes. He'll be furious, for sure, and I can't have you limping around because—"

The dragon hissed and retreated further.

Mia put her hands on her hips. "Don't you *dare* try to get away from me!"

The dragon recoiled and attempted just that. She chased him in a circle, Garnet squawking the whole time, but when she tripped over a vine he turned and stretched his wing to catch her. She seized the moment and smeared his wounds with the malodorous but she hoped efficacious mixture. He squirmed and growled, but Mia was fast and showed him no mercy.

"Hold still, you big baby! This won't hurt but for a second."

†††

"What's that horrible smell?" Kort murmured. Mild sunlight beat warm on his cheeks.

He opened his eyes. A sleeping face came into focus, that of an angel sent to liberate him he was sure. *Mia.* Garnet covered both her and Kort with his wings, snoring soundly. But what was that awful odor, and how did Mia sleep with all that racket?

They were deep in the woods, covered by a canopy of trees and thus hidden from sight from the air, so Kort breathed in a sigh of relief. The three of them were safe. But as he sat up, sniffing, the jagged crosshatched wounds on his arms pulled taut. A curse formed on his lips, but he suppressed it. He didn't want to wake Mia. He simply lay there and watched her sleep, watched her breathe, watched her exist and be what she was: a gift from Varik. But then…what was she doing here, risking her life for him? Hadn't he ordered her to stay at Castle Elias?

His father's voice loomed in the back of his mind, reminding him Chalvaren belonged to Mia too. Her willingness to sacrifice for the common good meant she got to protect him too, even though he was the one who should be doing the protecting. Mia Ansgar was a living, breathing contradiction. And she had a right to be here with him. She must be furious that Magnus was taken. He'd failed her. Failed the dragonlet. Hell, he'd failed everyone. He'd let Isa exist long enough to wreak all this havoc on the world when he should have gone and confronted her years before.

Another thought occurred. He should have listened to his mother regarding negotiations with the alliance territories. Instead of showing her nothing but his pigheaded rejections of her politics and demands for him to participate, what would it have cost him to don fine clothes now and then in the name of fellowship? He could have been one of Elissabet's best allies on the point of amassing an army and air force of alliance troops to take Isa out. Kort gritted his teeth together, and regret plagued him. But, wait, he still could do just that—thanks to Mia's quick thinking and her total disregard for his orders.

Her eyelids moved rapidly as she slept. Restless, she reached a hand up to cover her eyes and rolled over. He thought he saw sadness etched across her face as she did.

"I swear, Mia, I will avenge the dead. If it's at all possible, I'll see Magnus and Lucan home safe again," he whispered. "I will get us all home."

Dragon training. Magic training. Afternoon swims and lovemaking. Watching Mia read her father's journals to Magnus by firelight in the library while he and his father talked, Kort's younger brothers staring up rapt as they listened to strategy and politics.... The last few weeks had been gloriously wonderful despite the change from how his life was before Mia. Kort wanted that again, with his mother nearby reading to Brite, both dragons snoozing outside on the dragon-deck, the soldiers and inhabitants of Castle Elias close at hand for celebrations and everyday life. He wanted it all, and as he watched Mia sleep, he swore a vow that somehow he'd get it back.

She rolled over again, facing him, and he sighed. The Dragonstone bulged securely under her navy linen shirt. Lengths of her blonde hair framed her beautiful face, but it was...dark and clumpy in places?

Was *that* what he smelled? Kort twisted up on his elbows and blinked sleep from his eyes, then noticed a heavy ointment smeared across his right bicep. It was indeed what was caught in her hair, darkening it, and Mia's hands showed her work—she was covered in the greasy, vile medication up to her elbows. The greasy stench wafted to his nose. He sucked in a tight breath and gagged. Where the hell had she found this remedy? It was as if rotting vegetation was suspended in resin.

He wiped the slippery goo off as quickly as he could, but exposed to the air the jagged lacerations on his arms stung like viper bites. When he smeared the ointment back into place, the pain abated.

Ah.

Embarrassed, he glanced back at Mia, remembering the garden where he first met her. She'd tended healing herbs there, and she'd been discussing Chalvaren's flora for weeks with his mother and Thorvid. He'd commented that she would soon be providing salves for the entire castle, but he'd never expected her to heal him. Just as, he supposed, he hadn't expected a lot of things that happened since he met her.

He twisted and examined Garnet's hide. The dragon's cuts were smeared with the same sticky, wretched-smelling ointment, but the acrid aroma suddenly became soothing, a surprise, a gift he didn't understand but was grateful for all the same. If Mia's herb-craft could heal Garnet's wounds, only an idiot and an ingrate would protest, even if it stank to the far ends of Chalvaren.

Still, he crossed his arms over his chest and wrinkled his nose. *Damn* her. She'd come after him with an injured dragon in tow? One part of him wanted to spank her supple little ass for such a badly considered plan, but if Mia hadn't acted and totally disregarded his orders he'd be lying broken on the bottom of this canyon, dead.

Painful images rushed back, and Kort fought to breathe. Blood. Scars. Razor wire formed with black magic. The final image of Lucan's face hovering above his as the wizard cut him free then shoved him to what was ultimately his salvation. Kort covered his eyes with his arm and shook his head, trying not to cry.

When he sat back up, Mia was awake. Her emerald green eyes greeted him as she lay silent, staring. Tears flooded her eyes, which he reached out to dry.

"Stay still," she whispered.

He fought the pain of his cuts and thumbed away her tears then tried to make light of their situation. "What is that god-awful reeking concoction?"

She shrugged and gave a small smile. "From the looks of it your wounds have improved through the night. And his as well. Though, he injured that right wingtip when he crash-landed to save your life." She pointed at Garnet and pushed herself to a sitting position, exasperated. "I practically had to beat him with a stick to get him to hold still. Your fearsome dragon is really such a…little boy."

Kort smiled. "I'd have paid to see that."

Mia nodded and laughed. "So, how do you feel this morning? You look better, but…"

He closed the distance between them and she fell silent. Then she kissed him.

Kort's entire world brightened. Despite the remnants of his earlier pain he pulled her into an embrace and their tongues touched. He rubbed a hand up her arm, down her throat, over her breast and she responded with a throaty moan. His blue aura spiked.

She broke the kiss long. "We can't. Isa. She's got my dragon, Lucan, and who knows how many of your warriors. We have to go after her. We've a wizard to find, and I need your help."

Garnet stirred from his slumber and raised a wing, exposing them to more rays of morning sunlight spilling through the canopy above. Kort rose to his feet and stared down at Mia.

"What wizard?"

Mia stood and pointed. "Your mother tells me your dragon knows the way to Alastair Krogh."

"Krogh. No way, Mia. We're not going near him." Kort shook his head vehemently, but when he looked at her he realized she wasn't going to listen. "You don't understand. He won't help us no matter what we say. He refuses to get involved."

"Kort, we have to find him. Your mother told me he's got friends—the Others, or something like that—and that I should go to him if something happened to you. She said he's our best hope."

"I'm fine," Kort growled. "But there's bad blood between them, Mia. Alastair Krogh will never help us. This is a terrible idea. I wo—"

Mia turned and walked away, throwing her thumb over her shoulder at Garnet. "Your dragon and I are going to find that wizard. What happened to you *and your entire squadron* last night shows how bad things have gotten. Now, you can go home and try things your way if you want, but we're listening to Queen Elissabet."

Kort stood there gaping for a moment, fists on hips, but then Garnet nosed him in the chest. He scratched the dragon's chin…and then took an astonished step back when the beast spoke to him.

"I'm obligated to accompany your princess because there's bound to be danger along the way to Alastair's hideout"—the big fire-breather stared intensely at him—"and I promised your mother I'd see Mia safely there. If there's any hope that wizard will help us rescue Magnus, I'm not turning back. So, are you coming with us or what?"

Chapter 32

Kort gazed up at the sheer cliff face of solid quartz rock toward The Shrine, still reeling from the fact that his dragon could speak. Mia had seemed to take it in stride.

"Take us to the top, Garnet."

The dragon's injuries kept him from flying for much with both of them, but digging in deep with his mighty claws the fire-breather scaled the wall. The ascent was slow. Kort sensed his dragon was hurting and scowled in anger.

Mia held tight to his waist the whole time, and he imagined her fear. "Don't look down."

"No worries," she answered, her lips near his ear causing a shiver of pleasure down his spine.

The Dragon Shrine of Chalvaren was erected on a natural fault line, a giant crevasse that divided the continent east to west. It had seemed a natural stop on the way to Krogh's, because Kort owed it to Mia to help her understand all of what she was fighting for—and it wouldn't hurt to build up some divine goodwill with reflection and prayer.

"I originally wanted to show you this on a bright and cheery day," he admitted. "Not today. Not with everything devastated like this." Not with all they had to do. Still, he felt the time would be well spent. Unless…did she know the names of the dragons who died? Was that possible? Likely, no. He would reveal what her father had denied her by taking his family from Chalvaren.

"Garnet, can you make it?" Mia asked as the dragon paused, huffing. A low rumbling growl was her answer, and then a renewed climb up the sheer rock face.

"He's strong. He can do this," Kort said. As long as they didn't ask him to overburden his wounded wings.

The safety of flat ground dropped away beneath them, but Garnet finally reached a plateau and hauled them up over the edge. Mia looked over Kort's shoulder at the open-air temple that was revealed and asked, "What is this place?"

Kort smiled grimly but said nothing. She would soon learn.

Garnet lumbered across the grass toward the shrine. Round columns of bleached white stone supported its roof, each sculpted with an image of Chalvaren's deities, fierce guardians of this land with expectation carved in their stone eyes. This was one of the most significant places in this world, not only for Kort personally, but for almost every other elf ever. It was a painful reminder, but at least by the end of the night Mia would be whole in her knowledge of the history of their world.

"Kort?" Mia asked. "Is this a temple?"

Garnet stopped. Ahead were wide, terraced marble stairs.

Kort dismounted and took Mia's hands. He led her down Garnet's bended knee to the soft grass then gestured to the temple with his right hand. "Yes," he said. "This is where we ask for the blessings we need."

She looked up at him, her face filled with awe. She said nothing.

He pointed at her chest, then off across the meadow. "The crevasse where they harvested the Dragonstone is just over there, but this temple is where they chronicled it. I want you to read the story on the walls. Then I want you to join me and ask Varik for his blessing."

Mia peered up at the columns, pointed and called the sculptures of the elven deities by name. "Varik. Tempest. Octavianus. Kendelle. Lactacious. Marineth. Delsin. The gods of Chalvaren."

Kort pulled her hands to his lips, kissed them, and nodded. "You know them all."

"My father and mother taught me." She shifted to look at him, and he read gentle comprehension of shared heritage in their green depths. "My mother prayed every night. We recited their names together…but this…?" She strode forward, an expression of excitement in her green eyes.

He followed her up the wide, white stone stairs. Mia stopped at the top. Grand stone walls rose for at least seven stories around them, and an ornate, white granite altar occupied the shrine center.

"We should go inside," Kort said.

He followed her to the altar but stood back, letting her engage the shrine in silence. First she looked at the altar and sucked in a hard breath upon seeing the gifts that covered it, obscure offerings representing elven life and gratitude. A shard of valuable dragon ore rested amongst them. A fine carved arrowhead lay next to it. A golden chalice. Dried flower heads. A child's doll. Kort just stared and wished he'd brought something of value.

"I want to leave something for Varik," Mia announced. She reached into the leather pouch that dangled from her belt and retrieved three black dragon scales, each the size of her palm, which she'd collected and carried with her since the day she met Magnus. "I always thought they might be good luck."

She laid the scales on the polished granite altar alongside the other gifts. Kneeling, she bowed her head, steepled her hands and said, "For my dragon child—for Magnus, Varik. I offer these, and I beg for his safety."

Kort knelt beside her, mirroring her actions but raising his voice. "Protect Magnus until we find him, Varik. Show us the way to him. Show us the way. Chalvaren needs your blessing."

"*We* need your blessing, too," Mia said, reaching to take his hand. "Bless our union, Varik. I ask for your fortune to smile on our love, on our future. I offer the only things I have—my strength, my wisdom, my hope and my joy—and I offer you my fears and my worries of loneliness in exchange for your courage."

She squeezed Kort's hand, and Kort blanched, cowed. *Mia.* If this woman would pray beside him forever, he knew any future was possible. She was the other half of him. She was the better half of him. She was perfect.

"Show us the way to blend our auras for good," he added, remembering the problem that had distressed Mia so greatly. She gave him a grateful look, and then they closed their eyes and knelt in silence for moments that seemed to stretch out into eternity.

Kort finally opened his eyes. The Dragonstone sparkled on Mia's chest, tiny beads of multicolored light swirling around the artifact. *Ghostfire.* And it was growing. When he saw that, he dared let himself smile.

†††

A dragon roared, and Mia looked around.

"Was that Garnet?"

She'd assumed it was; he waited outside the temple on the wide white stones, and she'd thought she recognized the dragon's voice, his tenor, the vibrancy of his call. But it wasn't Garnet. It wasn't a single dragon at all but a chorus that emanated from the Dragonstone. A swirl of sparkling ghostfire wisped up out of the amethyst, so she pulled it from her neck and laid it on the altar.

Kort grasped her arm. "Watch out, Mia."

She let him tug her a few steps away, and they both watched the stone with rapt attention. Suddenly the temple was full of dragons— or rather of the souls of the dragons living in the Dragonstone. The beasts rose and took shape, their ghostly pale bodies outlined by the color of their breeds. Mia should have hid her face in fear, but these were the most ethereal and beautiful creatures she'd ever observed, and she couldn't look away. Strong. Defiant. Larger than life.

"The spirits of dragons," she whispered.

As each dragon soul swirled from the heart of the Dragonstone, a flash of an element corresponding to its type fired to life—wind, water, fire and earth—before it flew to a section of the shrine's stone wall, each coming to rest by a separate plaque. Above it all, the sculptures burst to life, animate and invigorated if still anchored to their pedestals. Mia scrambled to examine each.

"Oh, look at that!" she said.

Kort joined her, grasping her hand. She needed his strength as she read. She leaned into him while the stories on the Dragon Shrine's walls came to life, showing her the tragedy of the past twenty-five years, showing her the lost dragons and their heart's desires, showing her more than any history book could tell her.

"They all...died?"

Kort looked unable to answer, he was so overcome by awe. "These plaques and carvings were commissioned by my parents to honor the dragons and warriors lost in the battle against Malachai, and later those lost to Isa. I've never seen them come to life like this." He glanced over at her. "But the Dragonstone's never been in the temple until today."

Mia moved to the first section of carved story. "It's Isa." Her aunt was much younger and more beautiful, but a darkness surrounded her that seemed to ooze from the shadowy-seeming wizard looming next to her. "He corrupted her...?"

She felt Kort move close. "The story I was told as a child was that Malachai and Isa sent ten dragons into the crevasse to harvest the Dragonstone, all against Chalvaren law. Worse, the High Elven Magic Council suspected he'd entranced both dragons and elves with black magic. They demanded he stop and turn over his ill-gotten gains, not yet ready to pursue a more deadly punishment—mostly because they were afraid of him. And they had every right to be. He'd grown more powerful than they'd ever imagined."

Mia said nothing, just waited, horrified.

"Malachai refused to obey. He wanted the power of the Dragonstone so badly he was willing to sacrifice everything."

"All to rule Chalvaren? Even though he was already an impossibly powerful wizard?"

Kort nodded. "And so it came to war when he attempted to assassinate my father and corrupt the wizards on the Council."

Mia watched then, watched the various tales of the conflict unfold. The story of each dragon who died that day, each sacrifice for the sake of greed, was crushing. She pulled Kort along behind her.

"Such amazing creatures," she murmured. "And every single one lost to Malachai's greed and evil."

"Yes," Kort agreed.

"But your people and these dragons stopped him. The Council and—"

Kort pointed to the sixth section of wall, and a plaque. Lachlan Elias stood nearby, carved in stone, a magic bow in his hands. A ghostly water dragon twisted beneath the carving, and Mia read the name from the inscription. "'MacAndrew'...?"

"My father's dragon. Five years after Malachai died, Isa attacked Castle Elias. She came after the artifact."

"He...he died in the attack?"

"My father never took another dragon to his heart."

How horrible. Losing a dragon would be...

"No wonder Lachlan evaded my questions," Mia whispered. Images of Magnus yipping as Isa dragged him away surged through her mind, and she fisted her hands on her hips and pressed forward to the next panel.

"That's a silver," she guessed. "An ice dragon linked to the element of water like Isa's."

Kort's eyes flooded with tears and he didn't reply.

Mia knelt and traced her fingers in the runes on the plaque. "'Luxovious'... And 'Kort Elias.'"

She solemnly stood and studied the magnificent silver. Riderless, the dragon's ghost-like soul reared beside a carved image of a very young boy, which made Mia swing around and gasp. "*Your* dragon? You look like you're about five years old in this sculpture."

Kort hung his head, unable to look.

Mia grasped his arms. "What happened?"

"They refused to let me ride him, my mother forbade it, but Luxovious followed MacAndrew into battle against Isa."

"He...?" She tightened her grip on his forearm, but Kort still didn't look at her. "How sad. And he was just like VanZanz?"

Kort turned, his eyes burning. "They were nest-mates. Brothers."

Mia shook her head, seeing that he blamed himself. "You were only a child, Kort. Luxovious made his own choice. You did nothing wrong, yet you blame yourself?"

Kort pulled himself free of her grip. "I never should have listened to my mother. I could have saved him!"

"I see." It made sense now, his burning desire to protect dragons. Why he'd defined himself by his work with the Riders. Why he'd risked his life to find Magnus in the first place. Why he was so angry at his mother. "I see that your whole life has been about making that right."

He swallowed, hard. "I'd have still been the same person if it didn't happen...."

Mia shook her head, and she caressed his handsome face. Her heart ached for him. She shuddered at the thought of losing Magnus forever like that. "I love who you've become, but no. And when will you be able to let this go?"

Kort just looked away and tugged her toward the next set of carvings. "Never."

This wall was shocking to Mia. Theo Ansgar loomed above her, larger than life, a much younger man.

"My father," she whispered.

He was depicted as a fierce elven warrior clad in leather and mail, a heavy broadsword lifted above his head. Mia reached out to touch the sculpture, wanting to connect with him, wanting his soul to come to life, wanting to speak to him...but none of that happened. And when she narrowed her gaze on the dragon, she realized that it too was just a carving. And: "It's Garnet!"

"Your father led the fight against Isa when she came for the Dragonstone that day, and yes, he rode his dragon, Garnet. My father put Garnet and I together after Theo left. He thought that somehow we might save each other from our grief."

The pieces were all falling together, Mia decided. But as Kort's strong arms supported her, she heard the lonesome call of the mighty red dragon who awaited them at the edge of the shrine, and she knew for certain that he too still grieved for the vanished Theo Ansgar.

Chapter 33

Isa stood as the shadow elves brought the young black dragon to her shrine in Castle Cumberlae. The Aurora had not come easily, and the guards, though each strong and vicious, bore bloody bite marks. They'd eventually bound his claws and wings, and muzzled his mouth.

"So much vigor for one so young," Isa said with a smile. "Magnus, did he say his name was? So special. He'll be perfect for Malachai. Do not injure him. I don't want a single scale out of place."

The greenish-gray shadow elves muscled the amber-eyed dragonlet up close. Isa reached out to touch him, and Magnus lunged. If his mouth hadn't been chained shut, she'd have lost her arm. This drew a delicious smile to her face.

"Tonight, little one, you meet your destiny."

Magnus hissed and jumped backward, shaking off his captors. The shadow elves sprang to their feet and subdued him by working in tandem, grinding his head into the stone floor. Only as a growl of hatred bubbled up in the dragonlet's throat did Isa nod her approval.

"Let's get on with it, shall we?" she asked, striding along the altar and turning her attention to a leather-bound grimoire resting between the two golden urns. Tracing a finger down one page, Isa read the words aloud to a spell of conjuring. The two urns came to life, pulsing against the altar's red velvet cover.

Isa poured a pitcher of oil into a shallow dish and lit it. As she tossed in several strands of her ebony hair, the flaming bowl crackled to life.

"Yes," she called. "That's right. Come to me, Malachai!"

Magnus growled as the acrid smell of Isa's burning hair filled the chamber. Isa just kept chanting.

"Malachai!" she paused to call. "Revive our son and let me see you both! I bring you gifts, my love. An Aurora-class dragon, and the Dragonstone of Chalvaren!"

Black smoke wafted from the larger urn, and a voice. "Releeeeeeasssse meeee…"

Isa froze, ecstatic. She'd seen and felt vibrations before, but she'd never heard Malachai's voice. Her heart danced with anticipation, and she stole a glance back at the spirit dragon. "So, he *is* valuable. I thought so when I found he could talk."

Magnus struggled against the shadow elves. Isa curled her lip, walked over to them and plucked a scale from his neck. Magnus exhaled, shuddered, and tried to shake his head, but his captors held him tight. Isa drifted back to the altar and placed the iridescent black scale in the burning bowl. The fire surged higher and the dragon scale glowed.

"Yes," Isa hissed. "It's working. I offer you the conduit of ultimate power, Malachai!"

The ghostly voice came again. "Releeeeeeasssssse meeee…"

Isa watched with reverent glee as more black wisps drifted up from the ashes in the urn and twisted together midair. Her heart pounded as she turned her eyes on the smaller urn and tiny tendrils of smoke coiled up from the lip of the container. Her son. Her arms ached to hold him. The boy's essence couldn't yet re-form from his ashes, but maybe tonight…

With an unsteady voice she called out, "Come back to me, Son. Join your father."

Pivoting back to the grimoire, she read more words of magic and pulled the Dragonstone from around her neck. She held the jewel up to the altar and shouted, "Cross the plane of death, Malachai! Bring my son back to me!"

Magnus snorted and growled where he stood then whipped his tail around to bash one of the shadow elves with pointed spikes. The demonic guard grunted, knees buckling, but his partner took up the slack and strong-armed Magnus back into place.

Isa ignored them all. Placing the Dragonstone in the bowl of fiery oil, she chanted a few final words and braced herself for the answer to her prayers.

"Release them back to me!"

The flames and the oil twisted and bubbled. The Dragonstone surged with fire and then...lost its facets and melted into a shapeless mass of ooze, its purple color dissolving and rushing out into streaks in the oil. One final belch from the muck extinguished Isa's sacrificial fire, shadowy wisps of smoke disintegrated back into the two golden urns, and all hope squeezed out of her heart.

A bloodcurdling scream of rage filled Isa's altar room, and almost all of Cumberlae.

Chapter 34

As they left the Dragon Shrine, Kort saw a deep pool of mountain-fed river water. He insisted they stop their ride, saying, "Garnet needs to drink, and we both need a bath."

"A meal might do us good as well," Mia agreed.

She looked around for edible plants while he stripped down and got into the pool, letting the cold water ease his wounds. She joined him a short time later, while Garnet swam in the deepest section, drinking his fill of freshwater and gobbling down fish.

The dragon turned several fish over to Kort, who lit a fire and cooked them with the plants Mia harvested while she washed greasy ointment from her hair. A bright midday sun dried their clothes while they ate, and soon they were back on their way to finding Alastair Krogh.

"Garnet," Mia said, stroking the dragon's neck as he carried them through the forest. "Why didn't you ever speak before the attack last night? Many people didn't think you *could* speak. I certainly didn't."

Kort leaned in, eager to hear his dragon's voice again, eager to understand the change in the beast.

"When your father left, I lost my words...."

"You missed him too? So much that you took a vow of silence?" Mia asked.

It was a simple enough explanation, Kort thought, and the dragon's silence all these years spoke volumes of his love for Theo Ansgar.

He asked, "What changed, Garnet?"

The dragon's chest expanded with a sigh. "When Mia arrived with Magnus, *everything* changed. But when I was bound last night by the witch's black magic, when I realized your anguish that I might die…well, that startled my voice awake again."

Mia's hand found Kort's face behind her, and she sighed too. "I think he loves you," she said.

Kort placed a gentle kiss on her ear; then he let Mia place his hand on Garnet's neck so he could stroke the dragon's hide as well.

The journey did not take much longer. Their destination was an incredibly tall, sprawling house deep in the woods. Three dragons stood guard.

Kort assessed the house as Mia thrust her shoulders back and said, "So. This is where our friend is hiding. Alastair Krogh, the wizard responsible for killing Malachai and driving Isa insane before running off to be alone."

"He wasn't the only one involved, Mia," Kort pointed out. Malachai had needed to be stopped. He just should have been stopped earlier, and Isa with him. "The whole council made the decision together. And now Isa is killing them off one by one…."

Garnet walked up to the three dragons, who eyed him speculatively. One, a water dragon bearing green scales flecked with gold, spoke. It surprised Kort. Could all dragons speak, or only the primary elementals? Why didn't they? Did many have the capacity of language and choose not to bother?

"Our master doesn't tolerate visitors. What is your business here?"

Garnet regarded the green with respect and nodded, but he countered, "In this case he might consider an exception. Mia"—he gestured back with his head—"brings news about your master's brother, Lucan Brix."

The second dragon, white as the brightest moonlight, rustled his wings and took on an aggressive posture that Garnet copied. "I don't think we recognize the name."

Kort's heart hammered, and he assessed the home for a second entry. Would this escalate into a fight?

"What's your plan if they decide to engage?" he whispered to Mia.

"They won't. They *can't*. They must grant us permission to see Krogh." She strode forward as if the guardians had no choice. "I have everything they need to see right here."

Kort rushed to keep up. When he began to talk, Mia shushed him, tugging out the golden chain of the Dragonstone as she did. She held the gem high. "Dragons, forgive me, but I must see your master."

All three guardians bent their knees and lowered their heads, and Mia marched past. Kort followed under a tall arched walkway, glancing nervously at Krogh's dragons. Garnet fell in line, and soon they were all past.

Once they were through Alastair Krogh's guards, Mia dropped the Dragonstone back onto her chest and grasped the two circular knobs on the house's immense front doors. Yanking them open, she snatched a torch off the wall to light their way and waved it side to side in front of them.

"We'll go right," she decided.

"Send Garnet ahead. Just in case," Kort said, eyeing the incredible height of the ceilings.

"What do you think will happen? Isn't this your uncle?"

Kort took her torch then stepped in front of her. "I don't know what will happen, and I don't want to lose you. Not here or anywhere."

He took her hand, and they started down the corridor, her body pressed close to his. Despite the tingling warmth from her taut nipples grazing his back, he couldn't help muttering, "This is a bad idea."

"Get on with it, already," she hissed. "Worrying isn't going to help anyone."

The damp stone hallway wended downward. When Kort stopped once and called back to Garnet, the swish of a scaled tail on stone informed him all was well in the rear. Still, he held the torch up to his face and said, "Alastair won't help us, Mia. He's a coward."

She shrugged. "That may be true, but I intend to give him the chance to redeem himself. Your mother suggested this, and I trust her. Do you want to wait outside?"

Kort ground his teeth. "I'm not letting you go in there alone."

She smiled. "Then, Prince Charming, *get going.*"

Prince Charming? Kort suddenly wished Lachlan hadn't read him the story of Cinderella as a boy. Insulted, he pressed onward, and after another turn they found a tall arched wooden door with a green light glimmering underneath.

"This is it," Mia said, excited.

Kort raised his hand to knock, but Mia seized his fist. "No. We don't ask. Just go in. We're here because he owes us."

"Things don't work like that here on—"

He never got to finish his protest. Mia stalked inside, and Kort shuffled in behind her. The room was enormous, and Garnet easily followed.

Mia advanced, shoulders square, gait confident, long blonde hair cascading down around her hips. "I understand a wizard lives here. Is that true?" she called out.

Kort looked around, taking stock. Alastair Krogh actually had a ton of equipment and components, including toads in glass containers on shelves and cat-sized scorpions in haphazard wooden cages. He looked at the poisonous creatures with contempt. He didn't want one of those insects anywhere Mia. One sting could kill a man.

An older, silver-haired elf with a widow's peak stepped from the shadows. He was dressed in a cloak to fend off a chill in the room, brown trousers, and boots. Kort noticed the outline of a longsword at his side, which prompted a step closer to Mia. "A wizard? I'm just an old man with odd ways, I'm afraid. Who are you, young lady, and how did you get past my guards?"

"My name is Mia Ansgar, and your guardians can be charmed, wizard. But that is not the point." She stared the old man down. "I understand you might be of a mind to lend your services to Castle Elias. Would you finally be willing to sacrifice your life and your soul for what is right, Alastair Krogh?"

The wizard stepped back. Mia advanced and planted her palms on the middle of the table where his crystal ball held court with ancient maps of Chalvaren and a grimoire or two. Kort crossed his arms against his chest and admired her bluntness.

The wizard twisted his fingers haphazardly in the air. "I've gone down that road, Mia Ansgar. It doesn't pay well."

"What? How dare you?" Mia spat.

Alastair met her glare for glare. "How dare I *what*?"

Kort slammed his fist down on the table. Garnet rustled his wings, and a low growl bubbled up from the dragon's throat.

Alastair winced, his eyes narrow. "Ah. You must belong to Elissabet. How is our queen—Kort, is it? *Nephew.*"

Mia nodded. "We are here from Queen Elissabet, and she's prepared for you to name any price to help us, Alastair. It is time to end this madness that has embroiled Chalvaren for far too long."

Alastair's candles and the multicolored light from his crystal ball shone on Mia's face and lit up her green eyes, which sparkled with anger. Kort stared at her, more in love than ever. Mia held nothing back emotionally, and never had she looked so alluring, so bright and ethereal. Was it closeness to this man's obvious magic that refined her features and increased her beauty, or was it that their time in the Dragon Shrine changed her? She was certainly more self-assured than he'd ever seen. The swish of the dragon's tail behind him returned him to the moment.

"My plight is simple," Mia continued with a sigh, and she held out her hands. "An evil you conjured into being before I was born has taken something precious from me."

"I don't do theft," Alastair said indignantly. "Or evil."

His long silver hair sparkled in the light, but when he moved a hand toward the heavy broadsword at his hip, Kort jumped in front of Mia and jabbed a finger at him. "Garnet!"

The fire dragon came to life, lurching around Kort and toppling the wizard backward onto the floor, papers scattering in the wind created by his sudden movement. He pinned the wizard to the floor with two enormous claws and snarled, "She is my rider's chosen princess, and any threat to her is a threat to me. And the theft she speaks of is my offspring, Magnus. I trust it is your heart's desire to see us all reunited."

Krogh stared at the red dragon, wide-eyed. His jaw worked soundlessly, but his body remained frozen in place.

Mia made her way forward and shoved Garnet's head out of the way. "You're a liar. Your version of not doing theft or evil is a sham."

"Liar?" Alastair hissed. "I'm many things, but never a liar."

"You're a liar and a *coward*." Mia punched out her words with her index finger. "You and your worthless High Elven Magic Council. None of you did a damn thing to help Isa after you killed her husband. Malachai's death may have been justified, but your neglect afterward was not."

"Don't you dare speak to me about the principles of mercy." Alastair seethed, attempting to force himself free.

"*You* did this to Chalvaren. You just let Isa go insane. Your hiding and cowardice bred Chalvaren's perfect enemy. After killing her beloved—"

"Malachai needed to die," Alastair interrupted, squirming under Garnet's claws. "And I wasn't the only one there who agreed. This was justice. Chalvaren would never have survived if Malachai had killed Lachlan. If he'd corrupted the Council."

"You made Isa watch! You made her watch as all she cared about was destroyed!"

Alastair gazed at Mia with a crinkled squint. Mouth open, he gave a hesitant nod. "That was part of the punishment as well. There was little evidence she'd participated in the early crimes but…well, I'd hoped she would learn from his mistake. We all did."

Mia drew back, disgusted. "You created a monster. Why didn't you have the wisdom to shield her, to protect her from her grief? Maybe she was just a teenage girl who got caught up in something awful!"

Kort blinked. He'd only ever thought of Isa as a heartless witch, but perhaps she'd been something else once. Perhaps there was a time when she could have been brought back from the edge of insanity and evil.

Perhaps.

"She needed to internalize the penalty for practicing black magic," Alastair growled. "You weren't there. You could never understand the risk of letting Malachai live."

"I'm not *talking* about Malachai. You should not have made Isa watch. It would have been almost kinder to kill her."

"And wiser," Alastair hissed. "She was already insane by that point. Malachai turned her to darkness, and she fed off him like an addiction. Her brother could not change her. He tried, for Varik's sake. Nothing I did justifies Isa's actions. At any time she could have left Malachai, could have chosen a path of peace."

"But she didn't," Kort said.

"No, she didn't."

"But what would it have cost to show her some mercy?" Mia asked. "And what gain have you from forcing such misery upon her? What could that do but confirm what she was becoming? And, how long has Chalvaren suffered since? The dragons and elves she has killed...the eggs she has sacrificed... All of it! Perhaps it could have been avoided. Through mercy."

Alastair swung his gaze over to meet Kort's, and remorse showed in the wizard's face. Mia stood frozen, tears pouring down her cheeks.

"She was my aunt. She could have been better. Don't you see what your cowardice has cost me?"

Kort slid around Garnet's legs and grasped Mia by the waist. He pulled her backward, away from Alastair, but she continued to weep.

"He helped make Isa what she is, and he doesn't even care."

"Shh," Kort said. "Quiet now, Mia. Stop this at once. I told you he was a coward—that he'd never help us. Why do you think he ran in the first place?" He held her tight to his chest as she began thrashing. "All we can do is go forward."

She pulled back and stared at him. "But your mother... She said he'd help us."

Kort shook his head. "Remember what I showed you in the shrine. We must deal with Isa ourselves. We don't need Krogh. And, look." He pointed around the room. "He's paid the price of his sins, Mia, in the curse of having no one to love him, no one to share his days, no one to care about."

"What I saw in that shrine, Kort? Isa as a young girl. She was so beautiful then. I believe she could have been good. It's all his fault that—"

"No," Kort said, stopping her. "That's not true. He's right that she made her own choice. Isa still refuses to be redeemed. He may hold some culpability, but this isn't all Alastair's fault. She could have forgiven him. As we must. As we will."

Mia slumped in his arms. "I just want Magnus back, Kort. I... He's innocent. I won't see him sacrificed or turned into some shadowy killer. Isn't that why she would take him from us?"

"We'll get him back, Mia." Kort shook his head then turned her face to his. "I swear to you, we'll bring your Aurora home. Magnus will be free, or I will never ask another thing of you for all our years together. I will follow where you lead, and we will find happiness somehow. But I *will not fail*."

He thumbed away her hot, angry tears and cupped her face in a gentle loving embrace. She took his cheeks in her hands, and then she kissed him.

"An Aurora?" Alastair rumbled. "A spirit dragon hatched…?" He struggled to lift Garnet's claw. "You don't mean to tell me you let that crazy witch get her hands on it."

Mia lifted her hands. "Yes. Magnus is my dragonlet, an Aurora, and Isa Ansgar abducted him from Castle Elias last night—after slaughtering many others."

Alastair groaned and shoved again at Garnet's claw. "If she corrupts an Aurora he could call every dragon on Chalvaren into service. The danger of her would treble. Call off your dragon. Let me up. Let's see what I can do."

"Keep your claws ready, Garnet," Mia said, "but let's hear what the wizard has to say."

The red pulled away and let Alastair up.

Chapter 35

Magnus wailed out a cry of agony, fighting his bindings. Isa spun to face him. Her shadow elves rushed to her side, pulling her away from the red velvet–draped altar, upon which sat her failure in the form of the two golden urns. Even through her grief, she was pleased by their attention.

"No. Stop him," she growled.

But it was too late; they should never have left him unattended. Magnus tore at the chains on his muzzle, breaking them. He wrestled free from his other bindings then, and in one smoothly executed pounce he tore the head off her fiercest warrior. He gobbled it down, roared, and turned on the next.

Isa stepped back, afraid for the first time in ages. Her second warrior sacrificed his right arm to a bite, and Magnus snarled as he chewed. The dragon advanced, and the wounded shadow elf toppled Isa's altar in an attempt to get away.

"VanZanz!" Isa screamed.

The rampaging dragonlet turned, his long tail switching back and forth.

"VANZANZ!"

Magnus crouched and stalked Isa, his mouth full of bloody, spiky teeth. Isa tried to breathe but couldn't. He was *magnificent*. Even as the dragonlet keyed in on her, she relished his grandeur, his killing perfection, his focus.

He prowled across the floor and stared at her, then hesitated, whined, and stared. She gasped as he gave her one of the most intense—was it *forgiving*?—gazes she'd ever seen. And, was that sorrow she saw? It was as if this dragon saw into the depths of her soul and recognized her pain. Isa lost herself in his amber eyes, and she reached out to connect.

He snorted. She pulled back.

"What is this?" she murmured. "Are you reaching out to me?"

Why would he? She'd attacked his home, killed many dragons and elves there, maybe killed some of his family. Could this spirit dragon really see why she'd done it and forgive her? That sort of connection...frightened her.

"No. I've been here before, Aurora. Trust is for fools. As is forgiveness."

Magnus's gaze hardened, and then he pounced.

The chamber's double doors blasted open, and VanZanz burst through. His icy breath immobilized Magnus mid-leap. Isa sucked in a sharp breath, and then her dragon moved close and nosed her. She released the breath and reminded herself that forgiveness was for the weak. There was only power.

She bound the frozen dragonlet herself, perfectly, giving annoyed glances at the shadow elves who'd done a terrible job and allowed him to escape. One was dead and the other now lacked an arm. "Now I'll have to replace them too."

Magnus shivered and whined as the icy shell of VanZanz's elemental breath weapon melted, and he gave a low keening cry. The sound resonated deep in Isa's soul, so she caressed him and said, "I know you want freedom, little one, and you shall soon have it."

The dragonlet cried out and struggled against his leather and silver bindings.

"Don't feed your suffering, dragonlet. Your grief will pass," Isa growled, her eye twitching. She honestly hated the dragonlet's cries. While she despised almost every living soul on Chalvaren, dragons were different. She pitied this one. He simply wanted to return to his home and family. On so many levels, Isa understood.

However, she had no intention of allowing anything of the sort.

Disgustingly late, shadow elf guards rushed in. Isa fought back her annoyance and said, "Take him below to the holding area. Don't hurt him, though. He must be in perfect order for Malachai. Once I obtain the true Dragonstone, the spirit dragon will be my gift to him."

VanZanz roared in approval.

Isa turned back to the Aurora. "You are a lucky boy, Magnus. You will serve one of the greatest wizards Chalvaren has ever known."

Despite the muzzle, Magnus hissed and attempted to take off her arm. Only after VanZanz snapped his jaws in a direct warning did the dragonlet still.

The strangest noise suddenly sounded, bubbling up from the dragonlet's throat. Isa stepped back, amused, and reached out to steady herself on VanZanz.

"Is that a purr?"

Magnus locked stares with her dragon, still purring, and VanZanz stepped closer, cocking his head. Isa hated the look in his eyes, so she cuffed her silver hard under the chin. As VanZanz stumbled back she hissed, "Look away. Don't let him deceive you."

She glanced around at her shadow elves, who stood stupidly doing nothing, and sighed. "Guards, clean up this mess and get him settled." She turned back to her dragon. "Don't engage the Aurora again, VanZanz. But stick with me. I just might let you have a taste of Lucan's flesh before we kill him."

The Aurora returned to his high-pitched, keening vocalizations that made Isa's eye twitch.

Chapter 36

Alastair had run to the crystal ball in the center of the room. As Mia approached him and the swirling orb of magic, a tic pulsed erratically in the wizard's jaw.

She leaned against the sturdy, waist-high wooden table. Opening her hand, hoping to make some sort of peace with the wizard, she said, "My father bred Magnus, so I've learned. He and my mother combined magic to lure dragons together to mate, and the spells they used produced the Aurora."

Alastair glanced at Kort and sighed. "Lucan sent you to fetch her or her father, didn't he? He knew that without the Dragonstone no one would ever end Isa's threat. Maybe it's time to call the council back together."

Mia glanced at Kort, whose lips were pressed into a pale, thin line. He was clearly angry at having been manipulated by Lucan, if that's what had happened. Were they both pawns in games greater than they realized? It did not matter, Mia decided. Their destiny was to save Magnus. Still, she gripped the wizard's table until her fingers ached.

"Damn them," Kort growled. "How dare they scheme to use me like this? Did my mother and your brother have this in mind all along?"

"Perhaps. Lucan Brix would betray anyone. He betrayed me. *Everyone* betrayed me," Alastair added.

Mia shook her head. "Okay, say that's true. Say it's all true, this game of blaming other people. None of this helps. The entire kingdom will fall if we don't get Magnus back from Isa. So, here, let's focus on that." She pointed. "Your crystal ball? May I? Perhaps we can find Magnus if we tap into your magic."

The wizard stepped forward like a child protecting a toy, but Mia pushed past him.

"No," she said, drawing the Dragonstone from her shirt and extending purple ghostfire toward the crystal ball. This kind of magic made sense to her. It was purely intuitive, and she could use the Dragonstone as a focus. "We will use this to look. To locate him. Show us what we need to see. *Show me the Aurora.*"

Alastair's spinning crystal ball settled onto images that seemed to be the interior of Isa Ansgar's castle, shadow elves marching here and there. The wizard flinched as Lucan Brix's body was revealed, hanging at a strange angle on a torture table. With his head tilted downward, Lucan's face was ruddy and showed deep purple-red marks, and Isa knelt close to him, a pair of shears in her hands.

Mia's stomach twisted. Lucan's blood dripped down into a small brass bowl below him. One of the wizard's magnificent ears, the one he adorned with gold hoops and precious jewelry, was missing its tip. A diamond stud poked up awkwardly from the center of the brass bowl.

Alastair drew in a sharp breath and frowned, and Mia said, "You do care for him, no matter what you say." Still, the wizard's expression showed he harbored resentment for his brother, so she pressed onward and said to the crystal ball, "Show me the spirit dragon. Show us Magnus."

The image blurred, and glittery shards of blue and gold static appeared. Mia sucked in a sharp breath, hoping to settle her nervous belly, but the image resolved into her bound and struggling dragonlet and anger coagulated hot in her veins. She wanted to reach through the crystal and rescue Magnus, wanted to strangle Isa Ansgar with her own bare hands. Mercy became a word she almost didn't understand.

"We had no idea you were in our future. Does Isa know about you yet, Mia?" Alastair asked, interrupting her thoughts. She'd been palming the crystal orb as if she could somehow comfort her Aurora, but she pulled back her hand.

"Me? What does it matter? This isn't about me. This is about Magnus."

Alastair shook his head. "I…I cannot help you. She's grown too powerful." He gestured at Lucan's broken body as some sort of evidence.

Mia's heart broke with the finality of his statement. "What? You'll leave your brother to die and this kingdom to suffer? You just saw— What's wrong with you? What would it take to motivate you?"

The old man turned to leave, hesitating at the door.

Kort came to Mia and embraced her, shaking his head. "Let the coward go. How much time must we waste before you realize he's useless?"

She stared at him. "Kort, we need *some*one to—"

"It's apparently not going to be him. Now can we see anything else in that ball?"

†††

"Such a waste," Isa murmured, glancing around her torture room.

It was then that she felt the scrying, the essence of eyes upon her. She allowed the intrusion even as she scraped the last drops of blood from her shears. Being watched excited her and made her want to perform, so she continued, "Such a pity, Lucan. All your potential wasted on the wrong side of my cause."

The wizard was done for. He wasn't dead—not yet—but he was in shock, waiting for her next round of punishment. She'd cut him so many times that he was close to bleeding out, his once magnificent body limp against her stainless steel table. And that *was* a shame. She'd liked Lucan. He was handsome and powerful, and they'd had relations once, after all. But that was a lifetime ago. Knitting her brows, Isa reached out and trailed one fingertip down his chest. When he groaned through his haze of pain, she didn't feel any remorse.

"Do you want to know the reason I saved you and the queen for last?" she whispered. "I wanted you to enjoy what I could never have: everything. Taking it from you brings me pleasure, Lucan."

"You won't win," her enemy replied. Though weak, his gravelly voice filled the room. "You'll never rule all of Chalvaren."

Isa leaned close to his bloody ear and ignored him. "I'm glad you can hear me, Lucan. Tell me, does it hurt? You're in shock now, I suppose, and numb. But I have another session planned after I pray with Malachai. It involves more...intimate parts of your body." She traced her finger toward his groin and giggled as Lucan's stomach muscles tensed. "It really is too bad you won't join me. You're well equipped to satisfy a woman—and eager, as I recall."

Lucan struggled away from her. "Black arts won't do it, Isa. You've become more powerful, yes, but you'll never be great enough to bring your perverse lover ba—"

Isa struck out, clawing the wizard's face. Lucan didn't move or fight back; he simply wheezed and went limp, which allowed the burst of sudden fear Isa felt to diminish.

"You may be right, wizard. Black arts won't do it, but the real Dragonstone will. Castle Elias tricked me once, but not again. I shall raise Malachai. Then all Chalvaren will be ours."

✝✝✝

Alastair Krogh hesitated, his hand on the door, his ear cocked toward the sounds from his crystal ball. Mia watched, her heart fluttering. Was this it? Had he finally heard something that mattered to him?

"She truly plans to raise Malachai from the dead? After all this time?"

Garnet growled from his position behind Mia, low and deep, causing her to glance from the wizard to the dragon and back. Alastair's expression settled into resolution. Odd, that he wasn't moved enough when every wizard in Chalvaren was being murdered, nor when a unique spirit dragon was kidnapped for sacrifice, nor when his brother was tortured, but if Isa revived Malachai it was a different thing altogether…? Perhaps it was a perverted sense of justice. Or perhaps he'd finally become scared enough to become brave.

"Up until now I thought she'd fail," the silver-haired wizard whispered. "The loss of the others was great, yes, but if she raises Malachai our entire world is doomed. We have no choice but to oppose her."

"No. None," Mia agreed. She relaxed her hold on the table. She had Krogh, and she knew it. Isa had just revealed her hand, and her one statement was something the wizard couldn't live with. "Malachai back from the dead. If *we* don't stop her, who will?"

"Dear gods," Kort said, following Mia's cue and hammering the point home as the crystal ball dimmed. "She's trying to raise Malachai? That's unholy, and he's even more evil than she is! If she succeeds, none of us will be safe. No one. No one on the entire planet. Not even you will be able to find a place to hide, Alastair!"

The silver-haired wizard covered his face with his hands.

Mia edged forward, a spark of hope cresting in her belly. "What are we going to do to end this, Alastair? Queen Elissabet said you're our only hope."

The wizard looked up, his eyes haunted. "Isa cannot. If she releases that *thing*..." He shook his head, the tension in his body becoming clearer and clearer. "How much does she know about you, Mia?"

"I don't know." Mia glanced down at the stone floor. "She registered something back at Castle Elias. Some familiarity, maybe...? The only thing I know for sure is that she now knows I gave her a paste replica of the Dragonstone."

Alastair laughed, a surprisingly booming sound. "No wonder she's furious! Oh, my dear Mia, you have no idea—"

"Of *what*, wizard?" Kort stepped forward, clearly furious, and Mia was afraid his anger would snap the tenuous thread of familiarity she and Krogh had built over the last few moments.

She raised one finger, asking Kort to back off. If he messed this up now she'd never forgive him. They needed Alastair. They needed his anger. They needed his magic. They even needed whatever strange creatures he might summon to help them crush Isa's plans. Queen Elissabet had said so.

"If Isa raises Malachai...all will suffer," Alastair said. "You must take Mia home, Kort. Hide her away. If that witch gets her hands on Mia and the real Dragonstone... Do not fear the artifact will not work for her. Mia could be turned."

Mia stared at the wizard, furious. "I guarantee you that will never happen."

Alastair sucked in a tight breath. "You have no idea what you would do, Mia, if the fates of those you love are demanded in trade. Isa Ansgar may ask just that."

Kort stepped forward. Jabbing his index finger into the wizard's chest he said, "She is above reproach, Alastair. She won't succumb to her aunt. She knows there is nothing more important than the lives of the innocent. *All* of them. No one life more important than the others. It is the way of our people."

Alastair shook his head sadly. He glanced at her. "No? Then your princess has no idea she will someday rear kings—maybe sooner than she thinks."

Nausea gripped Mia. She felt the room tilt, and she clung to the edges of the table to stabilize herself. Kort turned, searching her face and seeing the way she was standing.

"What's wrong with you?"

"Nothing." Mia shook her head again as his jaw tightened. "I'm fine."

But she wasn't. Something was different. Not wrong, exactly, but she couldn't shake the waves of queasiness from her belly.

Garnet approached and sniffed around her body. He whined out a note of concern, and Mia turned slowly to Alastair and said, "Wait… Do you mean…?"

No. NO. No. No. No. NO! This couldn't be possible! She set her hands on the table to keep the room from spinning. She willed them not to move but couldn't stop them. She instinctively clutched her flat belly as Kort rushed to her side, and he took both her arms and rubbed them, peered into her eyes then lowered his gaze to her belly. Mia's stomach lurched further, and Alastair rubbed his weary eyes with long, gnarled fingers.

Kort looked stunned. "Are you pregnant?"

Mia shook her head. "No, certainly not. I don't think so. Why would you ask that? I'm…I'm just worried about *him*." She gestured to the crystal ball, though the tiny image of the muzzled dragonlet in chains had disappeared. It broke her heart to remember Magnus bound, but she also realized she couldn't fight the truth. A pleasant truth. An amazing truth. They hadn't taken precautions. All those nights and afternoons locked in Kort's arms, the ways he'd given her body everything it wanted but she was afraid to ask for, all that erotic passion… She'd always desired a family of her own, wanted her happily-ever-after, and now her One True Love had granted her heart's deepest wish. Even if the timing couldn't have possibly been worse. Kort Elias had planted his seed in her body, and she would indeed someday rear Elias kings.

Assuming the world survived Isa's madness. Was this the truth her mother's prophecy had foretold?

The silver-haired wizard smiled as if he shared her pleasure. "By Varik, Mia, I'm glad for you." He eyed Kort and threw out his hand.

"What have you done by bringing her here? You must take her home at once, back to Castle Elias. This is no place for a pregnant elf!"

"No," Mia said. "He did not bring me, and he has no choice about me going forward. I've come this far, and I mean to see Magnus returned and Kort protected. We're not going anywhere except to deal with her."

She poked her finger at the crystal ball for emphasis, but another wave of nausea rolled over her and she grabbed the table for support. At the same time, a warmth glowed inside her that hadn't been there before this conversation. She would never be alone again. Not really. Kort Elias had forever dispelled that gnawing fear.

She was pregnant with his child.

Chapter 37

Kort's world spun one hundred and eighty degrees.

"Pregnant?" A wellspring of pride drew a smile so big that his face hurt. When he kissed Mia's forehead she looked up at him, reflected his smile back and wrapped her arms around his waist, and a sudden possessiveness washed through him so that he sheltered her in his arms. "Of course this changes everything, Mia."

"You have to take her home, Kort." Alastair Krogh was holding the broadsword he'd pulled from the sheath on his belt. Carved fighting dragons twined on the hilt, and the blade buzzed with multicolored energy. Solid dragon ore. A very impressive enchanted weapon.

Alastair sheathed the sword and began strapping on silver armor he drew off the wall. Donning a cloak, he tied his grey hair back into a tail then looked over at the two of them and said, "Take my house for the night. You need to rest and tend to Mia, Kort. I'll see what I can do to round up the Others."

"What? Who?" Kort asked.

"My associates. A handful of mages—elves, humans and dwarves—from the seven kingdoms. Your mother is not the only one who tries to keep this world running smoothly, even if I do my work from solitude and in secret rather than from a large castle."

"Queen Elissabet talked about realigning the magic council," Mia spoke up.

"That may be possible," Alastair agreed. "When the Others find out the Dragonstone has returned and Isa wants to get her hands on it as a means to raise Malachai—well, not all of them are cowards, and if Elissabet is okay with building the Council with wizards from other countries…"

Kort's heart pounded with excitement. "With the right powerful wizards working in unison we could take Castle Cumberlae. We could drag Isa Ansgar out by her black hair!" The idea of a massive frontal onslaught appealed to him. "But, first things first. Alastair's right. I want to get you back to Castle Elias and out of harm's way, Mia." He laid a gentle kiss on her head as Krogh collected his things and walked to the door.

"I'll be back before morning light," the silver-haired wizard said. "Make yourself at home here. But know, Kort, this is going to cost you. These people don't work for free."

Mia spoke up. "I have Queen Elissabet's word that you and whomever you require will be paid."

Alastair hesitated and pointed at Kort. "I want his word as well. If we are summoning the greatest powers from all seven countries—"

Kort motioned impatiently to the door. "Go! Your price will be paid. A share of Isa's treasure will be divided equally among all those who help."

Mia raised her hand and interjected, "Only if the Aurora and the prince are delivered safely back to Castle Elias with me."

The wizard chuckled and regarded each of them with twinkling grey eyes. "It'll cost you more than treasure, Prince. Think land. *Lots* of Elias land. Alliances. Spots on the Council. The never-ending protection of Castle Elias. My people don't come cheap."

"Don't forget fame, wizard." Disdain laced Kort's words, for he couldn't help seeing why his mother and Lucan had cut ties with their brother. Anyone who spent years doing nothing and then would bargain for personal gain deserved little respect. "Your friends will have the distinction of being the crew who slew Isa Ansgar. That should motivate them also."

Alastair nodded and left, and Kort watched until he disappeared through the door. The wizard's help brightened their prospect of success. One thing was for damn sure, though: He'd see Mia back in the safety of the bunker at Castle Elias.

He couldn't bring himself to tell her or press the issue. Not yet. She'd be too resistant to the idea. Maybe things would be easier in the morning.

"Let's see if we can find somewhere comfortable to rest."

She nodded and followed him, her hand clasped tightly in his.

The guest bedroom they found contrasted sharply with the rest of Alastair's home. It was spotless, well-lit, and while it wasn't the same as their space in the Castle Elias west tower it was a welcome place to rest. Garnet took up a watchful guard just outside.

"This should do," Kort said, closing the door. Then he and Mia stripped off their filthy clothes and collapsed in each other's arms, snuggling down between the sheets of the soft, down-stuffed feather bed.

"I'm exhausted," Mia whispered, folding herself into the crook of his arm.

He kissed her ear. "Try to get some sleep."

Lying there, he grazed his hand over her flat belly. He had no idea what to expect except for what he'd seen as his father cared for his mother during her three pregnancies, and thinking of Mia being stressed in any way disturbed him.

"The little I know about pregnant women is that they need to rest, need to be cared for, and like to eat. After we rest, I'm taking you back to the castle so Thorvid can fatten you up. Then I'll rejoin Alastair to deal with Castle Cumberlae—with reinforcements."

"Kort…" Mia turned to face him. "You could just let Alastair handle things. In fact, you *should*. Promise me you won't go."

"I love you, my beautiful Mia," Kort whispered, "but part of loving you means protecting you, especially now. And I promised to bring back Magnus!"

Her eyes got hard, as if she were preparing to argue. He didn't want that, so he kissed her instead. She cuddled closer. He nuzzled her soft, warm neck and thought about…how much he didn't know! To be honest, the entire notion of her pregnancy terrified him. What did he understand of being a father? Of being a husband to someone who was pregnant? Would Mia grow more fragile, like a tender flower that would die if she were touched in the wrong way? His mother had—

"Kort," Mia said, her voice clear and strong.

He turned. "Yes?"

"You're thinking too hard, sweetheart."

"What do you mean?"

"Your body is tense. You're holding me so tight I can barely breathe. What's wrong?"

He eased his vise-like grip on her. He'd wanted to protect her, and he intended to do so even though he didn't want to fight about it with her right now. She was so precious to him. He'd never wanted anything the way he wanted Mia at his side, and it rattled him.

When he began apologizing profusely she giggled and said, "Stop worrying! *Please,*" she added, nestling closer to his chest. Clasping his arm she said, "I have a solution. If you'll agree to let me come with you to Cumberlae, I'll promise to stay out of your way. I'll...go free Magnus while you and Alastair and his band of misfits handle Isa."

"No," Kort said. "That will put you in danger."

"So I'm to listen to you just like that? No discussion? No debate? Your word is final in this relationship?"

He heaved a deep breath. The last thing he was going to do was let her anywhere near Castle Cumberlae, not even if he had to tie her to Garnet's back with instructions for the beast to carry her out of harm's way. "Do you have any idea how wrong I was not to listen to you back at the castle when you asked me to see reason, to not go off into the night after her? I see that now, Mia, and I want you to see it too."

"I'd never intentionally put our child in danger, but I can help you get Magnus out by being sneaky. I—"

He silenced her with a kiss, and she relaxed when he cradled her face in his hands and stroked her jaw with his fingertips. But when he broke the kiss, Mia giggled.

Kort furrowed his brow. "What's so funny?"

She shrugged. "Nothing. Nothing at all. I was just remembering the last conversation I had with your mother before Garnet and I came after you." She yawned and smiled. "Something about kings needing strong queens or some such nonsense."

"Don't tell me you're starting to listen to my mother," he said, rolling his eyes.

"You know, you don't have to do everything. I'm right here, and I'm not so fragile I'm going to break."

"Good." Her words filled his heart with hope. "Mia, I want you here with me always."

"Me too," she said. "I really do."

He snuggled her closer and kissed her neck, pleased that she was seeing reason. "I'm glad."

"Yes." She wiggled closer to his raging erection. "I can tell."

He didn't know whether he was supposed to be mortified or totally happy. He chose to go with the latter.

"By the way," she continued, "we'll get married as soon as Alastair and his people extinguish the threat, okay?"

Kort laughed. "Finally, she officially accepts."

Mia laughed too, and he loved the sound, loved the expression in her eyes, loved every part of her. He lifted her left hand—the one that bore his grandmother's ring—and kissed it. But as his lips lingered there, Mia raised winged brows and added, "On one condition."

He stared at her. "Name it, woman."

"Make love to me."

Oddly enough, the idea gave him pause. "Er, do you think that's safe? I mean, what if…?"

She smiled. "If there's a child he'll be absolutely okay. He'll be even better if his mother feels safe and secure and loved in the arms of his father."

Kort's heart beat fast, and something primal washed through his chest. "Or her?"

Mia gave him a soft smile, drifted her fingers along his jaw and nodded. "Or her."

They knew each other's bodies now, and the urgent demands they'd felt before tonight were lessened. Kort eased himself into Mia's body softly, gently, with all the tenderness his heart and his body could deploy. She kissed him slowly, deeply, and her soft moans of pleasure, the way she said his name, filled him with hope. And auras melding or not—he couldn't bring himself to pay attention—the next few hours showed what a lifetime of this kind of love promised both of them.

Chapter 38

To hell with Lucan Brix. He was a pawn in this anyway. Still, damn him for what he'd said.

Isa swung her head back and forth, mulling over the situation and clenching her fists. She slipped through Castle Cumberlae, back to her private quarters, her head swimming with images. One was Malachai returned and vibrant, the thing she wanted more than life itself. Another was the faces of the wizards she hated.

"Damn hypocrites," she sneered. "They'll see. Once I get my hands on that Dragonstone, they'll all kneel. Once Malachai and our child are back we can start to set this world aright. I'm going to see Alastair Krogh pay, and I will ruin Elissabet Elias too. The first step is getting my hands on her offspring. Now, how can I do that?"

She slammed her fist into her palm and eyed her shard of the Dragonstone. Since it scorched her hand she'd relegated it to a stand constructed of shriveled dragon claws where it couldn't blister her skin. She could use its magic from here, though, and she intended to look in on those who'd been spying on her. With the right spell, she knew how to get to them. As long as Alastair activated his crystal ball.

†††

Mia awoke to the sound of Kort snoring softly beside her, which made her turn to face him. So handsome. So perfect. Everything she'd always hoped for in those days of solitude and loneliness on Earth.

She touched his square jaw and inhaled a deep breath of contentment before hearing Garnet snoring loudly outside. The noise reminded her of Magnus and made her smile, which dissolved into a grimace when she thought of what the Aurora might be going through in Isa's clutches. It was insupportable.

Twisting away from Kort, she considered what to do. A memory surfaced of her desire to reach through Alastair's crystal ball and grab Magnus, to throttle Isa where she stood. Could such a thing be done? Could the globe be used as a portal rather than a scrying device? Maybe, if Mia used the Dragonstone... At the very least she could see what was happening, and at the most she could reach through and bring back her dragonlet.

She tugged the sheets from her legs and sat up. If she could do that, see Magnus safely back here, then she and Kort would have nothing to argue about. Everything would be okay. Sure, they'd still have to mount a rescue effort for the others and destroy Isa, but... Her mind drifted to Pure and to Poseidon, to the captured Dragon Riders. How were they being treated? Were they bound like Magnus? Tortured like Lucan?

"Someone's got to end this," she murmured. First things first, though. She had to get her hands on Magnus.

She dressed quietly and sneaked back to the chamber with the crystal ball. Her mind was awash with plans to open a portal and bring Magnus back, and the possibility seemed more and more exciting with every breath. Her dragonlet returned, she and Kort could go back home. Alastair and his crew of Others could take care of the dirty work on their own. She'd make certain they were paid, and everything would be fine.

The ball sat quiet and cloudy, but Mia focused in. Her aura leapt from her hands onto it, shimmering images she longed for springing to life and spinning around the globe's expansive interior. Sunny days. Dragons protecting Castle Elias. She and Kort and everyone at peace. She even saw a vision of their child, a tiny version of both of them with blonde hair who sat in the shelter of Kort's strong arms.

Tears filled her eyes at such happy thoughts.

"God, *that's* what's inspiring all these emotions." Her hand instinctively found her belly as she added, "That's what I want. All of us together. Forever."

Yes, she wanted peace and home and family, her dragon on one side of her, her prince on the other, their extended family nearby, rejoicing, living in the sunshine, growing and prospering like the elves of old that her father once spoke of.

"I want all of that to come true," she murmured, "I want that to be a reality and not just a fairy tale. And my father spoke the truth on so many other topics, so I know it can happen."

Mia tapped her finger on the crystal ball, wondering about something else that had been bothering her. Isa was the one link left to her father. She'd made many horrible decisions, but Isa was powerful and...perhaps she could be reformed. Perhaps her aunt could make reparations and become a force for good. It was unlikely, but imagine the triumph of such an accomplishment. Imagine what could be achieved working *with* a woman who could summon shadow demons and capture entire squadrons of dragons with a single spell. What goal of peace and prosperity couldn't be realized?

Of course, she was being overly optimistic, Mia knew. Hope was an ethereal thing, and every single person she'd met on Chalvaren said it couldn't be done; Isa Ansgar could not be reasoned with. Remembering the wraiths that appeared from the possessed elf in the interrogation chamber of Castle Elias was a sobering reminder that maybe they were right. Still, Alastair Krogh had imagined the worst from the start and nothing good had come of his choice, either. Drawing in a deep breath, Mia promised herself that, despite the dire warnings, she'd try to reason with Isa if she got the chance.

She turned her attention back to Alastair's crystal ball. Could she trust using it without him here? Lucan and Elissabet both had acted very particular about their possessions, in particular their magic paraphernalia. Yet, she just wanted one small glimpse, and if it was possible to pull Magnus back through the ball she would do so. Then she'd go back to bed and flee back to Castle Elias tomorrow like Kort asked. Like Alastair had—she grimaced—directed.

Mia pulled the Dragonstone out from under her linen shirt and summoned the intuitive magic she knew she could control. "*Luceat lux in Magnus.* Show me Magnus," she said.

The image distorted. Flecks swirled inside the ball.

"Show me Magnus in Isa's lair," Mia corrected, hoping that was the problem. The image stilled and her dragonlet came into view, still bound, still crying, still in jeopardy, so when a thought occurred, an instinct, she voiced it knowing that what she must do was save and comfort him.

"*Aperire porta ad Magnus.* Open a portal and let me touch my Aurora."

†††

Isa had waited expectantly, but this was beyond even her grandest hope. A blonde female elf had come for Magnus rather than Alastair, but, as the shimmering portal opened against the stone wall of her dungeon and the foolish girl peered through, Isa saw…she held the Dragonstone! It was nearly enough to make her come undone where she stood hidden behind the horse-sized Aurora.

She watched the young woman. Her spies had said this blond "Mia" was linked to the beast, that the two had imprinted and she couldn't bear to be away from him. She obviously loved the dragonlet, and that sentiment played wildly across her face. It would ultimately be her destruction.

Magnus came to life with a croak. Mia reached through the portal, tentatively, hopefully, moving as if to touch him, and Isa let her come.

The Aurora thrashed against his bindings and said, "Princess. My Mia."

Isa stepped back, startled. Would the spirit dragon give her away? At the moment he seemed too caught up in seeing Mia, who smiled and reached out for him.

"Come, Magnus. Come quickly!"

The dragon rushed forward but his chains pulled tight, as did Mia's face. When he cried out her name again, Mia advanced and Isa smiled. Mia cooed to the dragon and crossed fully through the portal.

"Magnus," she whispered. "I just want to touch you."

"Then you shall," Isa replied, laughing, and she swung a leather whip that coiled around the young woman's arm. Mia reared back, but Isa dragged her close. "Come and see to your dragonlet, child. Come and comfort him. He wants you."

"NO!" Mia shrieked, trying desperately to move back toward the glowing portal behind her, but it was too late; Isa would not let her go.

"Never underestimate the love of a mother," she mused. "Welcome to Castle Cumberlae, Mia. Your dragonlet child has brought you to me, and now there is no escape."

"NO!" she heard again, and she glanced at the portal back to Alastair's home. Untended, it was shimmering closed, but staring clearly through was Kort Elias. The prince's face was set in lines of rage and determination, and his powerlessness, his suffering, pricked Isa's heart for a moment. She understood it. Her Malachai had felt that way for her once, and she for him. That expression was love.

Which was something she could work with. Manipulate.

Smiling, Isa called out for the shadow elves who waited in the hall, intending to subdue the blonde girl as quickly as possible, but as the portal shimmered closed Mia acted, spinning and tearing the Dragonstone from her neck. Pitching the fist-sized artifact toward Kort she screamed, "Take it!"

"No!" Isa shouted at the same time as Kort. She lunged for the amethyst…and grabbed the chain just in time.

The portal sizzled shut.

†††

"MIA! NO!" Kort screamed again as his beautiful princess disappeared into Isa's lair. By the gods, what had she done?

Garnet burst into the room as Kort slammed his fists against the wall, trying to get through and bring Mia back. Alastair followed the dragon, and only then did Kort notice sunlight streaming in the window. He'd woken and Mia was gone, so he'd followed an instinct and come back here. Just in time to see her taken.

"What in the name of—?"

"Isa took Mia!" Kort turned, seized the wizard's crystal ball, and brandished it. "You left this thing here? You let this happen!" In his rage, he hurled the artifact at the floor.

"No!" Alastair roared, reaching out, but he was too late. It shattered into a million pieces.

"You petulant ass!" the wizard said, eyes wide as he spun on Kort. "We could have been killed. More importantly, we could have used it to open another door to maybe save her." He knelt and tried in vain to collect the shards, but his expression showed the act was useless.

Kort advanced on the wizard and seized him by the neck.

"No," Alastair rasped, suffocating.

"My family! My Mia!"

Alastair scrabbled at Kort's fingers and then clawed at his arms. His face turned an ugly blue. It was only when Garnet growled then spoke to him that Kort realized what he was doing.

"You don't want to kill the wizard, Kort. You want to kill Isa."

Rational thought returned. Kort relaxed his grip on Alastair. He shoved the wizard onto the floor amongst the remains of his precious crystal ball, a half sob escaping him as he did.

"The Others," Alastair gasped. "They're coming. We'll help you. We'll get... We'll fight to get Mia and Magnus back and—"

"I'm not waiting another second," Kort growled. "Garnet, let's go."

Alastair rose to his knees and clasped Kort's legs. "No. Wait. You're no match for her alone. Let us help you!"

Kort kicked the wizard away. "Magic. Wizards. What good do any of you do the rest of us?" He turned and pointed to the door, and at his command Garnet joined him in heading outside.

"Wait! Take my sword!"

Alastair unbuckled his belt and tossed the sheathed weapon to Kort, who turned and caught the wizard's offering in midair. Then he and Garnet rushed through the maze of Alastair's home, burst outside through the huge front doors and surprised the wizard's guardian dragons. The three watched in mute bewilderment as Kort mounted; then Garnet took two steps and launched himself up into the air, spreading his wings and taking flight.

The next stop was Castle Cumberlae.

Chapter 39

Mia realized the enormity of her folly as Isa held the Dragonstone up to the light and peered into it. What had she done? By Varik, she'd killed them all.

Isa turned, eyes narrowed in a cold smile. She stood there dressed in skintight black leather, with waist-length blue-black hair that swirled around her muscular body like an angry mane, and Mia winced. The woman resembled her father.

"So glad you joined us, Mia. My spies have told me all about you."

"Have they?" Mia answered cautiously. "I'm Mia. Mia *Ansgar*."

Isa pointed to the jewel. "So, you have returned what your father stole from me. For that, I'll spare your life."

Mia's belly knotted in anxiety. The strength her aunt exuded threatened and intrigued her all at once. She gripped her shaking hands behind her back and stood straighter, facing Isa and forcing all uncertainty from her face. Yet, what was the point? Trapped here in Isa's lair, what hope did she have of getting back to Kort?

At least she had made it to Magnus. She turned away from Isa and went to the dragonlet, who struggled against his bindings. She touched the scales on his nose. He bolted forward. Coldness and sadness and sorrow and terror lingered about him, and her aura flared out, purple energy from inside her heart that spread over him from nose to tail. He shuddered and nuzzled her hands and whined.

"Mia. My Mia," he wheezed despite the silver chains of his muzzle.

She wrestled with his bonds, desperate to free him. Finally, she loosened one chain, then another. She dragged the muzzle from his head and touched the soft scales under his chin, curling her fingers in his favorite scratching spot. Her heart hammered at the sight of his injuries, and she turned her rage on Isa. "How dare you injure my dragon? Release him. I want to take him home. Dragonlets deserve better care," she growled, her voice barely containing her rage. "I'm so sorry, Magnus."

"Home?" Isa laughed. "You think Castle Elias is your home? *This* was your father's home not so long ago."

Mia searched the room, but if Theo Ansgar had once stayed here Isa must have driven all evidence away.

"This could be your home now, Mia. Join me and I'll see that you never want for anything." Isa gestured to the Dragonstone. "You could help me rule the new Chalvaren. We are family, after all."

Mia caressed Magnus's chin, thinking. Slowly she shook her head and suggested, "It's not too late, Isa."

"Too late for what?" Isa cocked her head, curious.

"Let us go. Turn yourself in to King Lach—"

"It's definitely too late for that," Isa snapped then wagged a finger. "You are so naive, Mia. You think you have the power to make all this go away? You're just like your father. Optimistic. Hopeful. *Delusional.*"

Isa approached. As she did, Mia spotted something black and sinister flutter out of Isa's mouth and ear and pop up onto her shoulder. The crow-like demon bounced and cawed out victory, and pecked vigorously at the Dragonstone. A shadow wraith? Her stomach clenched at the nauseating aroma of decay, but she bit the inside of her cheek, refusing to show fear.

The black thing lingered there, gazing back at her. Mia's skin crawled, so she diverted her eyes, shaking her head.

"No," she agreed. "It's never going to go away, what you've done." She forced herself to look her aunt in the eye and add, "You killed all those men. And dragons!"

Isa tapped her chest. "I harvested their magic."

Mia glared at her aunt and said nothing.

"I'll never bow to Lachlan," Isa said. "Nor to Elissabet. But I am expecting the queen for a visit soon...."

The cold smile on her aunt's lips made Mia reconsider her plea, but still she had to try. "I'll stand beside you if you repent. You're the only link I have left to Theo. I can't promise the outcome, but I'll help you—"

"Is that what you want, Mia? To *save* me?" Isa's expression changed to one of disbelief, and her ivory skin pinkened.

"Yes. But if you won't bow to Castle Elias, I will see you in chains. Or worse."

Hard, hateful laughter erupted from Isa's lips. "Then we have a serious problem."

Mia's aunt turned and strode toward the door, the conversation clearly ended. She signaled to several shadow elves, who advanced on Mia. Nonetheless, Mia wanted to keep trying. She had to. In her heart she had to believe she'd done everything possible to salvage her aunt's misspent life.

She held up her hand, palm up. "Surely there must be a way to peace, Isa."

Her aunt hesitated, turned, and glowered. Something flickered in her eyes, though, and Mia thought she had made a connection for the briefest moment, but then Isa's expression hardened. She rubbed the Dragonstone with her long fingers and said, "The Eliases, those bastards to whom you grovel, are using you, Mia. They brought you here to—"

"That's not true," Mia interrupted. She'd once feared being their pawn, but the thought pained her no longer. She shook her head and rubbed her dragonlet's soft muzzle. Touching Magnus, keeping that connection, settled her jangled nerves.

Isa chuckled and shrugged, swinging the Dragonstone like a pendulum from its chain. "All right, niece. As you will. But a ritual awaits. Join me, and watch me change Chalvaren's history. You can be part of it, Mia, at any time. I'll see you with riches beyond your wildest dreams. Power. And your dragonlet."

Mia shook her head, defiant. "No. Give me the Dragonstone. I'll extract the shadow wraith feeding off the grief in your soul, we can talk and—"

"There's no time left for talk."

Isa spun and marched toward the door. She signaled, and the two shadow elves moved forward again to restrain her, but worse than that was what Mia saw next. Duncan and Shayleigh entered the room, traitors by their very presence. Traitors who somehow had fooled everyone into believing they were loyal to Chalvaren.

The shadow elves lurched forward and reapplied Magnus's chains and muzzle. At the same time, Duncan and Shayleigh raised double metal shackles Mia knew were meant to meant to bind her. And a gag.

Shayleigh shook her head and looked sad. "Please reconsider our mistress's offer, Mia. She wants you to join us. We heard. And she will be a good ruler."

Mia glared at her and then Duncan, but it did not stop the pair's advance. "What?" she asked. "Not even any shadow wraiths to bind you? Are you seriously doing this of your own accord? What did she promise you?"

"When she rules, all this will change. She's said that she just wants revenge on those who murdered her beloved, and to raise him from the dead. Now that she's recovered the Dragonstone, she can do just that. You should reconsider, Mia. We're on the winning side, so you should join us if you know what's good for you—and for that dragon you love so much."

"She will never win, Shayleigh," Mia spat. "Evil can never win for long."

"Really, such optimism," Shayleigh remarked with a laugh. "And such melodrama doesn't suit anyone. Be a good girl now. Let's get this gag in place."

Duncan eased in behind Mia, clearly expecting her to surrender. She whipped around and kneed him in the groin, knocking him backward. He cursed and grabbed himself, falling to his knees, but Shayleigh attacked and wrestled Mia to the ground. In two blinks she was bound and gagged, and dragged upright by her hair.

"If you hadn't shown up at Castle Elias when you did," Shayleigh snarled, "Duncan would have been matched to that spirit dragon. He would have obeyed Isa naturally. Now Isa's got the Dragonstone and she'll have to destroy him, overpower him or absorb his energy. Think about *this,* Mia. If you join her and convince him to help her unite all the dragons, she might let Magnus live."

Mia could hardly think. She struggled to get away. "You helped Isa attack the castle. You helped her steal my dragon! You've been traitors the whole time!"

Magnus lurched forward but couldn't reach her, bound and held by the pair of shadow elves. Duncan staggered to his feet and grasped a length of chain. "Fight us and I'll beat him with it," he warned.

Mia stopped struggling, broken. She should have listened to Kort and let him handle this; she never should have tried to do this alone. But sometimes knowledge came too late to be of use to anyone.

†††

Isa slammed the door to the dungeon and collapsed against it. She sucked in hot, short breaths and stared down at her palms.

"Pity she's such a fool," she muttered to herself. Had Mia really said those words? Had she really offered to stand beside Isa when they addressed the king?

She considered what it would look like: someone standing up for her, begging for mercy on her behalf before Lachlan's royal court, on her knees. A part of Isa wanted that, wanted Mia's version of the future, wanted all her grief to end with forgiveness and love. But then her black-winged shadow drake rose up beside her and she remembered Malachai and all she'd lost. Her child! The idea of mercy and redemption was a joke that she must drive down and bury in the depths of her heart. Mia could never fix what had been done to her and her family. No one could but Isa herself.

"No," she said. "Tonight I shall see Malachai returned. Tonight my grief finds its vengeance."

Chapter 40

Alastair Krogh circled Castle Elias on his coppery brown earth dragon then urged it to descend to the courtyard. His companions remained aloft, and their sudden presence was marked by blasts from horns on the east tower. This would be a tricky reunion, he realized. He could only hope they'd get what he came for.

He dismounted and ran forward as soon as he landed but found himself surrounded by guards. Furious expressions masked their faces, and they brandished swords and bows, so he bowed and stretched out his hands in a pose of surrender. The castle guards paused, murmuring amongst themselves.

"Call Queen Elissabet," he shouted. "Please. I must speak with her at once. Her son Kort is in great jeopardy, and I need her magic to save him."

Murmurs spread through the troops, and several of the elves ran toward the castle proper. Heavy wingbeats of more dragons cut through the night air behind him, and Alastair turned to see the first of The Others join him. Castle Elias's guards watched, nonplussed, as three cloaked and mighty-seeming wizards dismounted and stood beside their beasts, obviously waiting for word from Alastair.

When the Elias guards did not attack, several more surly characters joined the gathering from above. One was a dwarf with a red beard and carrying a heavy double battleaxe who slid off a smallish water dragon. Next was a dark-skinned elf, sword drawn.

Alastair turned to them. "Put down your weapons. We'll have cause to use them later, but on another. Right now we beseech the king and queen."

Two new voices cut through the night air, raised in vigorous argument, and Alastair pivoted to see his sister and brother-in-law in heated debate. Elissabet was dressed in a vest of thick leather armor and a skirt of chainmail that hung well below her knees. Boots were apparent on her long legs, and a thick silver broadsword dangled at her side. Her husband growled choice obscenities at her heels.

"Well, I'll be damned," Alastair said as the queen stormed into the yard. "My little sister's in rare form tonight."

His men chuckled. He hissed at them to hold their tongues as three Southern Alliance elves walked out of Castle Elias behind her and joined his ranks. Elissabet had never been one to laugh at herself.

His sister wheeled on her husband. "I *will* go with him. I have to bring Kort back."

King Lachlan reached for her arm, but she jerked away. He said, "I cannot lose you too, Elissabet. Be reasonable. Think about the other children."

Elissabet thrust out her arm. "Alastair's my brother, Lachlan. He's one of the most powerful wizards that ever lived, and you know that. He's finally found his courage again—or his greed—and he'll see to my safe return. Won't you, Alastair?"

"The situation has turned dire, Lachlan, and I cannot tolerate this escalation. Isa means to raise Malachai from the grave, and if she succeeds, your head on a spike is likely his first priority."

Lachlan wheeled on Alastair, his expression tight. He pressed Elissabet behind him possessively, started shaking his head no. "Then she stays here where I can protect her."

Alastair gestured broadly at the king. "I watched over her for years before she met you, majesty. I personally guarantee her return. And we'll return of your firstborn son as well... unless the Others and I die trying," he added in a somewhat more mumbly voice.

Lachlan stormed past Elissabet, stole her sword from its scabbard, and laid the razor-sharp blade against Alastair's bare neck. The king's blue eyes were wild with anger, and Alastair knelt before him. His men took a knee as well. He'd warned them this might happen.

Lachlan growled, "So help me Varik, Alastair..."

Alastair nodded and held up damp palms. "Isa has Lucan and Mia, all your Riders, their dragons and Magnus. And the Dragonstone. Kort went after Mia. I have brought together a group to help. Without Elissabet we will all certainly fail."

The king reeled and addressed his wife. "I do not wish to live without you at my side. Please, Elissabet, do not do this. Leave it to others who are not so precious to me. I love you too much to risk."

Her eyes flashed with defiance and she pointed to the castle. "See to our other children, my love. This is a long time coming. I'll be back before first light."

She swept her hand up his cheek and pressed a passionate kiss to his lips, and Lachlan let her sword clatter to the ground. Taking her face in his hands, he kissed his queen with wild abandon. The men cheered, and Alastair smirked.

Elissabet pulled back, retrieved and sheathed her sword, and leapt up onto Alastair's dragon. She screamed out a defiant "Ha!" and Alastair and the Others followed suit. When they were all mounted, the dragons took flight. The Others were headed into battle, and their mission was clear and intentional. Chalvaren's Isa-brought night must finally end.

Chapter 41

Kort and Garnet approached Castle Cumberlae. Garnet circled the roof twice so they could assess the best point of entry, then they glided downward, silent and cautious.

"See them?" Kort pointed out three seven-foot tall shadow elves. They were dressed in loincloths and boots, armed with jagged twelve-inch daggers, and they patrolled the battlements. It made him hope that magical alarms were unlikely. "You take the forward two, I'll take the third."

Garnet alit, soundless as a falling feather despite clamping down on adjacent roof tiles with iron-hard claws. Kort slid silently off his back, slipped down behind a guard and beheaded it with Alastair's borrowed sword. The dragon-ore blade sparkled in the dark, and its magic did its work. The hulking creature pitched forward off the wall, body falling noiselessly to the ground.

Garnet struck next, seizing one shadow elf in his front claws and tearing the thing in half with a bite. The second turned and lifted a dagger, but Garnet's breath roasted his flesh from his bones just as he looked about to shriek a warning of intruders.

Kort slipped back up Garnet's neck. "Good," he whispered. "Three down. Let's go see what's next."

Another group patrolled the courtyard, but it too failed to sound any alarm. Working in tandem, Kort and Garnet killed fifteen shadow elves then slunk inside the castle proper. Their first objective was Mia, and then Magnus; he'd secure them then wait for reinforcements. He prayed Alastair forgave him for his fury and brought the Others as he'd promised.

Close quarters required a different strategy, so Kort sized up the interior of the castle as they entered, Garnet moving surprisingly stealthily for his size. A central area led upward three stories of stone-decked balconies full of shadow elves. Coming and going, these warriors looked familiar.

His men—or what was left of them.

His gut pitched and grief rode him, but as several turned and saw him, he steeled his will and barked out an order. With no time to find the magic to save them, he had no choice.

"Light them up before they sound the alarm."

Garnet did as commanded. Kort wept bitter tears.

†††

Isa carried her prize to the altar and again set the stage. New warriors stood guard for her, and she acknowledged them with a dismissive nod, tucking long strands of blue-black hair behind her pointed ears as she imagined the glorious future to come.

"Malachai?" she whispered. "I found new offerings to lure you home tonight."

The Dragonstone lay against her chest, her racing heart. Ceremonial candle flames flickered atop the blood red velvet cloth–draped altar, and she savored the strike of the match and the fire that grew up in the sacrificial bowl of oil. Into it she offered three ebony hairs from her own head, and three blonde hairs she'd plucked from Mia's.

With trembling hands, she opened her grimoire to the marked page. She trailed her finger down the spell to return her family and let the trance of speaking the words engulf her. *"Venite ad me, mea lux, et dominabitur Chalvaren.* Come to me, my love, and we will rule Chalvaren."

The gold urns clattered and smoke wafted skyward. Joy bounded in her belly as Isa watched the spell take hold.

Yes, this is finally it!

She chanted the words of the spell so loudly that by the end her voice was scratchy from the strain. Ignoring her discomfort, she traced a loving finger over Malachai's urn and called to him.

"It is time, lover. Come and meet your destiny."

Smoke sifted out of his vessel, filling the air with the pungent smell of brimstone. As it did, she called out, "Yes! Malachai, your throne awaits!"

"Releeeeeassssse mee…," came his voice.

Her body trembled and she licked her lips. She nodded. She tore the Dragonstone from her neck and kissed it, placing it gently in the burning oil. Magic flames flared high, and bursts of color jumped out of the oil. Isa stumbled back, exultant.

"Twenty-five long years I've waited for you!" Waited to feel him caress her body, waited for him to make right what Alastair Krogh had despoiled. Images of that day manifested again in her memory, which Isa tried to shut out by closing her eyes: Malachai being drawn and quartered, Alastair and Lachlan's evil silver chains tied to Chalvaren's dragons, ripping her love limb from limb. She'd been a mere child and that devastation she'd witnessed...

Malachai's essence was coalescing before her, and she leaned forward and waved her hand through it. His handsome face materialized, and he blinked. Long ebony hair swirled about the tall, lean, muscular form she remembered. He still wore the leather battle armor he'd died in. Best of all, his eyes sparkled with adoration.

"Releasssssse me," the image hissed. Shadow wraiths swirled up around him, cawing, and Isa welcomed the sight of them. She threw her shoulders back and willed him to appear.

"Take my hand, Malachai," she commanded.

The Dragonstone glimmered in the bowl when she reached for him, and she smiled, but suddenly the flame that rolled across the oil sputtered and died. Again. Isa's lover dissolved along with the magic to bring him back. Again.

Isa did not scream. She simply stood in front of the altar, her heart flailing in her chest. She looked left then right. Her shadow warriors stood mute as Malachai's vessel clattered shut. Again.

She tapped her fingers against the altar, thinking. Finally an answer swept through her, and she screamed, "Guards! Bring me Mia Ansgar! And that goddamned dragonlet she loves so much!"

Warriors burst through the double wooden doors, but they seemed interested in something other than her most recent command. Isa wheeled around and saw flames burning outside in the main interior of the castle.

"Mistress! Intruders!" one smarter said. They drew their weapons and made to guard her.

Anger blackened Isa's vision. *No, not now. Not when I am so close.* What could possibly be here to stop her now? "Do I have to do *everything* myself?"

She stalked through the door, down the hall and onto a balcony to peer down. Kort sat his red dragon below, and their gazes locked. His glare was hateful.

Isa laughed. "What took you so long, Elias? *Spell et cum illis ligant tenebris*," she called. She flicked her wrists, and her razor-wire spell burst down across the three-story foyer.

"Garnet, move!" she heard. The dragon covered Kort with his wings and tried to duck under a balcony, but Isa's black and silver net dropped over their heads. Garnet's flames blasted in a cone upward, fighting it, but Isa knew the breath weapon was futile. She pulled back, laughing, as her razor-wire bound them and drove the mighty dragon to his knees.

Chapter 42

Duncan and Shayleigh dragged Mia down a torchlit hallway. At the end was a room with Isa, a wild look of fury on her aunt's face, and Mia jerked back, but with Duncan on one side and Shayleigh on the other she couldn't get away. Shadow elves struggled along behind her with a chained Magnus.

Isa curled her fingers, beckoning them all forward. Mia's gag scratched her face and dried her mouth, and she could hardly swallow let alone swallow the stone-like fear lodged in her throat.

"Come see what I've found in my castle, Mia. Your prince has come for you."

Duncan forced Mia forward, and her aunt fisted Mia's long blonde hair and pushed her against a stone railing. She saw Garnet below, bound by Isa's nets. It made Mia physically ill. Then furious.

She pivoted and rocketed her right shoulder up toward Isa's face. Her aunt almost lost her hold on Mia's hair but held tight, at the last moment pulling her away. Mia reared back, a cacophony of muffled curses spilling from her mouth. Her face burned with anger.

Isa dragged her close, so close that Mia felt her breath. "Yes. It *is* a pity, no? To see him like that, the great red beast on his knees trying to protect your prince. What would you do to save them, Mia?"

Anything, she realized. She struggled valiantly but ineffectually.

Isa gave a snakelike hiss of laughter that grew a stone of dread in Mia's belly. "Yes," she crowed. "Just what I'd hoped for. You love them."

Mia said nothing, just turned and stared daggers at her aunt.

"It is an honorable notion, Mia. We're not so unalike, you and I. I would be surprised by anything less."

Her aunt squeezed her neck with long icy fingers. Mia jerked against her grip and thrust her hip into Isa's side, knocking her back against the rail and trying to tip her over. She had to find some way out of this. Some way to save them. This violence was spiraling out of control.

Isa struck her face with a fist. "Do you want to save them? *Do you?* Or do you want them to die immediately?"

Mia thought of her unborn child, Kort's child, growing in her belly. She fisted her hands and forced herself to still.

"You would do anything to help them, wouldn't you child?" Isa drew a finger along Mia's cheek. "Wouldn't you?"

Mia lurched forward and head-butted her aunt. The impact nearly toppled Isa, but she recovered and stood taller, waggling a finger.

"You cannot hurt me, child. Alastair Krogh made me impervious to pain by stealing my Malachai. Now...look." She grasped Mia by the neck and forced her to stare back down over the railing. Garnet thrashed and tried to roar. "He's still intact...for the moment. Help me tonight, and I promise you'll see them live."

Mia went limp. She'd defied his sinister words at the time, but when it came to the lives of the ones she loved she realized Isa now had control. Alastair had been right. She'd say or do anything to help Kort and Garnet, to prevent their suffering.

She nodded, and Isa offered her a genuine smile. "So be it. Guards, take Mia and Magnus to my altar room, and take the intruders to the amphitheater."

Mia soon followed her aunt and her aunt's guards down the hall, wincing when Magnus whined in pain behind her. What could Isa want help with? But she knew. Isa needed her to activate the Dragonstone to wake Malachai.

She couldn't. She refused to have any hand in raising an evil wizard who threatened all of Chalvaren, who'd corrupted her aunt and begun this whole catastrophe. He'd been put to death for a reason, and no one except the mad Isa disputed that. Such an act would not be worthy. If Mia participated in any way, even to save Kort, she'd lose Kort; she knew it.

Tears pricked behind her eyes, and she suddenly realized Isa had led her into a chapel of sorts. Magnus gave another whimper, and Mia cast a forlorn glance behind her at the dragonlet.

Isa ordered her to her knees in front of the altar. Duncan and Shayleigh shoved her down onto the black cushions, and she tried for a glimpse into their eyes, maybe hoping some plea could help her. Did they have no loyalty to their homeland? Were they so lost with pride and greed they couldn't see what they were about to unleash?

"Stay still," Shayleigh shouted as Mia resisted.

The Dragonstone sat before her in a bowl of oil.

No, she told herself again. *I can't do it. I can't release him. Not even to save Kort.*

She lowered her head and squeezed her eyes shut, aching for him. If she went through with this, Kort would never forgive her. He couldn't. She'd be sacrificing the world for him, and he didn't believe in that sort of decision. Which made this her personal hell. She'd followed him here to find her happy-ever-after, to find heaven. She'd found that in his arms, and so much more. And now she was about to lose it.

Varik, see to Kort's life, she begged. *See to Garnet's as well. To Magnus. Take me, spare them.*

"Do it, Mia. Save your prince," Isa crowed, striding forward to the altar. She ripped the gag off Mia's mouth, unlocked her shackles and grasped her by the hair, wrenching her head back at a painful angle. "Activate it and save them."

"NO!" she shouted.

"*Malachai ad me, fili me.*" Isa mouthed the words of an ancient spell and again fisted Mia's hair. Wisps of smoke rose from two golden urns on the altar in front of them, floating together into elven forms. One man. One wriggling baby boy.

"Both of them!" Isa cried. "Release them, Mia! Say the words!"

Mia made a guttural sound of denial and threw herself backward.

The blackened wisps became a solid male mass, definitely the most sinister thing Mia had ever seen. His eyes glowed red, and his form sizzled with dark lightning that didn't belong to this world. Shadow wraiths flocked and cawed around his head and shoulders, and it was clear that his body fluttered between Hell and Chalvaren. His edges seemed formed of black sooty smoke.

Mia shook her head and screamed, rejecting the ritual. The image of the baby boy dematerialized as she did, and the associated curls of smoke fell back into the smaller urn. Isa's scream of sadness made tears spring to Mia's eyes.

Her aunt thrust Mia to the floor and encircled the tiny golden urn with her fingers. "I want him too," she shrieked.

Mia scrabbled backward. Terror shot white-hot adrenaline through her chest and she fell to the floor. "I *refuse* to be part of your horror show."

Isa turned and sprinted from the altar.

Surprised, Mia leapt to her feet. Had Isa changed her mind?

No. Of course not. Isa had rushed to one of her warriors, from whom she took a long curved blade. She grabbed Magnus's muzzled snout, exposing the soft tender hide of his neck where he loved to be scratched, and thrust the silver blade against it, baring her teeth. Her face and neck were blood red. A vein in her neck throbbed, and she glared at Mia, an animalistic growl tearing from her throat. She gestured to the altar. "Release my Malachai."

Beads of cold sweat sprang up on Mia's forehead. To give up her own life was one thing. To give up on Kort...well, that was unthinkable, but he would demand it if he were offered the choice himself. But to allow this monster to kill poor helpless Magnus... The Aurora was more important than any of them, was the future of Chalvaren. And he was completely innocent of any mistakes, wrongdoing or evil.

"Don't hurt him!" Mia cried.

And so she made her choice. Damn the consequences. Whatever evil had in store for the world tonight, they'd all face it together. Isa was going to kill Magnus. Mia couldn't let that happen, no matter what.

Dragging in rasping breaths, Mia's whole body shook as she lifted her hands and zinged her purple aura through the room. Onto the Dragonstone it flowed, and she called out, "Release Malachai."

The Dragonstone sizzled to life just as it had done in the Dragon Shrine, and ghostfire leapt from inside the artifact to sweep the room with brightly colored prisms of light. Mia looked away, only risking a glance at her dragonlet once she heard Malachai slip back into Chalvaren through the thin veil that shrouded him in the depths of Hell.

Mia heard a loud clatter. Isa had dropped her blade, slipped away from Magnus, and rushed to the altar. Her aunt's cry of "Yes!" barely reached Mia's ears as she stumbled forward to Magnus.

"Princess...," Magnus whispered. He strained against his chains.

Mia snatched up Isa's forgotten blade. The shadow elves nearby looked perplexed, unsure if she had fulfilled a bargain with their mistress. Or maybe they were just idiots. They scurried back when Mia swung at them, and soon she clasped her dragonlet around the neck in the biggest hug she could give.

She turned. Isa stood sheltered in her beloved's arms, completely absorbed with adoring him, and somehow that made Mia pity her. Isa had sacrificed her life for this, for him, for evil Malachai, her sanity and her goodness. Somewhere deep in her heart Mia empathized with such intense connection, because the burden of true love was that it demanded what it wanted. Just like she wanted Kort.

Isa gestured toward the altar, taking Malachai's hand. He appeared fully flesh and blood.

"Now. Our son," she said, her expression filled with a surprisingly beautiful maternal hope. It made Mia flatten a hand across her belly.

Malachai spoke. "How many wizards remain, Isa?" The question startled Mia.

"Three. But first, the child," Isa pleaded.

"No. We slay our enemies first. The boy can wait."

Mia caught the look of sadness in Isa's expression, but her aunt suppressed it just as fast and clasped Malachai's shoulders. "Elissabet's eldest son and his dragon wait in the arena for you now."

"What? Wait!" Mia fisted her hand. "You promised!"

Malachai turned and inspected her with a curious gaze. "Who's this?"

"Theo's daughter," Isa replied.

"Then she will know death first," Malachai said.

Drawing a sword, he lunged. Mia skipped back. Magnus cut him off before he could deliver a second attack, but Malachai struck the Aurora in the head with the hilt of his weapon, a severe blow that toppled the spirit dragon. Mia fell too, expecting to die. She draped her arms around her dragonlet's head.

The hurricane of force that was Malachai filled the chamber, yet Mia heard only laughter. "Yes," came his demonic voice, "much better. What was I thinking? We must draw this out. Bring them."

She glanced up to see Malachai and Isa stalk toward the door and several shadow elves moving toward her. Mia uttered a curse, dark and low, a vow of revenge. And yet, who was she kidding? She had no power. What had she done? She'd helped Isa free the devil himself. She had singlehandedly used the Dragonstone's magic to destroy Chalvaren.

Chapter 43

When Kort came to, he knelt in an enormous fighting arena and the silver leviathan before him seemed the clear favorite in what looked would be a match to the death.

How had he gotten here? One moment he was protected by Garnet's leathery wings, just barely safe from Isa's razor wire, the next her minions dragged him loose. Six of them had manhandled him into submission, into restraints, but it was only when they threatened his bound red dragon's heart with a six-foot spike that he'd given in. They'd covered his head with a sack then hit him over the head with something hard and he'd slipped into a black void.

"Garnet?" Kort said, looking around the amphitheater. His dragon lay motionless on the ground in front of him. The razor wire was gone, but Garnet's hide was covered with oozing cuts.

A short distance away, the silver snarled and dropped his massive horned head down in a promise of violence. As the creature approached Garnet, Kort flipped to his feet and lunged between the two.

"Get away from him, VanZanz."

A door opened on the opposite side of the arena. Kort turned his head to see four enormous shadow elves rolling a wooden-wheeled cart into the ring. Upon it was Magnus. The shadow elves dropped the lifeless dragonlet unceremoniously onto the arena floor, and their malicious laughter spiked prickles of icy dread through Kort.

He groaned. One very mad, hungry-looking silver dragon, and two of his own dragons down. It looked like he was on his own.

Straightening his spine, he thought of Mia and how he had yet to reach her. There was no time to feel bad for himself, no time to consider defeat.

I guess we'll just do this the old-fashioned way.

Twisting, he glanced around the arena in search of a weapon first, and then for a way out. Above were the amphitheater stands, but they were fenced off by evil-looking sharp wire. Cheers and applause roared down over him: Isa's remaining shadow elves, gloating. And there were more than he'd expected. Had she been kidnapping innocent villagers and infusing them with shadow wraiths? More abominations stood above him than fifty times the soldiers he'd sent to deal with Isa or the Riders she'd captured.

A new figure entered the ring, and Kort's heart was wrapped by ice-cold fingers. *Malachai.* He knew the elf by the ornate leathers he wore, the same ones he'd seen depicted on the walls of the Dragon Shrine, and by those double swords. He was even more terrifying in person than in Lucan's stories. Perhaps that was because he should have been dead.

Malachai strode across the dirt floor and flourished his arms wide, playing to the crowd. "Well, well, well. Look at him. The son of the king grovels before me."

A flush of humiliation burned his face, but Kort just glanced at Garnet, who was barely breathing, then Magnus. His muscles tensed for action as he fell into a low crouch, scouring the arena with his eyes for exits.

There's some way out of this. None of those I love will die tonight.

There had to be a way. There was always a way. His mother's voice drifted through his mind, and Kort cast his eyes up into the stands, through the wire squares of the fencing to the bloodthirsty crowd. In a particularly ornate spectator section, Isa settled into a thronelike chair.

Time and circumstance bore down on him. He had no weapons. He stood naked except for a ragged blue loincloth, which he fingered with a scowl. He had no dragons that could fight with him; both lay prone, awaiting the silver's teeth or a madman's magic.

Kort looked back up at Isa. The Dragonstone glittered on her chest, but there was something even more shocking.

"Mia...?"

His beautiful golden-haired princess sat down next to Isa. Had the witch truly turned her?

Cheers rose, so loud that they deafened him, and Kort thought surely the roof must lift off the arena. Somehow, Isa Ansgar's high tinkling laughter trickled through.

"The house of Elias will fall, Malachai. Finish the heir and we'll take the rest next!"

"That's not happening." Kort fisted his hands and glanced between his two downed dragons. Brite's tender laughter resonated in the back of his mind, and the hope and love his sister showed when speaking to Mia. That's what he would fight for tonight. For hope. For love. For family.

"Kill him, Malachai, and his dragons!" Isa was clapping wildly and laughing. "Elissabet will see their heads on spikes before we slaughter her remaining children."

Malachai's laughter boomed out, and he approached the dragons, using his magic to raise their unconscious bodies and move them like puppets, shouting ridiculous pleas of mercy in a high-pitched voice and entertaining the shadow elves filling the stands. VanZanz seemed caught up in it, too, for the beast began making chortling noises as the mock pleas became a list of all the hideous things Malachai would do to desecrate their corpses. The dark wizard seemed to grow more and more drunk with excitement.

Kort refused to listen. Instead he conjured Ian and Quinn's incessant chatter, their arguments about obscure dragon facts, their dreams of dangerous maneuvers they wanted to try. Those memories drowned out the shouts of bloodlust and he found momentary peace. And yet he ached to see the boys again, to watch them live and prosper and become the men he knew they would. He could not let Malachai or Isa harm them.

Lachlan's booming voice suddenly sounded in his head, correcting the youngsters, insisting they fall in line and stop worrying his mother. His father's words applied to him, too! Defiance filled his heart, and Kort fisted his hands and shut out all other thoughts, preparing for this final battle, knowing it was all or nothing, knowing the odds were against him but he could not allow himself to fail.

Then he heard one simple voice above them all. *Kort Elias, I love you. Come save me. We need you.*

"Mia?" He darted a glance up toward Isa's throne. Enthralled by the impending bloodbath, cheering and laughing like a maniac, the witch failed to notice the empty seat beside her. But Kort saw. His heart skipped a beat and then sputtered back to life as he searched the arena for her with his eyes, but he saw no blonde hair like hers. Then, turning, he thought he caught sight of a silver-haired wizard disappearing through an archway toward a dark arena staircase.

"Alastair?"

Three new figures appeared at the arch. Black robes disguised them, but the pulse of an orange aura hovered inside the hood of the one in the middle, and in the breadth of the instant it took him to identify his mother, they all disappeared.

Kort lowered his head, his heart beating faster with the thought of reinforcements and that Mia had been rescued. It gave him the determination he needed, and he slowly rose to his full height and turned to face the silver.

"What are you waiting for, cowards?"

VanZanz roared, and Malachai turned. The magically suspended bodies of Magnus and Garnet crashed to the ground as he mounted, and the dark wizard called out, "You are right! The time for talk is done!"

Kort jutted out his chin, but instead of approaching him Malachai steered the silver toward Magnus's limp form. As VanZanz lowered his head for feeding, Kort shouted, "You *are* cowards! He can't fight! Leave him alone. Take me!"

He sprang forward, vaulting up and over Magnus to put himself in harm's way.

Malachai laughed. "As you wish. Devour him slowly, VanZanz. Perhaps one limb at a time."

The beast lunged. Kort had played games like this while sleeping in the stalls with the dragons of Castle Elias, though, and he knew just the right timing. Or he hoped he did. Waiting until he sensed the chill of the silver's breath, he reached out, grabbed the prominent bony horn under the beast's chin and launched himself into the air. He kicked up, scissored his legs, and caught Malachai's neck between his knees.

"What? Stop him, dragon!" Malachai yelled, pulling at Kort's legs, but Kort locked them, muscles honed from twenty-five years of dragon riding, and he squeezed hard, aiming to snap the dark wizard's neck. He didn't quite manage.

VanZanz bucked. His thrashing propelled both men skyward. Kort kicked out, arms windmilling, and somersaulted into a freefall dismount. Malachai hit the ground awkwardly, but he rose, ready to fight, curling his fingers and sneering.

The crowd found their feet. Isa was already standing. Looking down at Kort standing alone against a dark wizard and a gargantuan ice dragon must have been less than entertaining, for thunderous applause and stomps of joy rose throughout the room as Malachai motioned for VanZanz to back away; he was going to handle this amusing princeling himself.

Malachai kicked out with a leather-booted foot, aiming for Kort's head and knocking him prone. Kort lunged as he fell, dizzy, but he caught Malachai's other leg and twisted. Shocked, the dark wizard screamed and crashed to the ground. Kort shoved his face into the dirt, grabbed him by the ears and gave his head a smash.

The silver gave himself away, his icy breath coating Kort's naked back, and Kort breathed a sigh of relief that any use of a breath weapon would harm Malachai as well. He spun to evade the dragon's bite, grabbed the beast's prominent chin horn and hurtled skyward, raking his fingernails across VanZanz's eye as he went. The silver roared and thrashed, furious as Kort landed to crouch on his head.

A second shake loosened Kort, launching him through the air. The crowd screamed with delight as he struck the arena floor chest first. The air was knocked out of him, and brilliant flashes of light burned behind his eyes as his head struck next. A mouthful of black dirt choked him, and Kort tasted his own blood.

He blinked. When he opened his eyes, the sight of Magnus, the innocent dragonlet lying still as death, brought a moment of weakness. He wanted to lie down like that, too. Blood filled his mouth, and he was *so* tired. But as blurry darkness threatened to steal his vision, he tensed his muscles and hefted his torso off the ground.

"Kort!"

Mia had appeared in front of him. She stood mere paces away, screaming his name. But she couldn't be here. Not in this ring. Not in reach of that silver…

"Get up! Kort! GET UP!" She tugged on his arm, waved her hand for him to rise and follow.

God, she was so beautiful. All he had to do was stand up. Then he could defend her. He reached out and tried to speak, tried to warn her about Malachai. About VanZanz. About Isa. Why hadn't VanZanz attacked? Would a bite tear Mia in two at any moment? Where were Isa and Malachai, and why hadn't they used their magic to finish this fight?

"Get away! Mia, run!"

"I'm not leaving without you." She planted white-knuckled fists on her hips, and he couldn't help but be amazed by her. His Mia. Defiant. Magnificent. Exquisite.

A great red wall rose behind her, a wall of crimson scales. Mia turned and stared, her face overcome with awe and delight. She pointed at Kort, and that red wall obscured her as it came for him. An iron-hard black claw soon appeared, and Kort grasped it. His vision was still blurry, and the ride from the ground to Garnet's neck was startling, but he shook off his confusion and surveyed the arena.

Mia was trying to wake Magnus, her purple aura glowing bright. More immediately important, however, Malachai waited atop VanZanz, a trickle of blood streaming down his forehead.

Kort pointed. "Ready for more of the same?"

Malachai waved him forward.

Chapter 44

An edgy, itchy feeling danced in Mia's belly as she stared at Magnus, limp and unmoving before her. She'd already tried to wake him magically, but she'd had no luck. If only she had the Dragonstone.

Thumping his side with the back of her hand she shouted, "Dragon, get up! Your sire needs you, Magnus."

The Aurora looked so fragile, so...*still*. Her heart lurched in her chest. Seeing Kort down had been terrifying, and the situation they faced was no less mortal. Malachai had risen and now threatened him on VanZanz. Worse, Isa needed to be destroyed. Whether her shadow wraith or something else was to blame, Mia's aunt was lost forever.

She had told Elissabet as much, told Alastair and the bizarre group of wizards who rescued her. They had agreed. Now they were nowhere to be seen, but she trusted that they were acting appropriately, searching the keep, breaking Isa's wards. She herself needed to save her dragonlet. They'd told her as much.

"Wake up, dragon!"

Magnus didn't budge, but that didn't hold Mia back. She shoved him, bent her knees, and threw her weight into lifting his heavy head, begging him, "Please, friend, we can't do this without you!"

Kort screamed out a war cry, and Mia turned to see the two great dragons advance on each other. Blasts of fire from the red met icy hoarfrost from the silver. The dragon's weapons neutralized each other, and the arena filled with boiling steam. The crowd raised cheers as the beasts finally engaged with tooth and claw, each leviathan seeking dominance.

Mia wiped moisture from her brow and turned back to Magnus.

"No. Please, Magnus. Don't do this. Wake up and help me!"

Nothing. His black scales were cold when she ran her fingers over them, and Mia's heart skipped two beats. It seemed like he was dying or dead, and she had nothing but her aura to save him. An aura that had already failed to wake him.

She glanced up into the stands. Isa still stood there, the Dragonstone secure on her chest. She looked somewhat quieter now as she watched Malachai fight Kort.

Mia turned up empty hands. Her tears spilled onto them. She focused on Magnus's face, desperate to see his amber eyes blinking up at her, to hear his voice saying her name. "Damn you, dragonlet, don't you dare leave me now!" She fell to her knees and gripped his head. "I need you, Magnus. You are my dragon, and you have a job to do. Please wake up!"

Nothing. Still nothing.

Raging anger, sorrow and fear burst through her, and her purple aura flared out fuller than before. "NO," she said. "I did not go through hell and back to see you lie here and die on me because of my aunt. You find it, Magnus, find whatever it is you need to come back and help me. I helped you on Earth, then I came here to help you on Chalvaren. To watch you grow and thrive and be everything you can be. You find it in yourself to come back and help *me*."

Her aura sizzled out from her hands, covering Magnus from snout to tail. "Varik, please," she said, remembering the tie of the god to her power, "help my dragon."

Her aura dimmed, and a new fear burst through her. Was this punishment for aiding Isa's black magic? Had she really condemned all of Chalvaren by her actions? Was Varik furious? Magnus's limp form seemed proof.

A crash sounded behind her, and a roar. VanZanz had knocked Garnet down. The red leapt back up and loosed a surprising breath of fire. The silver met it with ice, and sizzling steam rolled upward into the air.

Mia cringed and cried out another prayer. "Varik, give me back my dragon. I claim him in your name. I swear that all that was wrong shall be righted, that black magic shall not be cast again by those who pervert this land and take its power for their own. No more dragons shall be sacrificed, and my aunt shall be punished!"

Cruel laughter sounded behind her, and the sound of a door slamming shut. Mia's head shot up and she saw Isa at the opposite end of the arena, the Dragonstone swinging on her neck like a pendulum. Her aunt taunted her with it, swinging the jewel back and forth, her expression mocking.

"Lose something?"

Bile rushed up Mia's throat. She leapt over Magnus and ran forward, but hulking green shadow elves appeared, bursting through a door in the wall. These warriors surrounded her, jagged knives drawn, sniffing the air like rats. Behind them, Mia saw VanZanz knock Garnet to the ground again.

Isa brandished a silver sword and pointed it at Mia. To her guards she said, "Collect my slave and take her to the dungeon."

No! Mia burst through the circle of guards and raced back toward Magnus. This would be her last stand. She and Kort would die together. Where were Queen Elissabet and the Others?!

She ran faster, racing to get back to Magnus. "Wake up!" she cried as she reached him, but it was a vain shout, a vain hope. Magnus was dead. She and Kort were going to die. Their love had been sweet and fine, and it had shown her that she was not alone. Her mother's prophecy had been nothing to fear, as she had held the power all along. And now she would never be alone again.

Wait. Was that the flicker of an opening amber eye?

Isa was shouting orders. "Stop her! Leave the Aurora for Malachai and take the girl to the dungeons. Harm her as little as possible. I've been thinking, Mia. I've got a shadow drake to share with you tonight!"

Magnus rose. Mia threw herself upright and made a frantic leap for the dragonlet's neck. She caught and held on, and the dragonlet spun, crouching low, facing Isa and growling with determination.

"You're up," Mia whispered, and she lovingly caressed Magnus. "I was worried."

"Stop her!" Isa cried.

A real roar burst from Magnus's throat. He leapt forward and toppled the first shadow elf to reach him. Ripping off its head, he spat that out then used his claws to tear the heads off two others. Turning back toward Mia's aunt, he roared again.

Isa bolted behind another of her warriors, falling backward and chanting out a spell. Magnus roared again, and somehow the noise interrupted her cast. She scrambled backward, trying to get away, pointing at Mia. Her shadow drake erupted from her body and advanced.

"Don't stop!" Mia screamed as Magnus paused, and she kneed the Aurora forward.

Magnus obeyed. He tore the heads off three more shadow elves then raced through the drake with wide open jaws. Mia felt its smoky substance trying to invade her person, but her aura glowed brighter and the thing was rebuffed. She felt the light of Varik within her, the light of her promise from earlier, and she watched with fury as Isa scrambled backward.

"Stop her, Magnus. By all the gods of Chalvaren, we will end her tonight."

Magnus roared, lunged, and his jaws caught Isa around the chest.

"Malachai!" the witch howled, her final living word. With three vigorous shakes of his muscular neck, the dragonlet tore her in two.

Isa's shadow drake shot off toward Malachai. A flock of shadow wraiths flew up into the air and toward Mia, who flattened herself on Magnus's back. The dragonlet dropped Isa's body to the ground and lunged at each of the black bird ghosts, angry growls rumbling from his throat, but he was unable to harm them. They, however, were unable to harm him or Mia in return. The bright light of Varik's power resonated around them in her purple aura, and kept them safe.

Confused, Magnus careened to a sudden stop and landed in a spray of dust from the arena floor. Mia held on tight, dragging in much-needed air and surveying the chaos. Before her on the ground lay Isa, whose torso rose and fell with one final breath, her face set in a puzzled but hateful expression.

A sinister shriek like the death of a thousand birds drew Mia's ear, and she spun to learn the source. All at once came a mass exodus of shadow wraiths, their black forms lofting up from the bodies of the possessed, deserting them in unison. Every wraith wailed in horror, an ear-piercing sound that made Magnus claw at his ears and Mia clamp hands over her own. Then the shadowy demons flocked into the arena, diving toward Malachai and VanZanz.

Eyes wide, Mia whispered, "You did it, Magnus. You broke Isa's spell of darkness."

✝✝✝

His enemy loomed before him. The battle looked over, but Kort took heart as a shriek pierced the air and clouds of shadowy evil rushed out of the shadow elf spectators around the arena and swarmed toward him. Regular elves now stood in the stands, dazed but alive. Isa's spell on them was broken.

VanZanz paused. Atop him, Malachai stretched out his arms to welcome the shadow wraiths that flocked to him. He did not seem beaten. The bird-like creatures perched in multitudes along him like he was a tree of death.

Kort pointed to Isa's mutilated body. "You can't stay here without her!"

Malachai laughed. "I don't need her."

"Yes. Yes, you do. Without her to feed you our energy, you're nothing, wraith," Kort growled.

Garnet lunged. VanZanz flinched back, clearly disconcerted by Isa's body lying in two pieces across the ring. Rearing up and unseating Malachai, he thudded over to her.

Kort jumped down off Garnet's back as well. "You're not getting away, monster," he called to Malachai. "You're going back to Hell where you belong."

"And who's going to put me there, Prince Elias? You and your pitiful magic?" Malachai waggled his eyebrows and howled with laughter. "Your puny princess, who looks like she can't cast a spell except with the Dragonstone as a focus?"

The wizard thrust an armload of shadow wraiths toward Kort, who knelt and covered his head to deflect them. He threw out his aura out to protect himself, but he knew his magic wasn't strong enough to fight the devils off. The flock circled him, their essence turning his mouth dry as ash. He struggled to breathe. Memories of the fight in Castle Elias's interrogation chamber returned to him, and he knew he was going to die. Unless...

Mia and the others had been spectacular that day. United. Unstoppable. Undeniable. Varik's words drifted through his mind. Words about trusting others to be there for him, words about asking for help when it was needed. About ruling being an act of solidarity, not of independence and pride.

Like love.

He caught a glimpse of his dragon across the arena. Garnet had pursued VanZanz, who lunged wildly at Magnus seeking vengeance.

The Aurora dodged, and Kort's red took advantage of the silver's distraction. He clamped his jaws down on VanZanz's neck and then locked his legs, flapping his wings. The ice dragon struggled, but Garnet's jaws were too strong. A moment later the silver slumped to the floor of the arena, dead beside his mistress.

Shadow wraiths bit at Kort and tore at his flesh, their sooty wings still suffocating him. They attempted possession. Kort's aura spiked, and some of them scattered, singed by his magic. Still, he wasn't strong enough to break free. Not without help. And the bigger ones waited behind the smaller. Darker. Angrier. Scarier.

Mother. Mia. Alastair. Help me.

"By Varik, you will not take me!" he shouted. His aura sizzled forth, burning the nearest wraiths, but it was only for a moment.

He couldn't breathe. His muscles cramped and nausea rolled in waves through his gut. This was likely how the other wizards died, how his own warriors suffered when Isa seized their souls with her misuse of black magic. This was the horror Isa had intended for his mother, for all of his family.

"Mother! Help me!"

A burst of light flooded his eyes, a soothing orange warmth that he instantly recognized. He turned to find Queen Elissabet was indeed there, robed in black velvet, her hands open wide to project an aura of light against the shadows, calmly chanting a spell of protection. "*Lumen omnibus Chalvaren in Kort.* Shine the light of Chalvaren on my son!"

She stalked forward, the shield of light she created pushing the shadow wraiths before her. They screamed. She smashed them to the ground and they disintegrated.

Alastair Krogh and three of the ugliest, fiercest warriors Kort had ever seen appeared before him. They stood together in solidarity beside Elissabet. They opened their hands, and cones of light blasted forth. A kaleidoscope of color hit Kort's eyes and filled the arena. Their magic engulfed the wraiths, and more of Malachai's demons screamed and writhed and disintegrated in mid-air.

Kort was safe.

"Mia!" he screamed. "My Mia, where are you?

✝✝✝

She heard his scream.

"Kort? Magnus, get me over to him. Now!"

"Princess... The Dragonstone."

Mia bent down and recovered the gem, slipped the chain over her head and climbed back up onto Magnus. The Aurora flapped over Garnet and over VanZanz's carcass, and he and Mia joined the line of wizards squaring off with Malachai. The dragonlet hovered just above the ground, low enough that when Kort ran toward them and reached out for his tail he could vault himself up to land just behind Mia on his back.

"Let's do this!" Kort whispered, kissing Mia's neck as Magnus rose higher into the air. "Let's blend our auras and send that bastard back to Hell."

Mia shivered and half smiled, pleased. If ever they were united, this was the time.

She raised the Dragonstone aloft and chanted, *"Per Varik transmisimus, admonentes Malach et umbrae fit wraiths recta in infernum remittuntur.* By Varik, we send Malachai and his shadow wraiths straight back into Hell."

Ghostfire sprang up along the amethyst, joining Mia's purple aura. Kort's blue energy melded with both, and Mia directed a supercharged line of energy toward Malachai and his remaining demons. The dark wizard fell back, and he fell back even farther when below them all the wizards turned their magic upon the Dragonstone. Mia braced herself as the artifact lit up, and the blast of power, ten times what she'd ever channeled before, flowed through her and down at her enemy.

Ghostly outlines of the souls of Chalvaren's lost dragons burst from the gem and flew down along the beam, channeling a full rainbow of auras. The dragon souls rose up on liberated wings for a moment, gathering at the top of the amphitheater, then dove toward Malachai and his wraiths.

Malachai bellowed and turned to flee. Magnus gave a high-pitched keen, then barks that Mia couldn't help but sense as a command.

Earth dragon souls landed before the dark wizard, pounding their tails on the dirt floor and opening a crevasse, a hole to Hell that they tore wide with their claws. Fire dragons united and released a superheated blast to keep anything else from coming out. Wind dragons roared and blew up a wind that captured every wraith in its currents, and water dragons summoned torrents that poured down from above and pushed everything into the hole. Everywhere was the purple glow of Varik's magic, and Malachai howled, dragged back to Hell with every one of his wraiths.

It took some time. Mia shuddered at the chaos, but Kort held her close and together they watched Malachai destroyed. The water dragon souls roared and rained their deluge over the crevasse, and the earth dragons pushed mud over the hole to forever seal it shut. The wound in the earth was dried and cauterized by wind and fire, respectively.

The battle was over.

Chapter 45

"Kort!"

His mother called his name, and she and Alastair stared up at him and Mia on Magnus's back. "Are you all right?"

Magnus touched down beside the two, and the other wizards quietly moved to join them. Mia scrambled off the Aurora's back, and Kort followed, gathering her into his arms. He spun her around, lifting her feet off the ground, and she cupped his face with her hands.

"We did it! Together! You're alive!"

The joy in her voice lifted his heart. He set her back down and brushed his lips against hers, and for a moment the world was lost to their embrace.

His mother broke the reverie, unsurprisingly. She touched his arm. "Her victims, Kort. Those who were possessed. They must be confused."

Mia pulled away from him and looked up into the stands. "They were liberated when Magnus killed Isa. I saw the wraiths fly out of them. Look!"

Kort searched the stands with his eyes and saw it was true. Male and female elves stood where shadowy abominations had cheered on his imminent death. They looked befuddled but healthy. Saved.

"They're confused. Alarmed," Alastair said, a bit unnecessarily. "They need assistance."

Mia turned to Magnus. "Why don't you speak to them? It is your right."

The dragonlet whined and looked away.

Mia laughed and shook her head. Holding up the Dragonstone she said, "There's no getting out of it. This belongs to you, Aurora. You're the spirit dragon meant to protect these elves. Do this for me,

Magnus, if you're not ready yet to do it for yourself. Talk to them. Amaze them. Help them understand."

She lifted the artifact on its chain, which could only fit around the dragonlet's muzzle. When it touched him, however, her aura flared forth and the gem sizzled to life. The links expanded with her magic, and the chain grew until Mia was able to push it over the black dragonlet's head. Ghostfire sparkled across him, tinting everything in the amphitheater purple with its light.

Mia settled the jewel down over his neck to the hollow of his chest, smoothed Magnus's hide, and sighed lovingly. "I think it suits you. Now go. Do your work, dragon."

Magnus peered down at the jewel and then back into Mia's eyes. Garnet growled nearby and nosed Mia's shoulder, and the Aurora bowed to her, a gesture that was low and deep. Then he lifted up his neck and towered above everyone, stretching his black wings wide with purpose. Kort tugged Mia out of the way.

Magnus swept forward and addressed the crowd, many of whom stared with shock when they heard him speak. "People of Chalvaren! You are hereby liberated from the spell of Isa's black magic. Come and meet your new princess, Mia, and take heart and faith in the future. The seven kingdoms await your return."

A cheer slowly grew from the crowd, and the dragonlet puffed out his chest with pride, his tail swishing in anticipation. Garnet hovered behind him, watching intently.

Two of Kort's recently freed warriors moved down the stairs of the amphitheater and worked a control panel. The wire divider rolled back, and the newly restored elves flooded the arena floor. Every one knelt before Elissabet, Kort, and Magnus. Even Mia slid to one knee, which caused Kort some consternation.

Magnus nickered then bowed his head in a show of mutual respect. Alastair and The Others did the same. Kort lifted Mia to stand beside him, and the crowd erupted in cheers. Magnus raised his head to give a roar of satisfaction.

Alastair stood and touched Elissabet's arm. "We must find Lucan. We worked quickly to remove all of Isa and Malachai's spell protections during the fighting, but we were not able to find him."

Reminded of his uncle, Kort lurched toward the door back to the castle proper, but Mia grasped his hand and stopped him.

"He's here. I can sense him. But he's—"

A disturbance at the door caught his attention, and both Kort and Mia turned. One of Alastair's Others—a tall, dark-skinned elf in flowing white robes—marched Shayleigh and Duncan into the arena and forced the pair to their knees before Queen Elissabet.

"These two bore no shadow wraiths. They were here of their own volition."

"Both of them betrayed Castle Elias because Isa promised them power," Mia spoke up. "They told me as much while gloating about her victory."

Queen Elissabet's face hardened. "Duncan, Shayleigh. If you ever held any respect for my husband, for my house, lead us to my brother."

Duncan lowered his head and wept, but Shayleigh lunged at Mia. "You did this! You killed her! She was your blood and you betrayed her for them!" She whisked a sword from her captor's scabbard and thrust it forward, the blade meant for Mia's stomach, but Kort dragged Mia away just in time.

Garnet roared and charged. Magnus did the same, but it was the queen who avenged Shayleigh's perfidy. She swept her broadsword from its scabbard and buried it in the elf's back. Weapon clattering to the ground, Shayleigh feebly clutched the blade protruding from her chest. Elissabet gave a twist, and the traitor fell to her knees.

Kort stared, surprised. Mia met his eyes and then Elissabet's, and she said, "I caught her one day fingering the Dragonstone in my chamber. She told me she was dusting, but...my guess is that she's served Isa all along."

The queen drew forth her blade and wiped it clean upon Shayleigh's corpse. "She murdered the watchers in the east tower during Isa's assault. I suspect Duncan helped as well." The queen turned to look at him, but Castle Elias's former guard captain would not meet her eye.

"Lucan," Mia reminded them all. "He doesn't have much time."

Alastair jerked Duncan to his feet and pressed a blade to his throat. "Where's our brother?"

Duncan gestured back through the door. Alastair shoved him forward, and they all went to brave the dark halls of Castle Cumberlae.

†††

Mia bounded down the stone corridors. She sensed Lucan's failing heart and quickened her steps. "He's close. Lucan's *dying,* Kort."

Duncan stopped them in front of a set of double wooden doors. The doors were locked, heavy chains linked through the handles.

"Break them down, dragon," Kort commanded.

Mia backed into the shelter of his arms. Magnus kicked out powerful hind legs and shattered the great wooden doors inward, splintering them off their hinges. Then he sat back on his haunches and howled.

"Lucan!" Alastair called, charging through the debris. Queen Elissabet followed, stopping just inside the door, frozen.

"Dear gods in Heaven."

"What in Varik's name...?" Mia wondered. She scrambled in behind Elissabet but stopped dead in her tracks. Kort stood beside her. Garnet nosed in as well.

Mia blinked, and her belly tightened with horror. Everyone was silent. Four decapitated elf heads hung on the walls, prominently lit from above by magical spotlights. Surrounding each hung others less prominently mounted: women, children, brothers, sisters. Here were the four missing wizards of Chalvaren's once-great magic council, staring hideously down upon them. Under their preserved heads, plaques were labeled with each wizard's name inscribed in elven runes. Like prized animals. Like trophies in a collection.

"Oh, Varik," Mia said. It was the most horrible thing she'd ever seen. Everyone had been right that Isa was universes beyond redemption.

She clamped her hand across her mouth. Beside the dead hung three empty plaques, already labeled: ELISSABET ELIAS, ALASTAIR KROGH, and LUCAN BRIX.

An agonized moan built in Mia's throat, but Kort grabbed her elbow and dragged her away. "We can't do anything for them now," he said. "We can do something for *him.*" He squared her shoulders and pointed her at the metal table in the center of the room. Lucan lay there, still, his right ear missing, with black scratches on his cheek and bloody marks everywhere. The ugly gray color of his skin tore at Mia's heart.

"Lucan. Lucan!" Kort rushed forward, his strong voice booming through the chamber. He pulled and shook the chains that restrained the wizard, beginning to release him.

"No," Mia whispered, her aura flowing out around her. Sadness was intensifying it, anger and horror. "It can't end like this. He sacrificed himself to save you, Kort. He—"

And then she heard it, the sluggish heart of the wizard. Just a tiny sign of life, just one, but it beat, which meant they still had a chance.

Mia bolted forward. "We can help him. I can hear his heartbeat."

Kort worked Lucan's shackles, attempting to free him. Mia touched the wizard's chest, and Lucan groaned. It was a noise that petered out, sounding more like a death rattle than anything else.

Elissabet appeared, and Alastair. Alastair squinted his eyes, and he looked away from Lucan's face. A feeling of powerlessness rose up in the room, but Mia refuted it.

"No," she said. "Damn it. Help me save him."

Having finished his arms, Kort moved to Lucan's legs, tearing the shackles from his ankles. Neither Elissabet nor Alastair moved, frozen as they were with shock and misery. But Mia touched the arms of both wizards and said, "I will not allow this. This is not how this ends. I am grateful for everything you taught me, but now I'm going to teach you."

She opened her hands toward Lucan's body, showering him with her aura. Magnus growled and moved closer, sensing what she needed, and the Dragonstone flooded with light.

The queen moved then, raising both arms, and yellow-orange energy spilled onto Lucan. "*Nisi frater* Lucan, Varik," she sang. "*Nisi frater* Lucan."

Alastair came to life on Mia's left. His deep voice canted out a healing spell, and he threw his green aura into the mix. Energy spiked between the four of them, and Mia strained to use it, but she sensed there wasn't enough. How could it not be enough?

Kort stood at the end of the table. His blue aura seeped out, pouring onto Lucan's cold flesh. "Uncle! Godfather! Damn you, wake up! We need you! You and I are linked. We are family. We all love you."

Mia gasped, considering a new angle. "Look at me, Kort. *Mei sunt veri amoris.* I claim you as my One True Love. Bind your aura to mine. Forever. No matter what happens, I bind myself to you, and you must bind yourself to me. We are one, prince and princess. Eventually king and queen, if you still want that."

Kort eyed her for a fraction of a moment then smiled soberly and repeated the words. "*Mei sunt veri amoris.* My One True Love. Forever."

His aura burst forth and met Mia's, and as they touched the energies twined and blended, flooding the room in a way she had never seen. It had begun with their making love, grown as they realized how right they were for one another, and now their connection reached its pinnacle with a vow of eternity. Their bond was invincible, untamable, unstoppable.

Lucan's pelvis pitched up, his whole body pulled taut and suspended by sparkling magic. Mia moved down next to Kort, their powers fully united, their light lifting Lucan and turning him around, penetrating and soothing each injury. Varik had clearly decided this was not the day for Lucan to join the fallen.

The wizard's body touched back down on the table, and Mia sensed his heart began to beat. She counted, and the beat grew steadier.

Elissabet rushed in and touched her brother. Lucan's eyes flickered open and he sat up and glared at them, reaching out to finger his missing ear. Mia heaved a deep sigh and looked at Kort, who smiled down at her, gathered her in his arms, and kissed her. A sense of awe and wonderment filled her, and happiness.

They'd done it. They'd united their auras. Lucan Brix was alive.

Chapter 46

Outside, in the courtyard of Castle Cumberlae, the first rays of morning light caressed the victors. Kort shouted out orders, manhandled supplies, and directed his country's recovered lead dragons to corral Isa's captured ferals into a suitable flight wing back to Castle Elias while Magnus looked on with keen interest.

"Pure, make sure those young water dragons listen to Poseidon!"

The white wind dragon stormed across Cumberlae's fields to nip at the heels of several wiry dragonlets who darted to and fro, organizing them for the prince.

"Kristoff. Have you checked every room? I don't want a single prisoner left behind...," Kort said, and he tightened cargo straps on the underbelly of a green dragon meant to ferry home the rescued elves. All the liberated prisoners were gathered in the central courtyard of the manor, and Kort anticipated the long flight back to Castle Elias. "But I also don't want to wait another minute to get airborne."

"We've checked everywhere, and I think everyone feels the same," Kristoff replied, surveying the crowd with a small smile. "Think of the families who will reunite today, Kort. Men, women...to think that Isa was kidnapping them for as long as she was without notice! Just horrible. Elves that have been missing for years will finally see their loved ones again."

Kort smiled in response, but the expression barely hid his anger for their suffering.

He cinched tight the makeshift net that would help transport the survivors and bounded up into the harness to ensure it would hold. Glancing down at Kristoff he nodded. "Yes. We have work to do once we get back, returning everyone to their homes, but work's a good thing to have."

Below, Mia worked with Elissabet to secure a weakened but already cursing Lucan to a makeshift cot that would be strapped to the green dragon's back. Kristoff moved off to another project, and Kort surveyed the courtyard of the castle. His father had grown up here, and Mia's father as well, friends in an age before Isa and Malachai. Maybe his father would tell him that story someday over a game of cards. Nostalgia struck, and he craved Lachlan's company. Soon enough, Kort told himself. Soon enough.

He glanced around again at the survivors of this nightmare. The dragons had suffered the least, he supposed, those who hadn't been harvested for their energies. Still, Kort hated the crisscrossed scars across many of their scales. He glared at each painful reminder of capture and captivity, and then he looked at his own arm. Perhaps Lucan would tattoo a section of scar for him to remember always, and to commemorate the liberation of Chalvaren.

Poseidon, Magnus, and Garnet stood near each other, watching the other dragons. Seeing them reminded Kort of VanZanz, and he mourned the loss of the silver. Damn Isa, he thought. His first dragon's brother had never even had a chance to really live.

His thoughts went to Luxovious, but Kort shook off his grief. There was no time for it, and he jumped down to the ground and approached their lone prisoner.

Alastair stood watch over Duncan. With expert hands, Kort checked and tightened the elf's steel shackles. Castle Elias's former guard captain wept freely, his shoulders shaking. He kept his head lowered.

Kort spat on the ground and wiped his mouth, trying to remove the bitter taste of betrayal. "Keep him in chains, Alastair. When we get back home, you shall have your reward."

Krogh nodded, his dagger never far from Duncan's throat.

The guard captain moaned. "Kill me here."

"And deprive my father of the honor of looking you in the eye as he passes judgment?" Kort leaned forward, lifted Duncan's head by his dark brown hair, and growled into his ear, "Not a chance in hell." He let the traitor's head fall back and turned away to find any last task to solve.

Mia and one of Alastair's Others approached.

"Tell him," she said. "Kort. I want you to listen to her."

"We've found something you need to see, Prince Elias. Magical protections have come down and we found—"

Kort cut her off. "More atrocities? I don't want any more images in my head from this place. We have to leave now. We have to go home." He'd had enough of Isa's horrors taking down the heads of the wizards and their families, but her victims needed to be seen to and buried. That was the least he could do for them.

Mia stepped closer and touched his arm. "It's important. Trust me."

She tugged his hand, and against his better judgment Kort relented and followed. Seeing his mother standing nearby, however, he beckoned to her. "Mother, you're with us." If there were any lingering remnants of black magic, he wanted his mother at their side to assist.

The queen left Lucan with two female elves who seemed to be paying him a great deal of attention, and she fell in line behind Kort without comment. The group followed Alastair's wizard through the halls of Cumberlae, and Kort's gut clenched when he saw four elves standing guard outside a room at the end of the hall. How much more trauma would they have to endure before this day was done? What bizarre monstrosity waited inside this room?

"What's in here?" he asked.

The elves didn't answer. They just showed him inside an enormous hall that must once have been used for dining. Kort looked from side to side at Mia and Elissabet then clasped both their hands tight and steeled himself to learn what was so important.

"Oh. Look at that," his mother whispered, lifting her hand to her lips. Mia sucked in a gasp.

"I'll be damned. Would you look at that?" Kort repeated. His eyes ranged around the immense hall, the left side of which glittered with heaps of gold and silver, jewels, tapestries, paintings, ornate weapons, and at least a ton of twinkling dragon ore shards. He drew in a breath and then released a long exhale. "Whoa. Her treasure room. It's more than I ever imagined."

But the wealth wasn't what drew Elissabet and Mia. The women shot off to the right, opposite the chests of gold and treasure Isa had captured during her reign of evil, and Kort sucked in a breath as Mia and his mother shrieked with glee.

"Could it be...?" An unbidden smile found his face, and he followed them.

"Look! Holy hellfire of Chalvaren, your father will not believe this," Elissabet said, and she and Mia buzzed back and forth, assessing the real treasure of Castle Cumberlae.

"Dragons," Kort whispered. Dozens of nests lined the hall. Multicolored eggs, all of different clutches, waited to hatch. There were too many to count, unique dragons gestating together, a mismatched, eclectic assortment of various breeds, odd-sized eggs.

Mia took his hand and tugged him forward, pointing at the nests with trembling fingers. "Are these all key eggs? Kort, is that possible?"

Isa's vast nursery made Castle Elias's hatchery look like a closet. Kort's eyes scanned the long row of nests, and he multiplied the numbers of lost dragonlets in his head to imagine the impact on the dragon population of Chalvaren. "I've never seen anything like it.... Females lay at least four at a time, sometimes up to twelve." He shook his head sadly, realizing, "Each key egg here will never know his nest mates."

"These two have already hatched," his mother announced, and she plunged her hands down between two nests. She reared up in triumph, two tiny, wiggling, teal-and-green scaled water dragons clasped in her hands, just days old.

"Kort," Mia said. "What are we going to do with all these?"

He couldn't hold back his laughter. The sight of his mother cooing soft elven words at the two curious babies who hissed at her and flapped their wings thrilled him. He rushed forward to help her and cupped his hands around one of the tiny dragonlets. They were the burgeoning promise of Chalvaren's tomorrow.

"Hi there, little one," he whispered. "Is she holding you too tight?" He nuzzled the tiny dragon and turned to smile at both the queen and his princess. "What we're going to do is train them."

"Can we? Can we take them all back?" Mia asked, moving closer, inspecting the tiny winged babies.

Kort handed the tiny dragon to her, eased his arms around her waist and laid a gentle kiss on her ear. "Of course. They need us, and anything's possible when magic and dragons are combined."

Mia laid a careful kiss on the tiny dragon's head and laughed as the creature started to purr.

In that moment, Kort saw Mia. He'd seen her before, had registered her beauty and her strength and her value. But he hadn't, really. It was a thousandfold what he'd first imagined. She'd returned the Dragonstone to Chalvaren. She'd ensured Magnus would wear it forever, fulfilling the legend of peace associated with the artifact. She'd protected his kingdom and she'd made his heart whole.

"Look! Wind dragons!" Elissabet called, urging them to come see several milk-white eggs. Moving through a nest she lifted another with a red and gold shell. "And, oh, wow. Mia, come look! Kort, this is a fire dragon. Their eggs are exquisite!"

Elves poured in at that moment, as the guards outside couldn't stop them without force. Their faces were rapt and their exclamations quiet, and the chamber Kort had feared was now full of the sounds of elven happiness. Dragons would once again roam Chalvaren in packs, would be the crown jewels of a land of beauty and grandeur.

His mother glanced up and searched Kort's eyes. "Umm...send a messenger ahead to alert Lachlan. We're gonna need to adjust that load home, Son. We must find a way to ferry back the gold, but first I want each and every one of these eggs to land safely at Castle Elias, and it must all happen before nightfall."

Kort threw his head back and laughed. For once, he and his mother had exactly the same priorities.

"People of Chalvaren," he called out, "make way for all our new dragons!"

Chapter 47

Mia climbed up on Magnus's back. Kort sat behind her, wrapping strong arms around her waist.

"Let's go home," he said.

Magnus ran four steps then winged them up into the air, assuming a rear-flank position behind Garnet. The massive red flew lead, most of the larger eggs strapped securely to his red body in a cushioned cargo net. Pure flew in formation behind him with Elissabet riding proudly astride. Castle Elias's dragons filled the air, and seeing that warmed Mia, as did the sensation of wind in her face, but Kort's embrace warmed her more.

"I can't wait to see Castle Elias."

Kort nuzzled her neck, his lips lingering until shivers of passion awoke deep inside her. She turned her face into his warm embrace, so glad he was alive, so glad they were all alive. This dark tale had a happy ending, as did her mother's warning and prophecy. Mia let her hand trail up to her prince's pointed ear, and he moaned low and warm in response. She couldn't wait to get him home.

She looked down at a long line of marching elves below. These made their way by foot, destined for Castle Elias bearing Isa's stolen treasures. Kort had earmarked that wealth for proper distribution, for rebuilding, for rewards, for restitution.

"Do you think they'll be okay?" she murmured.

"Yes. And I'll send the dragons back to collect them as soon as our precious cargo rests securely in Castle Elias."

Mia squirmed with excitement. "I can't wait to show Brite what we found! She won't sleep for a week worrying over all these new eggs."

Kort chuckled, which sent a shiver of desire through her. "She'll be glad to see you home."

"And you," Mia agreed. She patted Magnus's neck and urged him higher, faster and forward to home.

Ahead, Queen Elissabet craned her neck to check on a load of smaller eggs nestled on her wind dragon's broad back. When she smiled, Mia pointed. "Look at her, Kort. Happiness suits your mother."

Beside Pure flew Poseidon, and Mia eyed his cargo with trepidation. She forced herself to relax and let out a deep breath.

Kort pulled her tight against him, one hand stretching across her belly in a gentle rub. "Are you well?"

She melted into his embrace and sighed. "I am. I can't wait to get back to the castle, back the west tower, back to the luxuries that await us. I'm tired of traveling. First, a bubble bath in that incredible tub. *Oh yeah.* Then a meal cooked by Thorvid." Her stomach growled, and she clutched Kort's hands. "I'm definitely feeling well right now."

He kissed her ear and said, "I've been savoring the thought of you in that king-sized bed...."

His voice was low and warm, and full of the promise of their infinite tomorrows. Mia turned and kissed his lips, looked up at his handsome face, and laughed. "I've got plans for that bed tonight myself."

"We'll sleep for days."

"I don't have much patience for sleeping, Kort."

"Me, neither, though we both need the rest. I can't wait to get you home."

Home? She blinked rapidly then stared at him. *Is that what I'm calling it now?*

It was.

Her emotions suddenly surged. "I'm angry." Anger, yes, anger flowed through her heart at what Isa and Malachai had conjured with their evil. "If only they'd cared about everyone else more than themselves. Like you. Like your mother and father. I'll never be able to forgive them for what they did to all those people," she announced.

"You have every right to your anger, Mia."

"But I'm curious too." Yes, she was curious about *so* much. "Did Lucan really send you after Magnus so that you could find me?"

"*I* asked him to send me after Magnus," Kort said, "but…well, now, thinking back, he didn't exactly discourage the idea before I asked. He must have had some idea of what was to come. He does have a bit of a way with a prophecy. I didn't think of that at the time."

Ah. Well, Mia meant to have a stiff discussion with the wizard once he recovered. Not that she could really complain about the way everything had turned out.

Kort shifted position and wrapped his leg around hers. "Mia…if Lucan did it intentionally, I'm going to have to shake his hand."

His words filled her with a sudden overwhelming sadness at what they'd all gone through, at the pain and suffering so many of Chalvaren's inhabitants had known, but she clasped her hands around Kort's neck and pulled his face to hers. "Any world without you in it would never work for me."

He took her lips in a hard, possessive kiss, and Mia trembled with the heat of his passion.

Unfortunately, they weren't about to satisfy themselves on dragonback, and a few minutes later her thoughts turned to what would happen once they returned to Castle Elias. "What about all those elves we've liberated? For some it's been years. How will you reunite them with their families?"

"Varik will show us the answer," was Kort's reply.

"Varik…" Mia repeated. Then: "Malachai infected my aunt with his darkness and ruined her. Do you think she could have been different if she'd been shown mercy? Could anyone have saved her? My father?"

Kort said nothing, and she was sure he was wondering the same thing.

Magnus flapped his wings and followed Garnet close. Mia turned her face into the wind and surveyed the forests and the mountains of Chalvaren. She wondered how Isa could have borne the weight of such sadness for twenty years, wondered how she could have harbored so much hatred for so long, wondered just what was the draw of ruling the world. But she knew some of it. She'd felt the power of the Dragonstone unleashed. All that potential, all that energy at her command…she could have taken anything she wanted. But the thing was, she *had* what she wanted.

"All I desire is you, Kort—and a family, and a place we can call our own."

"Then I'll see that you have those things, Mia. Always."

A thought occurred.

"If you'd lost me," she began. "If these elves turned against us and our unborn child, what would you do? What would *we* do?" She glanced down and encircled her belly with her hands. "Would I have done the same as Isa to return you from the dead, to save you at any cost?"

Again, Kort said nothing. She didn't think he could be corrupted.

She glanced around the incredible view surrounding her, the landscape with its flight of dragons, and she prayed. "Keep our souls, Varik. Protect us from mortal sin—from vengeance bred by grief. Shield us all from the hatred that lured Isa to the darkest side of revenge. Shield us from ourselves."

Suddenly, Magnus lofted upward and a brilliant beam from Chalvaren's rising sun exploded off the sea, blinding her. Through the sunlight her heart saw the goodness of world, the beauty that no one should trade for their own gain, no matter the reason. Chills of the sublime spread down her arm, along with a new emotion: hope. Yes, hope. Because evil had bred Isa's problems and evil was for the moment struck down. All that remained was blue sky and the steady and sure wingbeats of Chalvaren's dragons.

"Look, Kort. The west tower." Mia caught sight of the castle spires looming in the distance, the colorful blue and gold flags of Castle Elias whipping in the wind, welcoming weary travelers back to where they belonged. "Hurry, Magnus. Please take us home."

Chapter 48

Chalvaren had much to celebrate. Queen Elissabet had planned for the feast to last three days. Thorvid worked his staff in rotating shifts to keep everyone fed. The king's cellars were opened, and royal mead, wine and spirits flowed freely alongside all the good wishes the elves could give.

Mia's tummy quivered as she peered down from the dais upon a thousand elves gathered in the hall to hear her say the words, "I do." It wasn't that she didn't want to say them. She wanted to say them with all her heart. Public functions were simply not her strong suit.

"The hall of thrones looks exquisite today," she murmured. It was decorated for the event, and Queen Elissabet had garlanded the columns sculpted with the likenesses of the gods and goddesses of Chalvaren with strings of luminescent dragon ore.

"*You* look exquisite today, Princess," Kort replied, his blue eyes shimmering. He was dressed in a suit of rich clothes, over which lay an indigo fleece robe lined with white fur, the traditional dress of Chalvaren's royalty. King Lachlan had insisted.

Mia tried to breathe. Kort stood next to her and held her hand. The feel of his fingers interlocked with hers helped settle her down, and when she glanced up at him she couldn't help but smile. A thin golden crown graced his head and complemented his pointed ears and his long blond hair. *So handsome.* He was the one who looked exquisite.

The queen had dressed Mia in an ivory satin princess-styled gown overlaid with layers of hand-woven lace and glimmering with tiny sequins of dragon ore. Every time Mia glanced down, the beauty of the elegant gown took her breath away.

Of course, every elf in attendance today wore his best. The royal wedding was only one activity. Lachlan had personally decorated every warrior who'd returned to the castle with medals of gold. He'd stunned everyone by pardoning the repentant Duncan for his crimes, commuting his sentence from death to banishment—in order to show a mercy that might have headed off other recent mistakes, he said. And the best part, Mia thought, was all the reunited elven families. Lachlan honored all for their suffering, and he divided a portion of the recovered treasure to ease the hardships they'd endured.

The High Elven Magic Council had reconvened for the first time that morning, and Alastair sat proudly among his friends, richly rewarded. There were members from all the seven kingdoms, and Mia had joined their ranks—insisting beforehand that Magnus be given a seat alongside her, Garnet as well. This way, now that they could talk, the dragons of Chalvaren were ensured representation in decisions that would ultimately affect them.

She peeked down at the guests again, and at Magnus, Garnet, and Pure, who stood beside each other, watching the assembled elves with keen interest. Magnus wore the Dragonstone around his neck, and Mia could not imagine a better place for it.

"Look there, Kort!" she said when Magnus caught her eye and roared. The Aurora was seated next to Varik's column, and the noise had caused the god's image to come to life.

"He's here, Mia. He's come to bless our marriage," Kort whispered. He stood taller and spread his shoulders back with pride. "It happens rarely, but he's been known when pleased to show himself amongst elves he favors."

A mighty warrior elf himself, Varik didn't look all that different from any other elf in the room, but every elf in the hall bowed to him, even Elissabet and Lachlan. As well they should, Mia thought. His power made this world beautiful and wonderful.

Varik motioned for the priest standing in front of Kort and Mia to continue. The priest gestured to Mia and repeated his earlier question.

"Mia," Kort murmured, his voice low and sexy, dragging her out of her thoughts and back to the handsomeness of his face. His crystal-blue eyes twinkled, and she raised her brows when he looked expectant.

"Answer the question." He gestured with one of those strong, steady hands to the expectant priest who waited on her words.

Mia sucked in a breath, and her face burst into a smile. She said to the kind old priest, "I do. With all my heart, I do."

Next came a tricky part of the ceremony. Two other priests carried an enormous mantle of fur-lined indigo robes to the priest who'd just married them, and with great pomp and circumstance the three men laid the Castle Elias robe across her tight shoulders. It was supposedly a bad sign if it was dropped or mislaid.

Wow, the damn thing's heavy, she thought.

But the weight settled onto her shoulders just fine, and she expected somehow she'd come to like it with time. It was certainly soft and beautiful, and with power came responsibility. When Varik smiled at her, she couldn't help but think his nod was one of agreement.

King Lachlan and Queen Elissabet approached next. The head priest opened an ornately carved, cherry-colored wooden box, and the two peered inside together. They smiled in admiration, and Mia's breath caught.

Kort squeezed her hand. "Easy now, just like we practiced," he said, his strong hand reassuring.

They eased down onto their knees.

King Lachlan reached into the ornate box and lifted out a delicate golden tiara adorned with pearls, diamonds, and a central teardrop-shaped amethyst. He'd selected it himself, as the precious stone had been handed down through their family for generations, and now the king walked over and laid the crown on Mia's head. As he did, Kort squeezed her hand again to remind her he was by her side.

Mia thrilled with the weight of the crown. Kort and Mia stood, and Kort's father spread his arms wide to the crowd and called, "Loyal subjects of Castle Elias, I present your Prince Kort and Princess Mia!"

Kort thrust his chin out and squared his shoulders. Mia clenched his hand tighter, facing his people, facing *her* people she realized as every elf before them took a knee, touched their fists to their hearts and swore their allegiance to the crown. To her. To the future. To Chalvaren's ruling dynasty.

The three dragons roared. Applause thundered through the hall of thrones, and Mia finally allowed herself to breathe. At least until Kort embraced her. He would never fail to take her breath away.

Epilogue

Five days later, rays of morning sunlight drove into the Drakhos Mountains and illuminated the dark, forested wood. Mia opened her hand to shield her eyes and looked around the clearing, which didn't seem dark or scary at all. It was a crisp, beautiful day.

She looked toward the dragon's nest and bounced on her toes. Several of the eggs had already cracked, and the movement of new life stirred before her.

A few yards away, Magnus chattered and clicked in dragon language with the dam who guarded the nest. Today was really all about him, and his position as ambassador to the dragons of Chalvaren. He looked so dashing sporting the Dragonstone on his chest, Mia could hardly keep the smile of pride from her face.

Kort chuckled over her right shoulder. "She's amazing. See how she dares him to get any closer without her permission? The blue-green in her scales shows she's a water dragon. You girls don't get too close. Those are her babies, and she's very possessive."

Mia smiled in appreciation, while Brite tugged on her hand.

"Will she let us see the nest?"

Mia knelt beside the child. "I think Magnus is pleading our case. Do you want to see these baby dragons hatch?"

Brite wadded her pink skirt in her hands and nodded. "Not just that. I want one of them, Mia."

Now that the kingdom was peace, the princess was next in line to choose her dragon, assuming that dragon wanted to be chosen. Mia clasped the child's shoulders and reminded her, "A dragon is a huge responsibility. Are you certain you're ready? It will be a lot of work."

Brite bounced from side to side in anticipation. She smiled at Mia and nodded. "Will you show me how to take care of her?"

"'Her'?" Kort asked, kneeling beside them. "How do you know one is a girl?"

Brite's face lit up, and chills raced across Mia's skin. The child really was the cutest elf ever born. She wore her big brother's expression of seriousness, and her parents' expression of hope for their traditions. Somewhere inside her lived Quinn and Ian's ability to challenge everything, too.

"There *will* be girl dragons, Kort."

Mia watched Magnus work the dam, moving back and forth across the forest floor. He finally turned to Mia, left the mother dragon and approached. He sat on his haunches and folded his purple and teal-tipped wings tight against his maturing dragon scales, then regarded Mia with a nod.

"She'll allow it. She wants her younglings raised in the service of Castle Elias. On one condition…"

Mia stood and strode forward without listening to the rest, knowing she would agree to whatever Magnus reported. He really was good at this ambassador role, was always negotiating. The Dragonstone swung against his black, iridescent chest scales, and Mia raised her brows at the glimmer of ghostfire at the center of the stone.

She eyed the mother dragon, who hovered over her precious nest with wings spread wide. A spray of eggshell burst up into the air, and the dam nudged one of the eggs gently with her nose and softly cooed.

"What's her condition?"

"One of her offspring must serve the royal family."

Mia laughed and gestured to Brite. "If she'll allow us to witness the hatch, to participate and welcome the dragonlets, I'll promise her request will be fulfilled."

Magnus and the mother dragon exchanged vocalizations. Both relaxed after a moment, the dam looked over at Mia and lowered her head in a bow of welcome.

Mia turned to Kort, her fingers crossed. "Well, it looks like Brite will get her wish. Are you okay with this?"

Her husband hefted Brite up onto his hip. "Looks like you and I need to pick a dragonlet. Are *you* up for this, little girl?"

Brite giggled with glee and covered his cheek with her palm. "I'm ready."

Her husband smiled broadly, and Mia heaved a sigh of relief. She held out her hand, and he took it. She led them forward, just a step or two behind Magnus.

As they approached the nest, there came a distinct flutter of movement in Mia's own belly. It reached up and touched her heart, a moment of somehow impossible beauty and magnitude. The experience reminded her that in less than a year she'd be a mother herself, which would give her everything she'd ever wanted.

The dam bowed before them. Eggshells lofted up into the air again.

Mia leaned forward to see who was tossing all the shells. She reached out, and the dam nuzzled her hand. Mia grinned and asked, "May we attend your babies?"

The mother dragon purred.

The three elves took up positions on their knees around the nest. Brite squealed as they watched the miracle manifest. Kort shushed her, but he also smiled and showed her how to help dry the babies with the nesting materials.

Mia dove in and helped, too. The little dragons were wriggling and robust. One was red. The next was blue. A green one squawked out third.

Magnus nosed his way in to view the hatch.

"So tiny," Mia said to him, "but they'll grow fast—like you did."

Kort chuckled and reached into the straw to retrieve the third as the fourth dragonlet flung eggshells off his small wings, and Mia found her hands full of the little red one, which she cooed at and petted, enjoying his soft warm scales. He chirped out a little roar and wriggled in her hands, so full of life, so vigorous, and Mia stroked his chest.

The little green dragon wrapped a tail around Kort's robust forearm and called out. Brite leaned in, her eyes huge with anticipation. The two gazed at each other for a moment, and the child was speechless, a true feat.

The little dragon ruffled teal wings, still wet, not fully functional, and Magnus nickered his appreciation. The mother dragon cooed to all her babies, and they all peeped at the sound of her voice. Mia stroked the red dragonlet, but her eyes remained on Brite and the little water dragon.

"Thank you, Mia," Kort said beside her, and Mia was suddenly so glad she'd decided to stay. How foolish of her to ever consider leaving, no matter how much suffering had followed. All would be remedied by the years of enjoyment yet to come.

Brite's tiny green water dragonlet opened her mouth, cast back her head and roared, a tinkling sound as pure as a crystal-clear waterfall. Perfect.

"I want this one," the child said.

The dragonlet unwound her tail from Kort's arm and leapt onto Brite's, bounding up to the princess's shoulder. She nestled herself in the crook of Brite's neck and poked her pointed head in Brite's soft hair, and the dam looked on with what Mia imagined was a pleased look.

"I wonder what sort of magic and adventures these two will get into?" she whispered to Kort, clasping his hand in hers. As they touched, their auras sparkled to life and combined, as almost always happened now.

Kort pulled her to stand beside him. He brushed his lips against hers, and when he fanned his hand out against her growing belly, she grinned.

"Magic that sustains this kind of love is the only kind I want in our realm," he said. "It's worth everything."

"Mmmhmmm," Mia agreed, glancing over at her Aurora, more dragon than dragonlet now despite the fact that he had more to grow. Magnus and the dam chattered away at each other over the nest of tiny dragons. "The Dragonstone suits him. He looks so official wearing it."

"No regrets, Mia?" Kort asked. "About anything?"

She turned her attention to her husband's handsome face, pulled him closer and sighed. "Not a one," she said. "And you need never ask again."

They both turned and watched Kort's little sister, who found the soft spot underneath her new dragonlet's chin with her tiny fingers. She gently stroked the newborn's scales and giggled, and Chalvaren's newest royal dragonlet purred with the promise of a sweet tomorrow.

ABOUT THE AUTHOR

As a child growing up in Savannah, Georgia, where Spanish moss whispers tales in breezes from the Atlantic Ocean, Paula Millhouse soaked in the sunshine and heritage of historic cobblestones, pirate lore, and stories steeped in savory mysteries of the south. Now she works in the field of medicine by day and lives with her hero, her husband of twenty-five years, at the base of the Blue Ridge Mountains with their pack and pride of furry babies. She follows her muse by night on their quest for happily-ever-afters in thrilling romantic fiction.

In the tradition of southern storytellers, she loves sharing the lives of her characters with readers. She's a member of Romance Writers of America and the Fantasy, Futuristic, & Paranormal Writers specialty chapter.

Did you enjoy this book? Drop us a line and say so! We love to hear from readers, and so do our authors. To connect, visit www.boroughspublishinggroup.com online, send comments directly to info@boroughspublishinggroup.com, or friend us on Facebook and Twitter. And be sure to check back regularly for contests and new releases in your favorite subgenres of romance!

Are you an aspiring writer? Check out www.boroughspublishinggroup.com/submit and see if we can help you make your dreams come true.